MICROCOSMIC
GOD

Theodore Sturgeon, back row far right, at twenty-three years old, with his maternal grandmother and grandfather Dicker, other members of the Dicker family, his first wife, Dorothé, and their first child, Patricia, in Jamaica, 1941.

MICROCOSMIC GOD

Volume II:

The Complete Stories of

Theodore Sturgeon

Edited by

Paul Williams

Foreword by

Samuel R. Delany

North Atlantic Books
Berkeley, California

Microcosmic God
The Complete Short Stories of Theodore Sturgeon, Volume II

Published by
North Atlantic Books
P.O. Box 12327
Berkeley, California 94712

Cover art: *Returning Home,* © 1992 by Jacek Yerka. All rights reserved.
Cover and book design by Paula Morrison
Typeset by Catherine Campaigne

Printed in the United States of America

Microcosmic God is sponsored by the Society for the Study of Native Arts and Sciences, a nonprofit educational corporation whose goals are to develop an educational and crosscultural perspective linking various scientific, social, and artistic fields; to nurture a holistic view of arts, sciences, humanities, and healing; and to publish and distribute literature on the relationship of mind, body, and nature.

Library of Congress catalogue card number: 94-38047

2 3 4 5 6 7 8 9/98

CONTENTS

EDITOR'S NOTE

THEODORE HAMILTON STURGEON was born February 26, 1918, and died May 8, 1985. This is the second of a series of volumes that will collect his short fiction of all types and all lengths shorter than a novel. The volumes and the stories within the volumes are organized chronologically by order of composition (insofar as it can be determined). This second volume contains stories written between April 1940 and June 1941. Two are being published here for the first time; several others are appearing for the first time in book form.

For invaluable assistance in the preparation of this volume, the editor would like to thank Noël Sturgeon and the Theodore Sturgeon Literary Trust, Marion Sturgeon, Jayne Sturgeon, Ralph Vicinanza, Lindy Hough, Richard Grossinger, Debbie Notkin, Tom Whitmore, Samuel R. Delany, Dixon Chandler, Jeannie Trizzino, David G. Hartwell, Jonathan Lethem, Charles N. Brown, T. V. Reed, Cindy Lee Berryhill, Gordon Van Gelder, Sam Moskowitz, Robert Silverberg, Frank Robinson, and all of you who have expressed your interest and support.

Foreword

THEODORE STURGEON
by Samuel R. Delany

SOMETIME IN THE early fifties when I was ten or eleven, in a fat anthology of science fiction tales I read my first Theodore Sturgeon story—"Thunder and Roses."

Understand, I was a bright and profoundly unimaginative child: Much of what passes for intelligence in children is a stark deafness to metaphor coupled with a pigheaded literal-mindedness.

Roses didn't have much to do with thunder, so it was kind of a silly title. The story was largely about a singer named Starr Anthim, who mostly wasn't there and, when she was, sang a kind of anthem, which only made you think about the word itself, its sounds, and the way it kept fitting in with other words, instead of what was happening. And what *was* happening? Well, the tale was full of ordinary guys doing ordinary things like shaving and taking showers, all of which, for some reason, seemed disturbingly more vivid than I would have thought anyone could make such commonplace actions seem in a story, because it described the feel of warm water down the back of your neck between your shoulder blades and what it felt like, after the shower, when your clean foot landed on the bathroom tile half in and out of a puddle and a crinkled toothpaste tube lay on the glass shelf under the mirror. And the only other thing about it was that the world was coming to an end and everyone felt as powerless as a ten-year-old boy to stop it. And when I finished, I was crying ...

It couldn't have been very good, because that wasn't what stories—especially science fiction stories—were supposed to do ...

By the time I was twenty-one, Theodore Sturgeon was my favorite fiction writer of any genre, literary or paraliterary. And for all my lack of imagination at ten, Sturgeon's tales had taught me, as much as or more than those of any other writer, the incredible range of effects words could whip up, sharp and electric, in the human psyche.

Twenty-three years later, I *met* Sturgeon—in 1975. One afternoon while I was signing books at the Science Fiction Shop (then on Hudson Street in New York City), someone at the front desk called back, "Hey, there's a phone call for you, Chip," and, when I got there and lifted the receiver to my ear, for the first time I heard that tenor voice with a quality like the middle register of an A-flat clarinet and a pacing I want to call a drawl—only "drawl" connotes region and class, while what I heard over the phone that afternoon was much more a considered and personal rhythm, overlaid on a speech with such geographical variety lingering under its L's and R's and over the length of its O's and U's, that its articulate U.S. ordinariness put to shame the whole notion of "Midwestern Standard."

"Chip Delany . . . ? This is Ted Sturgeon . . . " He'd called to thank me for a passage I'd written in a novel, set some four thousand years in the future, in which a young poet speaks about a wonderful Twentieth Century writer.

The passage reads: "There was one ancient science fiction writer, Theodore Sturgeon, who would break me up every time I read him. He seemed to have seen every flash of light on a window, every leaf shadow on a screen door that I had ever seen; done everything I had ever done, from playing the guitar to laying over for a couple of weeks on a boat in Aransas Pass, Texas. And he was supposedly writing fiction, and that four thousand years ago. Then you learn that lots of other people find the same things in the same writer, who have done none of the things you've done and seen none of the things you've seen. That's a rare sort of writer . . . " *(Empire Star,* p. 83).

Sturgeon's comment to me about it? "That somebody might be reading something I've written forty—much less four thousand—years from now, that's the sort of thing a writer like me is afraid even to let himself *think* about." But he seemed very pleased that *I* had thought about it. And the fact is, if I had a single vote as to which SF writer from the decades of Sturgeon's finest productions would be read in the centuries to come, that vote would have to go to Sturgeon.

A few weeks after the signing, during a Lunacon SF convention, as I was walking through the hotel lobby, whose decor vacillated between scarlet and orange, Wina Sturgeon—Ted's diminutive then-companion—took my arm and said, "Chip, Ted would like to actually meet you. Why don't you come up for a few minutes? The kids are all there, of course. But if you don't mind ...?" and gave me a room number and left.

Minutes later, I took the elevator up, turned down the hall, knocked on the wood beside the painted metal laundry bin that hung outside, and inside heard kids laughing.

Someone said, "Come in." Then someone opened the lock.

Yes, the room was filled with Sturgeon children: Robin, Tandy, Noël, Timothy, Andros ... and Wina and a couple of other friends.

Sturgeon sat on the bed, back against the headboard, wearing some handmade embroidered pants—maybe sandals, I don't remember. A medium-height man and deeply tanned, he was on the upper side of middle-age, with gray hair grizzled on a thin chest. The only picture I'd ever seen of him was the portrait in the Ed Emsh fantasia that formed the cover for the special Sturgeon issue of *The Magazine of Fantasy and Science Fiction* for September, 1962. What I saw, there in the hotel room, was that face, with its beard and fine bones—described in one or another article I'd read as "Puckish" or "pixie-ish." But it was that face aged a decade. Sturgeon gave out a measured calm that glimmered through the confusion of the children's questions and visitors' comments, very natural and very winning. An impossible situation for conversation?

Not at all.

It was a pleasant and friendly evening, with lots of mutual good feeling; but all saying it makes me want to do is take the cliché "pleasant and friendly" and figure out some way to retrieve the meanings that have worn off the words from overuse: because what pleased that evening started like a warmth behind the knees and rose through the body till it reached the shoulders, letting loose—now at a bemused chuckle from Ted, now with someone's conversation about some situation two thousand miles way, now with a sterner word to a child and a hug to the same child a moment later—all the tensions that comprise what Freud called "unpleasure" (that includes those states where we do not feel good without actually being in pain), so that the expectation and nervousness and awe I'd brought with me could settle finally into the simpler and more intense feeling of friendliness. (Indeed, if, in vivid visual descriptions of the natural and social world, Sturgeon is surpassed—now and again just barely—by Nabokov or Gass—*no* other writer describes so accurately what it feels like to *have* a feeling—how feelings sit in or move through the body, tangling in its muscles, playing its nerves, wriggling under the skin or jarring its sensitive tissues.) A pleasant, friendly evening.

Sadly, it seemed a long time before I saw Ted again.

Our acquaintanceship—and I know Ted would have let me call it a friendship—was limited to the last decade of his life, during which I met him perhaps five times. Once he showed me the silver Q he wore on a chain around his neck—with the arrow through it. His personal emblem, it stood for, "Ask the next question"—his motto. I have two brief, warm letters from him, in answer to two of mine. Once I spent an afternoon with him while he recorded some of his stories at a midtown recording studio. Twice we made plans to get together, sit down and really talk—even going so far, the last time I saw him in Vancouver in June of '84, as to fix a summer date.

But somehow summer came and went. So did winter.

Then Ted was dead.

If I may strain a metaphor: Language is a sky we all live under. It's a total surround, both to thought and to action. "Poetry makes nothing happen," Auden wrote of Yeats. But once in a while, by luck or by skill, in poetry or in prose, a writer puts words together so that, if they *don't* make things happen, they make us *see* and *sense* things happening. The range of Sturgeon's work is an immense and astonishing galaxy of such dazzling and precise lights shining out against the twilight of ordinary rhetoric.

Theodore Sturgeon was the single most important science fiction writer during the years of his major output—the forties, fifties, and sixties. He was by no means the best known. He was popular—from

x

time to time, greatly so—but he never had the crossover appeal of a Robert Heinlein, Arthur Clarke, or Isaac Asimov. But the "crossover" machinery that took up the first two of these was film: Heinlein in 1950, with *Destination Moon,* and Clarke in 1968 with *2001: A Space Odyssey.* And Asimov's popular science books and official textbooks had far more to do with establishing him as a household name than did his science fiction—which, not counting reprints, comprises only some thirty-five titles out of his more than 300 volumes. But though on occasion *More Than Human* came close to reaching the sound stages, no film based on a Sturgeon story ever got done.

In no way am I suggesting that he displaces the other indubitable artists of our field ... Stanley Weinbaum, Alfred Bester, Philip Dick, or Cordwainer Smith. But if we can read Sturgeon, read him deeply, carefully, and with the nuance and insight his texts invite, then we can read any of these others; and our readings will be enriched by what we learn of science fictional language possibilities *from* Sturgeon.

This is not, however, a commutative proposition. For if we do *not* read Sturgeon, our readings of all these others will be deeply, and possibly irrevocably, impoverished: What our greatest SF artist—Sturgeon—does for the broader range of our art is takes what in other writers becomes dead convention or trope and, within a shared historical context, infuses it with life and demonstrates its vital use.

II

Sturgeon's theme was love. At least one of his methods was to physicalize the emotions and move them through the body, describing their weight and resistance, their frictions and trajectories. He articulated the ripplings in the tapestry of day that enwraps us all—articulated it with an economy and accuracy that again and again impinges on his reader with electric insistence. He loved the physical world of weather and scents, and, especially, machines—glittering in the sun, glimpsed through a laboratory window, rising blackly to block the stars, or rusting behind an old garage. He loved the commonsensical demands of the body—and, as well, had vast patience with the intricate excuses the mind raises against them.

More than half a dozen years ago, I first wrote:

> Right now there is a yawning fourfold need in Sturgeon schol-
> arship. First, we must have a reasonably and responsibly edited
> edition of Theodore Sturgeon's near 150 stories (more than a
> hundred of which are superb) as well as his half-dozen-plus
> novels.
>
> Second, someone must undertake a major, scholarly biog-
> raphy of Sturgeon.
>
> Third, efforts must be marshaled to preserve his letters,
> ephemera, and other writerly remains.
>
> Fourth, we must establish a Sturgeon Society and Sturgeon
> Newsletter to distribute information and inform those schol-
> ars and readers of Sturgeon of what is going on in Sturgeon
> studies.

The book you hold now, the second volume in a projected ten
volume set of Sturgeon's complete short fiction, reflects on all four
of those exhortations.

Spearheaded by Paul Williams and Noël Sturgeon (the fifth of
Sturgeon's children and the Trustee of his literary estate), The Sturgeon Project is an incipient Sturgeon Society. No regular newsletter
exists yet. But I know that will be coming. And anyone who has
looked at the first volume of these tales (*The Ultimate Egoist* [1994])
will be aware of how much the story notes for this series already
depend on the letters: the whole set will certainly have to be at the
center of any future biographical study.

Sturgeon was a superb artist: we've seen that from his writing
from the forties and fifties. But with the first volume of his earliest
work now available, we can see, with the rediscovered stories and
letters from his late adolescence, an artist who, in his commitment
to his work and in his perseverance, has much about him of the hero.

Robert Heinlein may be responsible for more technical innova-
tions, more rhetorical figures that have been absorbed into the particular practice of science fiction writing; his influence is certainly
greater. But if this is so, it is at an extremely high cost, both ethically
and aesthetically. (I use the terms in the same sense that allowed the

young Ludwig Wittgenstein to jot in his notebook, on the 24th of July, 1916, almost two years before Sturgeon was born, "Ethics and aesthetics are one and the same"—the very sense, I presume, that allowed the young Georg Lukacs to write, only a year before that, in his *Theory of the Novel,* that fiction is "the only art form in which the artist's ethical position *is* the aesthetic problem.") And if Alfred Bester's *The Stars My Destination* (1956) is regarded by many as the single greatest SF novel and therefore minimally outshines Sturgeon's *More Than Human* (1953), it is because Bester's book *is* a novel, whereas Sturgeon's is three connected novellas, two of which are superb and the third of which is merely fascinating.

To talk about science fiction with any sophistication, however, especially to talk about that science fiction which flowered in the forties and fifties, we must locate coequal forms. One, near-future science fiction, posits a familiar landscape, familiar social patterns, and familiar social surfaces. Into it the author intrudes one or a limited number of marvels. The game is to explore the resultant alterations in behavior. The other form, far-future science fiction, begins the game with a landscape where behavior patterns, social texture, and societal workings are already highly altered. Here, as the text proceeds, the game is to recognize which patterns of behavior—or, in the more sophisticated versions of this form, which abstracts of these behavior patterns—remain constant despite material reorganization. In this form of science fiction the question is: What is the human aspect of the structure of behavior—no matter how much the behavioral content or the context alters?

The newcomer to science fiction (often a young newcomer to science as well) is usually more at home with the near-future sort. The long-time reader, especially one at home with the technical underpinnings that support the multiple distortions of landscape in the far-future variety, often finds the second type the greater intellectual challenge.

When near-future science fictions fails, we usually dismiss the failure as "a gimmick story." When far-future science fiction fails, we usually call its degenerate form "space opera." But if we accept the division and acknowledge the fine and faulty examples on both sides, then we can go on to say that Sturgeon is *the* master of near-future science fiction (whereas *The Stars My Destination* is considered by many to be the pinnacle of the far-future variety).

Sturgeon was born February 26th, 1918, and grew up first on Staten Island, then in Philadelphia with his mother, his stepfather, and his older brother Peter. An adolescent career as a gymnast was ended by a bout of rheumatic fever. By and large to get away from a fraught relationship with his stepfather, Sturgeon, while still a teenager, entered the merchant marine. But his burning desire was to be a writer. His first fiction sale that we know about (for five dollars—on publication) was a short-short story called "Heavy Insurance" that appeared in the McClure Newspaper Syndicate, in *The Milwaukee Journal,* July 16th, 1938, when he was twenty. His story "A God in a Garden," written the following spring, marks Sturgeon's first sale to John W. Campbell, the great science fiction (and fantasy) editor, for whom Sturgeon was to become one of the prime members in his stable of writers during the later thirties and all through the forties. A contemporary fantasy, "A God in a Garden" appeared in the October *Unknown*—that extraordinary journal which, over the five years of its life, all but created the genre of contemporary urban fantasy. Sturgeon's first science fiction story, also sold to Campbell, was "Ether Breather." It appeared in *Astounding Science Fiction,* September 1939.

The Sturgeon *oeuvre* is magnanimous and expansive. If its verbal texture almost everywhere approaches the exquisite, its edges positively sprawl. The core of that work has been, to date, his four science fiction novels: *The Dreaming Jewels, More Than Human, Venus Plus X,* and *The Cosmic Rape.* And clearly on the SF border territory is his 1960 novella (published as a separate volume), *Some of Your Blood.* He also wrote an historical spoof, *I, Libertine* (1956) under the pseudonym of Frederick R. Ewing, a novel the tale of whose creation, at the inspiration of WOR-AM disc jockey Jean Shepherd, is a small fifties period comedy in itself. There is an Ellery Queen mystery that he ghosted, as well as some other film and TV novelizations to his credit. *(The King and Four Queens* [1956]; *Voyage to the Bottom of the Sea* [1961]). His final novel, *Godbody,* originally written at the end of the sixties for a publisher of erotica who eventually went out of business, only appeared posthumously in 1986 and is somewhere between fantasy, science fiction and erotic mysticism. At various times and in various circles, *More Than Human*—really a concatenation of three interconnected long stories—has been considered the greatest science fiction novel (certainly of the near-future variety) ever written, in spite of the weakness of its ending. But Sturgeon at his strongest is finally revealed—again and again—in the torrent of wonderful stories, which Paul Williams, in this series, has organized and annotated so brilliantly.

With the current project, the number both of the ordinary *and* the extraordinary tales has only risen. As far back as the special 1962 special issue of *The Magazine of Fantasy and Science Fiction* devoted to Sturgeon's work, Judith Merril wrote: "[a] quality of voice makes the most unevenly composed Sturgeon story compellingly readable." But it is astonishing to find that voice clear and recognizable in the very first handful of short-short stories he sold McClure as a twenty-year-old, who (after his first sale) had just broken away from the merchant marine.

One of the great paradoxes to me has always been that the general flaws one finds in commercial fiction are invariably in the line of plot and structure: The progression of incident in the vast majority of paraliterary fictions is simply and wholly unbelievable. Having done or felt A, it is simply unbelievable that character X would proceed to do B or C. What makes this paradoxical is simply that the explicitly stated esthetic of the writers of these stories is one that holds up craft over art, that says that surface is of a wholly secondary importance as to craft—which, by this esthetic is wholly a matter of a well-structured, well-motivated plot. If craft—specifically the structuring of believable fictions—can be learned, why can so few commercial writers learn it? Equally paradoxical is the fact that without exception, every truly memorable commercial writer, from Chandler and Hammett to Bradbury and Vance, Cordwainer Smith and Alfred Bester and—yes—Sturgeon is memorable because of a specific writerly surface that is so easily called "style."

These paradoxes have produced their share of critical embarrassments.

III

In the 1970s, for example, in the pages of *Science Fiction Studies*, Polish writer Stanislaw Lem attacked Sturgeon's story "Maturity," one of the most respected stories in the greater Anglo-American science fiction community. During the late forties, this story greatly excited the SF community of both readers and writers. It was much talked about and several times anthologized, quickly gaining a reputation as a "science fiction classic." Lem proceeded to point out the story's very real structural weaknesses. On the strength of those weaknesses, Lem proceeded to dismiss the story, Sturgeon, and the critical community that had held the story to be of value. Though Lem purposely skirted the story's good points, the flaws he picked out were—again—certainly there. But what Lem seemed wholly unaware of was the underlying cause of the excitement around the story in the first place. And that is: Sturgeon rewrote it.

SF stories had of course been rewritten before. Editors had often asked for changes, and even the sort of rewriting Sturgeon did is suggested in the memoirs of Isaac Asimov and others from the fine old days. All the same, in 1947 a draft of "Maturity" was published in *Astounding*. Sturgeon was not satisfied with it. (Presumably it wasn't mature enough ... ?) The story was reworked, and a new draft (mainly the ending differs) was published in an anthology. News of the whole process became generally known throughout that small and volatile group of writers, editors and fannish readers that composed the SF community (a tenth the size, in the late forties, of what it is today.) And the interest suddenly sparked. People wanted to see what an SF story rewritten by someone among them already acknowledged as a master wordsmith *looked* like.

To understand why they were so intrigued, however, we have to have some understanding of science fiction as a commercial writing field in the decade after the Second World War. We have to remember that the current respectability of science fiction is less than twenty-five years old. Many writers whose careers extend back before that period—among them many of our best—can still be heard to boast: "Me? No, I never rewrite. It all comes out first draft." Visitors from the world of mundane fiction, where the paradigms for fictive labor are the legendary travails of Joyce and Flaubert, tend to frown here. They *believe* these writers (though too frequently the writers who assert these first draft miracles are, to put it politely, overstating things); what bewilders mundane visitors (from a world where a boastful writer is much more likely to talk about how *much* work went into the text) is the underlying assumption to the boast. They miss the subtext that gives the boast its meaning. As one graduate English student once whispered to me a decade ago at a Science Fiction Writers of America party, where a number of our most eminent practitioners were deep in a round of I-work-less-on-my-best-stories-than-thou: "What enterprise do these men [the writers in question were all men] think they are involved in that *not* revising is something to *brag* about?"

The answer is not so difficult, however, as the graduate student might think.

Science Fiction is a highly affective mode of writing. Our audience gasps, applauds, rises stunned from its seats, falls back limp with hanging jaw—so that the writerly stance of the virtuoso is a valid one for us. The SF writer leaps up, momentarily casts a silhouette against the stars, effects a few breathtaking turns and recoveries, then lightly sets down, bows, and saunters off; and the little postperformance gesture—"See, it was nothing"—is, of course, just the final *part* of the performance.

Now there are literary writers—Nabokov, Borges—who are as pyrotechnic in their local effects as, well, Sturgeon—or, to cite another underrated star in our galaxy, Alfred Bester. But although they make our hearts leap as high in our breasts or our breath catch as sharply in our throats, all by a mere dazzle of words, we tend to express our appreciation of those effects by knowing smiles rather than by, as SF readers so often do, falling all over the floor.

We have all seen the SF reader at an SF convention, two o'clock in the morning, run shrieking from a hotel room, paperback waving, to halt, staggering, among the fans around the ice machine, gasping and panting: "*Read* that! Just *read* that paragraph there! I mean, isn't that *amazing*!" This is a very intense reaction.

For the SF writer to take on the public image of either a Borges (the rare work, produced over a vast period of time under the no doubt exquisitely painful pressure of a doubly distilled aesthetic sensibility and not a little political oppression) or a Nabokov (the rich novel written out on innumerable index cards, each individually and endlessly revised, interminably sorted over and, no doubt, cross-indexed, so that the text is finally the result of an unimaginable and eyestraining amount of sheer *work*) would seem, in light of such intense reader reaction, unseemly. The writer of literary fiction is traditionally the writer ignored or misunderstood. (Borges's work must wait twenty or twenty-five years for the world recognition we now consider its due; Nabokov becomes famous only through the fluke best-sellerdom of his tenth or so novel, because the public mistakenly considers it obscene.) Somehow it is meet for literary writers (or whoever proselytizes for them) to stress the pain and labor necessary to bring these writers' valuable works to the world. But that meetness is still proscribed by the career models of Joyce and Flaubert, both writers whose works were tried in court, the one waiting too long for recognition, the other too quickly forgotten.

SF writers and other practitioners of the paraliterary, within their circumscribed world, get all the recognition they can use and then some. And although recognition is not money, within the paraliterary world of SF writers, editors, and convention goers, those writers who do not start to establish reasonable reputations in their twenties are usually those who do not start writing till their thirties. With a background of such volatile appreciation, to downplay the pain and labor that goes into the work is simply a kind of good manners. The readers are quite impressed enough with the texts already. And though they clamor endlessly to ask, "Where do you get your ideas?" (a question I have never heard any SF writer worth her or his salt seriously try to answer), the question, "How do you put these ideas together?" (which, with a little thought and analysis, *is* sometimes answerable) is much rarer. I believe an SF reader asking, "Where do you get your ideas?" is simply the audience asking to be reassured that the hat is really empty and the rabbit really gone. But by and large in science fiction, the readers appreciate the trick enough to realize just how much (different for each of us) might be lost if the writer were to reveal how it was done. By comparison, the literary writer is continually in the position of having to say to a rather listless audience, "Well, you may not think much of the trick, but if you could only see what its mechanics are you'd appreciate it a lot more." And whether the mechanics to be explicated are the subtle recomplications of the textual surface itself, or a catalogue of the rigors, triumphs, traditions, or even personal tragedies that underlie the artist's personal training, the template is the same. Thus, what looks like befuddled vulgarity from the perspective of the literary world appears as a laudable aesthetic reticence from the perspective of the paraliterary landscape—the world of science fiction. But although this is the synchronic situation that contours such behavior from within the field, there is a diachronic (that is, historical) pressure as well from without, working toward the same end.

Literary fiction rises out of (or, more accurately, has since the early 19th century successfully appropriated) what Professor Stanley E. Fish calls "The Aesthetic of the Good Physician": literary fiction is good for you; its goal is a greater understanding of the world and of the passions, which understanding will make you a better person. If you are educated well enough, or lucky enough already to possess the proper temperament, the whole process may even give pleasure ... although more serious readers are chary of holding out even this much enticement. And with reason. Satisfaction, yes—but *pleasure...?* In the last few years at least two perfectly intelligent persons have told me, with a polemical glitter in their eye, "I never read for pleasure." One was an Oxford graduate specializing in Italian literature of the Resorgiamento. The other was the chairman of the comparative literature department for an upstate New York university. On the one hand, I can say that this sentence, as it concerns these two readers and as most SF readers would interpret it, is simply untrue. I have seen the first of these folk laugh aloud over one 17th-century lyric and be struck to wet-eyed muteness by another; the second, twenty-five minutes after he made the statement, was (as we shared the comparative privacy of Buffalo's Albright-Knox cafeteria) in tongue-tied rapture over an ironic trope in the third chapter of *Bouvard et Pécuchet*. On the other hand, their point on not reading *for* pleasure *is* polemical. I understand it, and I agree with its polemical intent. To have read and responded to the written word at a depth great enough to experience satisfaction/pleasure/rapture is *to have worked*. And if you are a writer, teacher, or critic, that work had best be done with a certain degree of conscientiousness, if not self-consciousness. Pleasure in reading is *not* innate. It is a learned response, as reading itself (i.e., all the conventions that contour pleasure in a text, from the meanings of individual words to the significance of larger fictive figures) is learned.

Fans—whether they are science fiction fans or opera fans—are people who, through education or exposure, have simply been able to establish the good working habits without really trying necessary to respond to the work. But unless fans keep up that work by fairly rigorous application, their enthusiasm falls away. They are able to enjoy less and less varied kinds of writing within their desired precincts; and finally none at all. And this atrophy of response is what the reader who reads "only for pleasure"—the reader who says, "I will make no conscious effort over any work aside from what my temperament and my education to date have rendered spontaneous"—always risks, always falls victim to. In this sense a reader must read *for* the work rather than for the pleasure, if pleasure is to be a rich and continuing experience in reading. The reader is rather like a dancer: s/he must be as committed to the practice session as s/he is to the performance to produce specular delights in either—a delight that even so laborious a reader as the author of *S/Z*, Roland Barthes, finally consents to call *The Pleasure of the Text*.

Now, as we have said, science fiction fans risk the same falling away if they do not work at their reading as do any other fans. But, because of the social matrix around science fiction (of which its extensive fandom, myriad fanzines, and hundred-odd yearly SF conventions are only the most conspicuous emblems), there is a much greater social pressure on SF fans to *do* the work than there is on most readers of literary fiction. (Outside the university, *where* is the pressure...?) From science fiction's initial self-presentation as an "intellectual" entertainment, to the various fictive conventions that must be learned for the reader to make any headway with the texts, to organized fandom, and finally to the rather flamboyant image most readers have of the delights to be achieved, everything allows us to take it on faith that in science fiction the work, to a surprising extent, is *done* by a large number of science fiction readers. Thus, in discussions of the field set within its borders, we are not so constrained to polemicize for that work by decrying the pleasure as are either our reader of 17th-century Italian or our Comp. Lit. chairman.

The larger point of all this is, of course, that science fiction does not grow out of "The Aesthetic of the Good Physician." It grows out of quite a different aesthetic, an aesthetic we could easily call Faustian—or even that of the Evil Charlatan.

It grows out of the dime novel, the pulp tradition, the borderline pornography of violence and romance. It grows out of a tradition that, for most of its history, was not only considered to be Not Good for You, but for much of its existence was considered to be downright deleterious. The Platonic ideal was—and still is—the dominant model by which art is judged, especially art for the young: Art is supposed to supply models for correct behavior. Thus, by definition, anything with too great an element of fantasy, anything that distorts the world, any text with any sort of larger-than-life romanticism, tends to be considered dangerous. This was especially true during the hardship years of the Great Depression, when brilliant men like Sturgeon's stepfather, William Dicky Sturgeon (whom Sturgeon and his older brother Peter called Argyll), master of half a dozen languages and a crack mathematician, were working well below their capacity at various elementary and high school teaching jobs, simply to hold a family together. It was a time when the good child was the silent child, the scared child, the child wholly intimidated by authority—the child who would do what he was told and could not possibly get into any sort of trouble. Sturgeon learned about this aesthetic at the hands of his stepfather, brutally and painfully. He describes the event in an autobiographical essay he wrote for a therapist, Jim Hayes, in 1965.

It was about this time that I discovered science fiction; a kid at school sold me a back number (1933 *Astounding*) for a nickel, my lunch money. I was always so unwary! I brought it home naked and open, and Argyll pounced on it as I came in the door. "Not in *my* house!" he said, and scooped it off my schoolbooks and took it straight into the kitchen and put it in the garbage and put the cover on. "That's what we do with garbage," and he sat back down at his desk and my mother at the end of it and their drink *(Argyll, 36)*.

At the same time, Argyll was reading to his stepson from such volumes as "*The Cloister and the Hearth, The White Company, Anthony Adverse, Vanity Fair, Tess of the D'Urbervilles,* Homer, Aristophanes, Byron *(Childe Harold), The Hound of Heaven, War and Peace, Crime and Punishment, Dead Souls,* God knows what all" *(Argyll, 29)*. And young Sturgeon "got most of it."

But Sturgeon also continued to read the forbidden pulp stories. He sought for a way to collect the magazines, and he expended a good deal of ingenuity figuring out a way to read them—in his desk drawer, while he was doing his homework, the sides waxed with a candle to keep them from squeaking—and to store them: Finding a trap door in the roof of his closet, young Sturgeon (he describes himself then as "twelve or fourteen") placed his magazines, two deep, between the attic beams—starting five beams away. He even went so far as to replace the dust on the beams after he had crawled across them, and did everything else to cover up the traces.

Two weeks later, however:

I breezed home from school full of innocence and anticipation, and Argyll looked up briefly and said, "There's a mess in your room I want you to clean up." It didn't even sound like a storm warning. He could say that about what a sharpened pencil might leave behind it.

The room was almost square, three windows opposite the door, Pete's bed and desk against the left wall, mine against the right. All the rest, open space, but not now. It was covered somewhat more than ankle deep by a drift of small pieces of newsprint, all almost exactly square, few bigger than four postage stamps. Showing here and there was a scrap of glossy polychrome from the covers.... This must have taken him hours to do, and it was hard to think of him in a rage doing it because so few of the little bits were crumpled. Hours and hours, rip, rip, rip.

It is hard to recapture my feelings at the moment. I went ahead and cleaned it all up and put it outside; I was mostly aware of this cold clutch in the solar plexus which is a compound of anger and fear (one never knew when one of his punishments was over, or if any specific one was designed to be complete in itself or part of a sequence)....

I do feel, however, that this episode had a great deal to do with my becoming a science fiction writer, and should be taken into account when evaluating the special interest that field has had for me (*Argyll*, 38).

But like many parents of the time who forbade their children to read "such trash," Argyll no doubt thought he was protecting his stepson from the pernicious influence of an evil antiart. But the larger point (in terms of writers like Sturgeon, who, through such firsthand encounters, knew this aesthetic to function at a strength that, say, someone like myself—whose childhood fell on the other side of the Second World War, in a time of greater affluence and general relaxation of moral rigidities—never had to deal with. When my parents walked in on me as an eight-year-old and found me reading a Batman comic, sometime in 1946, my father was, indeed, appalled. But my mother's response was: "But at least he's reading *something*...!" And so comics—and later science fiction—were allowed in the house with only comparatively minimal policing) is the effect of this aesthetic on the self-presentation of commercial SF writers at the time:

If I am doing something good for you that you must work hard to benefit from (the Good Physician Aesthetic speaking), then it is reasonable for me—or someone else, if I am too modest—to stress the work I have had to do, if only to urge you to do your part.

If, however, I am doing something bad for you—and, what's more, you have already worked hard to get hold of it (and in the early pulp years this meant not only the clandestinely purchased magazines, the parental disapproval, and—on my side of the War— the flashlight under the covers, the secret stash in the crawl space, but also *reading* all those texts, learning one's way around in a confusing and ill-set jargon, and learning to respond to a procession of conventions that were just forming and often in flux; so that whenever one of them was called up by no matter what distant or however fragmented metonymy, you knew what that convention meant, the way you know a word's meaning [rather than the way you know how to exegete a law or define a word—or explain a literary convention], in short, it meant work, a kind of work not so different in its basic form from that required of a scholar to become comfortable with the work of another century) then I have none of the privileges of the Good Physician. If I can get a consensus that, while what I am doing is bad for you, it's not all *that* bad (and, besides, I just tossed it off without much thought), then there is a possibility I may be judged a more or less forgivable scamp. If, however, not only is what I am doing bad for you, but it also becomes known that I worked on it, calculated its every effect, indulged dreams of glory over its possible success and sweated in agony over its possible failure, planned it endlessly and revised it incessantly, and, finally exhausted, let it go from me, sick over where it falls short of perfection and grimly smug over where it approaches it, then I am no longer a scamp.

I am a criminal.

This is the historical reason SF writers must play down the work that goes into their texts. Along with the synchronic reasons outlined above it, this is the historical background—far stronger in the thirties than it was in 1947 (and all but vanished today—though there is always the possibility for a resurgence), the date of "Maturity"—against which Sturgeon actually *revised* a story, revised it because of his own dissatisfaction with some Lukacsian ethical/aesthetic interface. This was the virtuoso stance suddenly cast aside. This was Faust admitting that the formula for his potion was really more complicated than the artificial sweeteners and fruit colorings listed in small print at the bottom of the label. This was not a commercial writer's acquiescence to some editorial exhortation to tone this down for propriety's sake or beef that up for excitement's. It was the acrobat, after the trick had been performed for all practical purposes successfully, as much a virtuoso as ever (it had been published, had it not?), suddenly shaking his head, going back into the ring, and doing it again—not for some effect of the performance, but out of commitment to what was being performed.

The effect—on a good deal of the audience—was stunning.

The temptation was, no doubt, to see this as simply an importation of "mainstream" behavior into science fiction. That some of Sturgeon's contemporaries saw it as such and thought it inappropriate no doubt added energy to the dialogue—which is why we can recall it today. Nevertheless, meanings are matters of context and metonymy: Faust, no matter the caduceus he wave aloft nor the bedside manner he assume, is *not* the Good Physician. And the whole occurrence was not caduceus-waving—it was real (that is, it was something the field *had* to deal with); it was perceived as authentic. What it did was to clear an area in that conceptual space that is science fiction (the texture of particular moments in that space expressed in—and as—particular SF texts) in which such commitment could now be recognized to exist and could continue to exist, if not with a terribly sophisticated critical vocabulary for talking about it then at least with a vocabulary of actions, situations, and responses through which it could be thought about dramatically. Such a clearing and defining reorganized the structure of a conceptual space in such a way that the structure recomplicates and expands through that space until the mental space of construction for the actual text (and thus the texture of the text) is changed.

A personal example, if it will help: My basic working method has been (at least up until the time of word processors) not extraordinary for an SF author making a living by writing. I instituted it with my first SF novel and, with minor variations, it remains my working method today: I write a longhand draft; from this I make a rough typescript, specifying, expanding, toothbrushing out redundancies, excising unnecessary adjectives and phrases, clarifying parallels as I go. From this I make a polished typescript, in which I can catch any missed details as well as do any doctoring necessary on those details thrown out of sync between the first and second layers. In my personal vocabulary this tri-layered process *is* my "first draft." Anything beyond this is "revision." And should that revision run over a sentence or two, it goes through the same tri-layered process. It is a highly utilitarian method: it makes for prose that stays in print. (Word processors have simply expanded the tri-layered process into a ten-or-more layered one.) Also, it acknowledges that the cleverest of us is extremely fallible, that a story is a very complex engine, and that in the best of them far too much is going on for even the author to keep all parts spinning in the air at any one time.

Why not allow a minimum of three?

This relates to Sturgeon in two ways. First, I probably would not have wanted to write science fiction if Sturgeon's work had not affected me the way it did. Second, I probably would not have hit on my working method—and certainly not hit on it for my first book—if the "Maturity" episode had not been part of our field's history, so that as a 19-year-old, twelve years after the fact, I could still be aware of its excitement, its energy, its message: science fiction *can* be revised, *can* command commitment, *can* strive for a stylistic clarity, concision, and invention beyond that of mere journalism. For science fiction to mature, this awareness had to grow out of science fiction's own space. It couldn't be imported—for the conceptual space of science fiction is finally far closer in organization to the performance space of the circus (with its extraordinary vertical as well as horizontal organization recalling science fiction's spaceships and alien worlds; with its audience surround and its oddly fuzzy distinction between backstage and performance area recalling SF writers' relation to their vociferous and ever-present fans; and the circus was the first art to insist openly that more must go on in the performance space than can possibly be seen at once) than it is to the staid divisions of the theater (backstage, stage, and audience), which, since Shakespeare, has constrained our view of "Literature." For it is precisely in the circus space that the virtuoso gesture is held out to tempt novices to trip over themselves in the rush to achieve it; whereupon they become victims of a derision far sharper and crueler than that which greets the clowns, who first lured them from their seats and into the ring with their parodic versions of all the splendor passing and twirling, roaring and soaring.

Looking back on the "Maturity" episode, two other general points might be made. First, this clearing of the conceptual space for this commitment could only have happened with a writer of the reputation Sturgeon had already garnered within the field by 1947. Second, given this late '40s setting, it could probably only have occurred around a story as profoundly safe as "Maturity": Any signs of daring or protest in the text itself would have immediately slanted the general interpretation of the supposed motivation for that subsequent revision away from one of pure ethical/aesthetic commitment. For we are talking of mythology now—not an actual writer with actual paper in an actual typewriter. But these myths, frustrating as they are for the man or woman at their core, have their formal importance. And "Maturity" is about as well-mannered a tale, by the conventions of ordinary '50s fiction, as someone is likely to find in the Sturgeon *oeuvre;* and the later version is slightly more well-mannered than the former. Anyone acquainted with the context, if not the text itself, should have been able to predict this. Certainly they should not have been, as Lem was, surprised by it. For that matter, all great writers have been concerned with good manners as their times define them. But to seek Sturgeon's greatness in a tale achieving notice in such circumstances and then to declare oneself put out at not finding it, as, in effect, Lem does, seems almost willfully obtuse. The careful analysis of a public success, however small that public, is always instructive. But by the same token—accepting public opinion as an essential given of someone's analytic insight, because public opinions are myths, and myths, as Cassirer and others have noted, are invariably conservative "if only through the committee nature of their composition"—the worst one can say of Lem is that, coming from a country with no pulp tradition of its own, he had no feel for the context and simply ignored or misread the contextual signs. The best one can say is that, well, giants will wrangle.

IV

But it is often the Sturgeon stories that gained notice, if not notoriety, in their day that seem now on the thin side. "The World Well Lost," for example, which despite its powerful picture of homophobia brushes rather pastel fingers over the subject of male homosexuality itself, was for a while frequently mentioned as an example of science fiction's growing "liberality" in matters sexual, along with Philip José Farmer's "The Lovers." Today the Farmer tale seems, at best, intriguingly troglodytic, and the Sturgeon only a step from rank conservatism—although it certainly made my eyes water when I first read it at fifteen. Another Sturgeon story much discussed in the few years after its publication was "Affair with a Green Monkey": however artful its opening, today we have to admit that its whole thrust is toward a rather trivial one-liner. A contemporary reader, finding the excited references to it that litter the fanzines and magazine letter columns of its day, is likely to ask: What was all the fuss? The only way to understand the fuss is, again, to reconstruct the surrounding situation, i.e., a social moment in which not only were the actions involved in these stories considered a sin, a sickness, and a crime by law, but the words themselves were forbidden to print. We can take an example from Sturgeon's science fiction novella, "To Marry Medusa" (1958—which Sturgeon later expanded into his briefest science fiction novel, *The Cosmic Rape* [1958]): "' ... an' him runnin' out an stickin' his head back in an' callin' me a—' Sanctimoniously, Al would not sully his lips with the word. And the rye-and-ginger by the door would be nodding wisely and saying, 'Man shouldn't mention a feller's mother, whatever,'" or, later on, from the novel's Chapter 12, "' ... Pop. Hey, Pop! Carol's sayin' summon a bish.' And Tony would say, 'Don't say that, Carol,' whereupon the lights of the oncoming vehicle would be upon him and in dedicated attention he would slit his eyes, set his jaw, and say precisely what Carol was trying to repeat." In light of today's realistic novel and film dialogue, readers tend to see these now as coy gestures toward a vanished piety. But what such passages actually are is ironic commentary on their epoch's very real and absolutely enforced (by law and threat of imprisonment) printing conventions—conventions that would not begin to relax till nearly a decade after the tales carrying such lines had been first published. Here we are again left with two points to make: first, verbal tropes such as the one-liner of "Affair with a Green Monkey" or the pastel touch in "The World Well Lost" are what that decade substituted for sex (of whatever persuasion) in print, while piously insisting that the clear discomfort these substitutions caused was precisely what was being avoided by eliding the sex itself.

We cannot be surprised if Sturgeon, the writer most sensitive to those years, was also, in the work of this period, very much of those years himself. But we should also note that when, for example in his Western story "Scars," Sturgeon dealt with some of the same material both "Affair With a Green Monkey" and "The World Well Lost" had focused on (i.e., men's dubiousness about masculine sexual expectations), he did so with much less heavy hands, to produce one of his strongest and most compassionate stories by today's standards.

But it is not in Sturgeon's well-mannered stories (be they conservatively or shockingly well-mannered) that today's reader is likely to find what is most interesting, most stimulating, most impressive, most obsessive, and most simply and awesomely beautiful in Sturgeon. The ten-year delay in finding a publisher for one of Sturgeon's earliest written stories (then the thousand-dollar first prize from *Argosy* magazine—a story by Graham Greene took second place—the vindication, the reputation: the story is "Bianca's Hands" [in *The Ultimate Egoist,* Volume I of The Complete Stories]) does not speak of well-mannered fiction as the times defined—although the story is beautifully wrought, and any nineteen-year-old (Sturgeon was nineteen when he wrote it) could be justly proud of it. "Die, Maestro, Die!," with its guitarist's amputated fingers (a passing obsession for Sturgeon? Compare this with the extraordinary self-mutilation scene involving the guitar-playing protagonist from *The Dreaming Jewels* [1950]) is not a polite tale at all. And while this second volume of stories contains a goodly number of Sturgeon stories that were particularly popular in their day ("Microcosmic God," "Shottle Bop," and "Poker Face" are all tales that came in for special praise when they first appeared—as did "Killdozer!", the story that will open the subsequent Volume III), the delight of this volume is that it contains so many stories that today's reader is bound to find even richer and *more* rewarding. Nor are "The Sex Opposite," "It Wasn't Syzygy," "The Other Celia," "Bright Segment," "A Way of Thinking," or "Mr. Costello, Hero" well-mannered stories by anybody's standards. And *these* are the tales in which a modern reader begins to encounter the unsurpassed, the incomparable, the magnificent Sturgeon.

The long-time Sturgeon reader has no doubt been patiently waiting through all this historical retrieval with a question. We ask it now: What are we to do with Sturgeon's frequently quoted assertion, "All my work is about love"? Well, I take the assertion seriously—but in the manner that I take seriously the innumerable strategies devised over the centuries by innumerable artists to reach into the centers of their own creativity. Such a statement may well represent Sturgeon's own key to working. But there is no necessity for it to be my key into the work. Where do I go for such a key? Where I go for the key into any other writer's work: to the text— and, because in science fiction there is such lively reader response, to the readers ... with a large margin for caution, translation, and evaluation.

Some six years before Heinlein's *Stranger in a Strange Land* (1961) supplied the term *grok* to the counterculture for a brief currency, Sturgeon's SF novel *More Than Human* gave a word to a circle of young readers (which included me) meant to combine aspects of blending and meshing: *blesh*. Perhaps it was simply because of my age, but *grok*—especially after someone (James Blish?) noted that its meaning was practically identical to the then-current meaning (it changes yearly) of the jazz term *dig*—somehow never entered my vocabulary.

Blesh did.

I still have to stop myself, now and then, from writing it down in the flow of the most formal nonfiction. And forty-five years after the publication of the novel in which it first appeared, a few friends of mine still use the term in conversation.

But I think this sound-image, bleshing, this order of *communitas* always on the verge of communion, expresses an inchoate need in the American psyche; as well, it relates to a gallery of images that recur through Sturgeon's texts. And the other single word—the biological image that the Sturgeon reader (and apparently for a while Sturgeon as well) most easily groups that gallery of images around as a metaphorical center—is, of course, the word denied in the title of one tale, explained in the text of another, and referred to in passing in any number of others: "syzygy."

Sturgeon himself describes it for one-celled organisms in "It Wasn't Syzygy": "Two of these organisms let their nuclei flow together for a time. Then they separate and go their ways again. It isn't a reproductive process at all. It's merely a way in which each may gain a part of the other." For biological accuracy, we can add that the cell walls merge and that cytoplasm as well as nucleoplasm, exchanges. After they separate, both cells quickly undergo fission twice (resulting in eight organisms). Although syzygy is not a reproductive process, besides allowing genetic mixing it triggers reproduction through two generations.

Looking at the range and power of this communion as it is presented again and again throughout Sturgeon's work, certainly I see love as one of its most important forms. Yet what has always struck me *vis-á-vis* Sturgeon's assertion is how much larger than love—love in any form I can recognize it—this communion is always turning out to be. It is almost always moving toward the larger-than-life, the cosmic, the mystical. In a number of places in Sturgeon's work— *More Than Human, The Cosmic Rape*—it comes to be one with evolution itself.

Dealing with such an awesome communion, Sturgeon might well want to keep himself oriented toward love. It would be rather heady, if not horrifying, to explore that communion without such a fixed point to home on—though a few times Sturgeon has given us a portrait of this communion with the orientation toward hate ("Die, Maestro, Die!" and "Mr. Costello, Hero"), and these are among his most powerful stories. Certainly the relationships presented in "Bianca's Hands" and "Bright Segment" begin as love; but although neither ever loses the name, both, by the end of their respective tales, have developed into something far more terrifying. Yet the intensity of effect, finally, allies that dark version to the brighter one of such tales as, say, "The (Widget), the (Wadget), and Boff" or "Make Room for Me."

Artists outgrow their terminology (not to mention their metaphors), and Sturgeon would soon leave syzygy behind—first as a word, then as a concept. But for the reader, the image of merging cells, fused in some imponderable union, closer than sex, with many aspects of sex about it but ultimately a replacement for sex among the essentially asexual, is a microstructure rich enough to begin organizing around it readings of the larger and more varied communions Sturgeon presents in one form or another in almost every tale.

Sturgeon wanted a world that worked differently from the one we live in; and that difference was that it had a place for love and logic both. What seemed to bolster him and give him personal patience and also artistic perseverance was his apprehension of the interconnectedness of all life's varied and variegated aspects.

For all the brilliance of its accomplishment, Sturgeon's career was by no means smooth or easy. He had three marriages (the second was annulled), two more long-term relationships, and seven children. Financially, there were times when he approached the level of middle class comfort, but not many. And his writing was broken by several extended periods when he could not write at all—even so much as a letter. Such periods were financially disastrous and deeply painful to the man—even as they troubled his readers. Because Sturgeon was as popular as he was, at the merest mention of a story or book idea from him, editors would rush into print with an announcement of a book or a story forthcoming, that finally would never appear. (The long, late tale "When You Care, When You Love" was trumpeted as the first section of a novel—never finished. And a tale called "Tandy's Story" that appeared in *Galaxy* in 1961 was supposed to be one of a series, one named for each of his children—never completed.)

There's a story that Sturgeon has told about himself and that others have repeated.

In the early fifties, during the midst of one of Sturgeon's several blocked periods, *Galaxy* editor Horace L. Gold finally broke through it. Sturgeon had explained to Gold that he was worrying so much about the terrifying oppression and fear emanating from Senator Joseph McCarthy, who was investigating "un-American" activity and destroying lives and reputations left and right in the process, Sturgeon couldn't bring himself to write a story that was simple entertainment. Unless it was something that told the world exactly how he felt about this evil madman, Sturgeon asked, how could he write anything. But a good story, he knew, couldn't simply be a sermon or a political Jeremiad.

Gold thought a moment, then responded: "You write me a story about a man who goes to meet his wife at a bus station to surprise her and who sees her come through the gate smiling at another man—and every *Galaxy* reader in the country will know exactly how you feel about that Washington demagogue."

The story with which Sturgeon responded, the story that ended his blocked period, was "Mr. Costello, Hero"—a beautifully indirect, yet scapularly astute, examination into the workings of "political" evil. But what Gold had perceived was, of course, precisely the interconnectedness (the communion) I referred to—the historically sensitive web on which the finest art plays its times in order to sound the richest music.

Sturgeon told the tale as a lesson on how to end writer's block.

But what he was too modest to say, and what I'm happy to be able to add, is that, for all its truth, I doubt there are very *many* writers to whom Gold would have given this advice.

Myself, I can only think of one.

And that is certainly one reason why, to us, today, Sturgeon is of such pristine and gemlike value.

Samuel R. Delany
New York, 1995

MICROCOSMIC GOD

Cargo

I HEARD SOMEBODY SAY she was haunted. She wasn't haunted. There's another name for what ailed her, and I'll tell you about it if you like. I was aboard her when it started, and before. I knew every sheared rivet on her. I knew her when she was honest, a drab and prosaic member of our merchant marine. I saw what happened to her.

She was one of those broad-shouldered old hulks built by the dozen during War I. Her sisters lay rotting and rusting and waiting for a national emergency to prove their unseaworthiness. O.K. They make good shrapnel. Her name was *Dawnlight,* she was seven thousand tons, a black oil tanker, limped like a three-legged dog, and was as beautiful as a wart. She could do nine knots downhill with a fair wind and an impossible current. When she was loaded she steered well until the loss of weight from burned fuel in the after bunkers threw her down by the head, and then she proceeded as will any tanker with a loss back aft; when she was light she drew seventeen feet aft and nothing forward, so that when the wind blew abeam she spun on her tail like a canoe.

Yes, I knew her of old. She used to carry casing-head. That's airplane gas that makes explosive vapors at around 40° F. So one day a fireman found casing-head seeping through the seams of No. 9 tank into the fireroom and evaporating there. He fainted dead away, and the crew took to the boats during the night. The Old Man woke up at noon the next day screaming for his coffee, put two and two together, and with the help of two engineers and a messman, worked her into a cove in a small island off Cuba.

It so happened that a very wealthy gentleman thereabouts turned up with a nice offer, with the result that the Old Man and his three finks made for Havana in a lifeboat with their pockets full of large bills and the ship's log, which contained an entry describing her explosion and sinking. After that she carried crude oil for the wealthy gentleman to war zones. Great sport.

What made it such great sport was that not only did the *Dawnlight* have no business being afloat, but she had no business being in her particular business. Her nationality was determined by the contents of the flag locker, and her current log looked like a set of the Encyclopaedia Britannica. They'd run up one flag or another, and pick a log to suit.

But she paid well and she fed well, and if you could keep away from the ocean floor and the concentration camps, you'd find her good shipping. If you must commit suicide, you might as well get rich doing it.

I caught her in a certain drydock that makes a good thing of doing quick work and asking few questions. Her skipper was a leathery old squarehead whose viscera must have been a little brown jug. Salt cracked off his joints when he moved. He was all man back aft and all devil on the bridge, and he owned our souls. Not that that was much of a possession. The crew matched the ship, and they were the crummiest, crustiest, hard-bitten bunch of has-been human beings ever to bless the land by going to sea. Had to be that way.

Any tanker is a five-hundred-foot stick of dynamite, even if she isn't an outlaw. If she's loaded, she'll burn forever and a week; and if she's light she'll go sky-high and never come down. All she needs is a spark from somewhere. That can happen easily enough any time; but imagine dodging subs and pocket battleships on both sides of the martial fence—swift, deadly back-stabbers, carrying many and many a spark for our cargoes. We had nothing for protection but luck and the Old Man. We stuck to him.

The *Dawnlight* was the only ship I'd have taken, feeling the way I was. Once in a while the world gangs up on a guy, and he wants an out. The *Dawnlight* was mine—she'd pulled me through a couple of dark spots in the past—once when a certain dope fell and cracked his silly skull in a brawl over a girl, and I had to disappear for a while, and once when I married the girl and she took to blackmailing me for a living. Aside from all this, though, the *Dawnlight* was the only ship I *could* get aboard. I carried an ordinary seaman's certificate, indorsed for wiper. The Department of Commerce was very lenient with me and let me keep those ratings after I ran a naval auxiliary tanker on the rocks. Passed out drunk on watch. Anyhow, the Old Man gave me the eight-to-twelve watch as third mate, papers or no papers. It was that kind of ship. He was that kind of a skipper. He had the idea I was that kind of a sailor.

We left the drydock (it's up North somewhere—that'll do!) and headed east and south. We were in ballast, carrying only two hundred big cases of farm machinery in the two dry cargo holds. Farm machinery with steel-jacketed noses and percussion caps. Nice chunky crates of tractors with rifled barrels. We followed the coastline pretty much, but stayed far off, out of the southbound steamer lanes. This wasn't long after the beginning of the war, when all hands ashore and afloat were excited about neutrality zones, so we wanted to keep our noses clean. However, we weren't too worried. We weren't the only gray-painted unidentified hulk at sea by any means, and anyway, we had the skipper.

We dropped down to about 33° and headed due east. It was early fall—the hurricane season—but the weather was fine and mellow. We kept the morning sun a point off the starboard bow, and in the evening we tore up the base of the shadow we threw ahead. The black gang talked of an unheard-of sixty-three revolutions per minute from the engine, when she hadn't done better than fifty-seven in the last twelve years. Every time I shot the sun or a star on my watch, the ship stood still and waited for me to get it, and I navigated as if I had a radio beam in my pocket. It didn't seem like the old *Dawnlight* any more, with her rotten gear and her chewing-gum calking. It was a pleasure to work her. Even Cajun Joe's sea bread stopped giving me heartburn.

Yes, it was too good to be true, so in the long run it didn't turn out to be true. After we reached longitude 30° everything about that ship went haywire. Nothing was really wrong, only—well, there was the matter of the sextants, for instance. Four of them—mine, and the first's, and the second's, but worst of all, the Old Man's ancient binocular-type monster. They all went just a little bit off—

5

enough to throw us eight or ten degrees off course. You see, after we passed 30°, we changed course a shade north to head us up toward Gibraltar; and no sooner had we done that than clouds popped up from nowhere and the weather got really thick.

Nights we sailed in a black soup, and days we sailed in a white one, and the compass was the only thing that would even admit where we might be. Things got screwy. The revolution counter said we were making a wabbly seven point two knots. The patent log claimed an even six. But it wasn't until the third day of fog, about five bells on my morning watch, that we really found out that we were being led astray. About the sextants, I mean.

There was a hole in the clouds, high on the starboard beam; I saw it coming up, figured it would show the sun, and whistled up the Old Man and the mate. I was right; it was a small hole, and as the three of us lined up on the wing of the bridge with our sextants, the second came bumbling sleepily up with his. Old Johnny Weiss was at the wheel, steadying the lubberline onto the compass card the way only an old shellback trained in sail can steer a ship.

"Watch the clock, Johnny," I said and got the image of that cloud hole on my mirror.

"Hi," he said, which was the nearest any of us came to "Aye-aye, sir" on that scow.

We froze there, the four of us, each sextant steady as a rock, waiting for the gleam. It came, and the Old Man said "Hup!" and we fixed our arcs.

We got the time from Johnny—the old clock in the wheelhouse was chronometer enough for us—and we broke out our tables. Our four sights came out close enough. Position, 31°17' N, 33°9'40"W—which landed us about four hundred miles due east of the Madeiras. We found that if we split the distance between the distance-run given by the deck and engine logs, we'd reach that position by dead reckoning. It looked good—too good. The *Dawnlight* was balky steering, what with her outmoded hydraulic telemotor and her screw-type steering engine. She'd never performed that way.

As soon as I was alone in the chart house I went over my figures. Everything was jake, but—the primary mirror on my sextant was askew. Slipped down a bit in its frame. Why, a thing like that could prove us a hundred and fifty miles off course! It had never happened before—it was a new sextant, and I took care of it. Now how in—

I slipped down to the Old Man's office and went in. He and the mate were bent over the desk. They straightened as I came in.

"Cap'n I—"

"Vot reading dit you get on your sun gun?" he asked me before I could finish my speech. I told him. He scratched his head and looked at the mate.

The mate said: "Yeah, me, too." He was a Boston Irishman named Toole; four foot eleven in his shoes. He was wanted for four very elaborate murders. He collected seventeenth-century miniatures. "I got the same thing, only my sextant's on the bum. That couldn't be right. Look—the eyepiece on the 'scope is off center."

"Look now here." The Old Man took down his behemoth and showed me a gradation plate sliding around loosely over its pulled rivets. "Yust py accident I gat the same."

"My gosh! That's what I came down to tell you, skipper. Look at this." I showed him the loose mirror on my instrument.

Just then Harry, the second mate, edged into the room. He always edged through doors on the mistaken assumption that he was thinner fore and aft than he was across the beam. It was hard to tell. Harry saw everything and said nothing, and if he was as innocent as he hugely looked, he would not have been aboard the *Dawnlight*. He said:

"Cap, m' readin' on that sight was off. My sextant—"

"—hass gone gebrochen. Don't tell me dis too."

"Why . . . yeh. Yeh."

"Four sextants go exactly the same amount off at the same time for four different reasons," said Toole, examining a bent arc track on Harry's sun gun. The captain sighed.

No one said anything for a minute, and we hardly noticed it when the captain's deck lamp winked off. The engine room speaking tube shrieked and I answered it because I was the nearest. I heard:

"Skipper?"

"Third mate."

"Tell the Old Man that No. 2 generator just threw its armature. Cracked the casing all to hell."

"What's the matter with No. 1?"

"Damfino. Fused solid two hours ago. And no spares for anything, and no cable to wind a new armature."

"O.K." I turned and told the skipper.

He almost laughed. "I vas yust going to say dot ve'd haf to take a radio bearing on Gibraltar and Feisal. Heh. Didn't y'u tell me, 'Arry, dot dere vas no acid for the batteries on the radio?"

"I did."

"Heh." The skipper drummed for a moment on his desk, looking at me without seeing me. Then he saw me. "Vot de dirty hell are y'u duing down here ven y'u're on vatch? Gat up dere!"

I got—there were times when you couldn't play around with the old boy.

Up on deck the weather looked the same. The sea was slick and the air was warm, and I had to fumble around to locate the bridge ladder. Johnny was steering steadily, easily, a couple of spokes each way every couple of minutes. He was the only man aboard that had the feel of that crazy ship, with her warped keel and her scored and twisted propeller. He looked up at me as I stepped into the wheelhouse and grunted.

"What's up, Johnny?"

"Reckon you know where we are, huh?"

"I reckon."

No sense in getting the crew talking. Sailors gossip like a bridge club, and for the same reason—grouped people with the same basic interests. I've seen three-quarters of a crew packed up and ready to leave because some wiseacre started the rumor that a ship was to be sold for scrap at the next port.

Johnny grunted, and I went into the chart room to monkey with that slipped glass in my sextant. The way the weather looked, I'd never have a chance to use it again, but then you can't tell about an African coastwise fog. What had made Johnny so quizzical? The more I tried to think of something else, the more that bothered me.

8

About ten minutes later, working on the theory that the last word said before a long pause is the one that sticks, I went back into the wheelhouse and asked:

"Why do you want to know?"

"Oh, nothin'." He spat, and the tobacco juice rang a knell on the cuspidor. "Jest thinkin'."

"Come on—give."

"Waal—seems to me we been steering east b' nor'east about two days—right?"

"So?"

"Youse guys was so busy peekin' through yer sextants at the Big Light that you didn't see it was in the wrong place."

"The sun? In the wrong place?"

"Yep. Steerin' east b' nor'east this time o' year, hereabouts, seems to me the sun'd show about broad on the bow at ten thirty in th' mornin'."

"Well?"

"So it shows up high an' dead abeam. Don't seem right, somehow."

He was right. I went and sat down on the pilot's stool. Radio dead, sextants haywire; all we have is the compass and good old Bowditch's dead-reckoning tables. And now—the compass?

"Johnny, are you sure you were on course when we took that sight?"

His silence was eloquent. Old Johnny Weiss could steer anything with a rudder unless it had a steering oar, and then he was better than most. If we had a radio, we could check the compass. We had no radio. If we could get a sun sight, we wouldn't need the radio. We couldn't get a sun sight. We were lost—lost as hell. We were steering a rock-steady compass course on a ship that was pounding the miles away under her counter as she had never done before, and she was heading bravely into nowhere.

An ordinary seaman popped in. "Lost the patent log, sir!"

Before I could say, "Oh, well, it didn't work, anyway," the engine room tube piped up.

"Well?" I said into it, in the tone that means "Now what?"

It was the third engineer again. "Is the skipper up there?"

"No. What is it?"

"A lot of things happen," wailed the third. "Why do they all have to happen to *me*?"

"You don't know, shipmate, you don't know! What's up?"

"The rev-counter arm worked loose and fell into the crank pit. The I.P. piston grabbed it and hauled counter and all in. Goddlemighty, what goes on here? We jinxed?"

"Seems as though," I said, and whistled down the captain's tube to report the latest.

Everything depended on our getting a sun sight now. We might have calculated our speed at least from the revolution readings, a tide chart and propslip table. The admiralty charts don't give a damn about this particular section of sea water. Why should they? There's supposed to be a deep around the Madeiras somewhere, but then again there's flat sand aplenty off Africa. Even the skipper's luck wouldn't pull us out of this. I had a feeling. Damn it, we couldn't even hail a ship, if we met one. It would be bound to turn out a q-ship or a sub-chaser, tickled to death to pinch our cargo. Farm machinery. Phooey!

The saloon messman came up carrying clean sheets for the chart-room cot. I knew what that meant. The bridge was going to be the skipper's little home until we got out of this—if we did. I was dead beat. Things like this couldn't happen—they *couldn't*!

We had a council of war that night, right after I came on watch, the captain and I. Nothing had happened all day; the sun came out only once, on the twelve to four, and ducked in again so quickly that Harry couldn't get to his sextant. He did set the pelorus on it, but the ship rolled violently because of some freak current just as he sighted, and the altitude he got was all off. There'd been nothing else—Oh yes; we'd lost three heaving lines over the side, trying to gauge our speed with a chip. The darnedest thing about it was that everything else was going as well as it possibly could.

The cook had found nine crates of really fancy canned goods in the linen locker—Lord knows how long they'd been there. It was just as if they'd been dropped out of nowhere. The engines ran without a hitch. The low-pressure cylinder lost its wheeze, and in the wash-rooms we got hot water when we wanted it instead of cold water or steam. Even the mattresses seemed softer. Only we just didn't know where we were.

The Old Man put his hand on my shoulder and startled me, coming up behind me in the darkness that way. I was standing out on the wing of the bridge.

"Vot's de matter; vorried about de veather?" he asked me. He was funny that way, keeping us on our toes with his furies and his—what was it?—kindnesses.

"Well, yes, cap'n. I don't like the looks of this."

He put his elbows on the coaming. "I tell y'u boy, ve ain't got nodding to fret about."

"Oh, I guess not, but I don't go for this hide-'n'-go-seek business." I could feel him regarding me carefully out of the corners of his eyes.

"I vant to tell y'u something. If I said dis to de mate, or Harry, or vun of de black gang, dey vould say: 'I t'ink de ol' squarehead is suckin' vind. He must be gettin' old.' But I tell y'u."

I was flattered.

"Dis is a old ship, but she is good. I am going to be sorry to turn her over to sumvun else."

"What are you talking about, skipper? You're not quitting when we get back?"

"No; before dat. Dass all I vorry about, y'u see. Dis vill be de first command I lost half a trip out. I vass master of thirty-two ships, but I alvays left dem in der home port. It von't be like dat now."

I was more than a little taken aback. I'd never seen the stringy old gun runner sentimental about his ship before. This was the first time I'd ever heard him mention it in printable terms. But what was all this about losing his command?

"What's the matter, cap'n—think we'll go to camp?" That was a *Dawnlight* idiom and meant being picked up by a warship of some kind.

"No boy—nodding like dat. Dey can't touch us. Nobody can touch us now. Ah—hear dat?"

He pointed far out to port. The night was very still, with hardly a sound but the continual seethe of millions of bursting bubbles slithering past the ship's side. But far out in the fog was an insistent splashing—that heavy smacking splash that every seaman knows.

"Porpoise," I said.

The skipper tugged at my elbow and led me through the wheelhouse to the other wing. "Listen."

There it was again, on the starboard side. "Must be quite a few of 'em," I said laconically, a little annoyed that he should change the subject that way.

"Dere is plenty, but dey are not porpoises."

"Blackfish?"

"Dey is not fish, too. Dey is somet'ing y'u have seen in books. Dey is vimmin with tails on."

"*What?*"

"O.K., I vas kidding. Call me ven y'u are relieved."

In the green glow from the starboard running light I saw him hand me a piercing gaze; then he shambled back to the chart room. A little bit short of breath, I went into the wheelhouse and lit a cigarette.

The cuspidor rang out, and I waited for Johnny to speak.

"The skipper ain't nuts," he said casually.

"Somebody is," I returned. "You heard him, then."

"Listen—if the skipper told me the devil himself was firing on the twelve to four, then the devil it would be." Johnny was fiercely loyal under that armor of easy talk. "I've heard them 'porpoises' of yours for three days now. Porpoises don't follow a ship two hundred yards off. They'll jump the bow wave fer a few minutes an' then high-tail, or they'll cross yer bow an' play away. These is different. I've gone five degrees off to port an' then to starboard to see if I could draw 'em. Nope; they keep their distance." Johnny curled some shag under his lip.

"Aw, that's . . . that's screwy, Johnny."

He shrugged. "You've shipped with the Old Man before. He sees more than most of us." And that's all he'd say.

It was about two days later that we began to load. Yeah, that's what I said. We didn't dock, and we didn't discharge our farm machinery. We took on—whatever it was our cargo turned out to be. It was on the four to eight in the evening when the white fog was just getting muddy in the dusk. I was dead asleep when the ship sat down on her tail, stuck her bow up and heeled over. The engines stopped, and I got up from the corner of my room where the impact had flung me.

She lay still on her side, and hell was breaking loose. Toole had apparently fallen up against the fire-alarm button, and the lookout forward was panicky and ringing a swing symphony on the bell. A broken steam line was roaring bloody murder, and so was the second mate. The whistle, at least, was quiet—it had fallen with a crash from the "Pat Finnegan" pipe.

I leaned against the wall and crouched into a pair of pants and staggered out on deck. I couldn't see a blasted thing. If the fog had been thick before, it was twenty times as thick now.

Someone ran into me, and we both went skittering into the scuppers. It was the mate on his way down to the captain's room. Why the Old Man wasn't on the bridge, I couldn't savvy, unless it had to do with that peculiar attitude of resignation about his imagined loss of command.

"What the hell?" I wanted to know.

Toole said: "Who is that—third mate? Oh. I don't know. We've hit something. We're right up on top of it. Ain't rocks; didn't hear any plates go. Isn't sand; no sand bank this size could stay this far from land."

"Where's the skipper?"

"In his room, far as I know. C'mon, let's roll him out."

We groped our way to the alleyway door and into the midship house. Light was streaming from the skipper's room, and as we approached the door we heard the rare, drawn-out chuckle. I'll never forget the shock of seeing this best of captains, a man who had never dented a bilge plate in his life, sprawled back in his tilted swivel chair with his feet on a tilted desk, chuckling into a tilted bottle of Scotch.

Toole squawked: "Cap'n! We've struck something!"

The skipper giggled. He had a terrific load on. I leaned past Toole and shook him. "Skipper! We've struck!"

He looked at us blearily. "Heh. Sid-down, boyss, de trip iss over. Ve have not struck. Ve is yust finished. Heh!"

"Clear the boats," Toole said aside to me.

The skipper heard him. "Vait!" he said furiously, and lurched to his feet. "I am still in command here! Don't lower no boats. Ve are not in distress, y'u hear? Heh! Ve are loading. I know all about it. Go an' see for y'uselfs, so y'u don't belief me!"

Toole stared at the captain for a moment. I stood by. If Toole decided the Old Man was nuts, he'd take over. If not, then the square-head was still running the show. Suddenly Toole leaned over and cut the master switch on the alarm system. It had a separate little battery circuit of its own, and was the only thing electrical aboard that still operated. The silence was deafening as the alarm bells throughout the ship stilled, and we could hear a bumble of voices from back aft as the crew milled about. They were a steady bunch; there would be no panic. Toole beckoned me out of the room and left. Once we were outside he said:

"What do you think?"

"I think he's—I dunno, Toole. He's a seaman first and a human being afterward. If he says we're not in distress, it's likely true. Course, he's drunk."

Toole snorted. "He thinks better when he's drunk. Come on, let's look around."

We dropped down the ladder. The ship lay still. She was careened, probably with her starboard side under water and the starboard rail awash.

Toole said: "Let's go to port. Maybe we can see what it is we've hit."

We had to go on all fours to get up there, so steeply was the deck canted. It did us no good; there was nothing to be seen anywhere but fog.

Toole clung with one arm to the chain rail and puffed, "Can't see a thing down there, can you?"

I hung over the edge. "Can't even see the water line."

"Let's go down to the starboard side. She must be awash there."

She was. I stepped ankle deep into sea water before I knew where

I was. The sea was dead calm, and the fog was a solid thing; and something was holding the ship heeled over. I tell you, it was a nasty feeling. If only we knew what was under us! And then—we saw the ship being loaded.

May I never see another sight like that one. As if to tease and torture us, the fog swirled silently away from the ship's side, leaving a little dim island of visibility for us to peer into. We could see fifty or sixty feet of deck, and the chain rails fore and aft dipping into the sea at our feet; and we could see a round patch of still water with its edges wetting the curtain of fog. And on that patch of water were footprints. We both saw them at the same time and froze, speechless. Coming toward us over the water they were—dozens of them. The water was like a resilient, glossy sheet of paving, and the impression of dozens—hundreds—of feet ran across it to the ship. But there was nothing making the footprints. Just—footprints. Oh, my God!

There were big splay ones and big slow ones, and little swift ones and plodding ones. Once something long and invisible crept with many legs up to the ship, and once little pointed feet, high-arched, tripped soundlessly over the chains and *something* fell sprawling a yard from where we stood. There was no splash, but just the indentation in the water of a tiny, perfect body that rolled and squirmed back onto its feet and ran over to the deck and disappeared. I suddenly felt that I was in the midst of a milling crowd of—of people. Nothing touched me, and yet, all around me was the pressure of scores of beings who jostled each other and pushed and shoved, in their eagerness to get aboard. It was ghastly. There was no menace in it, nor anything to fear except that here was a thing that could not be understood.

The fog closed down suddenly, and for a long moment we stood there, feeling the pressure of that mob of "passengers"; and then I reached out and found the mate's arm and tugged him toward the midship house. We crawled up the canted ladder and stood by the glow from the lamp in the captain's room.

"It's a lot of goddam nonsense," I said weakly.

"H-m-m."

I didn't know whether or not Toole agreed with me.

The skipper's voice came loosely from the porthole. "Heh! I cert'n'y t'ank y'u for de Scotch, I du. Vat a deal, vat a deal!" And he burst out into a horrible sound that might have been laughter, in his cracked and grating voice. I stared in. He was nodding and grinning at the forward bulkhead, toasting it with a pony of fire water.

"He's seein' things," said the mate abruptly.

"Maybe all the rest of us are blind," I said; and the mate's dazed expression made me wonder, too, why I had said that. Without another word he went above to take over the bridge, while I went aft to quiet the crew.

We lay there for fourteen hours, and all the while that invisible invasion continued. There was nothing any of us could do. And crazy things began happening. Any one of them might have happened to any of us once in a while, but—well, judge for yourself, now.

When I came on watch that night there was nothing to do but stand by, since we were hove to, and I set Johnny to polishing brass. He got his polish and his rag and got to work. I mooned at the fog from the wheelhouse window, and in about ten minutes I heard Johnny cuss and throw rag and can over the side.

"What gives, Johnny?"

"Ain't no use doin' this job. Must be the fog." He pointed to the binnacle cover. "The tarnish smells the polish and fades off all around me rag. On'y where I rub it comes in stronger."

It was true. All the places he had rubbed were black-green, and around those spots the battered brass gleamed brilliantly! I told John to go have himself a cup of coffee and settled down on the stool to smoke.

No cigarettes in the right pocket of my dungarees. None in the left. I *knew* I'd put a pack there. "Damn!" I muttered. Now where the—what was I looking for? Cigarettes? But I had a pack of cigarettes in my hand! Was I getting old or something? I tried to shrug it off. I must have had them there all the time, only—well, things like that don't happen to me! I'm not absent-minded. I pulled out a

smoke and stuck it in my chops, fumbling for a match. Now where—
I did some more cussing. No matches. What good is a fag to a guy
without a—I gagged suddenly on too much smoke. Why was I looking for a match? My cigarette was lit!

When a sailor starts to get the jitters he usually begins to think
about the girl he left behind him. It was just my luck to be tied up
with one I didn't want to think about. I simply went into a daze
while I finished that haunted cigarette. After a while Johnny came
back carrying a cup of coffee for me.

Now I like my coffee black. Wet a spoon in it and dip it in the
sugar barrel, and that's enough sugar for me. Johnny handed me the
cup, and I took the saucer off the rim. The coffee was creamed—on
a ship that means evaporated milk—and sweet as a soft caramel.

"Damn it, Johnny, you know how I like my coffee. What's the
idea of this?"

"What?"

I showed him. When he saw the pale liquid he recoiled as if there
had been a snake curled up on the saucer instead of a cup. "S'help
me, third, I didn't put a drop of milk in that cup! Nor sugar, neither!"

I growled and threw cup and saucer over the side. I couldn't say
anything to Johnny. I *knew* he was telling the truth. Oh, well, maybe
there happened to be some milk and sugar in the cup he used and
he didn't notice it. It was a weak sort of excuse, but I clung to it.

At six bells the second heaved himself up the ladder. "O.K.—
you're relieved," he said.

"At eleven o'clock? What's the idea?"

"Aw—" His huge bulk pulsed as he panted, and he was sweating. "I couldn't sleep, that's all. Shove off."

"I'll be damned! First time I ever heard of you rolling out before
you were called, Harry. What's the matter—this canting too much
for you?" The ship still lay over at about 47°.

"Naw. I c'n sleep through twice that. It was—Oh, go below,
third."

"O.K. Course 'n' speed the same—zero-zero. The wind is on the
weather side, an' we're runnin' between the anchors. The bow is
dead ahead and the smokestack is aft. The temperature—"

"Dry up, will ya?"

"The temperature is mighty hot around the second mate. What's eatin' you, Harry?"

"I'll tell you," he said suddenly, very softly, so Johnny couldn't hear. "It was my bunk. It was full of spikes. I could feel 'em, but I couldn't see 'em. I've got the blue willies, third." He mopped his expansive face.

I slapped him on the back and went aft laughing. I was sorry I had laughed. When I turned in to my bunk it was full of cold, wet worms that crept and crawled and sent me mooning and shuddering to the deck, to roll up in the carpet for some shut-eye. No, I couldn't see them.

We left there—wherever "there" was—about fourteen hours after we struck. What it was that had stopped the ship we never did find out. We took soundings all around and got nothing but deep water. Whatever it was that the ship was lying on was directly underneath the turn of the bilge, so that no sounding lead could strike it. After the first surprise of it we almost got used to it—it and the fog, thick as banked snow, that covered everything. And all the while the "loading" went on. When it began, that invisible crowding centered around the section of the starboard well deck that was awash. But in a few hours it spread to every part of the ship. Everywhere you went you saw nothing and you actually felt nothing; and yet there was an increasing sense of being crowded—jostled.

It happened at breakfast, 7:20. The skipper was there, and the mate, though he should have been on the bridge. Harry rolled in, too, three hundred pounds of fretful wanness. I gathered that there were still spikes in his bunk. Being second mate, his watch was the twelve to four, and breakfast was generally something he did without.

The captain lolled back in his chair, leaning against the canted deck and grinning. It made me sore. I refused the bottle he shoved at me and ordered my eggs from the messman.

"Na, don't be dat vay," said the skipper. "Everyt'ing is under control. Ve is all going to get a bonus, and nobody is going to get hurt."

"I don't savvy you, cap'n," I said brusquely. "Here we are high and dry in the middle of an African pea-souper, with everything aboard gone haywire, and you're tickled to death. If you know what's going on, you ought to tip us off."

The mate said, "He's got something there, captain. I want to put a boat over the side, at least, and have a look at what it is that's grounded us. I told you that last night, and you wouldn't let a boat leave the chocks. What's the idea—don't you want to know?"

The captain dipped a piece of sea bread into the remains of four eggs on his plate. "Look, boyss, didn't I pull y'u out of a lot of spots before dis? Did I ever let y'u down yet? Heh. Vell, I von't now."

The mate looked exasperated. "O.K., O.K., but this calls for a little more than seamanship, skipper."

"Not from y'u it don't," flared the captain. "I know vat goes on, but if I told y'u, y'u wouldn't believe it. Y'u'll make out all right."

I decided to take matters into my own hands. "Toole, he's got some silly idea that the ship is out of our hands. Told me the other night. He's seeing ghosts. He says we were surrounded by 'vimmin mit tails on.'"

The mate cocked an eyebrow at the Old Man. The captain lurched to his feet.

"Vell, it's true! An' I bat y'u y'ur trip's pay against mine dat I gat one for myself! Ve is taking on a cargo of—" He swallowed noisily and put his face so close to mine that our foreheads nearly touched. "Vare de hell y'u t'ink I got dis viskey?" he bellowed. "Somebody has chartered dis ship, and ve'll get paid. Vot y'u care who it is? Y'u never worried before!" He stamped out.

Harry laughed hollowly, his four pale chins bobbing. "I guess that tells you off, third."

"I'll be damned," I said hotly. "I trust the Old Man as much as anyone, but I'm not going to take much more of this."

"Take it easy, man," soothed Harry. He reached for the canned milk. "A lot of this is fog and imagination. Until the skipper does something endangering crew, ship or cargo we've got no kick."

"What do you call staying in his room when the ship rams something?"

"He seems to know it's all right. Let it go, mate. We're O.K., so far. When the fog clears, everything will be jake. You're letting your imagination run away with you." He stared at Toole and upended the milk can over his cup.

Ink came out.

I clutched the edge of the slanting table and looked away and back again. It was true enough—black ink out of a milk can I'd seen the messman open three minutes before. I didn't say anything because I couldn't. Neither Toole nor Harry noticed it. Harry put the can on the table and it slid down toward Toole.

"All right," said Toole, "we'll keep our traps shut until the skipper pulls something really phoney. But I happen to know we have a cargo consigned to a Mediterranean port; and when and if we get off this sandbank, or whatever it is, I'm going to see to it that it's delivered. A charter is a charter." He picked up the can and poured.

Blood came out.

It drove me absolutely screwball. He wouldn't watch what he was doing! Harry was working on a pile of scrambled eggs, and the mate was looking at me, and my stomach was missing beats. I muttered something and went up to the bridge. Every time there was some rational explanation developing, something like that had to happen. Know why I couldn't pipe up about what I had seen? Because after the ink and the blood hit their coffee it was cream! You don't go telling people that you're bats!

It was ten minutes to eight, but as usual, Johnny Weiss was early. He was a darn good quartermaster—one of the best I ever sailed with. A very steady guy, but I didn't go for the blind trust he expressed in the skipper. That was all right to a certain extent, but now—

"Anything you want done?" he asked me.

"No, Johnny, stand by. Johnny—what would you do if the officers decided the captain was nuts and put him in irons?"

"I'd borry one of the Old Man's guns an' shoot the irons off him," said my quartermaster laconically. "An' then I'd stand over him an' take his orders."

Johnny was a keynote in the crew. We were asking for real trouble if we tried anything. Ah, it was no use. All we could do was to wait for developments.

At eight bells on the button we floated again, and the lurch of it threw every man jack off his feet. With a splash and a muffled scraping, the *Dawnlight* settled deeply from under our feet, righted herself, rolled far over to the other side, and then gradually steadied. After I got up off my back I rang a "Stand-by" on the engine room telegraph, whistled down the skipper's speaking tube, and motioned Johnny behind the wheel. He got up on the wheel mat as if we were leaving the dock in a seaport. Not a quiver! Old Johnny was one in a million.

I answered the engine room. "All steamed up and ready to go down here!" said the third engineer's voice. "And I think we'll have that generator running in another twenty minutes!"

"Good stuff!" I said, and whistled for the skipper. He must have felt that mighty lurch. I couldn't imagine why he wasn't on the bridge.

He answered sleepily: "Vell?"

"We're afloat!" I spluttered.

"So?"

"What do you want to do—lay here? Or are we going some place?"

There was silence for a long time—so long that I called and asked him if he was still on the other end of the tube.

"I vas getting my orders," he said. "Yes, ve go. Full speed ahead."

"What course?"

"How should I know? I'm through now, third. Y'u'll get y'ur orders."

"From Toole?"

"No!"

"Hey, if you ain't captain, who is?"

"I vouldn't know about dat. Full speed ahead!" The plug on his end of the tube clicked into place, and I turned toward Johnny, uncertain what to do.

"He said full ahead, didn't he?" asked Johnny quietly.

"Yeah, but—"

"Aye, aye, sir," he said with just a trace of sarcasm, and pulled the handle of the telegraph over from "Stand-by" to "Full ahead."

I put out my hand, and then shrugged and stuck it in my pocket. I'd tell Toole about it when I came off watch. "As you go," I said, not looking at the compass.

"As she goes, sir," said Johnny, and began to steer as the shudder of the engines pounded through the ship.

The mate came up with Harry at noon, and we had a little confab. Toole was rubbing his hands and visibly expanding under the warmth of the bright sun, which had shone since three bells with a fierce brilliance, as if it wanted to make up for our three days of fog. "How's she go?" he asked me.

"Due west," I said meaningly.

"*What?* And we have a cargo for the Mediterranean?"

"I only work here," I said. "Skipper's orders."

Harry shrugged. "Then west it is, that's all I say," he grunted.

"Do you want to get paid this trip?" snapped Toole. He picked up the slip on which I had written the ship's position, which I'd worked out as soon as I could after the sun came out. "We're due south of the Madeiras and heading home," he went on. "How do you think those arms shippers are going to like our returning with their cargo? This is the payoff."

Harry tried to catch his arm, but he twisted away and strode into the wheelhouse. The twelve-to-four quartermaster hadn't relieved Johnny Weiss yet.

"Change course," barked the mate, his small, chunky body trembling. "East-nor'east!"

Johnny looked him over coolly and spat. "Cap'n changes course, mate."

"Then change course!" Toole roared. "The squarehead's nuts. From now on I'm running this ship!"

"I ain't been told of it," said Johnny quietly, and steadied on his westerly course.

"Well, by God, I'm the mate!" Toole said. "You've had no orders from that lunatic to disregard a command of a superior officer. Steer east!"

Weiss gazed out of the wheelhouse window, taking his time about thinking it over. The mate had made his point; to refuse further would be rank insubordination. Though Johnny was strong in his loyalty to the skipper, he was too much of a seaman to be pig-headed about this until he knew a little better where he stood.

"East it is, sir," he said, and his eyes were baleful. He hauled at the wheel, and a hint of a grin cracked his leathery face. "She— won't answer, sir!"

I saw red. "Go below!" I growled, and butted him from behind the wheel with my shoulder. He laughed aloud and went out.

I grasped the two top spokes, hunched my shoulders and gave a mighty heave. There was suddenly no resistance at all on the wheel, and my own violence threw me heels over crupper into the second mate, and we spun and tumbled, all his mass of lard on top of me. It was like lying under an anchor. The wind was knocked out of him, and he couldn't move. I was smothering, and the mate was too surprised to do anything but stare. When Harry finally rolled off me it was a good two minutes before I could move.

"Damn that quartermaster," I gasped when we were on our feet again.

"Wasn't his fault," wheezed Harry. "He really tried to spin the wheel."

Knowing Johnny, I had to agree. He'd never pull anything like that. I scratched my head and turned to the mate. He was steering now, apparently without any trouble at all. "Don't tell me you can turn the ship?"

He grinned. "All it needed was a real helmsman," he ribbed me. And then the engines stopped, and the telegraph rang and spun over to "Stop," and the engine room tube squealed.

"Now what?"

"I dunno," came the third's plaintive voice. "She just quit on us."

"O.K.; let us know when you've shot the trouble." The engineer rang off.

"Now what the hell?" said the mate.

I shrugged. "This is a jinxed trip," I said. I verified the "Stop" signal on the telegraph.

Harry said: "I don't know what's got into you guys. The skipper said somethin' about a new charter. He don't have to tell us who gave it to us."

"He don't have to keep us in the dark, either," said Toole. Then, glancing at the compass, he said, "Looka that! She's swingin' back to west!"

I looked over his shoulder. Slowly the ship was turning in the gentle swell, back to due west. And just as she came to 270° on the card—the engines began to pound.

"Ah!" said the mate, and verified the "Full ahead" gong that had just rung.

The third whistled up again and reported that he was picking fluff off his oilskins. "I'm going on the wagon," he said. "She quits by herself and starts by herself, an' I'm gonna bust out cryin' if it keeps up!"

And that's how we found out that the ship, with this strange cargo, insisted on having her head. For every time we tried to change course, the engines would stop, or a rudder cable would break, or the steering engine would quit. What could we do? We stood our watches and ran our ship as if nothing were the matter. If we hadn't we'd have gone as mad as we thought we already were.

Harry noticed a strange thing one afternoon. He told me about it when we came off watch.

"Y'know that box o' books in the chart room?" he asked me.

I did. It was an American Merchant Marine Library Association book chest, left aboard from the time the ship was honest. I'd been pretty well all through it. There were a few textbooks on French and Spanish, half a dozen detective novels, a pile of ten-year-old magazines, and a miscellaneous collection of pamphlets and unclassifiable.

"Well, about three o'clock I hear a noise in the chart room," said Harry, "an' I have a look. Well, sir, them books is heaving 'emselves up out of the chest and spilling on th' deck. Most of 'em was just tossed around, but a few was stackin' in a neat heap near the bulkhead. I on'y saw it for a second, and then it stopped, like I'd caught someone at the job, but I couldn't see no one there." He stopped and licked his lips and wheezed. "I looks at that pile o' books, an' they was all to do with North America an' the United States. A coupla history books, an atlas, a guidebook to New York City, a book on th' national parks—all sech. Well, I goes back into the wheelhouse, an' a few minutes later I peeks in again. All them books on America was open in different places in the chart room, an' the pages was turnin' like someone was readin' them, only—there just wasn't nobody there!"

What the *hell* was it that we had aboard, that wanted to know about the United States, that had replaced our captain with a string of coincidence, that had "chartered" the ship? I'd had enough. I firmly swore that if I ever got back to the States, police or no, I'd get off this scow and stay off her. A man can just stand so much.

About three days out the torpedo boat picked us up. She was a raider, small and gray and fast and wicked, and she belonged to a nation that likes to sink arms runners. One of the nations, I mean. I had just come off watch, and was leaning on the taffrail when I saw her boiling along behind us, overtaking.

I ran forward, collaring an ordinary seaman. "Run up some colors," I said. "I don't give a damn what ones. Hurry!"

Pounding up the ladder, I hauled Toole out of the wheelhouse, pointed out the raider and dived for the radio shack, which was some good to us now that the generator was going again.

I sat down at the key and put on a headset. Sure enough, in a second or two I heard: "What ship is that? Where from? Where bound?" repeated in English, French, German and Spanish. I'd have called the skipper, but had given him up as a bad job. Toole came in.

"They want to know who we are," I said excitedly. "Who are we?"

"Wait'll I look at the flag the kid is running up," he said. He went to the door, and I heard him swear and whistle. "Give a look," he said.

Flying from the masthead was a brilliant green flag on which was a unicorn, rampant. I'd seen it—where was it? Years ago—oh, yes; that was it! In a book of English folk tales; that was supposed to be the standard of Oberon and Titania, King and Queen of ... of the fairies, the Little Folk!

Dazed, I turned to the key and began pounding. I didn't even realize what I was sending. Some imp controlled my hand, and not until it was sent did I realize I had said, "S.S. *Princess of Birmingham,* Liverpool, bound for Calais with a load of airplane parts."

"Thank you!" said the raider, and put a shell across our bow. Toole had gone back to the bridge, and I sat there sweating and wondering what the hell to do about this. Of all stupid things to say to an enemy raider!

The engine vibration suddenly became labored and the ship slowed perceptibly. Oh, of course, the old wagon would pick a time like this to become temperamental! I beat my skull with my fists and groaned. This was curtains.

The raider was abeam and angling toward us. "Heave to!" she kept buzzing through my phones. Through the porthole beside me I could already see the men moving about on her narrow decks. I turned to my key again and sent the commander of the raider some advice on a highly original way to amuse himself. In answer he brought his four swivel guns to bear on us.

The bridge tube whistled. Toole said, "What the hell did you say to him? He's fixin' to sink us!"

"I don't know," I wailed. "I don't know nothing!"

I ripped off the headset and put my elbows on the port ring across the room, staring out to sea with my back to the swiftly approaching raider. And there in the sunny waves was a conning tower, periscope and all!

Now get this. Here we were, lying helpless, going dead slow with crippled engines between a surface raider and a sub. We were meat for anyone working for any government. Most of us were Americans; if the raider took us it would mean an international incident at a time when no one could afford one. If the sub took us, it was the concentration camp for us. Either might, and probably would, sink us. We were outlaws.

I went up on the bridge. No sense doing anything now. If we got into boats, we'd likely be cut down by machine-gun bullets. Toole was frantically tugging at the handle of the engine room telegraph.

"I'm trying to stop her!" he gasped. "She's going dead slow; there's something wrong with the engines. They're making such a racket back there that the first assistant can't hear the tube whistle. The telegraph is jammed! The helm won't answer! Oh, my God!"

"Where's your quartermaster?"

Toole jerked a thumb toward the bridge ladder. "I sent him aft to run down to the engine room, and he tripped and fell down to the boat deck! Knocked himself out!"

I ran to the port wing and looked out at the sub. True to her kind, she was attacking without asking questions. There was a jet of spume, and the swift wake of a torpedo cut toward us. At the rate we were going, it would strike us just between the after dry-cargo hold—where the "farm machinery" was stowed—and the fire room. It would get both the explosives and the boiler—good night nurse!

And then our "coincidental commander" took a hand. The crippled, laboring engines suddenly raced, shuddered and took hold. Grumbling in every plate, the *Dawnlight* sat down on her counter, raised her blunt nose eight feet, and scuttled forward at a speed that her builders would have denied. In fifty seconds she was doing fourteen knots. The torpedo swept close under our stern, and the raging wash of the tanker deflected it, so that it hurtled—straight toward the raider!

It struck just aft the stem piece, blowing away the gunboat's bow and turning her on her beam ends. She righted slowly lying far down by the head, and lay helpless. The sub, seeing her for the first time, came to the surface and men tumbled out of the hatches to man her four-incher. She began blasting away at the torpedo boat as fast as she could load, and the raider answered her, two shots to the sub's one. And there we left them, and for all I know they are blasting away yet, far too busy to pay attention to a crummy old tankship. And Toole and I—well, we cried on each other's shoulders for twenty minutes, and then we laughed ourselves sick.

The next four days were straight sailing, but for the pranks that were played on us. The skipper stuck to his cabin; we found out why later, and I can't really blame him. There was still no sign of the mob of beings that could be felt aboard, but for—again—the pranks that were played on us. We stood our watches and we ate our meals and we painted and chipped and scraped as usual. But for the—but I said that before.

Like the time the buff-colored paint the day gang was laying on the after bulkhead turned the steel transparent for forty-eight hours.

Behind the bulkhead was the crew's washroom. The view from up forward was exquisite. As the four-to-eight fireman expressed it: "I wouldn't give a damn if the washroom was just fer washin'."

And lots of little things, like a spoonful of salt turning to thumbtacks in the Cajun's best gumbo soup, and live lobsters in the linen locker, and toadstools in the bos'n's stores, and beautiful green grass, an acre of it, with four concentric fairy rings, growing on a flaked hawser in the forward cargo hold; and then there were the dice that, in the middle of a crap game, developed wickedly humorous caricatures of the six ship's officers—including me. That might not seem like much to you; but when you remember how clever they were, and when you could never meet one of your crew without his bursting into fits of laughter when he saw your face—well, it wasn't the best thing in the world for discipline.

About the captain—We got curious, Toole and I, about how he was getting on. He had locked himself in his room, and every once in a while would whistle for more food. He ate fish almost exclusively, in enormous quantities. We decided to do something about it. Some minor pretext to get a peek into his room. He wouldn't come to the door if we knocked; the portholes were the answer. Now, how could we get the curtain off from the outside without the irascible old man's coming out with a gun in each hand? We finally hit on something ideal. We'd get a broken spar with a snaggy end from somewhere, carry it past his porthole, and "accidentally" stick it in, tearing off the curtain and giving us a good look.

I'm sorry we did. We'd no business looking into the Old Man's private life that way. After all, we decided when we batted the wind about it afterward, the Old Man had a right, if he wanted to, to have a ... a mermaid in his room! We saw her without being seen, and the skipper must have been in the inner room. She was very lovely, and I got a flash of scales and golden hair, and felt like a heel for looking.

Toole and I talked it over one afternoon as we neared the coast. The two of us had seen more of the whole screwy business than anyone else, and besides, Toole was an Irishman. No one will ever know if he was right or not, but his explanation is the only one that will fit all the facts. Pieced together from a two-hour conversation, this is about what he said, and now—I believe him:

"Third, this is a silly trip, hey? Ah, well. There are many things that you or I can't understand, and we're used to them, like the northern lights and the ways of a woman. I think that the skipper sold us out. No; no harm to us." He dragged on his cigar and stared out to sea as he talked. "Something, or somebody, made a deal with him the day after we sailed. Listen; hear that?"

Far out on the beam sounded the steady *smack-splash* of huge schools of porpoise. Oh, yes; they *might* have been porpoise.

"You told me what the skipper said to you about those critters. And they don't act like porpoises. I don't know if it was one of them or not; maybe it was something we couldn't see that talked. I think the skipper could. He's a squarehead, and they're seagoing people, and they know the sea from 'way back. He's been to sea half again as long as the oldest sailor aboard; you know that. I don't have to tell you that the sea is something that we'll never really understand. You can't know *all* about anything, even an atom; and the sea is so *damn* big.

"Well, he was made an offer; and it was probably a lifetime supply of whiskey and a week or so with that m-mermaid we—thought we saw in his room. What was the deal?

"That he should turn over his ship, and the crew to work it, to whatever party it was that wanted it for a trip from the African coast to America. There must have been provisions, if I know the skipper; he's a downy bird. He must have provided that the ship was to be protected against weather and bullets, mines and torps. He must have stipulated that no one aboard was to be harmed permanently, and—I'm sure of this—that ship and cargo were to be returned to him at the end of the trip. Everything else I've guessed at has turned out, hasn't it? Why not that? The only thing that really bothers me is the loss of time, because time is really big money in this racket. But you can bet that the squarehead wasn't beaten down. We'll find out—I'm certain of it.

"Now, about the passengers. Laugh at me and I'll dry up like a clam; but I believe I have the answer. The old country has inhabitants that men have dreamed and sung and written and told about a great deal, and seen more than seldom. I've spent a lot of time off watch reading about 'em, and my mother used to tell me — bless her! Anyway, there was ghosts and pixies, goblins and brownies, and dervishes and fairies and nymphs and peris and dryads and naiads and kelpies and sprites; gnomes and imps and elves and dwarves and nixies and ghouls and pigwidgeons, and the legion of the leprechauns, and many another. And some were good and some were not, and some helped and some hindered; but all were mischievous as hell. They weren't too bad, any more than are the snakes and spiders that eat mosquitos, and many were downright beneficial.

"There's hell to pay in Europe now, third. You can't expect a self-respectin' pixie to hide in a shell hole and watch a baby torn to shreds. They sickened of it, and their boss man, whoever he is, got 'em together and made arrangements to ship 'em someplace where there's a little peace and quiet once in a while, where they can work their harmless spells on a non-aggressive populace. They can't swim worth a damn, and you couldn't expect the sea folk to ferry 'em over; they're an unreliable lot anyway, to all accounts.

"I read a book once about Ol' Puck, and how the Little People were brought to the British Isles from the Continent. They couldn't swim even that, and they got a blind man to row and a deaf mute to stand lookout, and never a word was said of it until Puck himself told of it. This is the twentieth century, and it's a big ocean they've got to cross, and there are many more of them. Did ye notice, by the way," he broke off suddenly, "that though our tanks are empty an' we've used fuel and water and stores for near two weeks, that we're *low in the water*?" He laughed. "We've many and many of 'em aboard.

"We'll unload 'em, and we'll get our pay for the job. But this I'll tell you, and now you may laugh, for you're in the same boat. We're r'arin', tearin' lawbreakers aboard here, third, and we don't give a damn, or we wouldn't be here. But if there's any kind of a good place for us to go at the end of the voyage, then we'll go there for this week's work. It was always a good thing to help a war refugee."

I didn't laugh. I went away by myself and chewed and swallowed that, and I thought about it a bit, and now I believe what I believe, and maybe a little bit more. It's a big world, and these are crazy times.

Well, almost as we expected, we unloaded, but it only took us three hours instead of fourteen. Yes, we struck fog off the Carolinas, and the ship nosed up and heeled over in it, and we could feel the pressure getting less aboard. And when the *thing* under the ship sank and floated us again, and the sun came out—

Well, this is the part that is hard to explain. I won't try it. But look: It was the twenty-third day of September when we sailed from the drydock. And when we lay off the coast that way, just out of the fog, it was the twenty-fifth. And it would have taken just three days for us to reach there from the drydock. Somewhere we lost a week. Yeah.

And the bunkers were full of fuel. And the lockers were full of stores. And the fresh-water tanks were full of water, just as they had been. But—there's a difference. Any fuel we use is—or acts like—high-grade stuff. And our food tastes better, and the work is easier. Yeah, we're lawbreakers—outlaws. But we take our ship where we please, when we please, and never a warship do we see, and never a shell or mine touches us. Oh, yeah; they say she's haunted. No; there's another word for it. She is—*enchanted*. We're paid, and we're being paid. And we'll go anywhere and do anything, because we have the best skipper a man ever sailed under, and because, more than any other men on earth, we need not be afraid of death.

But I can't forget that there'll be hell an' all to pay ashore!

Shottle Bop

I'D NEVER SEEN the place before, and I lived just down the block and around the corner. I'll even give you the address, if you like. "The Shottle Bop," between Twentieth and Twenty-first Streets, on Tenth Avenue in New York City. You can find it if you go there looking for it. Might even be worth your while, too.

But you'd better not.

"The Shottle Bop." It got me. It was a small shop with a weather-beaten sign swung from a wrought crane, creaking dismally in the late fall wind. I walked past it, thinking of the engagement ring in my pocket and how it had just been handed back to me by Audrey, and my mind was far removed from such things as shottle bops. I was thinking that Audrey might have used a gentler term than "useless" in describing me; and her neatly turned remark about my being a "constitutional psychopathic incompetent" was as uncalled-for as it was spectacular. She must have read it somewhere, balanced as it was by "And I wouldn't marry you if you were the last man on earth!" which is a notably worn cliché.

"Shottle Bop!" I muttered, and then paused, wondering where I had picked up such oddly rhythmic syllables with which to express myself. I'd seen it on that sign, of course, and it had caught my eye. "And what," I asked myself, "might be a Shottle Bop?" Myself replied promptly, "Dunno. Toddle back and have a look." So toddle I did, back along the east side of Tenth, wondering what manner of man might be running such an establishment in pursuance of what kind of business. I was enlightened on the second point by a sign in the window, all but obscured by the dust and ashes of apparent centuries, which read:

WE SELL BOTTLES

There was another line of smaller print there. I rubbed at the crusted glass with my sleeve and finally was able to make out

With things in them.

Just like that:

WE SELL BOTTLES
With things in them.

Well of course I went in. Sometimes very delightful things come in bottles, and the way I was feeling, I could stand a little delighting.

"Close it!" shrilled a voice, as I pushed through the door. The voice came from a shimmering egg adrift in the air behind the counter, low-down. Peering over, I saw that it was not an egg at all, but the bald pate of an old man who was clutching the edge of the counter, his scrawny body streaming away in the slight draft from the open door, as if he were made of bubbles. A mite startled, I kicked the door with my heel. He immediately fell on his face, and then scrambled smiling to his feet.

"Ah, it's good to see you again," he rasped.

I think his vocal cords were dusty, too. Everything else here was. As the door swung to, I felt as if I were inside a great dusty brain that had just closed its eyes. Oh yes, there was light enough. But it wasn't the lamp light and it wasn't daylight. It was like—like light reflected from the cheeks of pale people. Can't say I enjoyed it much.

"What do you mean, 'again'?" I asked irritably. "You never saw me before."

"I saw you when you came in and I fell down and got up and saw you again," he quibbled, and beamed. "What can I do for you?"

"Oh," I said. "Well, I saw your sign. What have you got in a bottle that I might like?"

"What do you want?"

"What've you got?"

He broke into a piping chant—I remember it yet, word for word.

For half a buck, a vial of luck
  Or a bottle of nifty breaks
Or a flask of joy, or Myrna Loy
  For luncheon with sirloin steaks.

Pour out a mug from this old jug,
  And you'll never get wet in rains.
I've bottles of grins and racetrack wins
  And lotions to ease your pains.

Here's bottles of imps and wet-pack shrimps
  From a sea unknown to man,
And an elixir to banish fear,
  And the sap from the pipes of Pan.

With the powdered horn of a unicorn
  You can win yourself a mate;
With the rich hobnob; or get a job—
  It's yours at a lowered rate.

"Now wait right there!" I snapped. "You mean you actually sell dragon's blood and ink from the pen of Friar Bacon and all such mumbo-jum?"

He nodded rapidly and smiled all over his improbable face.

I went on—"The genuine article?"

He kept on nodding.

I regarded him for a moment. "You mean to stand there with your teeth in your mouth and your bare face hanging out and tell me that in this day and age, in this city and in broad daylight, you sell such trash and then expect me—me, an enlightened intellectual—"

"You are very stupid and twice as bombastic," he said quietly.

I glowered at him and reached for the doorknob—and there I froze. And I mean froze. For the old man whipped out an ancient bulb-type atomizer and squeezed a couple of whiffs at me as I turned away; and so help me, *I couldn't move!* I could cuss, though, and boy, did I.

The proprietor hopped over the counter and ran over to me. He must have been standing on a box back there, for now I could see

34

he was barely three feet tall. He grabbed my coat tails, ran up my back and slid down my arm, which was extended doorward. He sat down on my wrist and swung his feet and laughed up at me. As far as I could feel, he weighed absolutely nothing.

When I had run out of profanity—I pride myself on never repeating a phrase of invective—he said, "Does that prove anything to you, my cocky and unintelligent friend? That was the essential oil from the hair of the Gorgon's head. And until I give you an antidote, you'll stand there from now till a week text Neusday!"

"Get me out of this," I roared, "or I smack you so hard you lose your brains through the pores in your feet!"

He giggled.

I tried to tear loose again and couldn't. It was as if all my epidermis had turned to high-carbon steel. I began cussing again, but quit in despair.

"You think altogether too much of yourself," said the proprietor of the Shottle Bop. "Look at you! Why, I wouldn't hire you to wash my windows. You expect to marry a girl who is accustomed to the least of animal comfort, and then you get miffed because she turns you down. Why does she turn you down? Because you won't get a job. You're a no-good. You're a bum! He, he! And you have the nerve to walk around telling people where to get off. Now if I were in your position I would ask politely to be released, and then I would see if anyone in this shop would be good enough to sell you a bottle full of something that might help out."

Now I never apologize to anybody, and I never back down, and I never take any guff from mere tradesmen. But this was different. I'd never been petrified before, nor had my nose rubbed in so many galling truths. I relented. "O.K., O.K.; let me break away then. I'll buy something."

"Your tone is sullen," he said complacently, dropping lightly to the floor and holding his atomizer at the ready. "You'll have to say 'Please. Pretty please.'"

"Pretty please," I said, almost choking with humiliation.

He went back of the counter and returned with a paper of powder which he had me sniff. In a couple of seconds I began to sweat,

and my limbs lost their rigidity so quickly that it almost threw me.
I'd have been flat on my back if the man hadn't caught me and solic-
itously led me to a chair. As strength dribbled back into my shocked
tissues, it occurred to me that I might like to flatten this hobgoblin
for pulling a trick like that. But a strange something stopped me—
strange because I'd never had the experience before. It was simply
the idea that once I got outside I'd agree with him for having such
a low opinion of me.

He wasn't worrying. Rubbing his hands briskly, he turned to his
shelves. "Now let's see ... what would be best for you, I wonder?
Hm-m-m. Success is something you couldn't justify. Money? You
don't know how to spend it. A good job? You're not fitted for one."
He turned gentle eyes on me and shook his head. "A sad case. *Tsk,
tsk.*" I crawled. "A perfect mate? Nup. You're too stupid to recognize perfection, too conceited to appreciate it. I don't think that I
can—Wait!"

He whipped four or five bottles and jars off the dozens of shelves
behind him and disappeared somewhere in the dark recesses of the
store. Immediately there came sounds of violent activity—clinkings
and little crashes; stirrings and then the rapid susurrant grating of a
mortar and pestle; then the slushy sound of liquid being added to a
dry ingredient during stirring; and at length, after quite a silence, the
glugging of a bottle being filled through a filtering funnel. The proprietor reappeared triumphantly bearing a four-ounce bottle without a label.

"This will do it!" he beamed.

"That will do what?"

"Why, cure you!"

"Cure—" My pompous attitude, as Audrey called it, had returned
while he was mixing. "What do you mean cure? I haven't got
anything!"

"My dear little boy," he said offensively, "you most certainly
have. Are you happy? Have you ever been happy? No. Well, I'm
going to fix all that up. That is, I'll give you the start you need. Like
any other cure, it requires your cooperation.

"You're in a bad way, young fellow. You have what is known in the profession as retrogressive metempsychosis of the ego in its most malignant form. You are a constitutional unemployable; a downright sociophagus. I don't like you. Nobody likes you."

Feeling a little bit on the receiving end of a blitz, I stammered, "W-what do you aim to do?"

He extended the bottle. "Go home. Get into a room by yourself—the smaller the better. Drink this down, right out of the bottle. Stand by for developments. That's all."

"But—what will it do to me?"

"It will do nothing *to* you. It will do a great deal *for* you. It can do as much for you as you want it to. But mind me, now. As long as you use what it gives you for your self-improvement, you will thrive. Use it for self-gratification, as a basis for boasting, or for revenge, and you will suffer in the extreme. Remember that, now."

"But what is it? How—"

"I am selling you a talent. You have none now. When you discover what kind of a talent it is, it will be up to you to use it to your advantage. Now go away. I still don't like you."

"What do I owe you?" I muttered, completely snowed under by this time.

"The bottle carries its own price. You won't pay anything unless you fail to follow my directions. Now will you go, or must I uncork a bottle of jinn—and I don't mean London Dry?"

"I'll go," I said. I'd seen something swirling in the depths of a ten-gallon carboy at one end of the counter, and I didn't like it a bit. "Good-by."

"Bood-gy," he returned.

I went out and I headed down Tenth Avenue and I turned east up Twentieth Street and I never looked back. And for many reasons I wish now that I had, for there was, without doubt, something very strange about that Shottle Bop.

I didn't simmer down until I got home; but once I had a cup of black Italian coffee under my belt I felt better. I was skeptical about it at last. I was actually inclined to scoff. But somehow I didn't want to scoff too loudly. I looked at the bottle a little scornfully, and there was a certain something about the glass of it that seemed to be star-

37

ing back at me. I sniffed and threw it up behind some old hats on top of the closet, and then sat down to unlax. I used to love to unlax. I'd put my feet on the doorknob and slide down in the upholstery until I was sitting on my shoulder blades, and as the old saying has it, "Sometimes I sets and thinks, and sometimes I just sets." The former is easy enough, and is what even an accomplished loafer has to go through before he reaches the latter and more blissful state. It takes years of practice to relax sufficiently to be able to "just set." I'd learned it years ago.

But just as I was about to slip into the vegetable status, I was annoyed by something. I tried to ignore it. I manifested a superhuman display of lack of curiosity, but the annoyance persisted. A light pressure on my elbow, where it draped over the arm of the chair. I was put in the unpleasant predicament of having to concentrate on what it was; and realizing that concentration on anything was the least desirable thing there could be. I gave up finally, and with a deep sigh, opened my eyes and had a look.

It was the bottle.

I screwed up my eyes and then looked again, but it was still there. The closet door was open as I had left it, and its shelf almost directly above me. Must have fallen out. Feeling that if the damn thing were on the floor it couldn't fall any farther, I shoved if off the arm of the chair with my elbow.

It bounced. It bounced with such astonishing accuracy that it wound up in exactly the same spot it had started from—on the arm of the easy chair, by my elbow. Startled, I shoved it violently. This time I pushed it hard enough to send it against the wall, from which it rebounded to the shelf under my small table, and thence back to the chair arm—and this time it perched cozily against my shoulder. Jarred by the bouncing, the stopper hopped out of the bottle mouth and rolled into my lap; and there I sat, breathing the bittersweet fumes of its contents, feeling frightened and silly as hell.

I grabbed the bottle and sniffed. I'd smelled that somewhere before—where was it? Uh—oh, yes; that mascara the Chinese honky-tonk girls use in Frisco. The liquid was dark—smoky black. I tasted it cautiously. It wasn't bad. If it wasn't alcoholic, then the old man in the shop had found a darn good substitute for alcohol. At the second sip I liked it and at the third I really enjoyed it and there wasn't any fourth because by then the little bottle was a dead marine. That was about the time I remembered the name of the black ingredient with the funny smell. Kohl. It is an herb the Orientals use to make it possible to see supernatural beings. Silly superstition!

And then the liquid I'd just put away, lying warm and comfortable in my stomach, began to fizz. Then I think it began to swell. I tried to get up and couldn't. The room seemed to come apart and throw itself at me piecemeal, and I passed out.

Don't you ever wake up the way I did. For your own sake, be careful about things like that. Don't swim up out of a sodden sleep and look around you and see all those things fluttering and drifting and flying and creeping and crawling around you—puffy things dripping blood, and filmy, legless creatures, and little bits and snatches of pasty human anatomy. It was awful. There was a human hand afloat in the air an inch away from my nose; and at my startled gasp it drifted away from me, fingers fluttering in the disturbed air from my breath. Something veined and bulbous popped out from under my chair and rolled across the floor. I heard a faint clicking, and looked up into a gnashing set of jaws without any face attached. I think I broke down and cried a little. I know I passed out again.

The next time I awoke—must have been hours later, because it was broad daylight and my clock and watch had both stopped— things were a little better. Oh, yes, there were a few of the horrors around. But somehow they didn't bother me much now. I was practically convinced that I was nuts; now that I had the conviction, why worry about it? I dunno; it must have been one of the ingredients in the bottle that had calmed me down so. I was curious and excited, and that's about all. I looked around me and I was almost pleased.

The walls were green! The drab wallpaper had turned to something breathtakingly beautiful. They were covered with what seemed to be moss, but never moss like that grew for human eyes to see before. It was long and thick, and it had a slight perpetual movement—not that of a breeze, but of growth. Fascinated, I moved over and looked closely. Growing indeed, with all the quick magic of spore and cyst and root and growth again to spore; and the swift magic was only a part of the magical whole, for never was there such a green. I put out my hand to touch and stroke it, but I felt only the wallpaper. But when I closed my fingers on it, I could feel that light touch of it in the palm of my hand, the weight of twenty sunbeams, the soft resilience of jet-darkness in a closed place. The sensation was a delicate ecstasy, and never have I been happier than I was at that moment.

Around the baseboards were little snowy toadstools, and the floor was grassy. Up the hinged side of the closet door climbed a mass of flowering vines, and their petals were hued in tones indescribable. I felt as if I had been blind until now, and deaf, too; for now I could hear the whispering of scarlet, gauzy insects among the leaves and the constant murmur of growth. All around me was a new and lovely world, so delicate that the wind of my movements tore petals from the flowers, so real and natural that it defied its own impossibility. Awestruck, I turned and turned, running from wall to wall, looking under my old furniture, into my old books; and everywhere I looked I found newer and more beautiful things to wonder at. It was while I was flat on my stomach looking up at the bed springs, where a colony of jewellike lizards had nested, that I first heard the sobbing.

It was young and plaintive, and had no right to be in my room where everything was so happy. I stood up and looked around, and there in the corner crouched the translucent figure of a little girl. She was leaning back against the wall. Her thin legs were crossed in front of her, and she held the leg of a tattered toy elephant dejectedly in one hand and cried into the other. Her hair was long and dark, and it poured and tumbled over her face and shoulders.

I said, "What's the matter, kiddo?" I hate to hear a child cry like that.

She cut herself off in the middle of a sob and shook the hair out of her eyes, looking up and past me, all fright and olive skin and big, filled violet eyes. "Oh!" she squeaked.

I repeated, "What's the matter? Why are you crying?"

She hugged the elephant to her breast defensively, and whimpered, "W-where are you?"

Surprised, I said, "Right here in front of you, child. Can't you see me?"

She shook her head. "I'm scared. Who are you?"

"I'm not going to hurt you. I heard you crying, and I wanted to see if I could help you. Can't you see me at all?"

"No," she whispered. "Are you an angel?"

I guffawed. "By no means!" I stepped closer and put my hand on her shoulder. The hand went right through her and she winced and shrank away, uttering a little wordless cry. "I'm sorry," I said quickly. "I didn't mean ... you can't see me at all? I can see you."

She shook her head again. "I think you're a ghost," she said.

"Do tell!" I said. "And what are you?"

"I'm Ginny," she said. "I have to stay here, and I have no one to play with." She blinked, and there was a suspicion of further tears.

"Where did you come from?" I asked.

"I came here with my mother," she said. "We lived in lots of other rooming houses. Mother cleaned floors in office buildings. But this is where I got so sick. I was sick a long time. Then one day I got off the bed and came over here, but then when I looked back I was still on the bed. It was awful funny. Some men came and put the 'me' that was on the bed onto a stretcher-thing and took it—me—out. After a while Mummy left, too. She cried for a long time before she left, and when I called to her she couldn't hear me. She never came back, and I just got to stay here."

"Why?"

"Oh, I got to. I—don't know why. I just—got to."

"What do you do here?"

"I just stay here and think about things. Once a lady lived here, had a little girl just like me. We used to play together until the lady watched us one day. She carried on somethin' awful. She said her little girl was possessed. The girl kept callin' me, 'Ginny! Ginny! Tell Mamma you're here!'; an' I tried, but the lady couldn't see me. Then the lady got scared an' picked up her little girl an' cried, an' so I was sorry. I ran over here an' hid, an' after a while the other little girl forgot about me, I guess. They moved," she finished with pathetic finality.

I was touched. "What will become of you, Ginny?"

"I dunno," she said, and her voice was troubled. "I guess I'll just stay here and wait for Mummy to come back. I been here a long time. I guess I deserve it, too."

"Why, child?"

She looked guiltily at her shoes. "I couldn' stand feelin' so awful bad when I was sick. I got up out of bed before it was time. I shoulda stayed where I was. This is what I get for quittin'. But Mummy'll be back; just you see."

"Sure she will," I muttered. My throat felt tight. "You take it easy, kid. Any time you want someone to talk to, you just pipe up. I'll talk to you any time I'm around."

She smiled and it was a pretty thing to see. What a raw deal for a kid! I grabbed my hat and went out.

Outside things were the same as in the room to me. The hallways, the dusty stair carpets wore new garments of brilliant, nearly intangible foliage. They were no longer dark, for each leaf had its own pale and different light. Once in a while I saw things not quite so pretty. There was a giggling thing that scuttled back and forth on the third floor landing. It was a little indistinct, but it looked a great deal like Barrel-head Brogan, a shanty-Irish bum who'd returned from a warehouse robbery a year or so ago, only to shoot himself accidentally with his own gun. I wasn't sorry.

Down on the first floor, on the bottom step, I saw two youngsters sitting. The girl had her head on the boy's shoulder, and he had his arms around her, and I could see the banister through them. I stopped to listen. Their voices were faint, and seemed to come from a long way away.

He said, "There's one way out."

She said, "Don't talk that way, Tommy!"

"What else can we do? I've loved you for three years, and we still can't get married. No money, no hope—no nothing. Sure, if we did do it, I just *know* we'd always be together. Always and always—"

After a long time she said, "All right, Tommy. You get a gun, like you said." She suddenly pulled him even closer. "Oh, Tommy, are you sure we'll always be together just like this?"

"Always," he whispered, and kissed her. "Just like this."

Then there was a long silence, while neither moved. Suddenly they were as I had first seen them, and he said:

"There's only one way out."

And she said, "Don't talk that way, Tommy!"

And he said, "What else can we do? I've loved you for three years—" It went on like that, over and over and over.

I felt lousy. I went on out into the street.

It began to filter through to me what had happened. The man in the shop had called it a "talent." I couldn't be crazy, could I? I didn't *feel* crazy. The draught from the bottle had opened my eyes on a new world. What was this world?

It was a thing peopled by ghosts. There they were—storybook ghosts, and regular haunts, and poor damned souls—all the fixings of a storied supernatural, all the things we have heard about and loudly disbelieved and secretly wonder about. So what? What had it all to do with me?

As the days slid by, I wondered less about my new, strange surroundings, and gave more and more thought to that question. I had bought—or been given—a talent. I could see ghosts. I could see all parts of a ghostly world, even the vegetation that grew in it. That was perfectly reasonable—the trees and birds and fungi and flowers. A ghost world is a world as we know it, and a world as we know it must have vegetation. Yes, I could see them. But they couldn't see me!

O.K.; what could I get out of it? I couldn't talk about it or write about it because I wouldn't be believed; and besides, I had this thing exclusive, as far as I knew; why cut a lot of other people in on it?

On what, though?

No, unless I could get a steer from somewhere, there was no percentage in it for me that I could see. And then, about six days after I took that eye-opener, I remembered the one place where I might get that steer.

The Shottle Bop!

I was on Sixth Avenue at the time, trying to find something in a five-and-dime that Ginny might like. She couldn't touch anything I brought her but she enjoyed things she could look at—picture books and such. By getting her a little book of photographs of trains since

43

the "DeWitt Clinton," and asking her which of them was like ones she had seen, I found out approximately how long it was she'd been there. Nearly eighteen years. Anyway, I got my bright idea and headed for Tenth Avenue and the Shottle Bop. I'd ask that old man—he'd tell me. And when I got to Twenty-first Street, I stopped and stared. Facing me was a blank wall. The whole side of the block was void of people. There was no sign of a shop.

I stood there for a full two minutes not even daring to think. Then I walked downtown toward Twentieth, and then uptown to Twenty-first. Then I did it again. No shop. I wound up without my question answered—what was I going to with this "talent"?

I was talking to Ginny one afternoon about this and that when a human leg, from the knee down, complete and puffy, drifted between us. I recoiled in horror, but Ginny pushed it gently with one hand. It bent under the touch, and started toward the window, which was open a little at the bottom. The leg floated toward the crack and was sucked through like a cloud of cigarette smoke, reforming again on the other side. It bumbled against the pane for a moment and then ballooned away.

"My gosh!" I breathed. "What *was* that?"

Ginny laughed. "Oh, just one of the Things that's all 'e time flying around. Did it scare you? I used to be scared, but I saw so many of them that I don't care any more, so's they don't light on me."

"But what in the name of all that's disgusting are they?"

"Parts." Ginny was all childish *savoir-faire*.

"Parts of what?"

"People, silly. It's some kind of game, *I* think. You see, if someone gets hurt and loses something—a finger or an ear or something, why, the ear—the *inside* part of it, I mean, like me being the inside of the 'me' they carried out of here—it goes back to where the person who owned it lived last. Then it goes back to the place before that, and so on. It doesn't go very fast. Then when something happens to a whole person, the 'inside' part comes looking for the rest of itself. It picks up bit after bit—Look!" she put out a filmy forefinger and thumb and nipped a flake of gossamer out of the air.

44

I leaned over and looked closely; it was a small section of semi-transparent human skin, ridged and whorled.

"Somebody must have cut his finger," said Ginny matter-of-factly, "while he was living in this room. When something happens to um— you see! He'll be back for it!"

"Good heavens!" I said. "Does this happen to everyone?"

"I dunno. Some people have to stay where they are—like me. But I guess if you haven't done nothing to deserve bein' kept in one place, you have to come all around pickin' up what you lost."

I'd thought of more pleasant things in my time.

For several days I'd noticed a gray ghost hovering up and down the block. He was always on the street, never inside. He whimpered constantly. He was—or had been—a little inoffensive man of the bowler hat and starched collar type. He paid no attention to me—none of them did, for I was apparently invisible to them. But I saw him so often that pretty soon I realized that I'd miss him if he went away. I decided I'd chat with him the next time I saw him.

I left the house one morning and stood around for a few minutes in front of the brownstone steps. Sure enough, pressing through the flotsam of my new, weird coexistent world, came the slim figure of the wraith I had noticed, his rabbit face screwed up, his eyes deep and sad, and his swallowtail coat and striped waistcoat immaculate. I stepped up behind him and said, "Hi!"

He started violently and would have run away, I'm sure, if he'd known where my voice was coming from.

"Take it easy, pal," I said. "I won't hurt you."

"Who are you?"

"You wouldn't know if I told you," I said. "Now stop shivering and tell me about yourself."

He mopped his ghostly face with a ghostly handkerchief, and then began fumbling nervously with a gold toothpick. "My word," he said. "No one's talked to me for years. I'm not quite myself, you see."

"I see," I said. "Well, take it easy. I just happen to've noticed you wandering around here lately. I got curious. You looking for somebody?"

45

"Oh, no," he said. Now that he had a chance to talk about his troubles, he forgot to be afraid of this mysterious voice from nowhere that had accosted him. "I'm looking for my home."

"Hm-m-m," I said. "Been looking for a long time?"

"Oh, yes." His nose twitched. "I left for work one morning a long time ago, and when I got off the ferry at Battery Place I stopped for a moment to watch the work on that new-fangled elevated railroad they were building down there. All of a sudden there was a loud noise—my goodness! It was terrible—and the next thing I knew I was standing back from the curb and looking at a man who looked just like me! A girder had fallen, and—my word!" He mopped his face again. "Since then I have been looking and looking. I can't seem to find anyone who knows where I might have lived, and I don't understand all the things I see floating around me, and I never thought I'd see the day when grass would grow on lower Broadway—oh, it's terrible." He began to cry.

I felt sorry for him. I could easily see what had happened. The shock was so great that even his ghost had amnesia! Poor little egg—until he was whole, he could find no rest. The thing interested me. Would a ghost react to the usual cures for amnesia? If so, then what would happen to him?

"You say you got off a ferryboat?"

"Yes."

"Then you must have lived on the Island ... Staten Island, over there across the bay!"

"You really think so?" He stared through me, puzzled and hopeful.

"Why sure! Say, how'd you like me to take you over there? Maybe we can find your house."

"Oh, that would be splendid! But—oh, my, what will my wife say?"

I grinned. "She might want to know where you've been. Anyway, she'll be glad to see you back, I imagine. Come on; let's get going!"

I gave him a shove in the direction of the subways and strolled along behind him. Once in a while I got a stare from a passer-by for walking with one hand out in front of me and talking into thin air.

It didn't bother me very much. My companion, though, was very self-conscious about it, for the inhabitants of his world screeched and giggled when they saw him doing practically the same thing. Of all the humans, only I was invisible to them, and the little ghost in the bowler hat blushed from embarrassment until I thought he'd burst.

We hopped a subway—it was a new experience for him, I gathered—and went down to South Ferry. The subway system in New York is a very unpleasant place to one gifted as I was. Everything that enjoys lurking in the dark hangs out there, and there is quite a crop of dismembered human remains. After this day I took the bus.

We got a ferry without waiting. The little gray ghost got a real kick out of the trip. He asked me about the ships in the harbor and their flags, and marveled at the dearth of sailing vessels. He *tsk, tsked* at the Statue of Liberty; the last time he had seen it, he said, was while it still had its original brassy gold color, before it got its patina. By this I placed him in the late '70s; he must have been looking for his home for over sixty years!

We landed at the Island, and from there I gave him his head. At the top of Fort Hill he suddenly said, "My name is John Quigg. I live at 45 Fourth Avenue!" I've never seen anyone quite so delighted as he was by the discovery. And from then on it was easy. He turned left again, straight down for two blocks and again right. I noticed— he didn't—that the street was marked "Winter Avenue." I remembered vaguely that the streets in this section had been numbered years ago.

He trotted briskly up the hill and then suddenly stopped and turned vaguely. "I say, are you still with me?"

"Still here," I said.

"I'm all right now. I can't tell you much how much I appreciate this. Is there anything I could do for you?"

I considered. "Hardly. We're of different times, you know. Things change."

He looked, a little pathetically, at the new apartment house on the corner and nodded. "I think I know what happened to me," he said softly. "But I guess it's all right. . . . I made a will, and the kids were grown." He sighed. "But if it hadn't been for you I'd still be wandering around Manhattan. Let's see—ah; come with me!"

He suddenly broke into a run. I followed as quickly as I could. Almost at the top of the hill was a huge old shingled house, with a silly cupola and a complete lack of paint. It was dirty and it was tumble-down, and at the sight of it the little fellow's face twisted sadly. He gulped and turned through a gap in the hedge and down beside the house. Casting about in the long grass, he spotted a boulder sunk deep into the turf.

"This is it," he said. "Just you dig under that. There is no mention of it in my will, except a small fund to keep paying the box rent. Yes, a safety-deposit box, and the key and an authority are under that stone. I hid it"—he giggled—"from my wife one night, and never did get a chance to tell her. You can have whatever's any good to you." He turned to the house, squared his shoulders, and marched in the side door, which banged open for him in a convenient gust of wind. I listened for a moment and then smiled at the tirade that burst forth. Old Quigg was catching real hell from his wife, who'd sat waiting for over sixty years for him! It was a bitter stream of invective, but—well, she must have loved him. She couldn't leave the place until she was complete, if Ginny's theory was correct, and she wasn't really complete until her husband came home! It tickled me. They'd be all right now!

I found an old pinchbar in the drive and attacked the ground under the stone. It took quite a while and made my hands bleed, but after a while I pried the stone up and was able to scrabble around under it. Sure enough, there was an oiled silk pouch under there. I caught it up and carefully unwrapped the strings around it. Inside was a key and a letter addressed to a New York bank, designating only "Bearer" and authorizing the use of the key. I laughed aloud. Little old meek and mild John Quigg, I'd bet, had set aside some "mad money." With a layout like that, a man could take a powder without leaving a single sign. The son-of-a-gun! I would never know just what it was he had up his sleeve, but I'll bet there was a woman in the case. Even fixed up with his will! Ah, well—I should kick!

It didn't take me long to get over to the bank. I had a little trouble getting into the vaults, because it took quite a while to look up the box in the old records. But I finally cleared the red tape, and found myself the proud possessor of just under eight thousand bucks in small bills—and not a yellowback among 'em!

Well, from then on I was pretty well set. What did I do? Well, first I bought clothes, and then, I started out to cut ice for myself. I clubbed around a bit and got to know a lot of people, and the more I knew the more I realized what a lot of superstitious dopes they were. I couldn't blame anyone for skirting a ladder under which crouched a genuine basilisk, of course, but what the heck—not one in a thousand have beasts under them! Anyway, my question was answered. I dropped two grand on an elegant office with drapes and dim indirect lighting, and I got me a phone installed and a little quiet sign on the door—Psychic Consultant. And, boy, I did all right.

My customers were mostly upper crust, because I came high. It was generally no trouble to get contact with people's dead relatives, which was usually what they wanted. Most ghosts are crazy to get in contact with this world anyway. That's one of the reasons that almost anyone can become a medium of sorts if he tries hard enough; Lord knows that it doesn't take much to contact the average ghost. Some, of course, were not available. If a man leads a pretty square life, and kicks off leaving no loose ends, he gets clear. I never did find out where these clear spirits went to. All I knew was that they weren't to be contacted. But the vast majority of people have to go back and tie up those loose ends after they die—righting a little wrong here, helping someone they've hindered, cleaning up a bit of dirty work. That's where luck itself comes from, I do believe. You don't get something for nothing.

If you get a nice break, it's been arranged that way by someone who did you dirt in the past, or someone who did wrong to your father or your grandfather or your great-uncle Julius. Everything evens up in the long run, and until it does, some poor damned soul is wandering around the earth trying to do something about it. Half of humanity is walking around crabbing about its tough breaks. If you and you and you only knew what dozens of powers were begging for the chance to help you if you'll let them! And if you let them, you'll help clear up the mess they've made of their lives here, and free them to go wherever it is they go when they've cleaned up. Next time you're in a jam, go away somewhere by yourself and open your mind to these folks. They'll cut in and guide you all right, if you can drop your smugness and mistaken confidence in your own judgment.

I had a couple of ghostly stooges to run errands for me. One of them, an ex-murderer by the name of One-Eye Rachuba, was the fastest spook I ever saw, when it came to locating a wanted ancestor; and then there was Professor Grafe, a frog-faced teacher of social science who'd embezzled from a charity fund and fallen into the Hudson trying to make a getaway. He could trace the most devious genealogies in mere seconds, deduce the most likely whereabouts of the ghost of a missing relative. The pair of them were all the office force I could use, and although every time they helped out one of my clients they came closer to freedom themselves, they were both so entangled with their own sloppy lives that I was sure of their services for years.

But do you think I'd be satisfied to stay where I was making money hand over fist without really working for it? Oh, no. Not me. No, I had to big-time. I had to brood over the events of the last few months, and I had to get dramatic about that screwball Audrey, who really wasn't worth my trouble. It wasn't enough that I'd proven Audrey wrong when she said I'd never amount to anything. And I wasn't happy when I thought about the gang. I had to show them up.

I even remembered what the little man in the Shottle Bop had said to me about using my "talent" for bragging or for revenge. I figured I had the edge on everyone, everything. Cocky, I was. Why, I could send one of my ghostly stooges out any time and find out exactly what anyone had been doing three hours ago come Michaelmas. With the shade of the professor at my shoulder, I could backtrack on any far-fetched statement and give immediate and logical reasons for backtracking. No one had anything on me, and I could out-talk, out-maneuver, and out-smart anyone on earth. I was really quite a fellow. I began to think, "What's the use of my doing as well as this when the gang on the West Side don't know anything about it?" and "Man, would that half-wit Happy Sam burn up if he saw me drifting down Broadway in my new six-thousand-dollar road-ster!" and "To think I used to waste my time and tears on a dope like Audrey!" In other words, I was tripping up on an inferiority complex. I acted like a veridam fool, which I was. I went over to the West Side.

It was a chilly, late winter night. I'd taken a lot of trouble to dress myself and my car so we'd be bright and shining and would knock some eyes out. Pity I couldn't brighten my brains up a little.

I drove up in front of Casey's pool room, being careful to do it too fast, and concentrating on shrieks from tires and a shuddering twenty-four-cylinder roar from the engine before I cut the switch. I didn't hurry to get out of the car, either. Just leaned back and lit a fifty-cent cigar, and then tipped my hat over one ear and touched the horn button, causing it to play "Tuxedo Junction" for forty-eight seconds. Then I looked over toward the pool hall.

Well, for a minute I thought that I shouldn't have come, if that was the effect my return to the fold was going to have. And from then on I forgot about everything except how to get out of there.

There were two figures slouched in the glowing doorway of the pool room. It was up a small side street, so short that the city had depended on the place, an old institution, to supply the street light-ing. Looking carefully, I made out one of the silhouetted figures as Happy Sam, and the other was Fred Bellew. They just looked out at me; they didn't move; they didn't say anything; and when I said, "Hiya, small fry—remember me?" I noticed that along the dark-ened walls flanking the bright doorway were ranked the whole crowd of them—the whole gang. It was a shock; it was a little too casu-ally perfect. I didn't like it.

"Hi," said Fred quietly. I knew he wouldn't like the big-timing. I didn't expect any of them to like it, of course, but Fred's dislike sprang from distaste, and the others from resentment, and for the first time I felt a little cheap. I climbed out over the door of the road-ster and let them have a gander at my fine feathers.

Sam snorted and said, "Jelly bean!" very clearly. Someone else giggled, and from the darkness beside the building came a high-pitched "Woo-woo!"

I walked up to Sam and grinned at him. I didn't feel like grinning. "I ain't seen you in so long I almost forgot what a heel you were," I said. "How you making?"

"I'm doing all right," he said, and added offensively, "I'm still *working* for a living."

The murmur that ran through the crowd told me that the really smart thing to do was to get back into that shiny new automobile and hoot along out of there. I stayed.

"Wise, huh?" I said weakly.

They'd been drinking, I realized—all of them. I was suddenly in a spot. Sam put his hands in his pockets and looked at me down his nose. He was the only short man that ever could do that to me. After a thick silence he said:

"Better get back to yer crystal balls, phony. We like guys that sweat. We even like guys that have rackets, if they run them because they're smarter or tougher than the next one. But luck and gab ain't enough. Scram."

I looked around helplessly. I was getting what I'd begged for. What had I expected, anyway? Had I thought that these boys would crowd around and shake my hand off for acting this way?

They hardly moved, but they were all around me suddenly. If I couldn't think of something quickly, I was going to be mobbed. And when those mugs started mobbing a man, they did it up just fine. I drew a deep breath.

"I'm not asking for anything from you, Sam. Nothing; that means advice; see?"

"You're gettin' it!" he flared. "You and your seeanses. We heard about you. Hanging up widow-women for fifty bucks a throw to talk to their 'dear departed'! P-sykik investigator! What a line! Go on; beat it!"

I had a leg to stand on now. "A phony, huh? Why I'll bet I could put a haunt on you that would make that hair of yours stand up on end, if you have guts enough to go where I tell you to."

"You'll bet? That's a laugh. Listen at that, gang." He laughed, then turned to me and talked through one side of his mouth. "All right, you wanted it. Come on, rich guy; you're called. Fred'll hold stakes. How about ten of your lousy bucks for every one of mine? Here, Fred—hold this sawbuck."

"I'll give you twenty to one," I said half hysterically. "And I'll take you to a place where you'll run up against the homeliest, plumb-meanest old haunt you ever heard of."

The crowd roared. Sam laughed with them, but didn't try to back out. With any of that gang, a bet was a bet. He'd taken me up, and he'd set odds, and he was bound. I just nodded and put two century notes into Fred Bellew's hand. Fred and Sam climbed into the car, and just as we started, Sam leaned out and waved.

"See you in hell, fellas," he said. "I'm goin' to raise me a ghost, and one of us is going to scare the other one to death!"

I honked my horn to drown out the whooping and hollering from the sidewalk and got out of there. I turned up the parkway and headed out of town.

"Where to?" Fred asked after a while.

"Stick around," I said, not knowing.

There must be some place not far from here where I could find an honest-to-God haunt, I thought, one that would make Sam back-track and set me up with the boys again. I opened the compartment in the dashboard and let Ikey out. Ikey was a little twisted imp who'd got his tail caught in between two sheets of steel when they were assembling the car, and had to stay there until it was junked.

"Hey, Ike," I whispered. He looked up, the gleam of the compartment light shining redly in his bright little eyes. "Whistle for the professor, will you? I don't want to yell for him because those mugs in the back seat will hear me. They can't hear you."

"O.K., boss," he said; and putting his fingers to his lips, he gave vent to a blood-curdling, howling scream.

That was the prof's call-letters, as it were. The old man flew ahead of the car, circled around and slid in beside me through the window, which I'd opened a crack for him.

"My goodness," he panted, "I wish you wouldn't summon me to a location which is traveling with this high degree of celerity. It was all I could do to catch up with you."

"Don't give me that, professor," I whispered. "You can catch a stratoliner if you want to. Say, I have a guy in the back who wants to get a real scare from a ghost. Know of any around here?"

The professor put on his ghostly pince-nez. "Why, yes. Remember my telling you about the Wolfmeyer place?"

"Golly—he's bad."

"He'll serve your purpose admirably. But don't ask me to go there with you. None of us ever associates with Wolfmeyer. And for Heaven's sake, be careful."

"I guess I can handle him. Where is it?"

He gave me explicit directions, bade me good night and left. I was a little surprised; the professor traveled around with me a great deal, and I'd never seen him refuse a chance to see some new scenery. I shrugged it off and went my way. I guess I just didn't know any better.

I headed out of town and into the country to a certain old farmhouse. Wolfmeyer, a Pennsylvania Dutchman, had hanged himself there. He had been, and was, a bad egg. Instead of being a nice guy about it all, he was the rebel type. He knew perfectly well that unless he did plenty of good to make up for the evil, he'd be stuck where he was for the rest of eternity. That didn't seem to bother him at all. He got surly and became a really bad spook. Eight people had died in that house since the old man rotted off his own rope. Three of them were tenants who had rented the place, and three were hobos, and two were psychic investigators. They'd all hanged themselves. That's the way Wolfmeyer worked. I think he really enjoyed haunting. He certainly was thorough about it anyway.

I didn't want to do any real harm to Happy Sam. I just wanted to teach him a lesson. And look what happened!

We reached the place just before midnight. No one had said much, except that I told Fred and Sam about Wolfmeyer, and pretty well what was to be expected from him. They did a good deal of laughing about it, so I just shut up and drove. The next item of conversation was Fred's, when he made the terms of the bet. To win, Sam was to stay in the house until dawn. He wasn't to call for help and he wasn't to leave. He had to bring in a coil of rope, tie a noose in one end and string the other up on "Wolfmeyer's Beam"—the great oaken beam on which the old man had hanged himself, and eight others after him. This was an added temptation to Wolfmeyer to work on Happy Sam, and was my idea. I was to go in with Sam, to watch him in case the thing became too dangerous. Fred was to stay in the car a hundred yards down the road and wait.

I parked the car at the agreed distance and Sam and I got out. Sam had my tow rope over his shoulder, already noosed. Fred had quieted down considerably, and his face was dead serious.

"I don't think I like this," he said, looking up the road at the house. It hunched back from the highway, and looked like a malign being deep in thought.

I said, "Well, Sam? Want to pay up now and call it quits?"

He followed Fred's gaze. It sure was a dreary-looking place, and his liquor had fizzed away. He thought a minute, then shrugged and grinned. I had to admire the rat. "Hell, I'll go through with it. Can't bluff me with scenery, phony."

Surprisingly, Fred piped up, "I don't think he's a phony, Sam."

The resistance made Sam stubborn, though I could see by his face that he knew better. "Come on, phony," he said and swung up the road.

We climbed into the house by way of a cellar door that slanted up to a window on the first floor. I hauled out a flashlight and lit the way to the beam. It was only one of many that delighted in turning the sound of one's footsteps into laughing whispers that ran round and round the rooms and halls and would not die. Under the famous beam the dusty floor was dark-stained.

I gave Sam a hand in fixing the rope, and then clicked off the light. It must have been tough on him then. I didn't mind, because I knew I could see anything before it got to me, and even then, no ghost could see me. Not only that, for me the walls and floors and ceilings were lit with the phosphorescent many-hued glow of the ever-present ghost plants. For its eerie effect I wished Sam could see the ghost-molds feeding greedily on the stain under the beam.

Sam was already breathing heavily, but I knew it would take more than just darkness and silence to get his goat. He'd have to be alone, and then he'd have to have a visitor or so.

"So long, kid," I said, slapping him on the shoulder, and I turned and walked out of the room.

I let him hear me go out of the house and then I crept silently back. It was without doubt the most deserted place I have ever seen. Even ghosts kept away from it, excepting, of course, Wolfmeyer's. There was just the luxurious vegetation, invisible to all but me, and the deep silence rippled by Sam's breath. After ten minutes or so I knew for certain that Happy Sam had more guts than I'd ever have credited him with. He had to be scared. He couldn't—or wouldn't —scare himself.

I crouched down against the walls of an adjoining room and made myself comfortable. I figured Wolfmeyer would be along pretty soon. I hoped earnestly that I could stop the thing before it got too far. No use in making this any more than a good lesson for a wiseacre. I was feeling pretty smug about it all, and I was totally unprepared for what happened.

I was looking toward the doorway opposite when I realized that for some minutes there had been the palest of pale glows there. It brightened as I watched; brightened and flickered gently. It was green, the green of things moldy and rotting away; and with it came a subtly harrowing stench. It was the smell of flesh so very dead that it had ceased to be really odorous. It was utterly horrible, and I was honestly scared out of my wits. It was some moments before the comforting thought of my invulnerability came back to me, and I shrank lower and closer to the wall and watched.

And Wolfmeyer came in.

His was the ghost of an old, old man. He wore a flowing, filthy robe, and his bare forearms thrust out in front of him were stringy and strong. His head, with its tangled hair and beard, quivered on a broken, ruined neck like the blade of a knife just thrown into soft wood. Each slow step as he crossed the room set his head to quivering again. His eyes were alight; red they were, with deep green flames buried in them. His canine teeth had lengthened into yellow, blunt tusks, and they were like pillars supporting his crooked grin. The putrescent green glow was a horrid halo about him. He was a bright and evil thing.

He passed me completely unconscious of my presence and paused at the door of the room where Sam waited by the rope. He stood just outside it, claws extended, the quivering of his head slowly dying. He stared in at Sam, and suddenly opened his mouth and howled. It was a quiet, deadly sound, one that might have come from the throat of a distant dog, but, though I couldn't see into the other room, I knew that Sam had jerked his head around and was staring at the ghost. Wolfmeyer raised his arms a trifle, seemed to totter a bit, and then moved into the room.

I snapped myself out of the crawling terror that gripped me and scrambled to my feet. If I didn't move fast—

Tiptoeing swiftly to the door, I stopped just long enough to see Wolfmeyer beating his arms about erratically over his head, a movement that made his robe flutter and his whole figure pulsate in the green light; just long enough to see Sam on his feet, wide-eyed, staggering back and back toward the rope. He clutched his throat and opened his mouth and made no sound, and his head tilted, his neck bent, his twisted face gaped at the ceiling as he clumped backward away from the ghost and into the ready noose. And then I leaned over Wolfmeyer's shoulder, put my lips to his ear, and said:

"*Boo!*"

I almost laughed. Wolfmeyer gave a little squeak, jumped about ten feet, and, without stopping to look around, high-tailed out of the room so fast that he was just a blur. That was one scared old spook!

At the same time Happy Sam straightened, his face relaxed and relieved, and sat down with a bump under the noose. That was as close a thing as ever I want to see. He sat there, his face soaking wet with cold sweat, his hands between his knees, staring limply at his feet.

"That'll show you!" I exulted, and walked over to him. "Pay up, scum, and may you starve for that week's pay!" He didn't move. I guess he was plenty shocked.

"Come on!" I said. "Pull yourself together, man! Haven't you seen enough? That old fellow will be back any second now. On your feet!"

He didn't move.

"Sam!"

He didn't move.

"*Sam!*" I clutched at his shoulder. He pitched over sideways and lay still. He was quite dead.

I didn't do anything and for a while I didn't say anything. Then I said hopelessly, as I knelt there, "Aw, Sam. Sam—cut it out, fella."

After I minute I rose slowly and started for the door. I'd taken three steps when I stopped. Something was happening! I rubbed my hand over my eyes. Yes, it is—it was getting dark! The vague luminescence of the vines and flowers of the ghost world was getting dimmer, fading, fading—

But that had never happened before!

No difference, I told myself desperately, it's happening now, all right. *I got to get out of here!*

See? You see. It was the stuff—the damn stuff from the Shottle Bop. It was wearing off! When Sam died it ... it stopped working on me! Was this what I had to pay for the bottle? Was this what was to happen if I used it for revenge?

The light was almost gone—and now it was gone. I couldn't see a thing in the room but one of the doors. Why could I see the doorway? What was that pale-green light that set off its dusty frame?

Wolfmeyer! *I got to get out of here!*

I couldn't see ghosts anymore. Ghosts could see me now. I ran. I darted across the dark room and smashed into the wall on the other side. I reeled back from it, blood spouting from between the fingers I slapped to my face. I ran again. Another wall clubbed me. Where was that other door? I ran again, and again struck a wall. I screamed and ran again. I tripped over Sam's body. My head went through the noose. It whipped down on my windpipe, and my neck broke with an agonizing crunch. I floundered there for half a minute, and then dangled.

Dead as hell, I was. Wolfmeyer, he laughed and laughed.

Fred found me and Sam in the morning. He took our bodies away in the car. Now I've got to stay here and haunt this damn old house. Me and Wolfmeyer.

Yesterday Was Monday

HARRY WRIGHT ROLLED OVER and said something spelled "Bzzzzhha-a-aw!" He chewed a bit on a mouthful of dry air and spat it out, opened one eye to see if it really would open, opened the other and closed the first, closed the second, swung his feet onto the floor, opened them again and stretched. This was a daily occurrence, and the only thing that made it remarkable at all was that he did it on a Wednesday morning, and—

Yesterday was Monday.

Oh, he knew it was Wednesday all right. It was partly that, even though he knew yesterday was Monday, there was a gap between Monday and now; and that must have been Tuesday. When you fall asleep and lie there all night without dreaming, you know, when you wake up, that time has passed. You've done nothing that you can remember; you've had no particular thoughts, no way to gauge time, and yet you know that some hours have passed. So it was with Harry Wright. Tuesday had gone wherever your eight hours went last night.

But he hadn't slept through Tuesday. Oh no. He never slept, as a matter of fact, more than six hours at a stretch, and there was no particular reason for him doing so now. Monday was the day before yesterday; he had turned in and slept his usual stretch, he had awakened, and it was Wednesday.

If *felt* like Wednesday. There was a Wednesdayish feel to the air.

Harry put on his socks and stood up. He wasn't fooled. He knew what day it was. "What happened to yesterday?" he muttered. "Oh—yesterday was Monday." That sufficed until he got his pajamas off. "Monday," he mused, reaching for his underwear, "was quite a while back, seems as though." If he had been the worrying type, he would have started then and there. But he wasn't. He was an easygoing sort, the kind of man that gets himself into a rut and stays there until he is pushed out. That was why he was an automobile mechanic at twenty-three dollars a week; that's why he had been one for eight years now, and would be from now on, if he could only find Tuesday and get back to work.

Guided by his reflexes, as usual, and with no mental effort at all, which was also usual, he finished washing, dressing, and making his bed. His alarm clock, which never alarmed because he was of such regular habits, said, as usual, six twenty-two when he paused on the way out, and gave his room the once-over. And there was a certain something about the place that made even this phlegmatic character stop and think.

It wasn't finished.

The bed was there, and the picture of Joe Louis. There were the two chairs sharing their usual seven legs, the split table, the pipe-organ bedstead, the beige wallpaper with the two swans over and over and over, the tiny corner sink, the tilted bureau. But none of them were finished. Not that there were any holes in anything. What paint there had been in the first place was still there. But there was an odor of old cut lumber, a subtle, insistent air of building, about the room and everything in it. It was indefinable, inescapable, and Harry Wright stood there caught up in it, wondering. He glanced suspiciously around but saw nothing he could really be suspicious of. He shook his head, locked the door and went out into the hall.

On the steps a little fellow, just over three feet tall, was gently stroking the third step from the top with a razor-sharp chisel, shaping up a new scar in the dirty wood. He looked up as Harry approached, and stood up quickly.

"Hi," said Harry, taking in the man's leather coat, his peaked cap, his wizened, bright-eyed little face. "Whatcha doing?"

"Touch-up," piped the little man. "The actor in the third floor front has a nail in his right heel. He came in late Tuesday night and cut the wood here. I have to get it ready for Wednesday."

"This is Wednesday," Harry pointed out.

"Of course. Always has been. Always will be."

Harry let that pass, started on down the stairs. He had achieved his amazing bovinity by making a practice of ignoring things he could not understand. But one thing bothered him—

"Did you say that feller in the third floor front was an actor?"

"Yes. They're all actors, you know."

"You're nuts, friend," said Harry bluntly. "That guy works on the docks."

"Oh yes—that's his part. That's what he acts."

"No kiddin'. An' what does he do when he isn't acting?"

"But he—Well, that's all he does do! That's all any of the actors do!"

"Gee—I thought he looked like a reg'lar guy, too," said Harry. "An actor? 'Magine!"

"Excuse me," said the little man, "but I've got to get back to work. We mustn't let anything get by us, you know. They'll be through Tuesday before long, and everything must be ready for them."

Harry thought: this guy's crazy nuts. He smiled uncertainly and went down to the landing below. When he looked back the man was cutting skillfully into the stair, making a neat little nail scratch. Harry shook his head. This was a screwy morning. He'd be glad to get back to the shop. There was a '39 sedan down there with a busted rear spring. Once he got his mind on that he could forget this nonsense. That's all that matters to a man in a rut. Work, eat, sleep, payday. Why even try to think anything else out?

The street was a riot of activity, but then it always was. But not quite this way. There were automobiles and trucks and buses around, aplenty, but none of them were moving. And none of them were quite complete. This was Harry's own field; if there was anything he didn't know about motor vehicles, it wasn't very important. And through that medium he began to get the general idea of what was going on.

Swarms of little men who might have been twins of the one he had spoken to were crowding around the cars, the sidewalks, the stores and buildings. All were working like mad with every tool imaginable. Some were touching up the finish of the cars with fine wire brushes, laying on networks of microscopic cracks and scratches. Some, with ball peens and mallets, were denting fenders skillfully, bending bumpers in an artful crash pattern, spider-webbing safety glass windshields. Others were aging top dressing with high-pressure,

needlepoint sandblasters. Still others were pumping dust into upholstery, sandpapering the dashboard finish around light switches, throt-
tles, chokes, to give a finger-worn appearance. Harry stood aside as
a half dozen of the workers scampered down the street bearing a
fender which they riveted to a 1930 coupé. It was freshly bloodstained.

Once awakened to this highly unusual activity, Harry stopped,
slightly open-mouthed, to watch what else was going on. He saw
the same process being industriously accomplished with the houses
and stores. Dirt was being laid on plate glass windows over a coat
of clear sizing. Woodwork was being cleverly scored and the paint
peeled to make it look correctly weather-beaten, and dozens of leather-
clad laborers were on their hands and knees, poking dust and dirt
into the cracks between the paving blocks. A line of them went down
the sidewalk, busily chewing gum and spitting it out; they were followed by another crew who carefully placed the wads according to
diagrams they carried, and stamped them flat.

Harry set his teeth and muscled his rocking brain into something
like its normal position. "I ain't never seen a day like this or crazy
people like this," he said, "but I ain't gonna let it be any of my affair.
I got my job to go to." And trying vainly to ignore the hundreds of
little, hardworking figures, he went grimly on down the street.

When he got to the garage he found no one there but more swarms
of stereotyped little people climbing over the place, dulling the paint
work, cracking the cement flooring, doing their hurried, efficient little tasks of aging. He noticed, only because he was so familiar with
the garage, that they were actually *making* the marks that had been
there as long as he had known the place. "Hell with it," he gritted,
anxious to submerge himself into his own world of wrenches and
grease guns. "I got my job; this is none o' my affair."

He looked about him, wondering if he should clean these inter-
lopers out of the garage. Naw—not his affair. He was hired to repair
cars, not to police the joint. Long as they kept away from him—
and, of course, animal caution told him that he was far, far outnumbered. The absence of the boss and the other mechanics was no
surprise to Harry; he always opened the place.

He climbed out of his street clothes and into coveralls, picked up a tool case and walked over to the sedan, which he had left up on the hydraulic rack yester—that is, Monday night. And that is when Harry Wright lost his temper. After all, the car was his job, and he didn't like having anyone else mess with a job he had started. So when he saw his job—his '39 sedan—resting steadily on its wheels over the rack, which was down under the floor, and when he saw that the rear spring was repaired, he began to burn. He dived under the car and ran deft fingers over the rear wheel suspensions. In spite of his anger at this unprecedented occurrence, he had to admit to himself that the job had been done well. "Might have done it myself," he muttered.

A soft clank and a gentle movement caught his attention. With a roar he reached out and grabbed the leg of one of the ubiquitous little men, wriggled out from under the car, caught his culprit by his leather collar, and dangled him at arm's length.

"What are you doing to my job?" Harry bellowed.

The little man tucked his chin into the front of his shirt to give his windpipe a chance, and said, "Why, I was just finishing up that spring job."

"Oh. So you were just finishing up on that spring job," Harry whispered, choked with rage. Then, at the top of his voice, "Who told you to touch that car?"

"Who told me? What do you—Well, it just had to be done, that's all. You'll have to let me go. I must tighten up those two bolts and lay some dust on the whole thing."

"You must *what*? You get within six feet o' that car and I'll twist your head off your neck with a Stillson!"

"But—It has to be done!"

"You won't do it! Why, I oughta—"

"Please let me go! If I don't leave that car the way it was Tuesday night—"

"When was Tuesday night?"

"The last act, of course. Let me go, or I'll call the district supervisor!"

"Call the devil himself. I'm going to spread you on the sidewalk outside; and heaven help you if I catch you near here again!"

The little man's jaw set, his eyes narrowed, and he whipped his feet upward. They crashed into Wright's jaw; Harry dropped him and staggered back. The little man began squealing, "Supervisor! Supervisor! Emergency!"

Harry growled and started after him; but suddenly, in the air between him and the midget workman, a long white hand appeared. The empty air was swept back, showing an aperture from the garage to blank, blind nothingness. Out of it stepped a tall man in a single loose-fitting garment literally studded with pockets. The opening closed behind the man.

Harry cowered before him. Never in his life had he seen such noble, powerful features, such strength of purpose, such broad shoulders, such a deep chest. The man stood with the backs of his hands on his hips, staring at Harry as if he were something somebody forgot to sweep up.

"That's him," said the little man shrilly. "He is trying to stop me from doing the work!"

"Who are you?" asked the beautiful man, down his nose.

"I'm the m-mechanic on this j-j—Who wants to know?"

"Iridel, supervisor of the district of Futura, wants to know."

"Where in hell did you come from?"

"I did not come from hell. I came from Thursday."

Harry held his head. "What *is* all this?" he wailed. "Why is today Wednesday? Who are all these crazy little guys? What happened to Tuesday?"

Iridel made a slight motion with his finger, and the little man scurried back under the car. Harry was frenzied to hear the wrench busily tightening bolts. He half started to dive under after the little fellow, but Iridel said, "Stop!" and when Iridel said, "Stop!" Harry stopped.

"This," said Iridel calmly, "is an amazing occurrence." He regarded Harry with unemotional curiosity. "An actor on stage before the sets are finished. Extraordinary."

"What stage?" asked Harry. "What are you doing here anyhow, and what's the idea of all these little guys working around here?"

"You ask a great many questions, actor," said Iridel. "I shall answer them, and then I shall have a few to ask you. These little men are stagehands—I am surprised that you didn't realize that. They are setting the stage for Wednesday. Tuesday? That's going on now."

"Arrgh!" Harry snorted. "How can Tuesday be going on when today's Wednesday?"

"Today isn't Wednesday, actor."

"Huh?"

"Today is Tuesday."

Harry scratched his head. "Met a feller on the steps this mornin'—one of these here stagehands of yours. He said this was Wednesday."

"It *is* Wednesday. Today is Tuesday. Tuesday is today. 'Today' is simply the name for the stage set which happens to be in use. 'Yesterday' means the set that has just been used; 'Tomorrow' is the set that will be used after the actors have finished with 'today.' This is Wednesday. Yesterday was Monday; today is Tuesday. See?"

Harry said, "No."

Iridel threw up his long hands. "My, you actors are stupid. Now listen carefully. This is Act Wednesday, Scene 6:22. That means that everything you see around you here is being readied for 6:22 AM on Wednesday. Wednesday isn't a time; it's a place. The actors are moving along toward it now. I see you still don't get the idea. Let's see ... ah. Look at that clock. What does it say?"

Harry Wright looked at the big electric clock on the wall over the compressor. It was corrected hourly and highly accurate, and it said 6:22. Harry looked at it amazed. "Six tw—but my gosh, man, that's what time I left the house. I walked here, an' I been here ten minutes already!"

Iridel shook his head. "You've been here no time at all, because there is no time until the actors make their entrances."

Harry sat down on a grease drum and wrinkled up his brains with the effort he was making. "You mean that this time proposition ain't something that moves along all the time? Sorta—well, like a road. A road don't go no place—You just go places along it. Is that it?"

"That's the general idea. In fact, that's a pretty good example. Suppose we say that it's a road; a highway built of paving blocks. Each block is a day; the actors move along it, and go through day after day. And our job here—mine and the little men—is to ... well, pave that road. This is the clean-up gang here. They are fixing up the last little details, so that everything will be ready for the actors."

Harry sat still, his mind creaking with the effects of this information. He felt as if he had been hit with a lead pipe, and the shock of it was being drawn out infinitely. This was the craziest-sounding thing he had ever run into. For no reason at all he remembered a talk he had had once with a drunken aviation mechanic who had tried to explain to him how the air flowing over an airplane's wings makes the machine go up in the air. He hadn't understood a word of the man's discourse, which was all about eddies and chords and cambers and foils, dihedrals and the Bernoulli effect. That didn't make any difference; the things flew whether he understood how or not; he knew that because he had seen them. This guy Iridel's lecture was the same sort of thing. If there was nothing in all he said, how come all these little guys were working around here? Why wasn't the clock telling time? Where was Tuesday?

He thought he'd get that straight for good and all. "Just where is Tuesday?" he asked.

"Over there," said Iridel, and pointed. Harry recoiled and fell off the drum; for when the man extended his hand, it *disappeared!*

Harry got up off the floor and said tautly, "Do that again."

"What? Oh—Point toward Tuesday? Certainly." And he pointed. His hand appeared again when he withdrew it.

Harry said, "My gosh!" and sat down again on the drum, sweating and staring at the supervisor of the district of Futura. "You point, an' your hand—ain't," he breathed. "What direction is that?"

"It is a direction like any other direction," said Iridel. "You know yourself there are four directions—forward, sideward, upward, and"—he pointed again, and again his hand vanished—"*that* way!"

"They never tole me that in school," said Harry. "Course, I was just a kid then, but—"

Iridel laughed. "It is the fourth dimension—it is *duration*. The actors move through length, breadth, and height, anywhere they choose to within the set. But there is another movement—one they can't control—and that is duration."

"How soon will they come ... eh ... here?" asked Harry, waving an arm. Iridel dipped into one of his numberless pockets and pulled out a watch. "It is now eight thirty-seven Tuesday morning," he said. "They'll be here as soon as they finish the act, and the scenes in Wednesday that have already been prepared."

Harry thought again for a moment, while Iridel waited patiently, smiling a little. Then he looked up at the supervisor and asked, "Hey—this 'actor' business—what's that all about?"

"Oh—that. Well, it's a play, that's all. Just like any play—put on for the amusement of an audience."

"I was to a play once," said Harry. "Who's the audience?"

Iridel stopped smiling. "Certain—Ones who may be amused," he said. "And now I'm going to ask you some questions. How did you get here?"

"Walked."

"You *walked* from Monday night to Wednesday morning?"

"Naw—From the house to here."

"Ah—But how did you get to Wednesday, six twenty-two?"

"Well I—Damfino. I just woke up an' came to work as usual."

"This is an extraordinary occurrence," said Iridel, shaking his head in puzzlement. "You'll have to see the producer."

"Producer? Who's he?"

"You'll find out. In the meantime, come along with me. I can't leave you here; you're too close to the play. I have to make my rounds anyway."

Iridel walked toward the door. Harry was tempted to stay and find himself some more work to do, but when Iridel glanced back at him and motioned him out, Harry followed. It was suddenly impossible to do anything else.

Just as he caught up with the supervisor, a little worker ran up, whipping off his cap.

"Iridel, sir," he piped, "the weather makers put .006 of one percent too little moisture in the air on this set. There's three-sevenths of an ounce too little gasoline in the storage tanks under here."

"How much is in the tanks?"

"Four thousand two hundred and seventy-three gallons, three pints, seven and twenty-one thirty-fourths ounces."

Iridel grunted. "Let it go this time. That was very sloppy work. Someone's going to get transferred to Limbo for this."

"Very good, sir," said the little man. "Long as you know we're not responsible." He put on his cap, spun around three times and rushed off.

"Lucky for the weather makers that the amount of gas in that tank doesn't come into Wednesday's script," said Iridel. "If anything interferes with the continuity of the play, there's the devil to pay. Actors haven't sense enough to cover up, either. They are liable to start whole series of miscues because of a little thing like that. The play might flop and then we'd all be out of work."

"Oh," Harry oh-ed. "Hey, Iridel—what's the idea of that patchy-looking place over there?"

Iridel followed his eyes. Harry was looking at a corner lot. It was tree-lined and overgrown with weeds and small saplings. The vegetation was true to form around the edges of the lot, and around the path that ran diagonally through it; but the spaces in between were a plane surface. Not a leaf nor a blade of grass grew there; it was naked-looking, blank, and absolutely without any color whatever.

"Oh, that," answered Iridel. "There are only two characters in Act Wednesday who will use that path. Therefore it is as grown-over as it should be. The rest of the lot doesn't enter into the play, so we don't have to do anything with it."

"But—Suppose someone wandered off the path on Wednesday," Harry offered.

"He'd be due for a surprise, I guess. But it could hardly happen. Special prompters are always detailed to spots like that, to keep the actors from going astray or missing any cues."

"Who are they—the prompters, I mean?"

"Prompters? G.A.'s—Guardian Angels. That's what the script writers call them."

"I heard o' them," said Harry.

"Yes, they have their work cut out for them," said the supervisor. "Actors are always forgetting their lines when they shouldn't, or remembering them when the script calls for a lapse. Well, it looks pretty good here. Let's have a look at Friday."

"Friday? You mean to tell me you're working on Friday already?"

"Of course! Why, we work years in advance! How on earth do you think we could get our trees grown otherwise? Here—step in!" Iridel put out his hand, seized empty air, drew it aside to show the kind of absolute nothingness he had first appeared from, and waved Harry on.

"Y-you want me to go in there?" asked Harry diffidently.

"Certainly. Hurry, now!"

Harry looked at the section of void with a rather weak-kneed look, but could not withstand the supervisor's strange compulsion. He stepped through.

And it wasn't so bad. There were no whirling lights, no sensations of falling, no falling unconscious. It was just like stepping into another room—which is what had happened. He found himself in a great round chamber, whose roundness was touched a bit with the indistinct. That is, it had curved walls and a domed roof, but there was something else about it. It seemed to stretch off in that direction toward which Iridel had so astonishingly pointed. The walls were lined with an amazing array of control machinery—switches and ground-glass screens, indicators and dials, knurled knobs and levers. Moving deftly before them was a crew of men, each looking exactly like Iridel except that their garments had no pockets. Harry stood wide-eyed, hypnotized by the enormous complexity of the controls and the ease with which the men worked among them. Iridel touched his shoulder. "Come with me," he said. "The producer is in now; we'll find out what is to be done with you."

They started across the floor. Harry had not quite time to wonder how long it would take them to cross that enormous room, for when they had taken perhaps a dozen steps they found themselves at the opposite wall. The ordinary laws of space and time simply did not apply in the place.

They stopped at a door of burnished bronze, so very highly polished that they could see through it. It opened and Iridel pushed Harry through. The door swung shut. Harry, panic-stricken lest he be separated from the only thing in this weird world he could begin to get used to, flung himself against the great bronze portal. It bounced him back, head over heels, into the middle of the floor. He rolled over and got up to his hands and knees.

He was in a tiny room, one end of which was filled by a colossal teakwood desk. The man sitting there regarded him with amusement. "Where'd you blow in from?" he asked; and his voice was like the angry bee sound of an approaching hurricane.

"Are you the producer?"

"Well, I'll be damned," said the man, and smiled. It seemed to fill the whole room with light. He was a big man, Harry noticed; but in this deceptive place, there was no way of telling how big. "I'll be most verily damned. An actor. You're a persistent lot, aren't you? Building houses for me that I almost never go into. Getting together and sending requests for better parts. Listening carefully to what I have to say and then ignoring or misinterpreting my advice. Always asking for just one more chance, and when you get it, messing that up too. And now one of you crashes the gate. What's your trouble, anyway?"

There was something about the producer that bothered Harry, but he could not place what it was, unless it was the fact that the man awed him and he didn't know why. "I woke up in Wednesday," he stammered, "and yesterday was Tuesday. I mean Monday. I mean—" He cleared his throat and started over. "I went to sleep Monday night and woke up Wednesday, and I'm looking for Tuesday."

"What do you want me to do about it?"

"Well—couldn't you tell me how to get back there? I got work to do."

"Oh—I get it," said the producer. "You want a favor from me. You know, someday, some one of you fellows is going to come to me wanting to give me something, free and for nothing, and then I am going to drop quietly dead. Don't I have enough trouble running this show without taking up time and space by doing favors for the likes of you?" He drew a couple of breaths and then smiled again. "However—I have always tried to be just, even if it is a tough job sometimes. Go on out and tell Iridel to show you the way back. I think I know what happened to you; when you made your exit from the last act you played in, you somehow managed to walk out behind the wrong curtain when you reached the wings. There's going to be a prompter sent to Limbo for this. Go on now—beat it."

Harry opened his mouth to speak, thought better of it and scuttled out the door, which opened before him. He stood in the huge control chamber, breathing hard. Iridel walked up to him.

"Well?"

"He says for you to get me out of here."

"All right," said Iridel. "This way." He led the way to a curtained doorway much like the one they had used to come in. Beside it were two dials, one marked in days and the other in hours and minutes.

"Monday night good enough for you?" asked Iridel.

"Swell," said Harry.

Iridel set the dials for 9:30 PM on Monday. "So long, actor. Maybe I'll see you again some time."

"So long," said Harry. He turned and stepped through the door.

He was back in the garage, and there was no curtained doorway behind him. He turned to ask Iridel if this would enable him to go to bed again and do Tuesday right from the start, but Iridel was gone.

The garage was a blaze of light. Harry glanced up at the clock— It was fifteen seconds after nine-thirty. That was funny; everyone should be home by now except Slim Jim, the night man, who hung out until four in the morning serving up gas at the pumps outside. A quick glance around sufficed. This might be Monday night, but it was a Monday night he hadn't known.

The place was filled with the little men again!

Harry sat on the fender of a convertible and groaned. "Now what have I got myself into?" he asked himself.

He could see that he was at a different place-in-time from the one in which he had met Iridel. There, they had been working to build, working with a precision and nicety that was a pleasure to watch. But here—

The little men were different, in the first place. They were tired-looking, sick, slow. There were scores of overseers about, and Harry winced with one of the little fellows when one of the men in white lashed out with a long whip. As the Wednesday crews worked, so

71

the Monday gangs slaved. And the work they were doing was different. For here they were breaking down, breaking up, carting away. Before his eyes, Harry saw sections of paving lifted out, pulverized, toted away by the sackload by lines of trudging, browbeaten little men. He saw great beams upended to support the roof, while bricks were pried out of the walls. He heard the gang working on the roof, saw patches of roofing torn away. He saw walls and roof both melt away under that driving, driven onslaught, and before he knew what was happening he was standing alone on a section of the dead white plain he had noticed before on the corner lot.

It was too much for his overburdened mind; he ran out into the night, breaking through lines of laden slaves, through neat and growing piles of rubble, screaming for Iridel. He ran for a long time, and finally dropped down behind a stack of lumber out where the Unitarian church used to be, dropped because he could go no farther. He heard footsteps and tried to make himself smaller. They came on steadily; one of the overseers rounded the corner and stood looking at him. Harry was in deep shadow, but he knew the man in white could see in the dark.

"Come out o' there," grated the man. Harry came out.

"You the guy was yellin' for Iridel?"

Harry nodded.

"What makes you think you'll find Iridel in Limbo?" sneered his captor. "Who are you, anyway?"

Harry had learned by this time. "I'm an—actor," he said in a small voice. "I got into Wednesday by mistake, and they sent me back here."

"What for?"

"Huh? Why—I guess it was a mistake, that's all."

The man stepped forward and grabbed Harry by the collar. He was about eight times as powerful as a hydraulic jack. "Don't give me no guff, pal," said the man. "Nobody gets sent to Limbo by mistake, or if he didn't do somethin' up there to make him deserve it. Come clean, now."

"I didn't do nothin'." Harry wailed. "I asked them the way back, and they showed me a door, and I went through it and came here.

72

That's all I know. Stop it, you're choking me!"

The man dropped him suddenly. "Listen, babe, you know who I am? Hey?" Harry shook his head. "Oh—you don't. Well, I'm Gurrah!"

"Yeah?" Harry said, not being able to think of anything else at the moment.

Gurrah puffed on his chest and appeared to be waiting for something more from Harry. When nothing came, he walked up to the mechanic, breathed in his face. "Ain't scared, huh? Tough guy, huh? Never heard of Gurrah, supervisor of Limbo an' the roughest, toughest son of the devil from Incidence to Eternity, huh?"

Now Harry was a peaceable man, but if there was anything he hated, it was to have a stranger breathe his bad breath pugnaciously at him. Before he knew it had happened, Gurrah was sprawled eight feet away, and Harry was standing alone rubbing his left knuckles— quite the more surprised of the two.

Gurrah sat up, feeling his face. "Why, you ... you hit me!" he roared. He got up and came over to Harry. "You hit me!" he said softly, his voice slightly out of focus in amazement. Harry wished he hadn't—wished he was in bed or in Futura or dead or something. Gurrah reached out with a heavy fist and—patted him on the shoulder. "Hey," he said, suddenly friendly, "you're all right. Heh! Took a poke at me, didn't you? Be damned! First time in a month o' Mondays anyone ever made a pass at me. Last was a feller named Orton. I killed 'im." Harry paled.

Gurrah leaned back against the lumber pile. "Dam'f I didn't enjoy that, feller. Yeah. This is a hell of a job they palmed off on me, but what can you do? Breakin' down—breakin' down. No sooner get through one job, workin' top speed, drivin' the boys till they bleed, than they give you the devil for not bein' halfway through another job. You'd think I'd been in the business long enough to know what it was all about, after more than eight hundred an' twenty million acts, wouldn't you? Heh. Try to tell *them* that. Ship a load of dog houses up to Wednesday, sneakin' it past backstage nice as you please. They turn right around and call me up. 'What's the matter with you, Gurrah? Them dog houses is no good. We sent you a list o' worn-out items two acts ago. One o' the items was dog houses. Snap out of it or we send someone back there who can read an' put you on a tote-line.' That's what I get—act in and act out. An' does it do any good to tell 'em that my aide got the message an' dropped dead before he got it to me? No. Uh-uh. If I say anything about that, they tell me to stop workin' 'em to death. If I do that, they kick because my shipments don't come in fast enough."

He paused for breath. Harry had a hunch that if he kept Gurrah in a good mood it might benefit him. He asked, "What's your job, anyway?"

"Job?" Gurrah howled. "Call this a job? Tearin' down the sets, shippin' what's good to the act after next, junkin' the rest?" He snorted.

Harry asked, "You mean they use the same props over again?"

"That's right. They don't last, though. Six, eight acts, maybe. Then they got to build new ones and weather them and knock 'em around to make 'em look as if they was used."

There was silence for a time. Gurrah, having got his bitterness off his chest for the first time in literally ages, was feeling pacified. Harry didn't know how to feel. He finally broke the ice. "Hey, Gurrah—How'm I goin' to get back into the play?"

"What's it to me? How'd you—Oh, that's right, you walked in from the control room, huh? That it?"

Harry nodded.

"An' how," growled Gurrah, "did you get inta the control room?"

"Iridel brought me."

"Then what?"

"Well, I went to see the producer, and—"

"Th' *producer!* Holy—You mean you walked right in and—" Gurrah mopped his brow. "What'd he say?"

"Why—he said he guessed it wasn't my fault that I woke up in Wednesday. He said to tell Iridel to ship me back."

"An' Iridel threw you back to Monday." And Gurrah threw back his shaggy head and roared.

"What's funny?" asked Harry, a little peeved.

"Iridel," said Gurrah. "Do you realize that I've been trying for fifty thousand acts or more to get something on that pretty ol' heel, and he drops you right in my lap. Pal, I can't thank you enough! He was supposed to send you back into the play, and instead o' that you wind up in yesterday! Why, I'll blackmail him till the end of time!" He whirled exultantly, called to a group of bedraggled little men who were staggering under a cornerstone on their way to the junkyard. "Take it easy, boys," he called. "I got ol' Iridel by the short hair. No more busted backs! No more snotty messages! *Haw haw haw!*"

Harry, a little amazed at all this, put in a timid word, "Hey— Gurrah. What about me?"

Gurrah turned. "You? Oh. *Tel-e-phone!*" At his shout two little workers, a trifle less bedraggled than the rest, trotted up. One hopped up and perched on Gurrah's right shoulder; the other draped himself over the left, with his head forward. Gurrah grabbed the latter by the neck, brought the man's head close and shouted into his ear, "Give me Iridel!" There was a moment's wait, then the little man on his other shoulder spoke in Iridel's voice, into Gurrah's ear, "Well?"

"Hiyah, fancy pants!"

"Fancy—I beg your—Who is this?"

"It's Gurrah, you futuristic parasite. I got a couple things to tell you."

"Gurrah! How—*dare* you talk to me like that! I'll have you—"

"You'll have me in your job if I tell all I know. You're a wart on the nose of progress, Iridel."

"What is the meaning of this?"

"The meaning of this is that you had instructions sent to you by the producer an' you muffed them. Had an actor there, didn't you? He saw the boss, didn't he? Told you he was to be sent back, didn't he? Sent him right over to me instead of to the play, didn't you? You're slippin', Iridel. Gettin' old. Well, get off the wire. I'm callin' the boss, right now."

"The boss? Oh—don't do that, old man. Look, let's talk this thing over. Ah—about that shipment of three-legged dogs I was wanting you to round up for me; I guess I can do without them. Any little favor I can do for you—"

—"you'll damn well do, after this. You better, Goldilocks." Gurrah knocked the two small heads together, breaking the connection and probably the heads, and turned grinning to Harry. "You see," he explained, "that Iridel feller is a damn good supervisor, but he's a stickler for detail. He sends people to Limbo for the silliest little mistakes. He never forgives anyone and he never forgets a slip. He's the cause of half the misery back here, with his hurry-up orders. Now things are gonna be different. The boss has wanted to give Iridel a dose of his own medicine for a long time now, but Irrie never gave him a chance."

Harry said patiently, "About me getting back now—"

"My fran'!" Gurrah bellowed. He delved into a pocket and pulled out a watch like Iridel's. "It's eleven forty on Tuesday," he said. "We'll shoot you back there now. You'll have to dope out your own reasons for disappearing. Don't spill too much, or a lot of people will suffer for it—you the most. Ready?"

Harry nodded; Gurrah swept out a hand and opened the curtain to nothingness. "You'll find yourself quite a ways from where you started," he said, "because you did a little moving around here. Go ahead."

"Thanks," said Harry.

Gurrah laughed. "Don't thank me, chum. You rate all the thanks! Hey—if, after you kick off, you don't make out so good up there, let them toss you over to me. You'll be treated good; you've my word on it. Beat it; luck!"

Holding his breath, Harry Wright stepped through the doorway.

He had to walk thirty blocks to the garage, and when he got there the boss was waiting for him.

"Where you been, Wright?"

"I—lost my way."

"Don't get wise. What do you think this is—vacation time? Get going on the spring job. Damn it, it won't be finished now till tomorra."

Harry looked him straight in the eye and said, "Listen. It'll be finished tonight. I happen to know." And, still grinning, he went back into the garage and took out his tools.

Brat

"It's strictly a short order proposition," said Michaele, tossing her searchlight hair back on her shoulders. "We've got to have a baby eight days from now or we're out a sweet pile of cash."

"We'll get one somewhere. Couldn't we adopt one or something?" I said, plucking a stalk of grass from the bank of the brook and jamming it between my front teeth.

"Takes weeks. We could kidnap one, maybe."

"They got laws. Laws are for the protection of people."

"Why does it always have to be other people?" Mike was beginning to froth up. "Shorty, get your bulk up off the ground and think of something."

"Think better this way," I said. "We could borrow one."

"Look," said Mike. "When I get my hands on a kid, that child and I have to go through a short but rigorous period of training. It's likely to be rough. If *I* had a baby and someone wanted to borrow it for any such purpose, I'd be damned if I'd let it go."

"Oh, you wouldn't be too tough," I said. "You've got maternal instincts and stuff."

"Shorty, you don't seem to realize that babies are very delicate creatures and require the most skilled and careful handling. I don't know *anything* about them. I am an only child, and I went right from high school into business college and from there into an office. The only experience I ever had with a baby was once when I minded one for an afternoon. It cried all the time I was there."

"Should've changed its diapers."

"I did."

"Must've stuck it with a pin then."

"I did not! You seem to know an awful lot about children," she said hotly.

"Sure I do. I was one myself once."

"Heel!" She leaped on me and rolled me into the brook. I came up spluttering and swearing. She took me by the neck, pulled me half up on the bank and began thudding my head on the soft bank.

"Let go my apple," I gasped. "This is no choking matter."

"Now will you cooperate? Shorty, quit your kidding. This is serious. Your Aunt Amanda has left us thirty grand, providing we can prove to her sister Jonquil that we are the right kind of people. 'Those who can take care of a baby can take care of money,' she used to say. We've got to be under Jonquil's eye for thirty days and take care of a baby. No nursemaids, no laundresses, no nothing."

"Let's wait till we have one of our own."

"Don't be stupid! You know as well as I do that that money will set you up in a business of your own as well as paying off the mortgage on the shack. *And* decorating it. *And* getting us a new car."

"*And* a fur coat. *And* a star sapphire. Maybe I'll even get a new pair of socks."

"*Shorty!*" A full lip quivered, green eyes swam.

"Oh darling, I didn't mean— Come here and be kissed."

She did. Then she went right on where she had left off. She's like that. She can puddle up at the drop of a cynicism, and when I apologize she sniffs once and the tears all go back into her eyes without being used. She holds them for when they'll be needed instead of wasting them. "But you know perfectly well that unless we get our hands on money—lots of it—and darn soon, we'll lose that little barn and the garage that we built just to *put* a new car in. Wouldn't that be silly?"

"No. No garage, no need for a car. Save lots of money!"

"Shorty—please."

"All right, all right. The fact that everything you say is correct doesn't help to get us a baby for thirty days. Damn money anyway! Money isn't everything!"

"Of course it isn't, darling," said Michaele sagely, "but it's what you buy everything with."

A sudden splash from the brook startled us. Mike screamed, "Shorty—grab him!"

I plunged into the water and hauled out a very tiny, very dirty—baby. It was dressed in a tattered romper, and it had an elfin face, big blue eyes and a golden topknot. It looked me over and sprayed me—*b-b-b-b-b-br-r-r*—with a combination of a mouthful of water and a Bronx cheer.

"Oh, the poor darling little angel!" said Mike. "Give him to me, Shorty! You're handling him like a bag of sugar!"

I stepped gingerly out of the brook and handed him over. Michaele cradled the filthy mite in her arms, completely oblivious to the child's effect on her white linen blouse. The same white linen blouse, I reflected bitterly, that I had been kicked out of the house for, when I pitched some cigar ashes on it. It made me feel funny, watching Mike handle that kid. I'd never pictured her that way.

The baby regarded Mike gravely as she discoursed to it about a poor drowned woofum-wuffums, and did the bad man treat it badly, then. The baby belched eloquently.

"He belches in English!" I remarked.

"Did it have the windy ripples?" cooed Mike. "Give us a kiss, honey lamb."

The baby immediately flung its little arms around her neck and planted a whopper on her mouth.

"Wow!" said Mike when she got her breath. "Shorty, could you take lessons!"

"Lessons my eye," I said jealously. "Mike, that's no baby, that's some old guy in his second childhood."

"The idea." She crooned to the baby for a moment, and then said suddenly, "Shorty—what were we talking about before heaven opened up and dropped this little bundle of—" Here the baby tried to squirm out of her arms and she paused to get a better grip.

"Bundle of what?" I asked, deadpan.

"Bundle of joy."

"Oh! Bundle of joy. What were we talking about? Ba—Hey! Babies!"

"That's right. And a will. And thirty grand."

I looked at the child with new eyes. "Who do you think belongs to the younker?"

"Someone who apparently won't miss him if we take him away for thirty days," she said. "No matter what bungling treatment I give him, it's bound to be better than what he's used to. Letting a mere babe crawl around in the woods! Why, it's awful!"

"The mere babe doesn't seem to mind," I said. "Tell you what we'll do—we'll take care of him for a few days and see if anyone claims him. We'll listen to the radio and watch the papers and the ol' grapevine. If anybody does claim him, maybe we can make a deal for a loan. At any rate we'll get to work on him right away."

At this juncture the baby eeled out of Mike's arms and took off across the grass. "Sweet Sue! Look at him go!" she said, scrambling to her feet. "Get him, Shorty!"

The infant, with twinkling heels, was crawling—running, on hands and knees—down toward the brook. I headed him off just as he reached the water, and snagged him up by the slack of his pants. As he came up off the ground he scooped up a handful of mud and pitched it into my eyes. I yelped and dropped him. When I could see a little daylight again I beheld Michaele taking a running brodie into a blackberry bush. I hurried over there, my eyelids making a nasty grating sound. Michaele was lying prone behind the baby, who was also lying prone, his little heels caught tightly in Mike's hands. He was nonchalantly picking blackberries.

Mike got her knees and then her feet under her, and picked up the baby, who munched contentedly. "I'm disgusted with you," she said, her eyes blazing. "Flinging an innocent child around like that! Why, it's a wonder you didn't break every bone in his poor little body!"

"But I— He threw mud in my—"

"Pick on someone your size, you big bully! I never knew till now that you were a sadist with an inferiority complex."

"And I never knew till now that it's true what they say about the guy in the three-cornered pants—the king can do no wrong! What's happened to your sense of justice, woman? That little brat there—"

"Shorty! Talking that way about a poor little baby! He's beautiful! He didn't mean anything by what he did. He's too young to know any better."

In the biggest, deepest bass voice I have ever heard, the baby said, "Lady, I do know what I'm doin'. I'm old enough!"

We both sat down.

"Did you say that?" Mike wanted to know.

I shook my head dazedly.

"Coupla dopes," said the baby.

"Who— What are you?" asked Mike breathlessly.

"What do I look like?" said the baby, showing his teeth. He had very sharp, very white teeth—two on the top gum and four on the lower.

"A little bundle of—"

"Shorty!" Mike held up a slim finger.

"Never mind him," growled the child. "I know lots of four-letter words. Go ahead, bud."

"You go ahead. What are you—a midget?"

I no sooner got the second syllable of that word out when the baby scuttled over to me and rocked my head back with a surprising right to the jaw. "That's the last time I'm going to be called that by anybody!" he roared deafeningly. "No! I'm not a . . . a . . . what you said. I'm a pro tem changeling, and that's all."

"What on earth is that?" asked Mike.

"Just what I said!" snapped the baby, "A pro tem changeling. When people treat their babies too well—or not well enough—I show up in their bassinets and give their folks what for. Only I'm always the spitting image of their kid. When they wise up in the treatment, they get their kids back—not before."

"Who pulls the switch? I mean, who do you work for?"

The baby pointed to the grass at our feet. I had to look twice before I realized what he was pointing at. The blades were dark and glossy and luxuriant in a perfect ring about four feet in diameter.

Michaele gasped and put her knuckles to her lips. "The Little People!" she breathed.

I was going to say, "Don't be silly, Mike!" but her taut face and the baby's bland, nodding head stopped me.

"Will you work for us?" she asked breathlessly. "We need a baby for thirty days to meet the conditions of a will."

"I heard you talking about it," said the baby. "No."

"No?"

"No."

A pause. "Look, kid," I said, "what do you like? Money? Food? Candy? Circuses?"

"I like steaks," said the child gruffly. "Rare, fresh, thick. Onions. Cooked so pink they say, 'Moo!' when you bite 'em. Why?"

"Good," I said. "If you work for us, you'll get all the steaks you can eat."

"No."

"What would you want to work for us?"

"Nothin'. I don't wanna work for you."

"What are we going to do?" I whispered to Mike. "This would be perfect!"

"Leave it to me. Look—baby—what's your name, anyway?"

"Percival. But don't call me Percival! Butch."

"Well, look, Butch; we're in an awful jam. If we don't get hold of a sockful of money darn soon, we'll lose that pretty little house over there."

"What's the matter with *him?* Can't he keep up the payments? What is he—a bum?"

"Hey, you—"

"Shut up, Shorty. He's just beginning, Butch. He's a graduate caterer. But he has to get a place of his own before he can make any real money."

"What happens if you lose th' house?"

"A furnished room. The two of us."

"What's the matter with that?"

I tensed. This was a question I had asked her myself.

"Not for me. I just couldn't live that way." Mike would wheedle, but she wouldn't lie.

Butch furrowed his nonexistent eyebrows. "Couldn't? Y'know, I like that. High standards." His voice deepened; the question lashed her. "Would you live with him in a furnished room if there were no other way?"

"Well, of course."

"I'll help you," said Butch instantly.

"Why?" I asked. "What do you expect to get out of it?"

"Nothing—some fun, maybe. I'll help you because you need help. That's the only reason I ever do anything for anybody. That's the only thing you should have told me in the first place—that you were in a jam. You and your bribes!" he snapped at me, and turned back to Mike. "I ain't gonna like that guy," he said.

I said, "I already don't like you."

As we started back to the house Butch said, "But I'm gonna get my steaks?"

Aunt Jonquil's house stood alone in a large lot with its skirts drawn primly up and an admonishing expression on its face. It looked as if it had squeezed its way between two other houses to hide itself, and some scoundrel had taken the other houses away.

And Aunt Jonquil, like her house, was five times as high as she was wide, extremely practical, unbeautifully ornate, and stood alone. She regarded marriage as an unfortunate necessity. She herself never married because an unkind nature had ruled that she must marry a man, and she thought that men were uncouth. She disapproved of smoking, drinking, swearing, gambling, and loud laughter. Smiles she enjoyed only if she could fully understand what was being smiled at; she mistrusted innuendo. A polite laugh was a thing she permitted herself perhaps twice a week, providing it was atoned for by ten minutes of frozen-faced gravity. Added to which, she was a fine person. Swell.

On the way to the city, I sat through this unnerving conversation:

Butch said, "Fathead! Drive more carefully!"

"He's doing all right," said Mike. "Really. It surprises me. He's usually an Indian." She was looking very lovely in a pea-green linen jacket and a very simple white skirt and a buff straw hat that looked like a halo.

Butch was wearing a lace-edged bonnet and an evil gleam in his eye to offset the angelic combination of a pale-blue sweater with white rabbits appliquéd on the sides, and fuzzy Angora booties on which he had insisted because I was a wearing a navy-blue and he knew it would come off all over me. He was, I think, a little uncomfortable due to my rather unskilled handling of his diapering. And the reason for my doing that job was to cause us more trouble than a little bit. Butch's ideas of privacy and the proprieties were advanced. He would no more think of letting Mike bathe or change him than I would think of letting Garbo change me. Thinking about this, I said:

"Butch, that prudishness of yours is going to be tough to keep up at Aunt Jonquil's."

"You'll keep it up, son," said the infant, "or I'll quit working. I ain't going to have no women messin' around me that way. What d'ye think I am—an exhibitionist?"

"I think you're a liar," I said. "And I'll tell you why. You said you made a life's work of substituting for children. How could you with ideas like that? Who you trying to horse up?"

"Oh," said Butch, "that. Well, I might's well confess to you that I ain't done that kind of work in years. I got sick of it. I was gettin' along in life and . . . well, you can imagine. Well, about thutty years ago I was out on a job an' the woman was changin' my drawers when a half-dozen babes arrived from her sewin' circle. She left off workin' right where she was and sang out for them all to come in and see how pretty I looked the way I was. I jumped out o' th' bassinet, grabbed a diaper off th' bed an' held it in front of me while I called the whole bunch of 'em what they were and told them to get out of there. I got fired for it. I thought they'd put me to work hauntin' houses or cleanin' dishes for sick people or somethin', but no—they cracked down on me. Told me I'd have to stay this way until I was repentant."

"Are you?" giggled Mike.

Butch snorted. "Not so you'd notice it," he growled. "Repentant because I believe in common decency? Heh?"

We waited a long time after we rang the bell before Jonquil opened the door. That was to give her time to peep out at us from the tumorous bay window and compose her features to meet the niece by marriage her unfastidious nephew had acquired.

"Jonquil!" I said heartily, dashing forward and delivering the required peck on her cheek. Jonquil expected her relatives to use her leathery cheek precisely as she herself used a napkin. Pat. Dry surface on dry surface. Moisture is vulgar.

"And this is Michaele," I said, stepping aside.

Mike said, "How do you do?" demurely, and smiled.

Aunt Jonquil stepped back a pace and held her head as if she were sighting at Mike through her nostrils. "Oh, yes," she said without moving her lips. The smile disappeared from Mike's face and came back with an effort of will that hurt. "Come in," said Jonquil at last, and with some reluctance.

We trailed through a foyer and entered the parlor. It wasn't a living room, it was an honest-to-goodness front parlor with antimacassars and sea shells. The tone of the room was sepia—light from the background of the heavily flowered wallpaper, dark for the furniture. The chairs and a hard-looking divan were covered with a material that looked as if it had been bleeding badly some months ago. When Butch's eye caught the glassed-in monstrosity of hay and dead flowers over the mantelpiece, he retched audibly.

"What a lovely place you have here," said Mike.

"Glad you like it," acknowledged Jonquil woodenly. "Let's have a look at the child." She walked over and peered at Butch. He scowled at her. "Good heavens!" she said.

"Isn't he lovely?" said Mike.

"Of course," said Jonquil without enthusiasm, and added, after searching her store of ready-made expressions, "the little wudgums!" She kitchy-cooed his chin with her sharp forefinger. He immediately began to wail, with the hoarse, high-pitched howl of a genuine baby.

"The poor darling's tired after his trip," said Mike.

Jonquil, frightened by Butch's vocal explosion, took the hint and led the way upstairs.

"Is the whole damn house like this?" whispered Butch hoarsely.

"No. I don't know. Shut up," said Mike. My sharp-eared aunt swiveled on the steps. "And go to sleepy-bye," she crooned aloud. She bent her head over his and hissed, "And keep on crying, you little wretch!"

Butch snorted and then complied.

We walked into the bedroom, austerely furnished, the kind of room they used in the last century for sleeping purposes only, and therefore designed so that it was quite unattractive to anyone with anything but sleep on his mind. It was all gray and white; the only spot of color in the room was the bedstead, which was a highly polished pipe organ. Mike lay the baby down on the bed and stripped off his booties, his shirt and his sweater. Butch put his fist in his mouth and waited tensely.

"Oh—I almost forgot. I have the very same bassinet you used, up in the attic," said Jonquil. "I should have had it ready. Your telegram was rather abrupt, Horace. You should have let me know sooner that you'd come today." She angled out of the room.

"Horace! I'll be— Is your name Horace?" asked Butch in delight.

"Yes," I said gruffly. "But it's Shorty to you, see, little man?"

"And I was worried about you callin' me Percival!"

I helped set up the bassinet and we tucked Butch in for his nap. I managed to be fooling around with his bedclothes when Mike bent over dutifully to give him a kiss. I grabbed Butch's chin and held it down so the kiss landed on his forehead. He was mightily wroth, and bit my finger till it bled. I stuck it in my pocket and told him, "I'll see you later, bummy-wummy!" He made a noise, and Jonquil fled, blushing.

We convened in the kitchen, which was far and away the pleasantest room in the house. "Where on earth did you get that child?" Jonquil asked, peering into a nice-smelling saucepan on the old-fashioned range.

"Neighbor's child," I said. "They were very poor and were glad to have him off their hands for a few weeks."

"He's a foundling," Mike ingeniously supplemented. "Left on their doorstep. He's never been adopted or anything."

"What's his name?"

"We call him Butch."

"How completely vulgar!" said Jonquil. "I will have no child named Butch in my house. We shall have to give him something more refined."

I had a brain wave. "How about Percival?" I said.

"Percival. Percy," murmured Jonquil, testing it out. "That is much better. That will do. I knew somebody called Percival once."

"Oh—you better not call him Percival," said Mike, giving me her no-good-can-come-of-this look.

"Why not?" I said blandly. "Lovely name."

"Yeah," said Mike. "Lovely."

"What time does Percival get his dinner?" asked Jonquil.

"Six o'clock."

"Good," said Jonquil. "I'll feed him!"

"Oh no, Aunt J—I mean, Miss Timmins. That's our job."

I think Jonquil actually smiled. "I think I'd like to do it," she said. "You're not making an inescapable duty out of this, are you?"

"I don't know what you mean," said Mike, a little coldly. "We *like* that child."

Jonquil peered intently at her. "I believe you do," she said in a surprised tone, and started out of the room. At the door she called back, "You needn't call me Miss Timmins," and she was gone.

"Well!" said Mike.

"Looks like you won the war, babe."

"Only the first battle, honey, and don't think I don't know it. What a peculiar old duck she is!" She busied herself at the stove, warming up some strained carrots she had taken out of a jar, sterilizing a bottle and filling it with pineapple juice. We had read a lot of baby manuals in the last few days!

Suddenly, "Where's your aunt?" Mike asked.

"I dunno. I guess she's— Good grief!"

There was a dry-boned shriek from upstairs and then the sound of hard heels pounding along the upper hallway toward the front stairs. We went up the back stairs two at time, and saw the flash of Jonquil's dimity skirts as she disappeared downstairs. We slung into the bedroom. Butch was lying in his bassinet doubled up in some kind of spasm.

"Now what?" I groaned.

"He's choking," said Mike. "What are we going to do, Shorty?"

I didn't know. Mike ran and turned him over. His face was all twisted up and he was pouring sweat and gasping. "Butch! Butch— What's the matter?"

And just then he got his wind back. *"Ho ho ho!"* he roared in his bullfrog voice, and lost it again.

"He's laughing," Mike whispered.

"That's the funniest way I ever saw anyone commit sideways," I said glumly. I reached out and smacked him across the puss. "Butch! Snap out of it!"

"Ooh!" said Butch. "You lousy heel. I'll get you for that."

"Sorry, Butch. But I thought you were strangling."

"Guess I was at that," he said, and started to laugh again. "Shorty, I couldn't help it. See, that ol' vinegar visage come in here and started staring at me. I stared right back. She bends over the bassinet. I grin. She grins. I open my mouth. She opens her mouth. I reach in and pull out her bridgework and pitch it out the windy. Her face sags down in the middle like a city street in Scranton. She does the steam-siren act and hauls on out o' here. But Shorty—Mike"—and he went off into another helpless spasm—"you shoulda seen her *face!*"

We all subsided when Jonquil came in again. "Just tending to my petunias," she said primly. "Why—you have dinner on the table. Thank you, child."

"Round two," I said noncommittally.

Around two in the morning I was awakened by a soft thudding in the hallway. I came up on one elbow. Mike was fast asleep. But the bassinet was empty. I breathed an oath and tiptoed out into the hall. Halfway down was Butch, crawling rapidly. In two strides I had him by the scruff of the neck.

"*Awk!*"

"Shut up! Where do you think you're going?"

He thumbed at a door down the hall.

"No, Butch. Get on back to bed. You can't go there."

He looked at me pleadingly. "I can't? Not for *nothin'?*"

"Not for nothin'."

"Aw—Shorty. Gimme a break."

"Break my eyebrow! You belong in that bassinet."

"Just this once, huh, Shorty?"

I looked worriedly at Jonquil's bedroom door. "All right, dammit. But make it snappy."

Butch went on strike the third day. He didn't like those strained vegetables and soups to begin with, and then one morning he heard the butcher boy downstairs, singing out, "Here's yer steaks, Miss Timmins!" That was enough for little Percival.

"There's got to be a new deal around here, chum," he said the next time he got me in the room alone. "I'm gettin' robbed."

"Robbed? Who's taking what?"

"Youse. You promise me steaks, right? Listen, Shorty, I'm through with that pap you been feedin' me. I'm starvin' to death on it."

"What would you suggest?" I asked calmly. "Shall I have one done to your taste and delivered to your room, sir?"

"You know what, Shorty? You're kiddin'." He jabbed a tiny forefinger into the front of my shirt for emphasis. "You're kiddin', but I ain't. An' what you just said is a pretty good idea. I want a steak once a day—here in this room. I mean it, son."

I opened my mouth to argue and then looked deep into those baby eyes. I saw an age-old stubbornness, an insurmountable firmness of character there. I shrugged and went out.

In the kitchen I found Mike and Jonquil deeply engaged in some apparently engrossing conversation about rayon taffeta. I broke it up by saying, "I just had an idea. Tonight I'm going to eat my supper upstairs with Bu ... Percival. I want you to get to know each other better, and I would commune with another male for a spell. I'm outnumbered down here."

Jonquil actually did smile this time. Smiles seemed to be coming to her a little more easily these days. "I think that's a lovely idea," she said. "We're having steak tonight, Horace. How do you like yours?"

"Broiled," said Mike, "and well d—"

"Rare!" I said, sending a glance at Mike. She shut up, wonderingly.

And that night I sat up in the bedroom, watching that miserable infant eat my dinner. He did it with gusto, with much smacking of the lips and grunting in ecstasy.

"What do you expect me to do with this?" I asked, holding up a cupful of lukewarm and sticky strained peas.

"*I* don't know," said Butch with his mouth full. "That's your problem."

I went to the window and looked out. Directly below was a spotless concrete walk which would certainly get spattered if I pitched the unappetizing stuff out there. "Butch—won't you get rid of this stuff for me?"

He sighed, his chin all greasy from my steak. "Thanks, no," he said luxuriously. "Couldn't eat another bite."

I tasted the peas tentatively, held my nose and gulped them down. As I swallowed the last of them I found time to direct a great many highly unpleasant thoughts at Butch. "No remarks, *Percy,*" I growled.

He just grinned. I picked up his plates and the cup and started out. "Haven't you forgotten something?" he asked sleepily.

"What?" He nodded toward the dresser and the bottle which stood on.it. Boiled milk with water and corn syrup added. "Damned if I will!" I snapped.

He grinned, opened his mouth and started to wail.

"Shut up!" I hissed. "You'll have them women up here claiming I'm twisting your tail or something."

"That's the idea," said Butch. "Now drink your milk like a good little boy and you can go out and play."

I muttered something impotently, ripped the nipple off the bottle and gulped the contents.

"That's for telling the old lady to call me Percy," said Butch. "I want another steak tomorrow. 'Bye now."

And that's how it came about that I, a full-grown man in good health, lived for close to two weeks on baby food. I think that the deep respect I have for babies dates from this time, and is founded on my realization of how good-natured they are on the diet they get. What really griped me was having to watch him eat my meals. Brother, I was earning that thirty grand the hard way.

About the beginning of the third week Butch's voice began to change. Mike noticed it first and came and told me.

"I think something's the matter with him," she said. "He doesn't seem as strong as he was, and his voice is getting high-pitched."

"Don't borrow trouble, beautiful," I said, putting my arm around her. "Lord knows he isn't losing any weight on the diet he's getting.

And he has plenty of lung power."

"That's another thing," she said in a puzzled tone. "This morning he was crying and I went in to see what he wanted. I spoke to him and shook him but he went on crying for almost five minutes before he suddenly sat up and said, 'What? What? Eh—it's you, Mike.' I asked him what he wanted; he said nothing and told me to scram."

"He was kidding you."

She twisted out of my arms and looked up at me, her golden brows just touching over the snowy crevasse of her frown. "Shorty— he was crying—*real tears.*"

That was the same day that Jonquil went into town and bought herself a half dozen bright dresses. And I strongly suspect she had something done to her hair. She looked fifteen years younger when she came in and said, "Horace—it seems to me you used to smoke."

"Well . . . yes—"

"Silly boy! You've stopped smoking just because you think I wouldn't approve! I like to have a man smoking around the house. Makes it more homey. Here."

She pressed something into my hand and fled, red-faced and bright-eyed. I looked at what she had given me. Two packs of cigarettes. They weren't my brand, but I don't think I have ever been so deeply touched.

I went and had a talk with Butch. He was sleeping lightly when I entered the room. I stood there looking down at him. He was awful tiny, I thought. I wonder what it is these women gush so much about.

Butch's eyes were so big under his lids that they seemed as if they just couldn't stay closed. The lashes lay on his cheek with the most gentle of delicate touches. He breathed evenly, with occasionally a tiny catch. It made nice listening, somehow. I caught a movement out of the corner of my eye—his hand, clenching and unclenching. It was very rosy, and far too small to be so perfect. I looked at my own hand and at his, and I just couldn't believe it . . .

He woke suddenly, opening his eyes and kicking. He looked first at the window, and then at the wall opposite. He whimpered, swallowed, gave a little cry. Then he turned his head and saw me. For a long moment he watched me, his deep eyes absolutely unclouded; suddenly he sat up and shook his head. "Hello," he said sleepily.

I had the strange sensation of watching a person wake up twice. I said, "Mike's worried about you." I told him why.

"Really?" he said. "I—don't feel much different. Heh! Imagine this happening to me."

"Imagine what happening?"

"I've heard of it before, but I never... Shorty, you won't laugh at me, will you?"

I thought of all that baby food, and all those steaks. "Don't worry. You ain't funny."

"Well, you know what I told you about me being a changeling. Changelings is funny animals. Nobody likes 'em. They raise all kinds of hell. Fathers resent 'em because they cry all night. Mothers get panicky if they don't know it's a changeling, and downright resentful if they do. A changeling has a lot of fun bein' a brat, but he don't get much emotional sugar, if you know what I mean. Well, in my case ... dammit, I can't get used to it! Me, of all people!...well, someone around here ... uh ... loves me."

"Not me," I said quickly, backing away.

"I know, not you." He gave me a sudden, birdlike glance and said softly, "You're a pretty good egg, Shorty."

"Huh? Aw—"

"Anyway, they say that if any woman loves a changeling, he loses his years and his memories, and turns into a real human kid. But he's got to be loved for himself, not for some kid he replaces." He shifted uneasily. "I don't ... I can't get used to it happening to me, but ... oh oh!" A pained expression came across his face and he looked at me helplessly. I took in the situation at a glance.

A few minutes later I corralled Mike. "Got something for you," I said, and handed her something made of layette cloth.

"What's ... Shorty! Not—"

I nodded. "Butch's getting infantile," I said.

While she was doing the laundry a while later I told her what Butch had said. She was very quiet while I told her, and afterward.

"Mike—if there is anything in all this fantastic business, it wouldn't be you, would it, that's making this change in him?"

She thought it over for a long time and then said, "I think he's terribly cute, Shorty."

I swung her around. She had soapsuds on her temple, where her fingers had trailed when she tossed her bright hair back with her wrist.

"Who's number one man around here?" I whispered. She laughed and said I was silly and stood on tiptoe to kiss me. She's a little bit of a thing.

The whole thing left me feeling awful funny.

Our thirty days were up, and we packed. Jonquil helped us, and I've never seen her so full of life. Half the time she laughed, and once in a while she actually broke down and giggled. And at lunch she said to us, "Horace—I'm afraid to let you take little Percy back with you. You said that those people who had him were sort of ne'er-do-wells, and they wouldn't miss him much. I wish you'd leave him with me for a week or so while you find out just what their home life is like, and whether they really want him back. If not, I . . . well, I'll see that he gets a good place to live in."

Mike and I looked at each other, and then Mike looked up at the ceiling, toward the bedroom. I got up suddenly. "I'll ask him," I said, and walked upstairs.

Butch was sitting up in the bassinet trying to catch a sunbeam. "Hey!" I said. "Jonquil wants you to stick around. What do you say?"

He looked at me, and his eyes were all baby, nothing else.

"Well?"

He made some tremendous mental effort, pursed his lips, took a deep breath, held it for an unconscionable time, and then one word burst out. "Percy!"

"I get it," I said. "So long, fella."

He didn't say anything; just went back to his sunbeam.

"It's O.K. with him," I said when I got back to the table.

"You never struck me as the kind of man who would play games with children," laughed Jonquil. "You'll do ... you'll do. Michaele, dear—I want you to write to me. I'm so glad you came."

So we got our thirty grand. We wrote as soon as we reached the shack—*our* shack, now—that no, the people wouldn't want Percy back, and that his last name was—Fay. We got a telegram in return thanking us and telling us that Jonquil was adopting the baby.

"You goin' to miss ol' Butch?" I asked Mike.

"No," she said. "Not too much. I'm sort of saving up."

"Oh," I said.

The Anonymous

When Chloe hooked Gabe, there was quite a ripple about it. The ripple, as such things will, spread in widening circles from office to drugstore to nightclub to the society columns, and everyone said, "Oh, the lucky girl, to get such a handsome fiancé!" Or, conversely, "Imagine being married to a man as good-looking as that! The poor kid!"

No, they weren't society, but it hit print all the same. What notoriety—for such it was—surrounded the engagement was Gabe's. He was a Figure. He Stood for Something. Pictures were taken of him and published in magazines, and the pictures were clipped out and hoarded by unprepossessing girls of all ages. He was Glamour—he was the Unattainable. Men disliked him because he was a byword of masculine desirability among all the girls they knew. Girls went coiffure over leather-lifts about the gentleman, following him, pestering him, forming a living halo of studied spontaneity about him. Some said he was Hayundsome. Some said he was just too, too. Most just said, "Oh, my!" at the first glimpse of his noble profile, and lapsed into ecstatic sighs. Oh, he was a killer.

And Chloe—well, she got cuffed around plenty, behind her back. It was amazing the way her friends dropped away from her when the news got around. The girls wondered in noisy whispers how she had managed to catch him, with all her obvious flaws, none of which had been worth mentioning before. One said, "She must have compromised him. She couldn't possibly have done it any other way." Another agreed delightedly, for such is the feminine way, and said, "I don't know how she has the gall to face us. If I were her I'd blush to the dark roots of my blonde hair." A third chimed in wistfully, "But Gabe's so wonderful. Chloe is really lucky," and was so pitied for her attitude that she was frozen out of the conversation. As for

Chloe's men friends, they took the attitude that they were beaten, hopelessly outclassed, and might just as well take their efforts elsewhere.

Chloe was hardly deserving of such treatment. She was a taffy-blonde, with long green eyes and a build something on the order of a Coca-Cola bottle. She had brain-power and differed from the ordinary run of brainy women in that she used hers. She caught Gabe by the simple tactic of refusing to "Oh!" and "Ah!" his every word and gesture, and he found this so refreshing that he asked her to marry him. Her head whirled violently at that, and, by sheer power of will, she had the whirling generate centripetal force enough to keep her from flinging herself into his arms. She smiled tremulously and squeezed his hand, and that was that.

As for Gabe, he liked it—the whole idea of it. It was generally taken for granted that Gabe was one to be envied. He had everything, hadn't he? He had looks, and he had the kind of job that could keep him clothed to suit those looks, and he had the natural manner for clothes like that—he would have been a distinguished man even if he had a face like the hunchback of Notre Dame. As it was, he had the face of a Greek god after a beauty treatment.

It wasn't just his features, though Lord knows they were super-special enough, what with his olive skin and his arched, pomegranate lips and his inscrutable eyes, and his rich dark hair. It was the way he used them, too. He was credited with a thousand virtues he couldn't possibly have possessed. To look at a woman wasn't a mere matter of focussing his eyes on her. It was to look deep into her crystal orbs—under his glance a woman's eyes immediately became crystal orbs—with a gaze so full of deep intent, of subdued and thrilling passion, of such age-old understanding, of such fright-fraught desires, that the poor girl found herself—insisted on being—a willing slave to him. And it was most embarrassing to him, because he was quite without intentions of any sort except to be agreeable. Gabe, you see, was rather a simple soul.

And his voice—Why, the man was incapable of raising it without its being warmly vibrant, or of lowering it without transmitting unspoken messages. The tones of it were as the bugle to the military

man, the gong to a racehorse, as the piper's flute to the children—
and rats—of Hamelin. At the first sound of it, spinsters left their
crocheting, maidens their movie magazines, and wives their hus-
bands. And he had a hell of a time getting rid of them. If he tried to
be polite about it, they were sure he was being considerate of their
ex-current paramours, and that made him very noble and self-sac-
rificing, and they loved it. If he called a spade a spade, or even a dirty
old shovel, they thought he was being dominant, and loved that too.
If he tried making them jealous by going with another woman, why
then they got jealous, and he had the other woman on his hands.

But with Chloe it was different. She was that rare type of
woman—there are such—who carried a constitutional resentment
of magnificent men. Gabe was a bit more magnificent than most,
but she doggedly stuck by her guns and treated him the way she had
always treated what she called "his kind." She took for granted that
if a man were better-looking than average, he was correspondingly
more vain, more conceited, more narrow-minded, more self-cen-
tered and more stupid than one who had to rely on his personality
to ingratiate himself with her. Any man who treats extra-beautiful
women in this fashion has the right idea; but for a woman to take
this tack is dangerous, as it is not an invariable rule, and she can get
herself disliked by handsome men, categorically. She then has no
alternative but to be less finicky about the men she is unpleasant to,
and ultimately she will find all men desirable and all of them
detestable. Chloe was headed in that general direction when she
received Gabe's surprising proposal.

He made it in all sincerity. He was, as has been remarked, a simple soul, a sheep in wolf's clothing. He found it intoxicatingly refreshing to discover a girl who would slap him around—a girl who would
tell him to stop his nonsense when he inadvertently said something
sweet, and who would accuse him of unbearable ostentation every
time he chose a necktie; who would tell him to stop bragging if he
mentioned that he had had an egg for breakfast, and that he would
look better with a mustache because it would cover part of his face.
He was delighted by insults and charmed by disparagement, for here,
in a lifetime of being a beautiful baby and a lovely child and a hand-

some youth and a glamorous man, was the first time that a woman had ever spoken to him with anything but awed admiration. His reaction was precisely the same as that of a one-eyed dwarf with halitosis who has been gently treated by the most beautiful woman who ever lived; he fell hopelessly in love. She called him "you revolting swell-head," and he loved it. She told someone in his hearing that he was an insufferable, humorless bore, and he went out and bought her a diamond pendant which he could not afford, and which she exchanged immediately for a genuine dyed weasel mink coat, which he despised, and he loved her for her independence. He didn't even mind it when she began to run true to form. She did; after all, she was a woman, in spite of the fact that she was an unusual one. She began crabbing about the way other women acted toward him.

And they really acted. Anyone who has been publicly engaged knows that, for some obscure reason, an engaged man is considered prey, and is the recipient of more ogling glances in any given day of his engagement than he received during any week before. Gabe was badgered. He became familiar with the friendly type of girl—the one who says, "Do tell me all about your fiancée; can she cook? She must be a dear; do you think she'll be able to handle your money? I'm so glad for you. I do *hope* you'll be happy. Of course, marriage is such an important step, but if you think you've chosen the right girl, I guess you'll be all right."

All of which gave Gabe much food for thought. One, or two, or half a dozen "friendly" girls, all envious of the fiancée, all trying desperately to break things up between them by their innuendoes—any man can handle them, if the fiancée in question has him properly hooked. But with Gabe, there were scores of them. Every single female of his acquaintance worked her malicious wiles on him, until he was embroiled in a mass of dreary conjectures about Chloe. His mind was not very fast; things occurred to him with startling suddenness, and he brought himself up sharply after a particularly harrowing session with the realization that he had cold feet. He was actually becoming afraid of Chloe and the fast-approaching connubial state. He locked himself in his room and faced himself sternly. He was frightened by his own fright, and stubbornly began to beat it down, point by point. He was still in love, and so he reasoned as a lover, and therefore came to many satisfactory conclusions about her. If she couldn't cook, then they'd eat in restaurants or hire someone who could. If she turned out to be a bad manager, then he'd do the managing. He glossed over her more evident faults, excused those which might have existed, and forgot those he was tempted to investigate. It was a close thing, but he emerged again into the everyday world a man with an ideal—Chloe. "And," he swore dramatically to himself, "If I'm not good enough for Chloe, then by damn, I'll make myself over the way she wants me." Lousy technique. But then, what man who is truly in love can hang on to his technique?

So he became humble to Chloe, and defiant to the "friendly" girls who swarmed around increasingly as the wedding date approached. That was the cause of all his trouble—his stubborn determination to make himself over.

For Chloe, having achieved her goal, was foolish enough to believe that she could keep him by continuing to act the way she had to get him, not knowing that the girl who continually surprises her man is the one who marries him. She was persistently destructive in her comments and her conversation. Every time she was secretly thrilled by his word or gesture, she kept it a secret, and loudly demanded that he remove the thrilling characteristic. He looked absolutely stunning, for instance, in a dark green gabardine; and as soon as she saw it she refused to go out with him in it, saying that it was too informal-looking for the black cire satin she had on. She didn't like the red pinstriped serge he substituted after a frenzied and expensive taxi ride home and back, but she said nothing about it. She didn't particularly care whether or not she changed him for the better; so long as she changed him she was satisfied. She felt that he was happier with her if she was persistently waspish and bullying. She went, eventually, a little too far.

For after Gabe had completely replaced his wardrobe, changed his diction, acquired new reading habits, learned to play bridge, joined four lodges so she could force him to break off any time she wished it, and innumerable other impositions, there was nothing left for her to work on but the very thing about him that made him desirable—his looks. And she hadn't sense enough not to stop there. She criticized the color of his hair, his eyes, his skin. She accused him of vanity, of posing, and of playing to his feminine galleries. She—well, let's listen in to a conversation.

It was at Romany Joe's place, which Gabe didn't like, and to which Chloe had therefore dragged him. Romany Joe's was a gypsy restaurant whose cuisine was as authentically gypsy as chop suey is Chinese. It was complete with a string orchestra, flowing flowered organdies wrapped around cigarette girls, wandering violinists, and fortune tellers.

Chloe, radiant in something pale-green and fluffy, was in her stride, while Gabe diffidently yessed her. "Stop admiring your reflection in the waitresses' eyes," she said pleasantly, "And see if you can't get another wine. Your taste in wines is foul." She daintily pushed away a crystal goblet of genuine 1923 Oporto.

Gabe stirred uneasily—he had spent half the previous evening boning up on the subject. "All right, darling." Chloe fought down an impulse to fling herself into his arms at the gentle, caressing tones of his voice and said,

"Gabe, for once and all—you've got to learn to keep your endearments to yourself in public places. I won't have you making a spectacle of yourself any longer. Keep that sort of thing for when we're alone."

"But we're never alone," he said sadly.

"Well, we will be after we're married. Don't stare at me that way, just so you can turn your profile to that minx at the other table. She saw it when you came in."

Gabe sighed miserably and turned his head away. Chloe followed his gaze, rather hoping that it would be resting on something luscious enough to arouse her audible jealousy. But Gabe was looking at an old, old gypsy woman who hobbled down the line of booths, stopping at each to mumble a few words. Chloe turned over a couple of scathing remarks and finally settled on, "Gabe! You're disgusting! Stop your ogling—have you no age limit?"

Gabe looked at her apologetically, remembered her warning about the brunette over there with the profile-fixation, looked up at the old woman, and then dropped his eyes to his long brown hands, really not knowing what to do with his eyes. Chloe said, "Stop trying to look penitent. You know I can see through you." And just then the old gypsy stopped at their booth.

"I tal fortune, pretty lady? Gen-tul-mun?"

Gabe thought as rapidly as his permanently fuzzy mind would permit. Chloe would doubtless feel that to give the woman any money would be wanton extravagance, and that to listen to her mumbo-jumbo would be childish. He shook his head and said, "Thanks, no." So Chloe leaned over and whispered viciously in his ear, "What's the matter with you? Do you begrudge a poor old woman a living? Call her back, Gabe! Or is she too old for you to waste any time with her?" Gabe passed up this astonishing reversal and beckoned to the crone. She showed her gums and limped back.

"Will you tell the lady's fortune?" Gabe asked. The old woman stared at Chloe with bright button-eyes.

"Maybe the lady no like," she said.

"What do you mean?" asked Gabe.

"Maybe I tal true fortune, maybe true fortune not good. Maybe"—she raised her arms and let them fall—"the lady no like."

"Don't be silly," said Chloe, and laughed. "You fortune tellers are all alike. I'll take a trip, there's danger ahead but it'll be all right in the end, there will be two men in my life and one of them will win out, beware of—"

"Ax-cuze me, lady," said the old woman gently. "Bot you are not right. All fortune tellers are not alike, no. Many tal you zis stuff, but only I tal you true. I have—" she waved a floppy reticule "—real magics an' spells in zis bag. I can tal you what weel happen if you don't use one of my spells, an' what will happen if you do. I can make your wishes come true. You will see, no?"

"We will see, yes," said Chloe. "Gabe, cross the old palm with silver and let's see what happens."

Gabe reached into his pocket, but the gypsy put out her hand and stopped him. "Not yat, good mister," she said. "Wait first."

That radical departure from custom should have been proof enough to both of them that this gypsy was indeed not like other gypsies!

The old lady busily opened her bag and drew out several things which she laid on the table. There was a hank of coarse black hair, a gold button, a half-dozen odd-sized jars of salve, and four old sheepskin scrolls. She arranged them in the shape of an unequal pentagon, and then began making the motions of taking more objects out of her bag and placing them carefully in the air over those on the table. Gabe and Chloe watched, entranced by the seriousness with which she worked.

The gypsy paused a moment, to see if her invisible structure would stand firm without her steady old hands on it, and then swiftly reached out and ran a lock of Chloe's hair through her fingers. Chloe would be appalled to discover when she reached home and a mirror later that that one lock had returned to its natural shade, a striking but unfashionable red-gold.

"Ah!" she cackled, peering through what must have been an aperture in the unseen pile of intangibles on the table. "*Orel . . . orel . . . adartha cay. . . .*"

"Wh—?" asked Gabe.

"Shh. Is gypsy language. Lady has color-hair to make veree easy gypsy spells. This one good now—watch."

A man strolled close by playing a violin, and the old woman whirled and snatched at the air, tying swift, elaborate knots out of nothing and twining them about and through the Thing on the table. Gabe had the odd feeling that she was stringing out the notes from the violin, tying them into a strong, thin, sweet pattern.

"Now. Is ready. I tal you fortune." The gypsy stared through nothingness at Chloe for so long that the girl shifted uneasily in her chair and said lightly, "Well? What's going to happen to me?"

"You will make wan wish," said the gypsy. "An' the wish will come true. An' then you will be as you were, an' for years you will be sorry for what you have done."

Gabe and Chloe turned puzzled eyes to each other; and whether the old lady vanished into her house of mystic cards between them, or sank into the floor, or simply scuttled off, they never knew. But in the time it took them to look away and then look back, she was— gone.

"Well!" said Chloe.

"I didn't pay her yet," said Gabe, looking vainly around.

"Why should you?" snapped Chloe. "She didn't do anything to earn her money."

"But you just said I shouldn't begrudge—"

"I said nothing of the kind, and you have no right to put that interpretation on it if I did. Is that what life with you is going to be, Gabe—bickering all the time, and having you throw everything I've ever said in my face? You're a stupid arrogant fool, and I really fail to see why I—"

"Chloe!" he cried before she could get the cruel words out. "Oh, Chloe, don't ever say you're sorry! Darling, I'll do anything to be worthy of you. Please don't keep telling me how poor a match I make for you—please. I'll do anything—what do you want me to be? What's the matter with me?" The poor, lovely, love-lorn lug was positively abject. He was leaning close to her, pleading in his eyes and his voice and his pose; and then he made one of those perfectly sincere gestures which are sneered at by you and you as melodramatic and laughable— he buried his face in his hands, and his shoulders shook.

Chloe was touched, but she would stick by her guns until death parted her from them. She looked down her nose at the handsome back of his neck, and sneered. A complementary sobbing caught her ear; she turned and saw the brunette at the other table, who had been eagerly watching the discussion, sobbing quite openly with Gabe. She was a sympathetic soul, and then, of course, she was more than taken with Chloe's spectacular escort.

Chloe was furious. The cloying mass of females that circulated about Gabe's beautiful but disinterested head had bothered her many a time before, but never to this extent. Oh, why did he have to make such a hopeless idiot of himself? She leaned closely to him and snarled in his ear,

"All right, pretty boy, I'll tell you what's the matter with you. You're too wonderful-looking to be alive. You attract too much attention. You have too long a string of stupid females trailing around after you, and I'm sick and tired of it and—" here she waxed very intense and lost all pretense of being a lady "—*and I wish to God you had the most ordinary-looking mug on earth!"*

He raised his head and their eyes met; and then, up between them flared a cloud of blinding purple flame, shot with yellow and blue-white. It hung for a split second over the table—over the parapher-nalia the gypsy had left there; and even in that brief interval, Gabe saw that the flame was five-sided, irregular, exactly in the form of the thing the gypsy had built there. Then their eyes gave out. Chloe said "Eek!" and sat for a moment frozen, and Gabe said "Ulp!" and fol-lowed suit. When sight returned to Chloe, she was quite alone. She sat where she was, her hands on her cheeks, her eyes wide and fright-ened, watching the startled darknesses receding. That she couldn't see Gabe at first was, she thought, a trick of the light. Then the old oak seat showed itself, and then its grain and the soft play of the lamps on it, and Gabe just wasn't there.

It had taken but the tiniest fraction of moments, and only now she realized that the music had stopped, that people were chatter-ing and turning her way, and that two waiters and an unremarkable man were around her, asking questions.

"W'at ees eet, modom?"

"Are you hurt?"

"What happened?"

Chloe stared at them blankly. "I—wh-where's Gabe?"

One of the men put a hand on her shoulder and she shook it off. "Where did he go?" she demanded. She didn't like the business of people disappearing from the booth.

"Gayub?" queried one of the waiters. "Vat ees dis Gayub?"

The anonymous man leaned over to speak to her, his face work-ing. She rose and pushed him away. "The man who was with me," she said. "Find him!"

The waiter looked about and scurried off. Chloe stood, very much alone, amid the gathering crowd. Someone said something about a bomb, and there was a tidal movement toward the door. Chloe ceased to be interesting, the music began, so that in very little time she was standing fretfully by herself beside the booth. She felt a timid hand on her arm and turned to look distantly at the nondescript charac-ter beside her.

He was a man somewhere between five and a half and six and a half feet, medium build, dressed in clothes which suited his height and weight. His eyes were either blue or brown and his complexion was halfway between light and dark. His manner was not quite retiring and almost aggressive, and there was something annoying and something likable about him. And he said,

"I don't like it here. Let's go home."

She flared up at him. "How *dare* you! Leave me alone!" She picked up her bag and wrap and walked away from him, toward the door. The man followed her; she knew he was close by her, yet when she glanced over her shoulder he had mingled with the crowd, like a praying mantis on a bean-vine.

She was stopped by a large individual who presented the general effect of good axle-grease—refined slime. It was Romany Joe himself.

He said, "Excuse me, madam. You are the lady who had the so unfortunate experience just now over there?"

"Yes. Have you found my fiancé?"

"Ah—he was your fiancé, this so handsome gentleman? No, madam, we have searched everywhere. He must have left."

"That heel!" she gritted. "I knew that face of his was a false front. Running away like that! Well, I'm glad I found out what sort of coward he is. I'm glad, you hear?"

"I hear," said Romany Joe, who couldn't have avoided it if he were three blocks away. "I am so soree. Would madam be so kind as to leave her name and address in case this unhappy incident has further ramifications?"

Chloe said, "By all means. And if you find that living cameo I came in with, give him a message from me. Tell him *never* to bother me again. I'm through! And while you're on the subject, tell him that the next time I say as much as 'Good morning' to another Greek god, it will be over my dead body." She paused, panting, lost a little in the floods of vituperation crowding to her writing lips. The ubiquitous hand of the stranger touched her elbow again, and before he had a chance to open his mouth she whirled on him and gave him a tongue-lashing that sent him scuttling out of the place and stopped the music again. Romany Joe stood wringing his hands helplessly while everyone else in the place stood around Chloe and giggled. But there are times when a lady gets so all-fired mad that she cares not one whit how high her entertainment value gets. Yes, they managed to ship her out of there, crying and hysterical and still spouting out mouthfuls of epithets that can only be described as "cherce." The insult that was added to her injury was the receipt, the following morning, of a polite note from Romany Joe reminding her that the dinner and wine had not been paid for, and enclosing a bill for six dollars and thirty-eight cents. Joe was primarily a businessman, after all.

When the magic flame sprang up between them, Gabe's first reaction after being shocked into immobility was to leap to his feet and fight the menace. He leapt, but found himself standing rather foolishly beside the booth with no apparent menace to fight. He turned to Chloe, a newly-arrived waiter at each shoulder. He put out his hand and said, "Are you hurt?" and Chloe looked right past him. That stunned him a little, and then he reflected that she was probably upset by the flash. He was edged out by the waiters, who were busily engaged in their mercenary solicitude. He shook his head to clear it and pushed forward again. Chloe had just sent the waiters off on some errand.

"I don't like it here," said Gabe, a little plaintively. "Let's go home."

And to his utter surprise, Chloe turned viciously to him, snapped, "How *dare* you! Leave me alone!" He fell back, feeling like a kicked dog, and then was utterly astounded to realize that she was loudly demanding that he be hunted down. He pressed forward as she headed for the door, touched her arm once and was brushed off like a beetle, and listened in to her conversation with Romany Joe. When he tried to speak to her again she turned on him with such a blast of invective that he had to retreat in self-defense. He couldn't understand it—any of it. He had a strange idea that maybe he was invisible, but he could see that people casually made way for him as anyone will for anyone else. He walked right past the cashier and she never noticed him. He had far too much on his mind to think of stopping. He went right on out into the night, agonized, bruised through and through by Chloe's treatment of him. What had he done to deserve that strange, harsh treatment? What did Chloe mean by ignoring him so, addressing him as if he were a total stranger, and a masher at that? What was the idea of demanding that a search be instituted for him when he was standing right beside her all the time? Why wouldn't she give him a chance to explain himself? It wasn't fair and it couldn't be understood, and the only thing that seemed at all clear was that he had lost his beloved Chloe for ever and ever.

He reached into his pocket for a cigarette and then remembered that he had left them on the table at Romany Joe's. He paused a moment, tempted to go back for them. Maybe he'd run into Chloe and she'd let him take her home at least. But then suppose she acted the same way? He couldn't stand any more of it; he hadn't done anything. Through his trampled affections began to show a dim ray of resentment. Heck with her. She could go her way, he'd go his. That's the way she wanted it, apparently. And that's the way it would be.

For tonight anyway. Maybe tomorrow it would be different...

Gabe didn't know quite what to do with himself. He didn't want to go home and go to bed, just to lie awake and brood all night. Neither did he want to walk around the streets this way. He squared his shoulders and marched into an all-night drugstore. He needed cigarettes anyway. What did the guys in the movies do when they had had a soul-shattering blow? Well, they paid attention to the little details of living, and shook it off that way. All right, he would. Until morning anyway. He'd go in there and buy cigarettes just as if nothing had happened.

The sleepy clerk slid his pack across the counter and took the half-dollar Gabe handed him. He punched up fifteen cents on the cash register and gave Gabe a dime. Gabe was almost to the door when he realized that the man had given him change for a quarter, not a half. He turned back to the counter, congratulating himself on his attention to detail in the face of this overwhelming series of events.

"Hey, doc—you short-changed me a little," he said, not at all offensively.

The clerk blinked at him. "Huh?"

"I gave you a half for that pack of cigarettes," Gabe explained, "Not a quarter."

"When?" asked the clerk, eyeing Gabe suspiciously.

"Just now!" said Gabe, surprised. "My God, man, I didn't even walk out of the place!"

"Yeah?" said the clerk. "Better beat it, bud. I had that worked on me before. You watch some guy come in an' buy something, an' then when he's gone you come in and say you been short-changed. Me, I never forget a face. Far as I know, I never seen you before in my life."

"You never—listen, you can't get away with that! Look, pal, I don't want to start any trouble. Here's the cigarettes. Didn't you just sell a pack of this brand, three minutes ago?"

"Yep. That don't mean I sold 'em to you. You might have got them any place around here."

Gabe heaved a sigh, and said patiently, "Do you, by any chance, know how many half-dollars you have in the register now?"

"Yeah, sure. My relief gets here in a few minutes; I just counted up." He pulled a ruled slip from behind the register. There's—lessee—eight halves in the drawer."

"Okay—now look in and count 'em."

"You better hope you're right," said the clerk pugnaciously. He turned to the cash register, poked the "No Sale," and scooped up his halves. "Two—four—five—seven—eight." He swung to Gabe. "Eight, see, wise-guy? Now get the hell—"

"Hold on, fella," said Gabe evenly. "Look in the quarter compartment."

The clerk slung the halves back into their compartment and ran his fingers around the inside of the quarter section. "You're a lot of trouble, bud. I oughta—I'll be damned! You're right—there is a half-dollar in with the quarters!"

"Satisfied?" asked Gabe gently.

"Okay—okay. Here. But get this. I don't know how you found about this two bits, but you did. Lucky guess. If it made any difference to me, I'd never let you walk out of here with it. Hear?"

Gabe pocketed the quarter. "I'll guarantee that I'll never walk in here again," he snapped, and ignoring the clerk's "Suits me!", he left the store. He would have been interested in the clerk's account of the incident as told to his relief, a few minutes later. It wound up, "—you wanna watch for that bird, Charley."

"What's he look like?" asked Charley, slipping into a white coat.

"Oh, he's a guy about five foot—uh ... his hair is—Damn it, Charley, I don't remember *what* he looked like!"

Gabe stood on the corner outside for a moment, fuming at the sleepy stupidity of the clerk, and then hailed a taxi. He sat back in the seat and reminded himself of Chloe by firmly thinking of other things. And when the cab stopped at his address, and the driver flipped up the flag on the meter and opened the door, Gabe was startled to hear the man say, "Hey! What happened to that other guy?"

"What other guy?"

"The one who got in on Pleasant View and Thirteenth."

"That was me!"

"Yeah? Well I—I dunno. I coulda swore it was some other guy. Well—thanks mister. 'Night."

"'Night." Gabe stood for a moment on the curb, watching the cab whirl away altogether too fast. "Guy's seeing things," he grinned, and went up the steps.

Gabe lived in a very comfortable and very modern little light-housekeeping bachelor digs. He had a large room and kitchenette up on the seventh floor. Sometimes he used to wonder if Chloe would be able to keep house as efficiently as the maid that cleaned up so precisely every day. He thought of that now, and ached a little inside. Oh well—

The elevator operator said "Floor?" and closed the doors, looking at him inquiringly. Gabe stared back. "Always kidding, hey, Joe?"

"Suh?"

"You've been ferrying me up to the seventh floor for two years now, every single night. 'Smatter, boy; don't you recognize me?" Gabe asked flippantly. The boy shook his head slowly, his large ivory eyes fixed on Gabe's face, giving the impression that they were fastened to something invisible in front of him.

"I'm Jarret—Gabe Jarret!" said that irritated gentleman.

"Mist' Jarret? Wal, I swan, I do! I never rec'nize you!"

"I don't know what's the matter with everybody tonight," said Gabe worriedly as he got off at the seventh. The doors closed behind him; a thought struck him and he pushed the elevator button. The doors slid open and Joe peered owlishly out.

"Er—Joe, don't call me in the morning, hey? I'm going to take the day off."

"Yassuh. Whut's that room number again, suh?"

"*What?*"

"Ain't you that new feller moved in yestiddy?"

"Joe! For the second time in half a minute, I'm Gabe Jarret! Room 7C! What the devil's the matter with you?"

Joe scratched his head and looked sheepish. "'Deed, Mist' Jarret, I dunno. Guess I better have my eyes examined or somp'n. Okay, I don't ring your room in th' mornin'. 'N-night, suh." He retreated into his cage, and Gabe strode fuming down the corridor. "Must be an epidemic," he muttered under his breath as he let himself into his room. "Everyone in the city turned moron overnight." He snapped on the lights, walked over and stood in front of the full-length mirror on his closet door. "Couldn't be me," he said positively. He fingered his necktie and scowled. "Or—could it?"

He was changed, certainly. His decisive, handsome features were indescribably, subtly changed. His nose, though still essentially the same shape, was not distinctly Roman. As a matter of fact, it was not distinctly anything. It was just a nose. His eyes—weren't they as deeply set? Or had they moved closer together? Or—farther apart? Or was there a difference at all? And the line of his jaw—let's see; it used to go straight back to there and then turn up a little, didn't it? Or did it? Gabe shook his head. "I'm having a nervous breakdown," he said, and undressed and washed and went to bed.

Not to sleep, though, for a long while. He talked quietly to himself about it.

"I used to have a face, damn it. I used to stop traffic. My God— not one woman gave me the eye all evening, ever since that—that explosion at Joe's. That was a funny thing. Wonder what—Chloe sure raised hell. Shouldn't have left her alone there, but—I dunno. It's up to me to give her what she wants, and she sure didn't want

me around. Lord, what a tongue that girl has! Imagine living with—
what was that flash, anyway? Lessee—the old woman had just told
Chloe's fortune. Gave her a wish. Well, she didn't wish anything.
Funny if there was something in all this mumbo jumbo. Suppose she
had a chance to wish for something that would come true.... I wonder what Chloe wants, anyhow? She's a funny kid. Everything I did
or said was wrong, and I found that such a change—so damn original, that I fell for her. Suppose she had a chance to make a wish
come true; would she wish for money? We have enough, between
us; don't know what she'd do with any more. Would she wish for
more looks? Hell, she's all right. Love? She's got me; Lord knows I
showed her how much I loved her." Gabe heaved himself up on his
elbow, staring off into the dark. "How much difference did that make
to her? Every other woman I ever met seemed to want her innings,
but then Chloe is different from any other woman I ever met. Maybe
she didn't care after all." Overwhelmed by the alien thought, Gabe
gave himself up to his misery for a long moment. Then, "Holy Pete,
this is a mess. I took an awful lot from her and as far as she knew I
liked it. I—didn't." It was the first time he had admitted that to himself. "Imagine her calling me down like that in public. What was that
crack she made—something about me setting an age limit, when I
accidentally looked at that old woman? You know, that was raw.
And telling me I was conceited, and that I had lousy taste in clothes,
and—Yeah, that was strong—'I wish to God you had the most ordinary-looking mug on earth!' Yeah—me too. I have, judging from
the way she acted toward me after that explosion. Yeah, Chloe and
the cashier and the clerk in the drugstore and Joe the elevator boy.
Heh! They look at my face once, and when they see it again, they
don't recognize it. 'I wish to God you had the—' Heh! That was a
wish! Hell of a thing to come true. Why, a man with that kind of a
face would really be behind the eight-ball. Anyone who saw him
would never remember him the next time. Just like Joe, in the elevator. I guess he was just sleepy; didn't take notice. Like the guy in
the store—*My God!*" Gabe rolled out of bed and sat on the edge of
it. "That *was* a wish! And it was the first wish she made after the
old woman told her that her wish would come true!"

He stood up, sat down, stood up and began to pace the room. "That's a fairy story. It just couldn't *be!* Wishes coming true.... *Me,* without a *face?*" He ran to the wall switch and flipped it, turned up the table and bed lamps, and stood in a blaze of light before the mirror.

"It's—it's amazing," he said aloud. His face was blurred—just the slightest bit indistinct, like a molded jelly that has been standing in a warm room. It was a perfectly normal, unfrightening face. It was the face of the Great Average—the consolidated features of a mob. It was the face of the man who shines your shoes on a ferry-boat, as remembered two months later. It was the face of a fellow called Charley something, who was in your Latin class in your first year in high school. Gabriel Jarret, glamor-boy, was now—the Anonymous!

"What am I going to *do?*" he breathed, turning away and back to the mirror, away and back. It was a terrible thing, a horrifying, morbidly fascinating thing. What could he do? He was a salesman; his living depended on his ability to put up a memorable front. Why, they wouldn't even know him at the office. He'd have to introduce himself in the morning and every day when he came in from his calls! What about his regular customers, and—omigosh—his prospects? Suppose he entertained a buyer, and left him for a moment during the evening; the man wouldn't know him when he got back! He was through—washed up—ruined. How could he even get a job now, let alone keep the one he had?

He turned out half the lights and threw himself into an easy chair to think it over. What would life be like for an anonymous man? No more heads turning when he came into a restaurant or night-club or office. No more women on his doorstep, on his mind, in his hair. Say, that wouldn't be bad, at that. He had spent twenty-eight years in being admired, and he was as sick of it as is a man with a purple birthmark with his particular flaw. It was a flaw, you see, as anything must be when carried to an extreme. Good diction is an asset; perfect diction is annoying and affected. Pleasing features are help-ful to their possessor; perfect ones are a damn nuisance, to quote the late Valentino, who early learned that the art of un-wenching is a far more difficult one than that of amorous conquest. And Gabe had been the extreme, the outside edge of hyper-superlativity.

He grinned excitedly. He could actually walk into a whole roomful of high school girls and walk out again without having one of them gasp and flutter! Why, he could have a life of his own, unmarked, unremarkable!

And so it was that Gabe smacked his palm with his fist, laughed aloud, turned out the lights and dove into bed, a happy man. Of all men in the world, only he could have been delighted with such an affliction; of all lovers in the world, only he was foolish enough to believe that his precious Chloe would be happy to find him as he was now. Hadn't she persistently accused him of being too handsome? Hadn't she fervently wished that he had the most ordinary-looking mug on earth? Ah, now she was his; now he was all she could have wanted him to be.

That's what he thought.

He woke early the next morning, and like a kid running for his Christmas tree, he ran for the mirror. It was true—it was true!

"Hot damn," he grinned. "No glamour!"

He dressed carefully and sat down to write a few notes. One to his bank, informing them that hereafter he would deal with them by mail. One to his landlord, giving him notice. A few to various debtors, enclosing checks. One to his employers, a resignation. And one to Chloe, and that was the strangest:

"Darling:

"Forgive me for the way I acted last night; something has happened to me that I can't understand, but which has made me very happy. That explosion in our booth last night changed me into what you have said you wanted me to be. I want you to see it too. Please, beloved, meet me as usual at lunch. Same place, same time. And be prepared for a surprise!"

He marked it for a special messenger, took the sheaf of envelopes out and mailed them, and then headed for a restaurant. He ordered a substantial breakfast, thinking amusedly that if he ordered and then moved to another table, the waiter would never find him. He ate leisurely, picked up his check and reached in his pocket for a dime to leave on the table.

He'd forgotten to bring any money.

He said, "Damn!" and wondered whether to try explaining it to the cashier, or to—he ate here often; she'd know him. It would be no trouble.

Approaching the cashier's desk, he remembered that she wouldn't remember him at that. He paused again, rubbed the side of his cheek in perplexity, and then squared his shoulders, tossed the check on the desk, said, "Good Morning!" and sauntered out the door.

"Hey, mister!" called the cashier, a pert young blonde. "Hey— you didn't pay! Jim—catch that guy!"

A brawny gentleman dropped his mop and trotted after Gabe. Gabe, by this time, was twenty feet away from the door and still moving. The waiter's heavy hand fell on his shoulder; he stopped, turned, looked surprisedly up at the duty-bound face.

"You can't get away with that, bud," said the mopster.

"With what?" asked Gabe innocently.

"Come back in here and ask the cashier with what," said the man, pushing Gabe in that direction.

Gabe went, protesting. Once inside the restaurant, the man said, "I've got 'im, Molly."

The girl threw up her hands. "Jimmy, you're a double-barreled half-wit! You've got the wrong guy!"

The man loosed Gabe and shuffled uneasily. "You sure, Molly?"

"Sure I'm sure, you—you ox!" she snapped, and said to Gabe, "Gee, I'm sorry, mister. I wouldn't have had that happen for—"

"Skip it," grinned Gabe. "As for you, Muscles, watch your step. You can get into trouble doing things like that." The lug retreated; Gabe smiled at the girl and walked out like an honest citizen. And after that he didn't bother going home for his money. He didn't need money.

He walked along Beaufort St., feeling proud of himself. He thought of the great criminal masterminds of song and story, and of how the basic idea, that a man must be remarkable to be a phenomenon, had been plugged. Why, you don't need brains to break the laws of statute and custom; all you need is protective coloration. He was absolutely invulnerable, and the idea was intoxicating. He could do anything—absolutely anything, and get away with it. That redhead over there, for instance; a luscious creation. Motivated not entirely by scientific curiosity, he overtook her, spun her around, put his arms about her and kissed her lingeringly. He held her long enough for a sizable crowd to gather, which took about forty-five seconds, and then released her, breathless and choleric. She said, "You—you—" and then hauled off and swung at him. He laughed at her and ducked back into the crowd. She lost sight of him for a moment—which was, of course, forever. She peered angrily about, looking for her "attacker," and her eyes finally rested on Gabe.

Now there were a lot of people laughing in that crowd, but none more heartily than Gabe Jarret. He was having the time of his life. The redhead took note of this, and spat out at him,

"What are you laughing at? What's supposed to be so funny? If you had the guts God gave a goose, you'd have stopped that—that beast from doing that to me instead of standing there laughing!"

"Lady," gasped Gabe, "I could no more have stopped him than I could have stopped myself!" And, still joyful, he threaded his way through the crowd and on down the street, leaving the girl to give furious and vain descriptions of her assailant to a tardy policeman.

"This," said Gabe, "certainly has possibilities."

He strolled on up the street, casually stepping on people's feet and watching them glare past him for the guilty party; boldly pulling handkerchiefs out of dignified old gentlemen's breast pockets; having himself a hell of a time. He stole a revolver out of a policeman's holster, ran around a bystander and handed it back to the cop, saying, "Lucky for you I snatched this out of that crook's hand, officer." The cop positively blushed. It was altogether too fast for him. And he saw a face he didn't like and knocked some teeth out of it for that reason, then disappeared completely by moving ten feet. He stopped at a bar and moved along the mahogany a few inches after each of four drinks, and they were all on the house. Ultimately, then, he wound up at the fountain and restaurant where he had been used to lunching with Chloe.

And she was there. He was thrilled at the sight of her, and went over and sat at her table. She looked up at him, deadpan, and went back to her food. He hugged himself.

"Chlo—"

She started and looked around her. He said it again. She looked straight at him, sniffed coldly and did something with one shoulder which said, "Don't annoy me."

"Chloe—don't you recognize me?"

"I do not! Leave me alone!"

"Chloe—it's Gabe!"

She narrowed her eyes and stared. "Don't look at my face," he said. "Look at my hands. See that ring? Remember it—the signet I always wore?"

"Yes," she said, puzzled. "It's Gabe's, but—" and her eyes went back to his face.

"This scar on my wrist," he said. "This necktie—you chose it. Remember the red pin-stripe suit?"

She pushed her chair back, appalled. "Gabe! What's—happened to you?"

"Something you won't believe—but it happened anyway. Remember last night in Romany Joe's? Well—you can think what you like about it, but when that old gypsy said you could make a wish and have it come true, she was right. You made a wish, and—here I am!"

"I made a—what are you talking about?"

"You did. You were sore at me, I guess, and you wished I had the most ordinary face on earth. Well—this is it! It's so ordinary that nobody I've met so far can remember it for two consecutive seconds!"

"Gabe—that's—that's childish. Wishes, indeed! Come on, now—tell me what's changed you so!"

"I tell you, that's it! Darling, isn't that what was bothering you so? Didn't you tell me that the main thing wrong with me was my looks?" He leaned eagerly across the table to her. "Well, that's been taken care of! I'll guarantee, there'll never be another woman cooing over me again!"

She looked at him. "I can well believe that," she said nastily.

"Chloe—I've changed my clothes and my mind and my habits

for you, and it wasn't enough. Now I've changed my face—isn't that all you can ask?"

Chloe rose, her head whirling. What colossal joke was this? What was she doing even talking to this nondescript character? How could she listen to this drivel he was pouring out, about an engagement and love and—and marriage? Had she come as low as this, that she must marry such an unassuming creature? Certainly she could catch a man who looked like *somebody,* not like just—*anybody.*

She twisted the diamond from her finger. "Gabe—I can't for the life of me think why I took this at all, or why I didn't give it back to you weeks ago. Do I have to say anything more?" And she tossed it on the table in front of the now speechless Gabe, and ran from him. As she left the restaurant she turned and looked back. There was a man sitting at the table—a man whom, as far as she knew, she had never seen before. He was looking at something clutched in his hands and he was apparently crying into them. Chloe wondered vaguely where Gabe had gone so quickly, and then went back to her office, where she sat in front of a typewriter all afternoon doing nothing and silently shrieking out at the injustice of the monstrous fate that had taken her beautiful, beautiful Gabe away.

It was a little more than Gabe could stand, that jilting. He sat there for a long time, watching the diamond wink and glitter crazily through his tears; and then he got up and walked unnoticed out of the restaurant. He walked without purpose, through the teeming streets, back and back through the city until he brought up in the marketing district, where fat women in shawls and squalling brats dodged great refrigerator trucks. He stood there for an hour or so, seeing nothing, smoking constantly and without enjoyment, staring blindly into his empty heart. Resentment grew redly as he stood there, and when he took his last cigarette and hurled it into the gutter, straightened his shoulders and said, "Damn her!", he was a changed and bitter man. He looked up and down the cluttered street, got his bearings and strode rapidly off. "I'm this way, by God, and she don't like it. Well, I do, and I'm going to make it pay off."

The late afternoon and evening papers were filled with an amazing series of robberies. It was a one-man crime wave, but the papers didn't know that.

A pawn-shop was the first. An unidentified man had walked into the store, stepped behind the counter, scooped up a handful of large bills and a revolver, and had casually walked out again. He was chased, but had vanished into the crowd.

A man with a gun had held up a gas station a block away from the pawn shop. He had cleared out the till and disappeared under the very nose of the policeman on the beat.

Two patrol cars had responded to a call that a bank was being robbed. Technically, it was only the patrons who were held up, and forced at gunpoint to deliver up their larger bills. When the police arrived, they bumped into a "bystander" on his way out of the bank. He cried, "There's a robbery going on in there!" and as the police rushed in with drawn revolvers, he leaped into one of the patrol cars and roared off up the avenue, his siren going full blast. The police could find no one who could describe either the bank-robber or the man who had stolen the bandit-chaser, or who could determine whether or not they were the same man. The car was found abandoned two miles up the street; several people had seen a man in plain clothes get out quietly and walk away, but no one knew what he looked like. While the two patrolmen were dusting their repossessed car for fingerprints, the jewelry store across the sidewalk from them was robbed—cash only. They both saw him leave and duck into a side street. They were greatly helped by a man who said he saw the robber go into a certain house. Search of the house revealed—nothing; and no sign was found of their informant.

Oh, Gabe had a wonderful afternoon.

Chloe left the office early, pleading sickness. All during the long afternoon she had worried and fretted about Gabe. Perhaps she had been hasty, she thought. Maybe it was his idea of a joke—a lesson for her, perchance. Could he have achieved that amazing, subtle change in his face by makeup? She doubted it. It was too good.

She thought of his new face, frightened by the idea. Much careful thinking had yielded the fact that the man she saw sitting at her table as she left must have been Gabe, since only he would have been sitting there, staring at the ring. Yet at the time she could have sworn it was a total stranger! And now, she couldn't think of how he differed from the Gabe she had sat at lunch with, nor how that Gabe differed from the one who took her to Romany Joe's the night before. Chloe was one of those unimaginative girls whose philosophy is strictly on a Q.E.D. basis. That is, if a certain action produced a certain reaction, she was so guided from then on, and did not care how or why it had happened. The operation of the little convertible coupe she drove on weekends was as much a mystery to her as was the gypsy woman's irregular pentagon. She could believe the automobile's operation without understanding it—why not the spell? She could start her car, and she could stop it. She had inadvertently started a spell. She would go to Romany Joe's tonight.

She arrived fairly early, looking worried but very lovely; and by luck she managed to get exactly the same booth she had had the night before. She was grimly determined to undo last night's weird work, no matter what the cost. As soon as she was settled with a cup of wine, she called the waiter back.

"Meess?"

"I'm looking for a fortune teller," said Chloe.

"Immediately, meess," said the waiter, bowing and backing away.

"Wait a minute! I want one particular fortune teller—no other."

"Vat ees her name?"

"I don't know. She's a very old woman, and she carries a bag with her."

"Vairy old? I am sorry, meess, but ve have no such a one here."

"But she—" Chloe paused, and then wearily waved the man away. What was the use? She might have known it would be like this. The whole thing made no sense at all. She was sick through and through. She would—

"You were looking for me, modom?"

Chloe started violently. There, beside the booth, was her old fortune-teller.

"I—that is—the waiter said—"

"He is a fool. If you want me, I will come. I come the first time, and the second time, and then I come no more. Now what is it?"

Chloe almost cried with relief. Now to make an end to this crazy business. She spilled out the whole story, while the old woman stood quietly, missing not a word, watching each passing expression of Chloe's petulant face with her brilliant little eyes. When Chloe had finished, she said,

"You have made one wish, and it is true; it can not be un-made. What do you want me to do?"

"What *can* you do? Oh please—I'll give you anything if you'll make my Gabe as he was. I've got to have him back—I've got to!"

"You want his nize face, no? Nothing more of him?"

"Oh yes—yes! But I can't stand him now; what woman wants a husband that can't be found in a crowd? I'd have to—" she giggled hysterically—"Make him sign a register before I would dare let him in the house at night! Oh please—"

"Yes, I can give you one more wish, if you like. But you must be careful. You must remember that you wished before and now you are unhappy. If you wish again you may not be happy too, more."

"I don't care! If I had Gabe back, loving me the way he did, I'd *have* to be happy. You will help me? You will?"

In answer, the gypsy brought out her charms and began to lay them out. Chloe watched breathlessly. There was a slight commotion at the door which she didn't begin to notice. She watched the strange invisible pentagon take shape over the table, her eyes caught and held by the marvellous dexterity of the old fingers.

In just a few hours Gabe, in his half-crazed, desperate attempt to make his affliction amuse him, had become much sought after—more so, he reflected wryly, than he had ever been before he became so superbly homely. Probably because he was richer now, he grinned as he walked out of a downtown factory with the payroll in his inside pocket and half the police in the city running around him, bumping into him, shoving him out the way in their earnest effort to find him.

He was a little tired of helping himself to other people's valuables, particularly since he didn't need money. However, he'd buy himself a famous automobile or two and take it easy for a while without getting in anyone's hair.

He strolled around downtown with a good, unpaid-for dinner under his belt and thousands of dollars crammed into his pockets. He didn't know quite what to do with himself until he saw a brilliant neon display halfway down what had been a side street before said display had been installed. ROMANY JOE'S.

"Now," said Gabe with great glee, "By all that's unholy, Joe's place is the one place in the world that deserves to be robbed by me! I'll get even with the gypsies for doing this to me—may they prosper!"

He hitched up his trousers, got his hand on the revolver in his right coat pocket, and sauntered in.

"Table for one, sir?" asked Romany Joe, rubbing his hands.

"C'mere," ordered Gabe coldly, and without even looking at Joe, walked over to the cashier. Joe followed.

"What can I do for you, sir?"

"Your belly," said Gabe in his best movie-gangster style, "Reminds me of a great, big balloon. Now I'm a funny feller. I like to pop balloons. I like to pump bullets into them. I'm going to bust that one of yours unless you get back of that counter and shell out all the twenties and everything else bigger than a twenty. I ain't greedy—you can keep the rest. Now—*move!*" and he prodded Joe with the concealed gun. Joe moved. The cashier squeaked and then subsided, and it was her squeak that caused the rustle that Chloe couldn't hear, so engrossed was she in the gypsy's work.

The gypsy steadied the structure carefully, and then carefully withdrew her hand. "Now!" she said hoarsely. "Make your wish!"

Chloe's mind raced. She would restore Gabe's looks, if there was anything in this mumbo jumbo. And he would be all hers—all hers. She'd see to that! "I wish," she said, "that Gabe will be handsome again—*and that he will never be able to make love to another woman besides me!*"

The weird flame leaped up, blinding her. She was shocked into silence—her whole mind was silenced, not even able to exult. And through that silence knifed the gypsy's voice—frightened now; *"You wish too much! Ah, it is not good....*"

Romany Joe, trembling, pushed the pile of bills across the counter. Gabe smiled, reached for it, and then stiffened. In the mirror behind Romany Joe, he saw the reflection of a man—

A tall, handsome man. His features, his teeth, his hair, breathtakingly beautiful. It was—

Himself! Gabe Jarret!

Gabe backed away, gun in hand, stripped of his cloak of anonymity. His eyes darted to right and left, seeking a way out, trying subconsciously to merge himself into the crowd, utterly failing.

Romany Joe ducked down, came up with a blue automatic. Gabe's revolver coughed twice, twice again—Gabe stared at it, his hand clamped tight on the trigger, wondering hysterically why it had gone off. Romany Joe folded slowly down over the counter, slid behind it, his clawed fingernails shrieking on the marble. Gabe ran towards the door, found his way blocked by three waiters. He fired wildly, missed, and the gun was knocked out of his hand as he was tackled from two sides at once. He went down, and just before his head struck the floor and knocked him unconscious, he saw Chloe's drawn face, and heard her shriek, "Gabe! Oh God, Gabe!"

He had a fractured skull. It was very bad, and it took him a long time—more than a year—to get well enough to stand trial for the murder of Josef Blebenau, known as Romany Joe. And during all that time, and during the trial, and after, in the days in the death house when appeal after appeal was being fought, Chloe visited him constantly. He loved her, and she loved him, and, being where he was, he had no chance at all to make love to any other woman. No chance at all, for the rest of his life. He died on the chair.

Chloe got her wish, you see. He was handsome, and saw only her for the rest of his days. It was not what she wanted, but it was her wish. But then, of course, wants and wishes are not the same thing.

Two Sidecars

HENLEY REACHED OUT to push it back under those hills, out of his eyes; but it was eight and a half million miles away and busy making the dawn a pretty one. His quarrel wasn't with the sun anyway, he reflected, staring at it through meshed eyelashes. His quarrel was with a man whose name he didn't know yet, but he'd find out. Oh yes he would, and then there was going to be a party. Henley was going to have fun at the party, and the other guy was not. The other guy was going to get pushed around. . . . Henley gazed for a long moment at the great, straight band canted across the sky before he identified it as the top of his windshield. He lay staring complacently at it until he shivered, and then he realized that he was soaking wet. He could tell without trying that if he moved at all his head would begin to detonate blindingly. He weighed this knowledge against a growing curiosity as to his whereabouts, and it was some time before the curiosity was intense enough to justify the pain of sitting up. He moved himself gently, both hands to his face, pulling himself upright by his cheeks. The two-day stubble offended him.

He gritted his teeth and fumbled in the side pocket of the car for the large rag that was cached there. Shaking it out, he flung it over the windshield to shade his eyes. *There are two of me now,* he thought. *One has a honey of a hangover and wants to lie down and die, and the other is worried about Caroline and wants to move.* The part of him that wanted to lie still and pass out watched the other part passively, watched it gaze about the flats back of the city, at the back road, at the way the car was tilted off it into the ditch. The car was a convertible and the top was down and it must have rained hard while he slumped back of the wheel. He searched fumblingly for reasons for his being here, being drunk. The only thing he could find to base it all on was Caroline's leaving him, and while that was reason enough, it was no excuse. He couldn't bring her back by getting drunk. He couldn't find her or the man she was leaving with. He couldn't do anything until he could think clearly, and he wouldn't be able to think clearly until he had another sidecar.

Two sidecars.

He looked down at his hands. One was cut across the knuckles. They thought for him, the hands, darting out to twitch the rag away, finding the brake, the gearshift lever, as his thinking feet began their slow dance over the starter, accelerator, clutch. The engine raced and coughed and raced again cleanly, and the big car backed out of the ditch. The low rasp of a new tire against a crumpled fender rose to a moan and died and rasped again as he backed and stopped and shifted, and then he swept away toward the city, the tortured fender screaming. Henley didn't care about that now. He rode inside the car, deep inside himself, watching his reflexive driving, looking at an insane mental flash of himself choosing melodramatically between Caroline and a sidecar, taking the sidecar. He felt sick and drove very fast.

There was a man sweeping the sidewalk in front of DeMaio's when Henley pulled up. "Lousy," said Henley when the man asked how he was. "You a bartender?"

"I think so," said the man, watching Henley get out of the car. He thought it was a shame to use expensive clothes like that. "But the boss don't yet, so I'm a porter. Why?"

"Can you mix a sidecar?"

"We ain't open yet." Henley walked into the place and said, "If the doors are open the joint is open. Mix me a sidecar. Two side-cars." The man began to speak, then left his jaw dropped as he saw the bill Henley tossed on the counter. He went behind the bar.

Henley hung by his triceps for two and a half hours then, drinking sidecars. The only thing in his mind was "Why didn't Caroline tell me who he was? Maybe I wouldn't care then. Maybe I wouldn't be sore." It was in his mind so long because he said it over and over again. He was saying it half aloud when someone stopped beside him for a beer. Henley screwed his gaze over to the man. He knew him. Ruskin. "Hi."

Ruskin jumped. "Good God. Henley." His voice was deep and smooth. He was young and tall and clean. His beer came and he didn't look at it. He was seeing Henley, the way he looked, his wrinkled clothes, his two-day beard. Henley laughed in two syllables that hurt his throat. He struck Ruskin's beer; it slid two feet down the bar and turned over. "The ge'mun's with me," he told the barkeep who wiped it up. "Two sidecars."

"You're in a sweet shape, Henley."

"Got a right to be. What's South America like, Ruskin?" Ruskin would know. He had a station at Bahia. Was going back in a day or so.

Ruskin raised his eyebrows. "Big. What part?"

"Dunno," said Henley flatly. He drank, and then words spilled out. "Wife's going there. She sent me a note. Polite as hell." His voice turned falsetto. "I'm sorry but it just won't work. Don't hold it against anyone—me, the man I'm going away with, or even yourself. You can't help being what you are. This shouldn't bother you much; your girlfriends won't let you be lonely. I'm going to South America. Maybe I'll write someday."

"That the note?" asked Ruskin, and smiled. "You always did cut a lot of corners with her, Henley. Talked a lot about it. You know, I often used to wonder if you talked like that to Car—your wife. Seems you did. Women don't like that, Henley. Didn't you know?"

Henley started on Ruskin's drink. He wasn't listening. He was trying to think. When the sound of Ruskin's voice stopped, he said, "Yes, I'll kill the dirty—" The disgust on Ruskin's face reached him vaguely. "Don't like me, do you?" he spat. "Okay, okay. Beat it then. Go on away. Don't like me, don't have to stick around. Plenty other—"

Ruskin's face was pale. "I never realized what a heel you are," he half-whispered. "How in God's name could a woman like Caroline ever—" His taut arms relaxed and his hands fell against his thighs. He walked out. Henley glared after him. When he was gone he called, "Hey! Have another—" Then he shrugged and finished the drink.

He put his weight on his elbows and hung his head and rocked a bit. "Damn boy scout," he muttered. He was irritated because

Ruskin reminded him of Caroline. They were both tall, clean-looking like that. When he thought of them together, it was no trouble at all for him to realize who was taking his wife away to South America. He said *"Gha!"* with an intake of breath, choked on his saliva. He stood on the brass rail, pounded the counter furiously. "That's the guy, that Ruskin! He's the one, the—" He began to cough. The bartender reached over, held him by the armpits, steadied him down to the floor.

"Who's who?" asked the bartender soothingly.

"That guy was drinking with me. Him and my wife—you see? You get that?"

"Well?" The bartender's cheeks were tight, smiling inside. He kept holding Henley up.

Henley felt something die, down deep. It hurt. He should kill Ruskin. He should kill them both. He had the guts. He looked at the bartender for a long time and then saw him. He drew a deep breath.

"Two sidecars," he said.

Microcosmic God

HERE IS A STORY about a man who had too much power, and a man who took too much, but don't worry; I'm not going political on you. The man who had the power was named James Kidder, and the other was his banker.

Kidder was quite a guy. He was a scientist and he lived on a small island off the New England coast all by himself. He wasn't the dwarfed little gnome of a mad scientist you read about. His hobby wasn't personal profit, and he wasn't a megalomaniac with a Russian name and no scruples. He wasn't insidious, and he wasn't even particularly subversive. He kept his hair cut and his nails clean and lived and thought like a reasonable human being. He was slightly on the baby-faced side; he was inclined to be a hermit; he was short and plump and—brilliant. His specialty was biochemistry, and he was always called *Mr.* Kidder. Not "Dr." Not "Professor." Just Mr. Kidder.

He was an odd sort of apple and always had been. He had never graduated from any college or university because he found them too slow for him, and too rigid in their approach to education. He could not get used to the idea that perhaps his professors knew what they were talking about. That went for his texts, too. He was always asking questions, and didn't mind very much when they were embarrassing. He considered Gregor Mendel a bungling liar, Darwin an amusing philosopher, and Luther Burbank a sensationalist. He never opened his mouth without its leaving his victim feeling breathless. If he was talking to someone who had knowledge, he went in there and got it, leaving his victim breathless. If he was talking to someone whose knowledge was already in his possession, he only asked repeatedly, "How do you know?" His most delectable pleasure was taken in cutting a fanatical eugenicist into conversational ribbons.

So people left him alone and never, never asked him to tea. He was polite, but not politic.

He had a little money of his own, and with it he leased the island and built himself a laboratory. Now I've mentioned that he was a biochemist. But being what he was, he couldn't keep his nose in his own field. It wasn't too remarkable when he made an intellectual excursion wide enough to perfect a method of crystallizing Vitamin B1 profitably by the ton—if anyone wanted it by the ton. He got a lot of money for it. He bought his island outright and put eight hundred men to work on an acre and a half of his ground, adding to his laboratory and building equipment. He got messing around with sisal fiber, found out how to fuse it, and boomed the banana industry by producing a practically unbreakable cord from the stuff.

You remember the popularizing demonstration he put on at Niagara, don't you? That business of running a line of the new cord from bank to bank over the rapids and suspending a ten-ton truck from the middle of it by razor edges resting on the cord? That's why ships now moor themselves with what looks like heaving line, no thicker than a lead pencil, that can be coiled on reels like a garden hose. Kidder made cigarette money out of that, too. He went out and bought himself a cyclotron with part of it.

After that money wasn't money any more. It was large numbers in little books. Kidder used little amounts of it to have food and equipment sent out to him, but after a while that stopped, too. His bank dispatched a messenger by seaplane to find out if Kidder was still alive. The man returned two days later in a mused state, having been amazed something awesome at the things he'd seen out there. Kidder was alive, all right, and he was turning out a surplus of good food in an astonishingly simplified synthetic form. The bank wrote immediately and wanted to know if Mr. Kidder, in his own interest, was willing to release the secret of his dirtless farming. Kidder replied that he would be glad to, and enclosed the formulas. In a P.S. he said that he hadn't sent the information ashore because he hadn't realized anyone would be interested. That from a man who was responsible for the greatest sociological change in the second half of the twentieth century—factory farming. It made him richer; I mean it made his bank richer. He didn't give a rap.

But Kidder didn't really get started until about eight months after the messenger's visit. For a biochemist who couldn't even be called "Dr." he did pretty well. Here is a partial list of the things that he turned out:

A commercially feasible plan for making an aluminum alloy stronger than the best steel so that it could be used as a structural metal.

An exhibition gadget he called a light pump, which worked on the theory that light is a form of matter and therefore subject to physical and electromagnetic laws. Seal a room with a single light source, beam a cylindrical vibratory magnetic field to it from the pump, and the light will be led down it. Now pass the light through Kidder's "lens"—a ring which perpetuates an electric field along the lines of a high-speed iris-type camera shutter. Below this is the heart of the light pump—a ninety-eight percent efficient light absorber, crystalline, which, in a sense, *loses* the light in its internal facets. The effect of darkening the room with this apparatus is slight but measurable. Pardon my layman's language, but that's the general idea.

Synthetic chlorophyll—by the barrel.

An airplane propeller efficient at eight times sonic speed.

A cheap goo you brush on over old paint, let harden, and then peel off like strips of cloth. The old paint comes with it. That one made friends fast.

A self-sustaining atomic disintegration of uranium's isotope 238, which is two hundred times as plentiful as the old stand-by, U-235.

That will do for the present. If I may repeat myself: for a biochemist who couldn't even be called "Dr.," he did pretty well.

Kidder was apparently unconscious of the fact that he held power enough on his little island to become master of the world. His mind simply didn't run to things like that. As long as he was left alone with his experiments, he was well content to leave the rest of the world to its own clumsy and primitive devices. He couldn't be reached except by a radiophone of his own design, and its only counterpart was locked in a vault of his Boston bank. Only one man could operate it. The extraordinarily sensitive transmitter would respond only to

Conant's own body vibrations. Kidder had instructed Conant that he was not to be disturbed except by messages of the greatest moment. His ideas and patents, what Conant could pry out of him, were released under pseudonyms known only to Conant—Kidder didn't care.

The result, of course, was an infiltration of the most astonishing advancements since the dawn of civilization. The nation profited— the world profited. But most of all, the bank profited. It began to get a little oversize. It began getting its fingers into other pies. It grew more fingers and had to bake more figurative pies. Before many years had passed, it was so big that, using Kidder's many weapons, it almost matched Kidder in power.

Almost.

Now stand by while I squelch those fellows in the lower left-hand corner who've been saying all this while that Kidder's slightly improbable; that no man could ever perfect himself in so many ways in so many sciences.

Well, you're right. Kidder was a genius—granted. But his genius was not creative. He was, to the core, a student. He applied what he knew, what he saw, and what he was taught. When first he began working in his new laboratory on his island he reasoned something like this:

"Everything I know is what I have been taught by the sayings and writings of people who have studied the sayings and writings of people who have—and so on. Once in a while someone stumbles on something new and he or someone cleverer uses the idea and disseminates it. But for each one that finds something really new, a couple of million gather and pass on information that is already current. I'd know more if I could get the jump on evolutionary trends. It takes too long to wait for the accidents that increase man's knowledge— my knowledge. If I had ambition enough now to figure out how to travel ahead in time, I could skim the surface of the future and just dip down when I saw something interesting. But time isn't that way. It can't be left behind or tossed ahead. What else is left?

"Well, there's the proposition of speeding intellectual evolution so that I can observe what it cooks up. That seems a bit inefficient. It would involve more labor to discipline human minds to that extent than it would to simply apply myself along those lines. But I can't apply myself that way. No one man can.

"I'm licked. I can't speed myself up, and I can't speed other men's minds up. Isn't there an alternative? There must be—somewhere, somehow, there's got to be an answer."

So it was on this, and not on eugenics, or light pumps, or botany, or atomic physics, that James Kidder applied himself. For a practical man, he found the problem slightly on the metaphysical side; but he attacked it with typical thoroughness, using his own peculiar brand of logic. Day after day he wandered over the island, throwing shells impotently at sea gulls and swearing richly. Then came a time when he sat indoors and brooded. And only then did he get feverishly to work.

He worked in his own field, biochemistry, and concentrated mainly on two things—genetics and animal metabolism. He learned, and filed away in his insatiable mind, many things having nothing to do with the problem in hand, and very little of what he wanted. But he piled that little on what little he knew or guessed, and in time had quite a collection of known factors to work with. His approach was characteristically unorthodox. He did things on the order of multiplying apples by pears, and balancing equations by adding $\log \sqrt{-1}$ to one side and ∞ to the other. He made mistakes, but only one of a kind, and later, only one of a species. He spent so many hours at his microscope that he had to quit work for two days to get rid of a hallucination that his heart was pumping his own blood through the mike. He did nothing by trial and error because he disapproved of the method as sloppy.

And he got results. He was lucky to begin with, and even luckier when he formularized the law of probability and reduced it to such low terms that he knew almost to the item what experiments not to try. When the cloudy, viscous semifluid on the watch glass began to move of itself he knew he was on the right track. When it began to seek food on its own he began to be excited. When it divided and, in a few hours, redivided, and each part grew and divided again, he was triumphant, for he had created life.

He nursed his brainchildren and sweated and strained over them,

131

and he designed baths of various vibrations for them, and inoculated and dosed and sprayed them. Each move he made taught him the next. And out of his tanks and tubes and incubators came amoeba-like creatures, and then ciliated animalcules, and more and more rapidly he produced animals with eye spots, nerve cysts, and then—victory of victories—a real blastopod, possessed of many cells instead of one. More slowly he developed a gastropod, but once he had it, it was not too difficult for him to give it organs, each with a specified function, each inheritable.

Then came cultured mollusklike things, and creatures with more and more perfected gills. The day that a nondescript thing wriggled up an inclined board out of a tank, threw flaps over its gills and feebly breathed air, Kidder quit work and went to the other end of the island and got disgustingly drunk. Hangover and all, he was soon back in the lab, forgetting to eat, forgetting to sleep, tearing into his problem.

He turned into a scientific byway and ran down his other great triumph—accelerated metabolism. He extracted and refined the stimulating factors in alcohol, coca, heroin, and Mother Nature's prize dope runner, *cannabis indica*. Like the scientist who, in analyzing the various clotting agents for blood treatments, found that oxalic acid and oxalic acid alone was the active factor, Kidder isolated the accelerators and decelerators, the stimulants and soporifics, in every substance that ever undermined a man's morality and/or caused a "noble experiment." In the process he found one thing he needed badly—a colorless elixir that made sleep the unnecessary and avoidable waster of time it should be. Then and there he went on a twenty-four-hour shift.

He artificially synthesized the substances he had isolated, and in doing so sloughed away a great many useless components. He pursued the subject along the lines of radiations and vibrations. He discovered something in the longer reds which, when projected through a vessel full of air vibrating in the supersonics, and then polarized, speeded up the heartbeat of small animals twenty to one. They ate twenty times as much, grew twenty times as fast, and—died twenty times sooner than they should have.

Kidder built a huge hermetically sealed room. Above it was another room, the same length and breadth but not quite as high. This was his control chamber. The large room was divided into four sealed sections, each with its individual heat and atmosphere controls. Over each section were miniature cranes and derricks—handling machinery of all kinds. There were also trapdoors fitted with aid locks leading from the upper to the lower room.

By this time the other laboratory had produced a warm-blooded, snake-skinned quadruped with an astonishingly rapid life cycle—a generation every eight days, a life span of about fifteen. Like the echidna, it was oviparous and mammalian. Its period of gestation was six hours; the eggs hatched in three; the young reached sexual maturity in another four days. Each female laid four eggs and lived just long enough to care for the young after they hatched. The males generally died two or three hours after mating. The creatures were highly adaptable. They were small—not more than three inches long, two inches to the shoulder from the ground. Their forepaws had three digits and a triple-jointed, opposed thumb. They were attuned to life in an atmosphere with a large ammonia content. Kidder bred four of the creatures and put one group in each section of the sealed room.

Then he was ready. With his controlled atmospheres he varied temperatures, oxygen content, humidity. He killed them off like flies with excesses of, for instance, carbon dioxide, and the survivors bred their physical resistance into the next generation. Periodically he would switch the eggs from one sealed section to another to keep the strains varied. And rapidly, under these controlled conditions, the creatures began to evolve.

This, then, was the answer to his problem. He couldn't speed up mankind's intellectual advancement enough to have it teach him the things his incredible mind yearned for. He couldn't speed himself up. So he created a new race—a race which would develop and evolve so fast that it would surpass the civilization of man; and from them he would learn.

They were completely in Kidder's power. Earth's normal atmosphere would poison them, as he took care to demonstrate to every fourth generation. They would make no attempt to escape from him.

They would live their lives and progress and make their little trial-and-error experiments hundreds of times faster than man did. They had the edge on man, for they had Kidder to guide them. It took man six thousand years really to discover science, three hundred to put it to work. It took Kidder's creatures two hundred days to equal man's mental attainments. And from then on—Kidder's spasmodic output made the late, great Tom Edison look like a home handicrafter.

He called them Neoterics, and he teased them into working for him. Kidder was inventive in an ideological way; that is, he could dream up impossible propositions providing he didn't have to work them out. For example, he wanted the Neoterics to figure out for themselves how to build shelters out of porous material. He created the need for such shelters by subjecting one of the sections to a high-pressure rainstorm which flattened the inhabitants. The Neoterics promptly devised waterproof shelters out of the thin waterproof material he piled in one corner. Kidder immediately blew down the flimsy structure with a blast of cold air. They built them up again so that they resisted both wind and rain. Kidder lowered the temperature so abruptly that they could not adjust their bodies to it. They heated their shelters with tiny braziers. Kidder promptly turned up the heat until they began to roast to death. After a few deaths, one of their bright boys figured out how to build a strong insulant house by using three-ply rubberoid, with the middle layer perforated thousands of times to create tiny air pockets.

Using such tactics, Kidder forced them to develop a highly advanced little culture. He caused a drought in one section and a liquid surplus in another, and then opened the partition between them. Quite a spectacular war was fought, and Kidder's notebooks filled with information about military tactics and weapons. Then there was the vaccine they developed against the common cold— the reason why that affliction has been absolutely stamped out in the world today, for it was one of the things that Conant, the bank president, got hold of. He spoke to Kidder over the radiophone one winter afternoon with a voice so hoarse from laryngitis that Kidder sent him a vial of vaccine and told him briskly not to ever call him again in such a disgustingly inaudible state. Conant had it analyzed and again Kidder's accounts and the bank's swelled.

At first Kidder merely supplied them with the materials he thought the Neoterics might need, but when they developed an intelligence equal to the task of fabricating their own from the elements at hand, he gave each section a stock of raw materials. The process for really strong aluminum was developed when he built in a huge plunger in one of the sections, which reached from wall to wall and was designed to descend at the rate of four inches a day until it crushed whatever was at the bottom. The Neoterics, in self-defense, used what strong material they had in hand to stop the inexorable death that threatened them. But Kidder had seen to it that they had nothing but aluminum oxide and a scattering of other elements, plus plenty of electric power. At first they ran up dozens of aluminum pillars; when these were crushed and twisted they tried shaping them so that the soft metal would take more weight. When that failed they quickly built stronger ones; and when the plunger was halted, Kidder removed one of the pillars and analyzed it. It was hardened aluminum, stronger and tougher than molybd steel.

Experience taught Kidder that he had to make certain changes to increase his power over his Neoterics before they got too ingenious. There were things that could be done with atomic power that he was curious about; but he was not willing to trust his little superscientists with a thing like that unless they could be trusted to use it strictly according to Hoyle. So he instituted a rule of fear. The most trivial departure from what he chose to consider the right way of doing things resulted in instant death of half a tribe. If he was trying to develop a Diesel-type power plant, for instance, that would operate without a flywheel, and a bright young Neoteric used any of the materials for architectural purposes, half the tribe immediately died. Of course, they had developed a written language; it was Kidder's own. The teletype in a glass-enclosed area in a corner of each section was a shrine. Any directions that were given on it were obeyed, or else ... After this innovation, Kidder's work was much simpler. There was no need for any more indirection. Anything he wanted done was done. No matter how impossible his commands, three or four generations of Neoterics could find a way to carry them out.

This quotation is from a paper that one of Kidder's high-speed telescopic cameras discovered being circulated among the younger Neoterics. It is translated from the highly simplified script of the Neoterics.

"These edicts shall be followed by each Neoteric upon pain of death, which punishment will be inflicted by the tribe upon the individual to protect the tribe against him.

"Priority of interest and tribal and individual effort is to be given the commands that appear on the word machine.

"Any misdirection of material or power, or use thereof for any other purpose than the carrying out of the machine's commands, unless no command appears, shall be punishable by death.

"Any information regarding the problem at hand, or ideas or experiments which might conceivably bear upon it, are to become the property of the tribe.

"Any individual failing to cooperate in the tribal effort, or who can be termed guilty of not expending his full efforts in the work, or the suspicion thereof, shall be subject to the death penalty."

Such are the results of complete domination. This paper impressed Kidder as much as it did because it was completely spontaneous. It was the Neoterics' own creed, developed by them for their own greatest good.

And so at last Kidder had his fulfillment. Crouched in the upper room, going from telescope to telescope, running off slowed-down films from his high-speed cameras, he found himself possessed of a tractable, dynamic source of information. Housed in the great square building with its four half-acre sections was a new world, to which he was God.

Conant's mind was similar to Kidder's in that its approach to any problem was along the shortest distance between any two points, regardless of whether that approach was along the line of most or least resistance. His rise to the bank presidency was a history of ruthless moves whose only justification was that they got him what he wanted. Like an overefficient general, he would never vanquish an enemy through sheer force of numbers alone. He would also skillfully flank his enemy, not on one side, but on both. Innocent bystanders were creatures deserving no consideration.

The time he took over a certain thousand-acre property, for instance, from a man named Grady, he was not satisfied with only the title to the land. Grady was an airport owner—had been all his life, and his father before him. Conant exerted every kind of pressure on the man and found him unshakable. Finally judicious persuasion led the city officials to dig a sewer right across the middle of the field, quite efficiently wrecking Grady's business. Knowing that this would supply Grady, who was a wealthy man, with motive for revenge, Conant took over Grady's bank at half again its value and caused it to fold up. Grady lost every cent he had and ended his life in an asylum. Conant was very proud of his tactics.

Like many another who has had Mammon by the tail, Conant did not know when to let go. His vast organization yielded him more money and power than any other concern in history, and yet he was not satisfied. Conant and money were like Kidder and knowledge. Conant's pyramided enterprises were to him what the Neoterics were to Kidder. Each had made his private world; each used it for his instruction and profit. Kidder, though, disturbed nobody but his Neoterics. Even so, Conant was not wholly villainous. He was a shrewd man, and had discovered early the value of pleasing people. No man can rob successfully over a period of years without pleasing the people he robs. The technique for doing this is highly involved, but master it and you can start your own mint.

Conant's one great fear was that Kidder would someday take an interest in world events and begin to become opinionated. Good heavens—the potential power he had! A little matter like swinging an election could be managed by a man like Kidder as easily as turning over in bed. The only thing he could do was to call him periodically and see if there was anything that Kidder needed to keep himself busy. Kidder appreciated this. Conant, once in a while, would suggest something to Kidder that intrigued him, something that would keep him deep in his hermitage for a few weeks. The light pump was one of the results of Conant's imagination. Conant bet him it couldn't be done. Kidder did it.

One afternoon Kidder answered the squeal of the radiophone's signal. Swearing mildly, he shut off the film he was watching and crossed the compound to the old laboratory. He went to the radiophone, threw a switch. The squealing stopped.

"Well?"

"Hello," said Conant. "Busy?"

"Not very," said Kidder. He was delighted with the pictures his camera had caught, showing the skillful work of a gang of Neoterics synthesizing rubber out of pure sulphur. He would rather have liked to tell Conant about it, but somehow he had never got around to telling Conant about the Neoterics, and he didn't see why he should start now.

Conant said, "Er ... Kidder, I was down at the club the other day and a bunch of us were filling up an evening with loose talk. Something came up which might interest you."

"What?"

"Couple of the utilities boys there. You know the power set-up in this country, don't you? Thirty percent atomic, the rest hydroelectric, Diesel and steam?"

"I hadn't known," said Kidder, who as innocent as a babe of current events.

"Well, we were arguing about what chance a new power source would have. One of the men there said it would be smarter to produce a new power and then talk about it. Another one waived that; said he couldn't name that new power, but he could describe it. Said it would have to have everything that present power sources have, plus one or two more things. It could be cheaper, for instance. It could be more efficient. It might supersede the others by being easier to carry from the power plant to the consumer. See what I mean? Any one of these factors might prove a new source of power competitive to the others. What I'd like to see is a new power with *all* of these factors. What do you think of it?"

"Not impossible."

"Think not?"

"I'll try it."

"Keep me posted." Conant's transmitter clicked off. The switch was a little piece of false front that Kidder had built into the set, which was something that Conant didn't know. The set switched itself off when Conant moved from it. After the switch's sharp crack, Kidder heard the banker mutter, "If he does it, I'm all set. If he doesn't, at least the crazy fool will keep himself busy on the isl—"

Kidder eyed the radiophone for an instant with raised eyebrows, and then shrugged them down again with his shoulders. It was quite evident that Conant had something up his sleeve, but Kidder wasn't worried. Who on earth would want to disturb him? He wasn't bothering anybody. He went back to the Neoterics' building, full of the new power idea.

Eleven days later Kidder called Conant and gave specific instructions on how to equip his receiver with a facsimile set which would enable Kidder to send written matter over the air. As soon as this was done and Kidder informed, the biochemist for once in his life spoke at some length.

"Conant—you inferred that a new power source that would be cheaper, more efficient and more easily transmitted than any now in use did not exist. You might be interested in the little generator I have just set up.

"It has power, Conant—unbelievable power. Broadcast. A beautiful little tight beam. Here—catch this on the facsimile recorder." Kidder slipped a sheet of paper under the clips on his transmitter and it appeared on Conant's set. "Here's the wiring diagram for a power receiver. Now listen. The beam is so tight, so highly directional, that not three thousandths of one percent of the power would be lost in a two-thousand-mile transmission. The power system is closed. That is, any drain on the beam returns a signal along it to the transmitter, which automatically steps up to increase the power output. It has a limit, but it's way up. And something else. This little gadget of mine can send out eight different beams with a total horsepower output of around eight thousand per minute per beam. From each beam you can draw enough power to turn the page of a book or fly a superstratosphere plane. Hold on—I haven't finished yet. Each beam, as I told you before, returns a signal from receiver to transmitter. This not only controls the power output of the beam, but directs it. Once contact is made, the beam will never let go. It will follow the receiver anywhere. You can power land, air or water vehicles with it, as well as any stationary plant. Like it?"

Conant, who was a banker and not a scientist, wiped his shining pate with the back of his hand and said, "I've never known you to steer me wrong yet, Kidder. How about the cost of this thing?"

"High," said Kidder promptly. "As high as an atomic plant. But there are no high-tension lines, no wires, no pipelines, no nothing. The receivers are little more complicated than a radio set. Transmitter is—well, that's quite a job."

"Didn't take you long," said Conant.

"No," said Kidder, "it didn't, did it?" It was the lifework of nearly twelve hundred highly cultured people, but Kidder wasn't going into that. "Of course, the one I have here's just a model."

Conant's voice was strained. "A—model? And it delivers—"

"Over sixty-thousand horsepower," said Kidder gleefully.

"Good heavens! In a full-sized machine—why, one transmitter would be enough to—" The possibilities of the thing choked Conant for a moment. "How is it fueled?"

"It isn't," said Kidder. "I won't begin to explain it. I've tapped a source of power of unimaginable force. It's—well, big. So big that it can't be misused."

"What?" snapped Conant. "What do you mean by that?"

Kidder cocked an eyebrow. Conant *had* something up his sleeve, then. At this second indication of it, Kidder, the least suspicious of men, began to put himself on guard. "I mean just what I say," he said evenly. "Don't try too hard to understand me—I barely savvy it myself. But the source of this power is a monstrous resultant caused by the unbalance of two previously equalized forces. Those equalized forces are cosmic in quantity. Actually, the forces are those which make suns crush atoms the way they crushed those that compose the companion of Sirius. It's not anything you can fool with."

"I don't—" said Conant, and his voice ended puzzledly.

"I'll give you a parallel of it," said Kidder. "Suppose you take two rods, one in each hand. Place their tips together and push. As long as your pressure is directly along their long axes, the pressure is equalized; right and left hands cancel each other. Now I come along; I put out one finger and touch the rods ever so lightly where they come together. They snap out of line violently; you break a couple of knuckles. The resultant force is at right angles to the original force you exerted. My power transmitter is on the same principle. It takes an infinitesimal amount of energy to throw those forces out of line. Easy enough when you know how to do it. The important question is whether or not you can control the resultant when you get it. I can."

"I—see." Conant indulged in a four-second gloat. "Heaven help the utility companies. I don't intend to. Kidder—I want a full-size power transmitter."

Kidder clucked into the radiophone. "Ambitious, aren't you? I haven't a staff out here, Conant—you know that. And I can't be expected to build four or five thousand tons of apparatus myself."

"I'll have five hundred engineers and laborers out there in forty-eight hours."

"You will not. Why bother me with it? I'm quite happy here, Conant, and one of the reasons is that I've no one to get in my hair."

"Oh, now, Kidder—don't be like that—I'll pay you—"

"You haven't got that much money," said Kidder briskly. He flipped the switch on his set. *His* switch worked.

Conant was furious. He shouted into the phone several times, then began to lean on the signal button. On his island, Kidder let the thing squeal and went back to his projection room. He was sorry he had sent the diagram of the receiver to Conant. It would have been interesting to power a plane or a car with the model transmitter he had taken from the Neoterics. But if Conant was going to be that way about it—well, anyway, the receiver would be no good without the transmitter. Any radio engineer would understand the diagram, but not the beam which activated it. And Conant wouldn't get his beam.

Pity he didn't know Conant well enough.

Kidder's days were endless sorties into learning. He never slept, nor did his Neoterics. He ate regularly every five hours, exercised for half an hour in every twelve. He did not keep track of time, for it meant nothing to him. Had he wanted to know the date, or the year, even, he knew he could get it from Conant. He didn't care, that's all. The time that was not spent in observation was used in developing new problems for the Neoterics. His thoughts just now ran to defense. The idea was born in his conversation with Conant; now the idea was primary, its motivation something of no importance. The Neoterics were working on a vibration field of quasi-electrical nature. Kidder could see little practical value in such a thing—an invisible wall which would kill any living thing which touched it. But still— the idea was intriguing.

He stretched and moved away from the telescope in the upper room through which he had been watching his creations at work. He was profoundly happy here in the large control room. Leaving it to go to the old laboratory for a bite to eat was a thing he hated to do. He felt like bidding it good-by each time he walked across the compound, and saying a glad hello when he returned. A little amused at himself, he went out.

There was a black blob—a distant power boat—a few miles off the island, toward the mainland. Kidder stopped and stared dis- tastefully at it. A white petal of spray was affixed to each side of the black body—it was coming toward him. He snorted, thinking of the time a yachtload of silly fools had landed out of curiosity one afternoon, spewed themselves over his beloved island, peppered him with lame-brained questions, and thrown his nervous equilibrium out for days. Lord, how he hated *people!*

The thought of unpleasantness bred two more thoughts that played half-consciously with his mind as he crossed the compound and entered the old laboratory. One was that perhaps it might be wise to surround his buildings with a field of force of some kind and post warnings for trespassers. The other thought was of Conant and the vague uneasiness the man had been sending to him through the radiophone these last weeks. His suggestion, two days ago, that a power plant be built on the island—horrible idea!

Conant rose from a laboratory bench as Kidder walked in.

They looked at each other wordlessly for a long moment. Kidder hadn't seen the bank president in years. The man's presence, he found, made his scalp crawl.

"Hello," said Conant genially. "You're looking fit."

Kidder grunted. Conant eased his unwieldy body back onto the bench and said, "Just to save you the energy of asking questions, Mr. Kidder, I arrived two hours ago on a small boat. Rotten way to travel. I wanted to be a surprise to you; my two men rowed me the last couple of miles. You're not very well equipped here for defense, are you? Why, anyone could slip up on you the way I did."

"Who'd want to?" growled Kidder. The man's voice edged annoyingly into his brain. He spoke too loudly for such a small room; at least, Kidder's hermit's ears felt that way. Kidder shrugged and went about preparing a light meal for himself.

"Well," drawled the banker. "I might want to." He drew out a Dow-metal cigar case. "Mind if I smoke?"

"I do," said Kidder sharply.

Conant laughed easily and put the cigars away. "I might," he said, "want to urge you to let me build that power station on this island."

"Radiophone work?"

"Oh, yes. But now that I'm here you can't switch me off. Now—how about it?"

"I haven't changed my mind."

"Oh, but you should, Kidder, you should. Think of it—think of the good it would do for the masses of people that are now paying exorbitant power bills!"

"I hate the masses! Why do you have to build here?"

"Oh, that. It's an ideal location. You own the island; work could begin here without causing any comment whatsoever. The plant would spring full-fledged on the power markets of the country, having been built in secret. The island can be made impregnable."

"I don't want to be bothered."

"We wouldn't bother you. We'd build on the north end of the island—a mile and a quarter from you and your work. Ah—by the way—where's the model of the power transmitter?"

Kidder, with his mouth full of synthesized food, waved a hand at a small table on which stood the model, a four-foot, amazingly intricate device of plastic and steel and tiny coils.

Conant rose and went over to look at it. "Actually works, eh?" He sighed deeply and said, "Kidder, I really hate to do this, but I want to build that plant rather badly. Carson! Robbins!"

Two bull-necked individuals stepped out from their hiding places in the corners of the room. One idly dangled a revolver by its trigger guard. Kidder looked blankly from one to the other of them.

"These gentlemen will follow my orders implicitly, Kidder. In half an hour a party will land here—engineers, contractors. They will start surveying the north end of the island for the construction for the power plant. These boys here feel about the same way I do as far as you are concerned. Do we proceed with your cooperation or without it? It's immaterial to me whether or not you are left alive to continue your work. My engineers can duplicate your model."

Kidder said nothing. He had stopped chewing when he saw the gunmen, and only now remembered to swallow. He sat crouched over his plate without moving or speaking.

Conant broke the silence by walking to the door. "Robbins— can you carry that model there?" The big man put his gun away, lifted the model gently, and nodded. "Take it down to the beach and meet the other boat. Tell Mr. Johansen, the engineer, that this is the model he is to work from." Robbins went out. Conant turned to Kidder. "There's no need for us to anger ourselves," he said oilily. "I think you are stubborn, but I don't hold it against you. I know how you feel. You'll be left alone; you have my promise. But I mean to go ahead on this job, and a small thing like your life can't stand in my way."

Kidder said, "Get out of here." There were two swollen veins throbbing at his temples. His voice was low, and it shook.

"Very well. Good day, Mr. Kidder. Oh—by the way—you're a clever devil." No one had ever referred to the scholastic Mr. Kidder that way before. "I realize the possibility of your blasting us off the island. I wouldn't do it if I were you. I'm willing to give you what you want—privacy. I want the same thing in return. If anything happens to me while I'm here, the island will be bombed by someone who is working for me. I'll admit they might fail. If they do, the

United States government will take a hand. You wouldn't want that, would you? That's rather a big thing for one man to fight. The same thing goes if the plant is sabotaged in any way after I go back to the mainland. You might be killed. You will most certainly be bothered interminably. Thanks for your ... er ... cooperation." The banker smirked and walked out, followed by his taciturn gorilla.

Kidder sat there for a long time without moving. Then he shook his head, rested it in his palms. He was badly frightened; not so much because his life was in danger, but because his privacy and his work—his world—were threatened. He was hurt and bewildered. He wasn't a businessman. He couldn't handle men. All his life he had run away from humans and what they represented to him. He was like a frightened child when men closed in on him.

Cooling a little, he wondered vaguely what would happen when the power plant opened. Certainly the government would be interested. Unless—unless by then Conant was the government. That plant was an unimaginable source of power, and not only the kind of power that turned wheels. He rose and went back to the world that was home to him, a world where his motives were understood, and where there were those who could help him. Back at the Neoterics' building, he escaped yet again from the world of men into his work.

Kidder called Conant the following week, much to the banker's surprise. His two days on the island had gotten the work well under way, and he had left with the arrival of a shipload of laborers and material. He kept in close touch by radio with Johansen, the engineer in charge. It had been a blind job for Johansen and all the rest of the crew on the island. Only the bank's infinite resources could have hired such a man, or the picked gang with him.

Johansen's first reaction when he saw the model had been ecstatic. He wanted to tell his friends about this marvel; but the only radio set available was beamed to Conant's private office in the bank, and Conant's armed guards, one to every two workers, had strict orders to destroy any other radio transmitter on sight. About that time he realized that he was a prisoner on the island. His instant anger subsided when he reflected that being a prisoner at fifty thousand dollars a week wasn't too bad. Two of the laborers and an engineer thought differently, and got disgruntled a couple of days after they arrived. They disappeared one night—the same night that five shots were fired down on the beach. No questions were asked, and there was no more trouble.

Conant covered his surprise at Kidder's call and was as offensively jovial as ever. "Well, now! Anything I can do for you?"

"Yes," said Kidder. His voice was low, completely without expression. "I want you to issue a warning to your men not to pass the white line I have drawn five hundred yards north of my buildings, right across the island."

"Warning? Why, my dear fellow, they have orders that you are not to be disturbed on any account."

"You've ordered them. All right. Now warn them. I have an electric field surrounding my laboratories that will kill anything living which penetrates it. I don't want to have murder on my conscience. There will be no deaths unless there are trespassers. You'll inform your workers?"

"Oh, now, Kidder," the banker expostulated. "That was totally unnecessary. You won't be bothered. Why—" But he found he was talking into a dead mike. He knew better than to call back. He called Johansen instead and told him about it. Johansen didn't like the sound of it, but he repeated the message and signed off. Conant liked that man. He was, for a moment, a little sorry that Johansen would never reach the mainland alive.

But that Kidder—he was beginning to be a problem. As long as his weapons were strictly defensive he was no real menace. But he would have to be taken care of when the plant was operating. Conant couldn't afford to have genius around him unless it was unquestionably on his side. The power transmitter and Conant's highly ambitious plans would be safe as long as Kidder was left to himself. Kidder knew that he could, for the time being, expect more sympathetic treatment from Conant than he could from a horde of government investigators.

Kidder only left his own enclosure once after the work began on the north end of the island, and it took all of his unskilled diplomacy to do it. Knowing the source of the plant's power, knowing what could happen if it were misused, he asked Conant's permission to inspect the great transmitter when it was nearly finished. Insuring his own life by refusing to report back to Conant until he was safe within his own laboratory again, he turned off his shield and walked up to the north end.

He saw an awe-inspiring sight. The four-foot model was duplicated nearly a hundred times as large. Inside a massive three-hundred-foot tower a space was packed nearly solid with the same bewildering maze of coils and bars that the Neoterics had built so delicately into their machine. At the top was a globe of polished metal alloy, the transmitting antenna. From it would stream thousands of tight beams of force, which could be tapped to any degree by corresponding thousands of receivers placed anywhere at any distance. Kidder learned that the receivers had already been built, but his informant, Johansen, knew little about that end of it and was saying less. Kidder checked over every detail of the structure, and when he was through he shook Johansen's hand admiringly.

"I didn't want this thing here," he said shyly, "and I don't. But I will say that it's a pleasure to see this kind of work."

"It's a pleasure to meet the man that invented it."

Kidder beamed. "I didn't invent it," he said. "Maybe someday I'll show you who did. I—well, good-by." He turned before he had a chance to say too much and marched off down the path.

"Shall I?" said a voice at Johansen's side. One of Conant's guards had his gun out.

Johansen knocked the man's arm down. "No." He scratched his head. "So that's the mysterious menace from the other end of the island. Eh! Why, he's a hell of a nice little feller!"

Built on the ruins of Denver, which was destroyed in the great Battle of the Rockies during the Western War, stands the most beautiful city in the world—our nation's capital, New Washington. In a circular room deep in the heart of the White House, the President, three army men and a civilian sat. Under the President's desk a dictaphone unostentatiously recorded every word that was said. Two thousand and more miles away, Conant hung over a radio receiver, tuned to receive the signals of the tiny transmitter in the civilian's side pocket.

One of the officers spoke.

"Mr. President, the 'impossible claims' made for this gentleman's product are absolutely true. He has proved beyond doubt each item on his prospectus."

The President glanced at the civilian, back at the officer. "I won't wait for your report," he said. "Tell me—what happened?"

Another of the army men mopped his face with a khaki bandanna. "I can't ask you to believe us, Mr. President, but it's true all the same. Mr. Wright here has in his suitcase three or four dozen small ... er ... bombs—"

"They're not bombs," said Wright casually.

"All right. They're not bombs. Mr. Wright smashed two of them on an anvil with a sledgehammer. There was no result. He put two more in an electric furnace. They burned away like so much tin and cardboard. We dropped one down the barrel of a field piece and fired it. Still nothing." He paused and looked at the third officer, who picked up the account.

"We really got started then. We flew to the proving grounds, dropped one of the objects and flew to thirty thousand feet. From there, with a small hand detonator no bigger than your fist, Mr. Wright set the thing off. I've never seen anything like it. Forty acres of land came straight up at us, breaking up as it came. The concussion was terrific—you must have felt it here, four hundred miles away."

The President nodded. "I did. Seismographs on the other side of the Earth picked it up."

"The crater it left was a quarter of a mile deep at the center. Why, one planeload of those things could demolish any city. There isn't even any necessity for accuracy!"

"You haven't heard anything yet," another officer broke in. "Mr. Wright's automobile is powered by a small plant similar to the others. He demonstrated it to us. We could find no fuel tank of any kind, or any other driving mechanism. But with a power plant no bigger than six cubic inches, that car, carrying enough weight to give it traction, outpulled an army tank!"

"And the other test!" said the third excitedly. "He put one of the objects into a replica of a treasury vault. The walls were twelve feet thick, super-reinforced concrete. He controlled it from a hundred yards away. He . . . he burst that vault! It wasn't an explosion—it was as if some incredibly powerful expansive force inside filled it and flattened the walls from inside. They cracked and split and pow-dered, and the steel girders and rods came twisting and shearing out like . . . like—*whew!* After that he insisted on seeing you. We knew it wasn't usual, but he said he has more to say and would say it only in your presence."

The President said gravely, "What is it, Mr. Wright?"

Wright rose, picked up his suitcase, opened it and took out a small cube, about eight inches on a side, made from some light-absorbent red material. Four men edged nervously away from it.

"These gentlemen," he began, "have seen only part of the things this device can do. I'm going to demonstrate to you the delicacy of control that is possible with it." He made an adjustment with a tiny knob on the side of the cube, set it on the edge of the President's desk.

"You have asked me more than once if this is my invention or if I am representing someone. The latter is true. It might also interest you to know that the man who controls this cube is right now sev-eral thousand miles from here. He, and he alone, can prevent it from detonating now that I"—he pulled his detonator out of the suitcase and pressed a button—"have done this. It will explode the way the one we dropped from the plane did, completely destroying this city and everything in it, in just four hours. It will also explode"—he stepped back and threw a tiny switch on his detonator—"if any mov-ing object comes within three feet of it or if anyone leaves this room but me—it can be compensated for that. If, after I leave, I am molested, it will detonate as soon as a hand is laid on me. No bul-lets can kill me fast enough to prevent me from setting it off."

The three army men were silent. One of them swiped nervously at the beads of cold sweat on his forehead. The others did not move. The President said evenly:

"What's your proposition?"

"A very reasonable one. My employer does not work in the open, for obvious reasons. All he wants is your agreement to carry out his orders; to appoint the cabinet members he chooses; to throw your influence in any way he dictates. The public—Congress—anyone else—need never know anything about it. I might add that if you agree to this proposal, this 'bomb,' as you call it, will not go off. But you can be sure that thousands of them are planted all over the country. You will never know when you are near one. If you disobey, it means instant annihilation for you and everyone else within three or four square miles.

"In three hours and fifty minutes—that will be at precisely seven o'clock—there is a commercial radio program on Station RPRS. You will cause the announcer, after his station identification, to say 'Agreed.' It will pass unnoticed by all but my employer. There is no use in having me followed; my work is done. I shall never see nor contact my employer again. That is all. Good afternoon, gentlemen!"

Wright closed his suitcase with a businesslike snap, bowed, and left the room. Four men sat staring at the little red cube.

"Do you think he can do all he says?" asked the President.

The three nodded mutely. The President reached for his phone.

There was an eavesdropper to all of the foregoing. Conant, squatting behind his great desk in the vault, where he had his sanctum sanctorum, knew nothing of it. But beside him was the compact bulk of Kidder's radiophone. His presence switched it on, and Kidder, on his island, blessed the day he had thought of that device. He had been meaning to call Conant all morning, but was very hesitant. His meeting with the young engineer Johansen had impressed him strongly. The man was such a thorough scientist, possessed of such complete delight in the work he did, that for the first time in his life Kidder found himself actually wanting to see someone again. But he feared for Johansen's life if he brought him to the laboratory, for Johansen's work was done on the island, and Conant would most certainly have the engineer killed if heard of his visit, fearing that Kidder would influence him to sabotage the great transmitter. And if Kidder went to the power plant he would probably be shot on sight.

All one day Kidder wrangled with himself, and finally determined to call Conant. Fortunately he gave no signal, but turned up the volume on the receiver when the little red light told him that Conant's transmitter was functioning. Curious, he heard everything that occurred in the President's chamber three thousand miles away. Horrified, he realized what Conant's engineers had done. Built into tiny containers were tens of thousands of power receivers. They had no power of their own, but, by remote control, could draw on any or all of the billions of horsepower the huge plant on the island was broadcasting.

Kidder stood in front of his receiver, speechless. There was nothing he could do. If he devised some means of destroying the power plant, the government would certainly step in and take over the island, and then—what would happen to him and his precious Neoterics?

Another sound grated out of the receiver—a commercial radio program. A few bars of music, a man's voice advertising stratoline fares on the installment plan, a short silence, then:

"Station RPRS, voice of the nation's Capital, District of South Colorado."

The three-second pause was interminable.

"The time is exactly ... er ... *agreed*. The time is exactly seven PM Mountain Standard Time."

Then came a half-insane chuckle. Kidder had difficulty believing it was Conant. A phone clicked. The banker's voice:

"Bill? All set. Get out there with your squadron and bomb up the island. Keep away from the plant, but cut the rest of it to ribbons. Do it quick and get out of there."

Almost hysterical with fear, Kidder rushed about the room and then shot out the door and across the compound. There were five hundred innocent workmen in barracks a quarter mile from the plant. Conant didn't need them now, and he didn't need Kidder. The only safety for anyone was in the plant itself, and Kidder wouldn't leave his Neoterics to be bombed. He flung himself up the stairs and to the nearest teletype. He banged out, "Get me a defense. I want an impenetrable shield. Urgent!"

The words ripped out from under his fingers in the functional script of the Neoterics. Kidder didn't think of what he wrote, didn't really visualize the thing he ordered. But he had done what he could. He'd have to leave them now, get to the barracks, warn those men. He ran up the path toward the plant, flung himself over the white line and marked death to those who crossed it.

A squadron of nine clip-winged, mosquito-nosed planes rose out of a cove on the mainland. There was no sound from the engines, for there were no engines. Each plane was powered with a tiny receiver and drew its unmarked, light-absorbent wings through the air with power from the island. In a matter of minutes they raised the island. The squadron leader spoke briskly into a microphone.

"Take the barracks first. Clean 'em up. Then work south."

Johansen was alone on a small hill near the center of the island. He carried a camera, and though he knew pretty well that his chances of ever getting ashore again were practically nonexistent, he liked angle shots of his tower, and took innumerable pictures. The first he knew of the planes was when he heard their whining dive over the barracks. He stood transfixed, saw a shower of bombs hurtle down and turn the barracks into a smashed ruin of broken wood, metal and bodies. The picture of Kidder's earnest face flashed into his mind. Poor little guy—if they ever bombed his end of the island he would— But his tower! Were they going to bomb the plant?

He watched, utterly appalled, as the planes flew out to sea, cut back and dove again. They seemed to be working south. At the third dive he was sure of it. Not knowing what he could do, he neverthe- less turned and ran toward Kidder's place. He rounded a turn in the trail and collided violently with the little biochemist. Kidder's face was scarlet with exertion, and he was the most terrified-looking object Johansen had ever seen.

Kidder waved a hand northward. "Conant!" he screamed over the uproar. "It's Conant! He's going to kill us all!"

"The plant?" said Johansen, turning pale.

"It's safe. He won't touch *that*! But . . . my place . . . what about all those men?"

"Too late!" shouted Johansen.

"Maybe I can— Come on!" called Kidder, and was off down the trail, heading south.

Johansen pounded after him. Kidder's little short legs became a blur as the squadron swooped overhead, laying its eggs in the spot where they had met.

As they burst out of the woods, Johansen put on a spurt, caught up with the scientist and knocked him sprawling not six feet from the white line.

"Wh . . . wh—"

"Don't go any farther, you fool! Your own damned force field— it'll kill you!"

"Force field? But—I came through it on the way up—Here. Wait. If I can—" Kidder began hunting furiously about in the grass. In a few seconds he ran up to the line, clutching a large grasshopper in his hand. He tossed it over. It lay still.

"See?" said Johansen. "It—"

"Look! It jumped! Come on! I don't know what went wrong, unless the Neoterics shut it off. They generated that field—I didn't."

"Neo—huh?"

"Never mind," snapped the biochemist, and ran.

They pounded gasping up the steps and into the Neoterics' control room. Kidder clapped his eyes to a telescope and shrieked in glee. "They've done it! We've done it!"

"Who's—"

"My little people! The Neoterics! They've made the impenetrable shield! Don't you see—it cut through the lines of force that start up that field out there! Their generator is still throwing it up, but the vibrations can't get out! They're safe! They're safe!" And the overwrought hermit began to cry. Johansen looked at him pityingly and shook his head.

"Sure—your little men are all right. But we aren't," he added, as the floor shook to the detonation of a bomb.

Johansen closed his eyes, got a grip on himself and let his curiosity overcome his fear. He stepped to the binocular telescope, gazed down it. There was nothing there but a curved sheet of gray material. He had never seen a gray quite like that. It was absolutely neutral. It didn't seem soft and it didn't seem hard, and to look at it made his brain reel. He looked up.

Kidder was pounding the keys of a teletype, watching the blank yellow tape anxiously.

"I'm not getting through to them," he whimpered. "I don't know what's the mat— Oh, of *course!*"

"What?"

"The shield is absolutely impenetrable! The teletype impulses can't get through or I could get them to extend the screen over the building—over the whole island! There's *nothing* those people can't do!"

"He's crazy," Johansen muttered. "Poor little—"

The teletype began clicking sharply. Kidder dove at it, practically embraced it. He read off the tape as it came out. Johansen saw the characters, but they meant nothing to him.

"Almighty," Kidder read falteringly, "pray have mercy on us and be forbearing until we have said our say. Without orders we have lowered the screen you ordered us to rise. We are lost, O great one. Our screen is truly impenetrable, and so cut off your words on the word machine. We have never, in the memory of any Neoteric, been without your word before. Forgive us our action. We will eagerly await your answer."

Kidder's fingers danced over the keys. "You can look now," he gasped. "Go on—the telescope!"

Johansen, trying to ignore the whine of sure death from above, looked.

He saw what looked like land—fantastic fields under cultivation, a settlement of some sort, factories, and—beings. Everything moved with incredible rapidity. He couldn't see one of the inhabitants except as darting pinky-white streaks. Fascinated, he stared for a long minute. A sound behind him made him whirl. It was Kidder, rubbing his hands together briskly. There was a broad smile on his face.

"They did it," he said happily. "You see?"

Johansen didn't see until he began to realize that there was a dead silence outside. He ran to a window. It was night outside—the blackest night—when it should have been dusk. "What happened?"

"The Neoterics," said Kidder, and laughed like a child. "My friends downstairs there. They threw up the impenetrable shield over the whole island. We can't be touched now!"

And at Johansen's amazed questions, he launched into a description of the race of beings below them.

Outside the shell, things happened. Nine airplanes suddenly went dead-stick. Nine pilots glided downward, powerless, and some fell into the sea, and some struck the miraculous gray shell that loomed in place of an island, slid off, and sank.

And ashore, a man named Wright sat in a car, half dead with fear, while government men surrounded him, approached cautiously, daring instant death from a now-dead source.

In a room deep in the White House, a high-ranking army officer shrieked, "I can't stand it any more! I can't!" and leaped up, snatched a red cube off the President's desk, ground it to ineffectual litter under his shining boots.

And in a few days they took a broken old man away from the bank and put him in an asylum, where he died within a week.

The shield, you see, was truly impenetrable. The power plant was untouched and sent out its beams; but the beams could not get out, and anything powered from the plant went dead. The story never became public, although for some years there was heightened naval activity off the New England coast. The navy, so the story went, had a new target range out there—a great hemi-ovoid of gray material. They bombed it and shelled it and rayed it and blasted all around it, but never even dented its smooth surface.

Kidder and Johansen let it stay there. They were happy enough with their researches and their Neoterics. They did not hear or feel the shelling, for the shield was truly impenetrable. They synthesized their food and their light and air from the materials at hand, and they simply didn't care. They were the only survivors of the bombing, with the exception of three poor maimed devils who died soon afterwards.

All this happened many years ago, and Kidder and Johansen may be alive today, and they may be dead. But that doesn't matter too much. The important thing is that the great gray shell will bear watching. Men die, but races live. Some day the Neoterics, after innumerable generations of inconceivable advancement, will take down their shield and come forth. When I think of that I feel frightened.

The Haunt

JUST A GAG, that's all—a gag. I'm sure it was. It had to be. Heck, we were wise, Tommy and me. Tommy was a radio technician and a good one, and I knew the gadgets to the last hidden loudspeaker and the last Fahnestock clip almost as well as he did. Tommy was a funny egg, anyway. Foggy, you know—the kind of guy that shows up at work with one brown shoe and one black, or dunks his cafeteria check in his coffee and hands a doughnut to the waiter to punch. But—he knew his stuff, he had the apparatus, and the idea tickled him. I can see his point there. Scaring the living daylights out of a cool cookie like Miriam Jensen was a challenge to any man.

Her rock-hard nerves were by no means her only striking characteristic. She was smooth—smooth to look at, smooth to talk to, smooth in the way she thought and acted and moved. Tall, you know—dark brunette, long slim neck, small head and features; quite tall—that kind. A knockout. Brains, too, and she used them. I don't believe anything but hard exercise could raise her pulse more than one-two beats a minute. I know that the funny idea I had that it would be nice to be married to her didn't have her at all fluttery. She laughed me off. When I asked for her lily-white hand, did she say she'd be a sister to me? Did she tell me tenderly that we weren't suited? Did she say so much as "No"? Uh-uh. She said: "You're cute, Bill. Didn't anyone ever tell you how cute you were?" And she giggled. I stood there with my teeth in my mouth and my bare face hanging out, watching her walk away; and then and there I said to myself, "I'm going to shake her off her high horse, by all that's unholy, if I have to kill her to do it."

I came home—lived in an apartment hotel then—and met Tommy in the hall. I dragged him into my place, stuck a drink in his hand, and figuratively wept on his shoulder about it for the best part of an hour, while he sat there doddering his untidy hair up and down and watching the bubbles collect on the bottom of an ice cube.

"W-what do y-you want to do about it?" he asked.

"I told you—slap her down. If I could think of a way to slap her down so that it would do *me* some good, I'd do it, too. But you can't walk up to a woman, take a poke at her, and expect her to marry you for it."

"You can with s-some women," Tommy observed with the profundity of a confirmed celibate.

"Not with this one," I snorted. "No, I've got to scare the bustle cover off her, and then rescue her, maybe. Or show her that I'm not scared by the same thing. Or both. Got any ideas?"

"I th-think you're a ph-phony, Bill."

"I didn't mean your ideas about me. Come on—you're supposed to run to brains. Forget the personalities and let's have a brain wave or two."

Tommy stared at the ceiling and gravely ground out his cigarette two inches away from an ash tray. "What's she sc-sc-frightened of, do you think?"

I walked up and down for a couple of minutes, trying to frown out an answer to that one. "Nothing, as far as I've ever heard," I said. "Miriam will dive off a sixty-foot platform, or break a bronc, or drive a midget racer, and breathe no harder for it than she does after a fast conga. I tell you, that girl's nerves—if she has any—are made of iridium-plated piano wire."

"I bet she's superstitious," said Tommy.

"What? Ghosts, you mean? Huh. Could be, but what—"

"Easy." Tommy set his half-empty glass down on the floor from about waist height. "We'll make her some ghosts—you'll rescue her from them."

"Swell. What do we do—draw some magic squares on the hotel carpet around a pot of devil's brew or something?"

"N-no. We take a couple coils of wire and my little public-speaking s-system, and maybe a few colored lights and stuff. And we haunt a house. Th-then you bring your iridium girl friend in. J-just leave it to me."

"That sounds like quite something, Tommy," I said. I was so tickled with the idea that I remembered I hadn't had a drink and began pouring myself one. "Miriam's a sucker for a dare. But the Lord help me if she ever found out about this."

Tommy looked at me vaguely and grinned. "I don't know nothin', ch-chief," he said, and got up to go. "I'll l-let you know what I dream up on this, B-Bill. Night." He went through the door.

I thanked him, pulled him out of the bathroom, and saw him to the right door. I never did meet such a foggy fellow.

Inside of a week he had it rigged up and took me out there to look it over. The house was a chalet over a century old. It had hedges in front of it gone hog wild, and the once-green paint was a filthy gray. It had eleven-foot ceilings and Venetian shutters which were in the last stages of decay, full of tartar and cavities, as it were. I don't know how Tommy had gotten hold of it, but he had, and man, how he'd rigged it up!

"You s-see," he explained, "the old place has a history, too. There have been four murders here, and th-three suicides. The l-last guy who owned it starved to death in the cellar." He motioned me after him and started through the weeds toward the back. I looked up at the gloomy old pile and shuddered. "What are we going around the back for?" I asked.

"So the dust in the f-front hallway will look as if no one has been here in the last twenty years," he said, opening a cellar window. "G-go on—climb in."

I did, and he tumbled in after me. He threaded his way though large piles of rubbish until he came to a partition. He opened a door in it and we found ourselves inside a neatly arranged control room. Pointing, Tommy said, "See th-that board? There's a photo cell and relay laid across every door in the house. Any time anyone goes into a room I know which it is by the number underneath the light. There's my mike over there, and phonograph pick-up. There's a hot-air system in the house; I put the speaker in the furnace, and when I play my little collection of m-moans and groans and shrieks from those recordings, you c-can hear them all over the house. It sounds swell."

"It does," I grinned. "But why do you have to know which room we're going to be in?"

"For the l-lights," he said. He showed me a battery of half a dozen knife switches and a rheostat. "Some of the lights are ultraviolet, and they shine on fluorescent paint on the opposite wall. You s-see something there, and when you turn your flashlight on it, it's gone. Some of the lights are photo flashes. Oh, it'll be quite a sh-show."

"It sure will," I said, delighted.

"Now, when you b-bring your little lump of dry ice in," said Tommy—I gathered he was referring to Miriam—"take her in the front way. Here—I've typed out all the stories about p-people who died in this place, and all the dope about how and where they g-got knocked off. Tell her all the yarns and take her into all the rooms. You'll know what to expect. That's all I can do—you'll have to figure out the rest yourself."

"You've done enough," I said, slapping him on the back so that his glasses fell off and broke. He pulled another pair out of his pocket and put them on. "Don't worry," I said. "This ought to cut some of her ice."

He gave me a few more details and took me on a tour of the place. Then I took my typewritten sheets and went home to bone up on them. It should be a snap, I thought. Anyhow, it should have been.

I cornered Miriam two nights later. I came up behind her and whispered in her ear, "Will you marry me?"

She said, "Oh, hello, Bill," without even turning around.

"Miriam," I said hoarsely, "I asked you a question!"

She gently slid her shoulder out from under my hand. "And I said 'Hello, Bill.'" She grinned.

I gnashed my teeth and tried to be calm.

"Do you like ghosts?" I asked irrelevantly.

"Dunno. I never met one," she said. "Don't you ever ask girls to dance?"

"No," I said. "I sweep 'em off their feet onto the floor when I feel like dancing, which I don't right now. I want to talk about ghosts."

"A safe subject," she observed. I nodded my head toward one of those pieces of furniture euphemistically called love seats, and we threaded our way through the crowd of people—it was one of those parties that Reggie Johns used to throw for people he didn't know. That is, he'd invite six couples he knew and forty or fifty would arrive.

"In 1853," I said oratorically, "Joachim Grandt—spelled with a 'd'—was murdered by person or persons unknown in the first floor back of an old Swiss chalet up on Grove Street. A rumor circulated to the effect that the room was haunted. This so depreciated the value of the house and grounds that Joachim's great-nephew, Harrison Grandt—also spelled with a 'd'—tried to prove that it was not haunted by spending a night there. He was found the next morning by one Harry Fortunato, strangled to death in exactly the manner used by the aforementioned person or persons. Fortunato was so exercised by this strange turn of events that he rushed out of the house and broke his neck on the front steps."

"All this is quite bewildering," said Miriam softly, "but it seems to me that it is hardly the thing to whisper into my shell-like ear when we could be dancing."

"Damn it, Miriam—"

"—also spelled with a 'd,'" she interjected.

"Let me finish telling you about this. After Fortunato's death there were two more murders and two supposed suicides, all of them either stranglings or neck-breakings. Now, the house is supposed to be really haunted. They say you can really see the spooks and hear voices and rattles and so froth—all the fixin's. I found out where the place is."

"Oh? And what might that have to do with—"

"You? Well, I've heard tell that you aren't afraid of man, woman or beast. I just wondered about ghosts."

"Don't be childish, Bill. Ghosts live inside the heads of foolish people and pop out when the foolish people want to be frightened."

"Not these ghosts."

She regarded me amusedly. "Don't tell me you've seen them?"

I nodded.

She said, "That proves my point. Let's dance."

She half rose, but I caught her wrist and yanked her back. I don't think she liked it. "Don't tell me you're afraid to go and see for yourself, Iron Woman?"

"Nobody suggested it."

"I just did."

She stopped yearning toward the dance floor and settled back. "Ah—so that's the idea. Go on—let's have it," she said in a I-won't-do-it-but-I'd-like-to-hear-about-it tone of voice.

"We'd just go out there and investigate it," I said. "Frankly, I'd like to see your hair curl."

"Let me get this straight," she said. "You and I are going out at this time of night to a deserted house in a deserted neighborhood to catch us a ghost. Right?" Her raised eyebrow added, "Monkey business, hey?"

"No!" I said immediately. "No monkey business. My word on that." Of course, Tommy's electrical ghosts were monkey business, but that was not what she and her eyebrow meant by monkey business.

"Real ghosts," she mused. "Bill, if this is some kind of a joke—"

"With me, lady," I said, with real sincerity, "this is no joke."

She insinuated herself out of the love seat onto her feet and said, "Stand by, then, while I tell Reggie we're leaving. I came with Roger Sykes, but he doesn't have to know anything about it."

While she was gone I got some grinning done. Just like clockwork, it was—this was the night Tommy had said he'd pick to throw a scare into her. She'd fallen for the bait better than I ever could have hoped, and it certainly looked as if everything was breaking my way. Maybe if I could get her scared enough we could head for Gretna Green. Could be—could be.

I saw her at the door, waiting for me. She was dressed in something skintight and yet flowing, with a long white panel front and back, and black shoulders and sides—I dunno—I'm no dressmaker, but the dress was like the rest of her—smooth. And now she had slipped a great black cloak over her shoulders that fell away from her body and looked like wings. What a woman! I sighed, envying myself because I was going to have her to myself for a few hours.

We climbed into my ancient but efficient old struggle buggy. "Where is this place?" Miriam asked as I pulled away from the curb.

I glanced at her, taking in the way she wound her cloak about her and writhed deeper into it. Every move a miracle, I thought. "I told you," I said, keeping my thoughts to myself. "Up on Grove Street, on top of Toad Hill, across the street from a junk yard."

"I know about where it is," she said. "Tarry not, my fran'—pile some coal on and let's get there. I've always wanted to meet up with a ghost."

Her tone was one I'd heard before, once in a while. The time, for instance, that one of the boys had been trying to lasso a post with a length of clothesline and she had grabbed it from him impatiently, saying, "Dammit, Joe, you make me nervous. Here," and had whirled it once and snagged the post on the first cast. And that other time when one of the horses from the riding academy broke its leg taking a hedge. While half a dozen people looked on, she picked up an edged stone and with one clean blow killed the horse. "It was the only thing to do," she explained bluntly. "None of you blockheads have even started back to the academy for a gun yet. What do you want to do—leave the animal to lie here screaming for a solid hour?"

"What makes you that way?" I asked her. She looked at me questioningly. "I mean, why are you always ducking in to do more or less violent things? Why don't you learn to knit?"

"I can knit," she said shortly, in a voice that said, "Oh, dry up."

So I dried up, contenting myself with the joyful play of street lights on her darkened profile, and wondering if I were a heel to pull this sort of a trick. We drew up eventually in front of the house. Miriam got out and stared up at it. It loomed gray and forbidding in the light of a half-moon. Before it, striving their dark utmost to hide the front walk, were the tangled, twelve-foot hedges. The whole place had a greedily unkempt look—it was a dirty old panhandler of a house, begging the right to exist another moment. Miriam walked up to the hedge and stopped, and I don't know whether she was hesitating or just waiting for me. We went up the path together.

I noticed with satisfaction that Tommy had either taken a taxi or parked his car on another street. That had bothered me a little—he was damn clever, but a little short on foresight. When we reached the top of the steps I covertly touched the doorbell. There was no sound—it would light a bulb on Tommy's board so he'd know we were in. I handed Miriam one of the two flashlights I had stowed in the car and pushed open the door.

Miriam caught my arm. "Ladies first, you clod," she laughed, and slid in ahead of me.

The floor of the foyer settled two inches under her feet with a bump; she flailed one arm a little to get her balance and turned to me, smiling coolly. "Coming, Bill?"

We found ourselves in a high, narrow hallway containing a flight of stairs far too big for it.

"Hello-o-o! Who's the-e-e-ere—"

"Huh?" Miriam and I asked each other. The voice had been tiny, just the echo of an echo, but clear as a bos'n's pipe. "I didn't say anything," we chorused, and then Miriam said, "Either we're not the only investigators or the ghosts are wasting no time on us. Either way, I like it here. Where to first, Bill?"

She'll have to get a little more scared than that before I can show her up, I thought. "Upstairs," I said. "We'll start at the top and work down."

Side by side, we headed up the old steps, scything great lumps of darkness away with our lights. At the first landing, Miriam walked ahead, as the stairs narrowed here. As she crossed the landing, I saw her heel sink as her weight whipped a loose board up on end. I caught it just before it could belt the back of her head.

"Thanks, pal," she said evenly. "I'll do the same for you some time." Never turned a hair!

Almost to the top, I thought I heard something. "Don't look now," I said in a hushed voice, "but I don't want you to miss anything, and I think I hear someone laughing."

We froze and stopped breathing to give the faint sound a chance. "That isn't laughing," said Miriam.

I listened more carefully. "Check," I said, "but from the sound of it, whatever is being laughed about should be cried over. Good heavens, what a crazy sound."

It was a burbly noise, so quiet it was almost intimate, and it sobbed in peals. Miriam snorted as if she were trying to blow an evil smell out of her nostrils. I wiped sweat off the palms of my hands. Where the hell had Tommy picked up *that* recording?

We tiptoed across the second-floor hall and Miriam pushed open a door. Dust swirled up as it swung noiselessly back, far faster than was warranted, and a great dim shape loomed up out of it.

Smash!

A splintering crash behind us, and that unimaginable something ahead of us. I jumped to the right and Miriam to the left, and for a second the whole world was made of flailing electric beams and hidden menace. Miriam, to be frank, calmed down first; at least, enough to steady her flashlight on one of the sources of our panic. It was the old print that had been hanging in the hallway. Its nail had pulled out of the loose plaster, probably because of one of my dainty No. 10 footfalls, and it had fallen to the floor, smashing the glass in the picture frame. I shot my light at the open door. Just inside was a tall piece of furniture, an old-fashioned secretary desk, covered with a dusty white cloth.

"A little jumpy, aren't you, Bill?" called Miriam cheerfully as she came over to me.

I thrust my tongue between my teeth so they wouldn't chatter so loudly, and tried to grin doing it. In that crazy light I think I got away with it. Miriam must have thought I felt fine, because she rather readily let me lead the way into the room.

There was nothing much there but dust and a couple of broken chairs. At the back of the room was another door. With Miriam treading on my heels, I went through it. I stood just inside, fencing with the blackness with my torch and seeing nothing, stepped aside to let Miriam in. Something touched me lightly on the shoulder—

Bong! Whee-hoo! Bong! Whee-hoo! Bong!

Miriam said "Gha!" with an intake of breath and grabbed at my arm, making me drop my light. It thumped to the floor and went out, and she pawed at hers, accidentally flipped the switch. Darkness hit us so hard our knees sagged under the weight of it, and my cold-blooded darling wrapped both arms around my head, which was the first thing she contacted; and she began making a noise like a duck-ling at the ripe old age of two hours. The bonging and whee-hooing went right on, until Miriam's hand, in a convulsive contraction, turned on her light again. We found ourselves staring up at an old-style cuckoo clock. It and its cuckoo were telling us the falsehood that it was eleven o'clock. I must have bumped into the pendulum and set it off.

Miriam stood there with her arms around me until the silly wooden bird had finished and retired; and yet a moment longer. This was my moment, and by damn if I wasn't too upset to appreciate it. Then she let me go, and said through a funny little smile, "Bill—I think maybe this is comic. Laugh a bit, huh?"

I licked some moisture off my upper lip onto a dry tongue. "Ha, ha," I said without enthusiasm.

Miriam said firmly, "The laughing noise was water in a pipe some-where. That crash was a picture falling off the wall. We both saw it. The ... ah ... thing in the doorway was an old bookcase covered with a dust cloth. This last ghost of yours was a cuckoo clock. Right?"

"Right."

"And that 'Who's there' we heard when we came in was ... was—What was it, anyway?"

"Imagination," I said promptly. "Although I know damn well *I* didn't imagine it."

"I did, then," she said stubbornly, and added, "Enough for both of us." Her wry grin was a sight to behold.

"Must be," I said, picking up my flashlight and trying to make my fingers behave enough to unscrew the reflector and slip in a spare bulb. I managed it, somehow. "And are you by any slim chance imag-ining—*that,* too?" I pointed. She pivoted.

"That" was a blob of light on the wall, so dim it was all but in-visible. The beam from her torch had been on another wall, or I wouldn't have seen it at all. As I stared breathlessly, looking at its shades and shadowy outlines, I began to make out what it was.

"It looks like a ... a neck!" whispered Miriam, backing onto my feet. The thing was indeed a neck, flesh-pink and mottled with deep fingerlike gouges of blue-black. It held for just a few seconds and then faded out.

I gulped and said, "Pretty!"

Miriam whipped her light around and splashed it on the wall. The beam wasn't steady, and she didn't say anything.

"Miriam—I feel like dancing, I think."

"There's no music here," she said quietly. "We'd have to go somewhere else."

"Yeah," I said, and gulped. "We would, wouldn't we?" But neither of us moved.

Finally she shrugged and took a deep breath. "What are you waiting for, Bill? Let's go!"

"Go? Dancing, you mean?"

"Dancing!" she contraltoed scornfully. "We were going to explore this house, weren't we? Come on, then."

"Quite a feller, aren't you?" I said to her under my breath. I think she heard me, because she squared her shoulders and went out. I tagged along.

It occurred to me that it was all very well to put on this show for her, but I was damned lucky that I'd picked her to pull it on rather than some more impressionable female. The place was getting under my skin as it was. Suppose I'd been with some twist who fainted or got hysterical or lost or something? Suppose I got left alone in this place? I began stepping on Miriam's heels.

We gave the rest of the second floor the once-over and nothing much happened. That pep talk of hers helped a lot. We casually dismissed sundry creaks and groans and rattlings as the wind in the chimneys, banging shutters, and settling floors. Neither of us saw fit to mention that there was no wind that night, and that a one-hundred-twenty-five-year-old house does not settle. In other words, we thought that nothing was bothering us at all until that sob-laughing started up again. That was pretty awful. Miriam had been holding hands with me for ten minutes before I realized it, and I only knew it at all when I felt her bones grate together as I clutched her when the laughing started. It ran up and down a whole tone scale, sounding like a palsied madman playing on a piano full of tears.

"Still like it here?" I asked.

"I didn't like school," she said, "but I graduated."

We had to open a door to get on the stairs leading to the third floor. They were narrow with a turn in the middle, with a tiny square landing at the turn. I was in the lead—must have been a mistake, because you can bet I didn't ask for it, chivalry or no chivalry. Just before I reached the landing I saw a woman, a beautiful thing in diaphanous robes, walk gravely out of the wall at my right, across the landing and into the wall at my left. The only thing that detracted from her loveliness was the blood which spouted from her ears, and the fact that I could see the patchy wall though her quite easily. I gasped and stepped back on Miriam's instep.

"Oo-o! Dammit, Bill—" She stood on her uninjured foot and clutched at the banister, a section of which immediately broke loose and went crashing and somersaulting into the darkness below.

"You all right?" I said over the reverberations.

I clutched at her to keep her from falling and managed only to get my thumb into her eye. She said something that her mother didn't teach her. "Get away, Bill—you're a menace! What in the name of corruption did you step backward for?"

"Didn't you see her—it?" I said before I had sense enough to say nothing. She shook her head.

"Who?"

"A girl! She— Oh, skip it, Miriam. I guess I imagined that, too. Come on."

We started to climb again, and something possessed us both to look back. At any rate, when I looked, it was over Miriam's head, and she was staring at the transparent woman, who was crossing back again from wall to wall across the landing. This time she walked backward, and the blood ran into her ears. It was infinitely more horrible than the first time, and yet, after the first shock of it, I was comforted. For the first time Tommy had laid it on too thick. That reversed action was too cinematic to get over, I thought. And that's what it must have been—a film projected from somewhere, perhaps out from under one of the steps, run forward and then backward. That would easily account for the transparency of the girl's figure, since it was projected directly against the wall. But—damn it, how did he ever achieve that astonishing three-dimensional effect?

"That," Miriam was saying brokenly, "is something that I just am not going to believe! Bill—for Heaven's sake, what sort of place is this?"

"Regular haunt, isn't it?" I said cheerfully. I was feeling better now that I'd figured out one of the ghosts to my satisfaction. "Come on—we'll make our round and get out of here. The sooner the quicker, y'know!"

Her gait and her carriage and her expression, all I could catch in the sweeping beams of our torches, were almost meek. I suddenly felt overwhelmingly like a heel. This was a lousy thing to do to such a swell girl.

"Miriam," I said softly, catching her arms, "I—"

But just then the laughter reached a cold crescendo, and from downstairs came the most blood-freezing, ululating scream that it's ever been my sorrow to hear. It was the kind of sound to clamp a man's jaws so tight in terror that his gums bleed, and his skin goose-fleshes out like a woodrasp. The scream seemed to stop the laughter, for the stillness after it devoted itself to the scream's echoes; and we stopped breathing so that the sound of our breath would not keep the echoes alive. That scream didn't belong on this earth. Somewhere in hell is a damned soul which has been there long enough to be miserable enough and still stay strong enough to scream like that.

We pushed away from each other merely because it was the only movement we could make to thrust the remembrance of that sound from us a little. The desire to complete our tour of the chalet was something fevered and senseless and quite irresistible by now. We hurried to get it done—we made no slightest move to leave it partly finished. I couldn't have done it without my knowledge that no matter how extreme these horrors became, they were but the creations of Tommy's strange genius for handling electrical circuits. Miriam had her own iron nerve and the fact that so far I hadn't broken into a hysterical retreat.

The third floor wasn't bad—there was nothing there but odds and ends of old furniture, dust, and creaking floorboards. When we started downstairs we knew we were all but on our way out, and we grew almost cheerful. Almost. Not quite, because that noise began again—that creeping, tear-filled laughter. It went on and on and on, until we couldn't stand it anymore, and it passed that point and still went on. We walked down steps and trotted down corridors and broke and ran in and out of rooms, playing childishly at being casual, while the laughter grew, not louder, but more and more clear; and we couldn't tell whether it was following us or whether it was simply everywhere. It was so all-enveloping that we lost consciousness of the fact that it was in the house. It was all around us, more than a sound—it was something we breathed, something which pressed our clothing to our shrinking bodies with its pulsings. It filled the whole world and there would never, never be an end to it, and we couldn't escape it by fleeing the house. We couldn't ever get away from it. It was part of us now, in our blood, in our bones. Rounding a corner on the first floor, Miriam crashed into a door and reeled back into my arms. I turned my light on her face. Part of the sound—some of it, all of it, I don't know—*was coming from her!*

"Miriam!" I screamed, and slapped her face twice, and clamped my hand over her writhing mouth. The laughter receded into the upper part of the house, and she sank tremblingly closer to me. "Miriam—Why did I— Darling, come out of it. Listen to me! Mir—"

"Oh, Bill! Bill, I'm scared! I'm scared, Bill!" She said it quietly, in a small, very surprised voice; and then she began to cry, and I'll bet my eyeballs that it was the first time in her life she'd cried, because those tears came hard.

I picked her up in my arms and carried her into a room we hadn't yet visited. There was a monstrous old red plush and mahogany divan there, and I put her down on it. She put her arms around my neck and all of a sudden was a very little girl afraid of the dark. I bent over her, all choked up, and for all I know, I cried, too.

The laughter approached again.

"Bill!" she wailed. "Make it stop! Oh, please, please, make it stop!"

I couldn't keep up that pretense any longer. "Stick around, bud," I gritted; and, jamming one of the torches in an angle of the divan's rococo, I headed for the door.

Miriam sat up and screamed for me. I went back, put my arms

around her and kissed her. She was so surprised when I let her go that she just sat there with her hand to her mouth, wordless, while I tore out and along the corridor to the steps that led down into the cellar.

Tommy's carried this thing too damn far, I gritted to myself as I cut into the littered cellar room where he had hidden his controls. There was such a thing as doing a job too well, and I was about to tell a radio engineer that, complete with fireworks. I fumbled along the wooden partition until I found a knothole he had used for a door-knob. I jammed a finger into it, whipped the door open, stabbed a ray of light inside. There wasn't anyone there. There just wasn't any-one in there at all!

"Tommy?" I sagged up against the partition, gasping. "Tommy!" Nobody in there. No one working those lights, that switchboard, phonograph, no— "Tommy!" I quavered.

The laughter kept on. On and on. I looked at the phonograph. It was there, all right, with its crystal pick-up and the wires running to the speaker in the old furnace. But it wasn't operating. I crept up to it and put out my hand and turned it over with a crash, and the laughter wouldn't stop.

Tommy! The goon, where'd he get to? Maybe he'd been here up until a minute or so ago. Maybe he was hiding in the cellar some-where. I went to the door and called him. No answer. I came back, ran my hand over the bulb-studded board. That sob-laughing was still sounding all around me. I wasn't doing it, was I? I shook my head to clear it and tried to think. Could that foggy fellow have for-gotten to show up? *Hadn't he been here at all?*

Tuesday. Tuesday night. This was Tuesday night. Wasn't Tommy supposed to show up for the haunt tonight? That's what I thought. A vague memory flashed across my mind—Tommy telling me what night he wanted to pull his trick. He had gone, "Wuh-Wuh-Wuh-Wuh-Wuh—" for about thirty seconds before he got it out. But a guy doesn't make that noise when he's trying to say "Tuesday." He does it when he's trying to say "Wednesday." Oh, but that was too damn silly! Whatever in the world made me think it was Tuesday?

I knew he'd said something about Tue— Oh, yes! "C-contact your snow queen on Tuesday so you'll be sure to have her at the house on Wuh-Wuh-Wuh—" That was it!

I punched myself in the mouth, I was so sore. Well, it didn't matter—some son of a gun had been monkeying with these controls for the last hour or so, and I didn't care who it was! I rushed the beam over the wiring, located the power line and tore it away from the switchboard. That would do it.

That didn't do it. First I heard that laughter, and then I heard Miriam scream. I bolted for the door—straight for the door, even though it meant plowing through all of Tommy's electrical equipment. I hit the cellar room amid a shower of coils and broken bulbs and rheostats and headed for the stairs. As I reached them, another thought wound itself around my heart and tried to stop it. Miriam was in the first floor back room—the room into which I had carried her—the room where four people had been inexplicably but thoroughly strangled!

I really made time. I was running too fast to get through the door clean, and I left a piece of my shoulder on the doorpost and kept running. This was it. This was our little haunt. That house didn't need Tommy!

Miriam was lying on the divan with her head twisted crazily and blue marks on her throat.

I screamed and whirled and ran out. A doctor—a policeman— I had to get someone! Miriam—I'd done this to Miriam! If she was dead, then I killed her!

I flew down the hall, out through the foyer. The outer door stopped me for a moment because it opened inward. I wrestled it open, stood gasping at the top of the steps. This was the way it was, then. This was what had happened to Grandt, and Fortunato had found Grandt as I found Miriam. Fortunato was lucky. He broke his neck running out of the house. I wished my neck was broken, and then I wouldn't have to worry about killing Miriam. I looked hungrily down the steps. Three other men had died on them the same way—why not one more? The laughter behind me fell away and settled into a low, expectant gurgle. It was going to happen again. Strangle one person,

and break another's neck on the steps. That's the way it always had
been. That's the—

"*No!*" I sobbed, and turned and butted my way back into the
house. When I did, the laughter stopped within itself.

I went blindly back down the long corridor and into the first floor
back. Miriam still lay there, and I stood, all tired inside, looking at
her. I didn't want to go near, didn't want to touch, didn't want anything. I just looked at her woodenly, the way she was stretched there
and twisted, the way her head hung, and the way those blue marks
on her long white neck bit in and shifted and bit in again. And then
I saw that she hadn't been strangled at all, for—*she was being
strangled!*

With a hoarse bark I leaped in, seized her, lifted her. I had to pull
against something. I propped her up with one arm, felt around her
throat with the other hand. Nothing there! I picked her up and tried
to carry her away, and I couldn't because she was being held by the
neck! I clutched her to me and put everything I had into that effort
to tear her away, and I couldn't! Then I felt something give, and her
eyes rolled up out of sight. She looked ghastly in the crazy light from
the torch that still flung its bright shaft angling upward from where
I had jammed it. I knew it hurt her, and I could all but feel her pain.
Then everything let go, and by a miracle I stayed on my feet, and I
stumbled and bungled and carried her out of the room and out of
the house and into the car.

As soon as we were well away from there I pulled over to the
curb. She couldn't have lived through that—she couldn't! But why
was she moving, then, and whispering something? I pulled her to
me, chafed her wrist. She was saying my name. I almost laughed.
She began to swear in a deep, husky voice. I did laugh.

"Oh—boy!" she said, and licked her lips. "Have I been through
the mill!" She touched her neck weakly and grinned.

"Darling, I'm a heel to get you into that place. I don't know whatever got into me—"

"Shush," she said, and lay back.

She was so quiet for so long that I got frightened. "Miriam—"

"Apropos of nothing," she said, and her voice was so strong and normal that it was a shock to me, "there's a question you asked me that I've been dodging. I'll marry you if you like."

I was still feeling like a heel. "What *for?*" I asked in real amazement. She leaned over against me.

"Because," she said softly, "I always wanted to be married to a man who could tell me ghost stories on long winter evenings."

There are just two more things to tell. Tommy refused to be our best man because he was sore at me for wrecking his equipment. The other thing is that I bought the chalet on Grove Street and had it razed. We built our house there and we're very happy in it.

Completely Automatic

"WHAT THE DEVIL does he do for a living?" I asked as the petty officer left the mess room.

"Nothing," said the second officer. "Nothing at all."

"What do you carry him for, then?"

The second was a man in his middle forties with a very nice grin. He used it now. "We carry him just in case," he said. "He's the chemical supervisor. He stands no watches, makes no reports. He reports aboard before we take off and disappears when we make port. For that he knocks down six hundred and forty credits a month."

"Six—Holy Kit, that's a lot of change for doing nothing. I was always under the impression that the crew of a spaceship was streamlined down to practically nothing. Does every ship carry these ... these paid passengers?"

The second nodded as he filled my glass again. "There was a time, four or five hundred years ago, when a ship couldn't have done without them. They had no automatic machinery to speak of then. The ships were self-powered, and half their capacity was given over to fuel. Half the rest was driving machinery. They had no power beams then; they had to plot their courses and steer them every trip. Now, of course, with the power beams that both guide and drive the vessels, things are different. There are only two or three hundred men in the System that know the theory of astrogation nowadays, and they are either research scientists or doddering scholars. It's only tradition that keeps a crew aboard any more—that and the fact that the more jobs the Supreme Council can create, the better for everybody. I don't kid myself—I know damn well that I could be replaced in a minute by two switches and a rheostat on the control panel back on Earth. That goes for everyone else riding these ships, too. Only the passenger ships carry captains, and they are there to impress the passengers. Sort of glorified masters of ceremonies. No, space travel isn't what it used to be."

"That may be true," I said, "but at least you do something for a living. You stand a regular watch and supervise the stowage and the passenger lists and keep the log and give the passengers the idea that the ship is in competent hands—but what about that chem super? False front is false front, but it's usually attached to something solid. That guy hasn't even an excuse for being aboard."

"You don't think so? Granted, his work is taken care of entirely by automatic machinery that hasn't broken down once in the last three hundred years, but that isn't the point. Remember—I told you that he is here *just in case.*"

"In case of what?"

"Certain eventualities. Got an hour or so? I'll tell you a story about a chemical supervisor that might interest you."

"Go ahead," I said. "I've got three weeks with nothing to do, let alone an hour. Start spinning."

The second officer unzipped his collar, flipped a lever on his chair to tilt it back a little, and began.

The reason I think you in particular would be interested in this yarn is that it has to do with what happened when they did exactly what you say they should do—get rid of some hundred-odd thousand pieces of deadwood in the way of chem supers and their apprentices. Yeah, they did, about twenty-eight years ago. There was a great deal of noise about it at the time, because most of the old conservatives didn't like the idea of breaking an old space tradition that way. They said that spaceships should no more take off without chem supers than they should without lifeboats. The fact that no one within the memory of living man had ever used a lifeboat for anything but joyriding didn't faze them.

The machinery was foolproof, rigidly inspected every trip, and all of it either one hundred percent automatic or remote control. Supers simply were not needed. The boys that held down the jobs were, with a few exceptions, friends of somebody who had a friend in the office. Their qualifications were courtesy ones; a couple of oral questions were examination enough for them. Many skippers carried their relatives with them as supers. A lot of fellows grabbed the jobs because they were sincerely interested in space travel and that way they could have a good look around the ship to see how they liked it and what kind of work would suit them best. It was a set-up—harmless enough, to be sure, except for the fact that the supers got paid a high wage, and that made the rest of the crew a little sore because they had to work for a living.

This was before the days of the Functionalist government, when many of the space lines were privately owned and the big boys at the top were anxious to cut costs and increase profits without regard to the number of men they threw out of work. I don't have to tell you that space transportation is as big an industry as they come; to get rid of a chem super and his apprentice on every single ship in the System that ever left any atmosphere was a big jolt. A few hundred thousand men thrown out of work all at once played hell with the economic balance, close as it was. Besides, most of those supers were absolutely worthless—bums, parasites, drifters, trouble-makers.

It was a foolish move, and the Council knew it; but the pressure put on by the profit-drunk "efficiency" experts of the space companies was too strong. They bounced them out—every last one of them. It's interesting to know that it was that group of worthless ex-supers who, by the noise they made, were ultimately responsible for the new set-up, where men are hired and paid for jobs that could be done away with—my job, for instance. It's better that way. No one loses anything; the companies don't gain so much, that's all. They can afford it. And it has completely done away with unemployment.

But to get back to the supers. I know all about what happened because it happened aboard the *Maggie Northern,* my first ship—my first job on these cans. It was a first for the ship too—her first trip without a super.

I came aboard her—I was a teenage kid at the time—with a suitcase with a busted handle under my arm and more ignorance than sense under my hat. I got in a lot of people's way and was finally shunted into the rocket man's fo'c'sle. I stood in the middle of the floor feeling shy. I hadn't known a spaceship would be like this. Like every kid my age, I had filled myself full of stories about the trade, and thought it would be cramped and stuffy with tiered bunks and lacking every facility a he-man would sneer at. But this, one of the poorest-equipped freighters in the Great Northern ore fleet, had three men to a room, each with a bed with innerspring mattress, hot and cold running water—the works. Some bright soul had painted a garden scene on the windowless bulkhead and had rigged it up with a window frame, glass and curtains. There was a kid a couple of years older than me sitting on a bench looking sad. He looked up at me.

"Hi. You the new wiper?"

"Yeah."

He got up and stuck out a hand. He was a good-looking kid, very tall. Well set up. "My name's Hume. Welcome to our dirty little home."

"I'm Babson. It don't look so bad."

"Neither does Fuzzy here," said Hume as a burly individual, the third wiper, came into the room. "But, boy—wait till you get to know him."

Fuzzy stopped in his tracks as he saw me and waited while his apelike face lit up. Then he ambled over to me, looked into my face, circled me slowly. "I seen that hay spread on the gangplank an' I figgered they was goin' to coax somethin' like this aboard," he said as if to himself. "What they doin', Hume—shippin' hog-callers now that they got rid of the supers?"

I got sore right away, not knowing kidding when I ran against it. "I don't think I like this guy, Hume," I said, and squared off to this Fuzzy.

Fuzzy said, "Heh! It talks!" But he went over to the lockers and began being busy.

"Don't mind him," Hume told me. "He ain't happy. I was super on this scow, see, and he was tired of working for a living and was after my job. Darn near got it, too—didn't you, Fuzzy?"

Fuzzy grunted.

"Would have, too, only the Council wiped the job off the books. That's the only thing about losing my job I like—it didn't go to a heel like that."

Since Hume seemed to be getting away with talking behind Fuzzy's back to his face that way, I thought I might as well chime in. "What'd he do?"

"Started studying chemistry, of all things! He was all set to prove to the Board that he knew more about my job than I did. As if anyone cared about how much a chem super knew! Anyhow, he's all set to pull his little blitz on me when the job disappears. This scow, being an ore boat and notably ill-equipped, has no apprentice super. I get demoted to wiper; Fuzzy is still a wiper; you're another."

I laughed. Fuzzy swung around. "All right, you mugs. I'll get my chance to show you wise eggs up yet. Some day, that job's going back on the books. When it does, I get it."

"Not a chance," said Hume. "It took the Council three hundred years to get rid of the job. You'll be on a government pension before you ever hear of it again."

Fuzzy opened his mouth to say something else but the loudspeaker cleared its throat and announced the takeoff. The two wipers jumped to their bunks, threw up a lever and lay down. I followed suit; in a few seconds there was a grinding roar and our beds slid on quadrantal rollers up against the bulkhead. There was a moment of crushing weight, and just when I thought I'd never get the strength to draw in another breath, the beds slid back off the bulkhead and were parallel with the floor again. In those days the momentum screens were inoperable inside the Heaviside Layer, and during the few seconds it took to get outside, the acceleration was really rough. They could lay it on thick because it lasted such a short time, but I can tell you, the headache you carried around with you for a couple of hours after starting was one to stand up and sneer at all the other headaches on Earth, laid end to end.

I learned all I had to know about being a wiper within two days after starting. I had a station to keep clean, a few alleyways to sweep, and the 12 to 4 space man to keep entertained. His job was to clean another station, sweep the alleyways I didn't sweep, and entertain me. In the old days, you know, they had an engine room aboard, and a crew to run it; and they had a control room and another crew to run that. The Plotnick-Martin power beams took care of that now. The three space men held lifeboat tickets and the wipers didn't, and that was the crew. They stood watches, two at a time, four hours on and eight off, and then there was a pinheaded individual who used to wander around the alleyways at odd hours doing nothing that I could see. He answered to the title of captain and he carried papers certifying his ability as a stowage expert for this particular ship.

That ship was quite something. There may be a few of them left—bulky old KH-type ore carriers. The series has been discontinued now, but it seems to me I saw one or two of them on the inter-asteroid runs a few years ago. Her capacity was something like two hundred thousand tons net and she was loaded to the ceil-plates with granular magnesium and sodium for the Sun mirrors of Titan. I don't have to tell you about the seven two-mile-diameter orbital mirrors that circulate around the satellite, making it habitable. You may not know, though, that the girders are all solid mag, because great rigidity isn't needed out there, and mag is cheap. The mirrors are silvered with sodium, which is bright and easy to handle. They have a patrol for each of the mirrors, which patches up meteorite punctures when they occur, squirting liquid sodium around the holes until they fill, then shaving them down with N rays. Well, we were bringing them their stock in trade, and it was an interesting cargo to handle. The mag was flaked to facilitate melting and casting, and the sodium was melted on Earth and run right into the holds where it "froze." When we discharged it, we would simply heat up the holds and pump it out. As long as it was loaded in an atmosphere of nitrogen and pumped out in space, there was little danger from it. We had tanks of nitrogen under pressure aboard, because after the sodium solidified in the holds it contracted. The space it left had to be filled with something, and it better not be air or water! Hence the nitrogen.

After a couple of weeks of this kind of life I began to wonder about the stories I had read, and what happened to all the glamour and adventure the space service was steeped in. I even went so far as to ask Hume about it. He thought it was very funny.

"That whiffed out with the power beams," he told me. "There wouldn't be anyone aboard these ships if it weren't for the fact that someone has to keep the chrome clean and the books up to date. Then, of course, there are emergencies."

"What?" I asked hopefully.

"Oh—I dunno. I never heard of any. But just in case some of the machinery turned out not to be foolproof, which has never happened so far, or in case something happened to the ship—"

"But what *could* happen?"

"Well—aw, why worry about it? Nothing ever has. If it did, it would happen so quickly we'd never know about it, or the ship would take care of itself so fast that by the time we realized there was an emergency, it would be past history." He sat down on the mess room table and put his feet on the bench. "Look, kid, I might as well wise you up. This is no kind of a life for a human being. If any of us were worth a damn in any trade at all, we wouldn't be here. If the Board members weren't as worthless as we are, they'd build ships without crew's quarters. If you have any gumption, you'll get off as soon as we get back to Terra, and go back to raising castor beans or whatever else it was you were doing before you shipped aboard this mud hen. If you have no gumption, you'll stay here with the rest of us bums and pray that the world in general and the Space Commerce Board in particular doesn't get hep to what soft, soft cushions a space tradition has shoved under our fat—"

Crash!

It wasn't a loud noise, and it wasn't much of a lurch, but both were so utterly unexpected that both of us found ourselves thrown very hard and very flat.

Hume looked at me blankly. The lights went out, flashed on again as an automatic emergency circuit snapped in. He said in a weak voice, "Well, there's your emergency!" and fainted away.

A voice I had never heard before said sharply, through the speakers, "Emergency! Stand by!" I rightly assumed that this, too, was an automatic alarm. I shook Hume until he sat up.

"What do we do now?" I snapped at him. I rather think I was a little panicky.

"I only work here," he said with a sickly attempt at levity. There were voices in the alleyway outside. We drifted out there. It was the captain and two of the space men.

"How should I know? Who do you think I am—Plotnick?"

"Who's Plotnick?" asked one of the stooges. The fact that Plotnick had invented the power beam that Martin had adapted to interstellar commerce was just another of those things that those guys never got around to learning.

"Plotnick's dead," said the other stooge brightly.

"The captain ain't dead," said the first stooge even more brightly.

"Oh, go on back to bed," said the captain pettishly. "Something happened. I don't know what it was. It'll be fixed when we get to Titan. Pass the word."

There was no necessity for that since the whole crew was there by that time. Those not on watch went back to bed. Yeah—back to bed, in the most desperate emergency any of them were ever destined to live through.

I went on watch two hours later. I hadn't slept very well. Breathing was hard and my heart was racing violently. I dozed fitfully, not realizing what the trouble was until the sting of sweat got into my eyes and I came awake. Just then Fuzzy came in to call me.

"One bell, lug," he said. His usual shirt and dungarees had given way to a pair of underwear shorts, and he, too, was sweating profusely. What jolted me more than anything else was his voice. It had been a deep gas-on-the-stomach bass. Now it was a quavering tenor-baritone.

"Comin' up," I said, and rolled out. We stared at each other curiously. My voice had positively pipsqueaked. He opened his mouth, closed it again and went out. I noticed he was panting.

There was a red light blinking over the door. I'd never noticed it before. Somewhere an alarm siren began wailing. I didn't know what that meant either. I rolled out and headed for the mess room. They were all there. Everyone looked worried except the captain. He just looked unhappy. They were all asking him what had happened, what was happening. I gathered that everyone was having trouble breathing, and I know everyone's voice sounded like a recording speeded up three hundred percent.

It was hot as hell.

Came that throat-clearing sound from the annunciators. Everyone shut up. Here at last was the blessed voice of authority. "Air pressure falling," it said. "All hands into space suits. Look for leaks."

We looked at each other stupidly. No one had the slightest idea where a space suit might be found.

There was a whir and click from the alleyway. Someone looked out and reported, "An impenetron shield's blocked us off from the rest of the crew's quarters, cap."

"My word," said the captain.

"My cigarettes," said Fuzzy.

The captain started forward. We followed because there was nothing else for us to do. When we got to the control room another shield dropped quietly behind us.

"No more mess room," said Fuzzy sadly.

"Yeah. No more eats," said one of the stooges.

"I don't see what's so funny about this," I said. I was scared. I was more scared than I ever even heard of anyone being. I was wishing I was working in the mines instead of this. I was wishing I was home in bed.

"There isn't anything funny about this," said the captain worriedly. He began fumbling a door open. We trailed in.

Thank heavens the captain knew something about the ship. The room was lined with case upon case of supplies—food, weapons, coils of wire, masses of spare apparatus that none of us knew anything about. But we knew cases of food when we saw them. There was even a roomy refrigerator there for storage. Also—eight space suits. Spares.

The captain checked our rush for them. "The air's all right here," he said. "Those automatic gates must have cut off the sections where the leaks were. We'll just have to make ourselves comfortable here."

"Yeah," said one of the stooges. "No beds. Where am *I* gonna sleep?"

There was a babel over that childish question. I drew Hume aside. He was no gem, but he seemed a little more intelligent than the rest of them. "What's this all about?"

He scratched his ear. "I dunno." That seemed to be a reflex with these boys—'I dunno.' "I guess we hit something—or something hit us."

"That would account for the loss of pressure," I said, "but what about the heat?" He began to speak; I stopped him. "*Don't* say, 'I dunno.' Think, for a change!"

It was a new idea for Hume. He turned it over for a minute and then came out with, "Why should I worry about it? The ship can take care of us till we get to Titan, and then the repair crews can worry about it."

"O.K., O.K.," I said, sore. "Go on, worm, spin yourself a cocoon. Me, I'll do my worrying now. That heat isn't coming from just nothing. Seems to me if we were just punctured it'd be getting cold here, not hot. But—you ain't worried. So go ahead. Be happy." I walked away.

He stared after me for a second and then shrugged and started looking for a place to bunk. Twice, out of the corner of my eye, I saw him stop and stare at me. He seemed to be going through pangs of some sort. I had a hunch what it was. The birth of thought. The stirring of an awakening intellect. It isn't surprising. Brains atrophy when they're not used, same as arms or legs. Boy, he was a case.

It got hotter.

I went to the captain about it. He actually seemed to be listening to everything I had to say. He nodded sagely every time I paused for breath. I was a little more than annoyed when I realized that he was nodding because he didn't understand a word of what I was saying. In some kind of desperation I asked him if there was, by any chance, a manual aboard, describing the ship and its equipment. When I had finished he went right on nodding his head, realized I had asked him a direct question, and stopped, not knowing what to do with his little head. Not use it to think with, certainly. He was another. The things that happen in the name of civilization! Some people would call this kind of ship progress. I was calling it poison.

"Yes," he said uncertainly, "there ought to be some such thing around." He began fumbling through the stores. I had to keep on his tail or he'd have forgotten what it was he was looking for. "Don't know what you want it for. Can't imagine. Terribly dull reading," he kept muttering. Suddenly he came across a box of books. He pulled one out, looked at it—the son-of-a-gun could read, apparently—and exclaimed, "Now *here* is something!" He handed it over to me. It was a trilogy of romantic novels.

"What the hell's this for?"

"One of the finest books I ever read," he said, in a let-me-be-a-sister-to-you tone.

I threw it at his head, tipped the books out. The manual was there, all right. It was a thick volume, very efficient-looking. It was. It was streamlined. It consisted of column after column, page after page, of figures and letters and dozens of symbols I'd never heard of. I couldn't understand a letter of it. In the foreword it said something about a key. Apparently there was a twenty- or thirty-volume key somewhere which gave the definitions of all that spaghetti. There was, the captain informed me—in the after magazine.

The after magazine was closed off by those precious automatic gates.

I groaned and took myself and my manual off into a corner. Somewhere in that book must be what I was looking for—instructions on how to proceed when your ship seems to be burning up. I raised my head. Burning up? If something was burning—

But what could be burning? The ship was all steel and impenetron. The cargo—*magnesium. Sodium!*

I almost let out a shout, but I hadn't the heart to disturb all those happy, stupid, unworried drifters. What good would it do them to know what the trouble was? They wouldn't know what to do about it if I did tell them.

No one got in my way as I circulated around the control chambers, staring at the maze of dials and indicators banked around the walls. The ship's designers had had a shot of the interior decorator's virus mixed in with their blood, it seemed to me. There were more damn concealed closets and sliding panels than a dope addict could dream up. It was mostly by accident that I found what I was looking for—a panel studded with tiny centigrade dials, with a monel plate at the top bearing the inscription "Cargo Temperatures."

Now the *Maggie Northern* had seventy-six holds of various sizes. Our cargo was about one-sixth sodium, the rest mag. According to the dials—and there was no reason why they should lie about it—fourteen of the mag holds were at temperatures ranging from nine to eleven hundred-odd degrees. Fourteen of them, all on the starboard bilge. That was all I wanted to know. I called the captain over. He peered owlishly at the dials.

"There's your trouble," I said with the air of a man completing a very complicated card trick. He nodded and looked at me as if he expected me to say something else.

"Well, what's the matter with you?" I roared. "The mag's afire! We hit something—sideswiped it! The frictional heat raised the mag to its kindling temperature; there was a residue of air in the holds; the mag started to burn, softened the bulkheads, and the air pressure from alleyways and living quarters and other holds caved them in and fed more air to the burning mag!"

The captain shook his head in wonderment. "You certainly seem to have doped it out," he said admiringly.

I stared at him, unable to believe my own eyes and ears. "What's the matter with you?" I screamed. By this time the rest of them were gathered around us, looking like a flock of sheep just over the hill from blasting operations. "Radio in to Titan! Find out what to do about it!"

The captain looked about him blankly. "What's the use? The ship's duplicate indicator aboard has already told the Titans all about it. I can't imagine why they haven't already let us hear from them."

"Try it," I gritted.

"Why?" he said.

I plowed into him. I only got a couple of good ones in before Hume and Fuzzy piled on me and held me down. The captain ran into the storeroom and shut the door.

"You shouldn't have done that," said Hume amazedly.

I said something like "Ugh!" and shrugged loose.

Fuzzy's ape face was disgustingly slack. Those guys didn't have the guts God gave a goose.

I went over to what looked to me more like a visiscreen than anything else in the place. There was a switch beside it. I threw it. Nothing happened. "Where's the receiver and transmitter?" I growled.

One of the space men piped up. "That's my station," he said. "Starboard side, down below."

I had another look at the hold-temperature indicators. "Fused solid by this time," I grunted. "You know anything about radio?"

He shook his chowder head. So did everyone else. I felt like crying.

Somebody had to do something. I couldn't—I didn't know anything. If only I had—aw, what's the use! And then it was I had my bright idea. I turned to Hume.

"Listen—didn't you say you were chem controller aboard this ship?"

He nodded.

"Well—come on then—give. We got a fire aboard. Put it out!"

"Me?"

"You."

"Oh." He counted on his fingers in slow motion, which, I gathered, was his substitute for thought. Finally he came out with, "I don't know how."

"You don't know how." I was going to get started on a long diatribe about how he ever got to be a chemical controller when he didn't even know how to put a little fire out—a fire that would have us all well-done and tender a week before what was left of the ship reached Titan. I decided to try to be patient.

"Look," I said gently. "Unless something is done by somebody, and soon, you and you and you are going to be roasted alive in this pig. See? I don't suppose you've noticed it, but it's getting warm in here too, already. Look—Four more holds have gone. O.K. Sit around and tell each other some bedtime stories. Go on. Die. See if anyone cares. Wait until the air gets so hot in here you can't breathe it. Watch your lazy ignorant flesh slough off when it starts to cook. It won't be quick, you know. You'll stay alive a long time. You have plenty to eat, plenty to drink. It'll hurt some, but what do you care? You're too damn comfortable to do anything about it."

The boys looked definitely sober. After a while Fuzzy spoke up. "Come on, Hume—can't you think of something?"

Hume had suddenly become very important to all of them. And I think the guy was really trying to come through. "We could put water on it," he said finally.

"This ain't a house fire, you know," I said.

"So what?"

"So—nothing," I said in my ignorance. "Try it, anyway; try something."

We coaxed the captain out and explained what went on. It was all right with him. Anything was all right with him. He showed us the tank valves and the controls to the hold pipe lines. Luckily they were very plainly labeled. Hume went to work on No. 14 hold. It wasn't as hot as the others, according to the temperature readings. The hottest any of them got was around eleven hundred, for some reason. Fourteen was about eight hundred. That was the mean temperature for the hold; I gathered from that that it was part afire. After a lot of fumbling, Hume got the vents into the tank open and the water turned on. We could spare the water—all those ships stored themselves with a safety factor of five. Council law.

The hold had gotten fifty degrees hotter before Hume got the water in there. As soon as he turned his valve the needle bounced up to about two thousand and quivered there.

"Turn it off!" I squawked. "That mag likes water. It likes it very much. Look at that!" I pointed at the board. The next hold was getting hot.

"Now what?" said Hume worriedly.

Me, I didn't know what to say. Fuzzy saved me the trouble.

"Get out of the way," he spat, suddenly very much alive. "You call yourself a chem super! I wasn't far off when I got the idea I could push you out of that job! Let a man in there." He slammed Hume aside, began to be very busy with the valves. "The set-up's perfect," he said. "What's in a fire extinguisher? Water? No, dope—carbon dioxide. We have fire in an enclosed space—all we have to do to blank it is fill the hold with CO_2! Cap—give me a hand."

I just watched. It sounded all right to me. Hume looked ashamed of himself. The rest of the boys clustered around the temperature gauges.

"Try Hold No. 20," I said.

Fuzzy threw over a lever and turned a valve quickly. There was a new confidence in the way he worked that was like a breath of cool air in the control room. Only there wasn't any cool air in the control room. It was getting hotter. Seven pairs of eyes watched the needle, narrowed as it flickered, widened as it slid over the dial to two thousand plus.

"Cut!" I cried.

There was dead silence. Someone said unnecessarily, "It likes carbon dioxide, too."

"I don't understand it," said the captain. "I've been loading mag on this run for eight years now." He mopped his head. "I know all about it—specific gravity 1.75, boiling point 1100, melting point 632.7. But I guess no one ever thought I'd have to know how to put it out if it started to burn."

"And you never thought to look it up," I said.

He shook his head.

I'd noticed that Hume had been sulking a little too silently in a corner after Fuzzy had shoved him there. He suddenly let out a yip and dove for the valves.

"Now what?" I asked.

"That would-be over there," Hume said, nodding toward Fuzzy, "barked up the wrong stump. I've got it! We're safe! Look—when mag burns—when anything burns—it hooks up with oxygen—right? It burned the oxygen in the air. It burned the oxygen in the water. It burned the oxygen in the CO_2. But there ain't no oxygen in nitrogen!"

I turned it over gleefully, and slapped him on the back. He and the captain got busy hooking up the nitrogen tanks to the hold pipe lines. I called for No. 22. It took a little longer this time, due to Hume's accidentally turning the water valve on instead of off when he had finished turning a whole set of wrong valves, so that the nitrogen, under pressure, backed up into the water tanks. But we got that straightened out and proceeded.

Nothing happened. One of the stooges got hysterical and had to be locked in the storeroom. The needle wavered a little, went down twenty degrees, stayed there. In a few minutes it went up.

"It used up all the nitrogen!" wailed the captain.

Hume said, "Must have combined with it. Damn. That mag sure is hungry." He looked at me as if I were a policeman and he were a little lost boy.

"Don't look at me that way," I said. I glanced at the dials. More than half the mag cargo was either burning or ready to. I had a bright idea. "Dump the cargo!"

The captain spread his hands. "Can't. If the hatches are opened, the automatic relays will break the power beam. The ship can't take off, operate, or anything else with the hatches open."

"Oh." I started walking up and down. I took off my shirt. Everyone else already had. Some had gone further than that. These automatic controls might have some good points, but—boy, oh, boy! when they started working against you!

I whirled on the captain. "What about the lifeboats?"

He looked up hopefully and then shook his head. "There's one forward and one aft. But they're both aft of here; we're right up in the nose now. The impenetron shields have locked us in. There's an escape hatch here, but—no, the lifeboat locks can only be opened from the inside. We couldn't get to the boats if we went out in space suits."

Hume got excited then. "How about those space suits?" he rapped out. "When it gets too hot in here, couldn't we cling to the hull in suits until the ship docks?"

We streamed into the storeroom. On each of the space helmets was a tag describing the air, water and food rations for each suit. Enough for eight days. We wouldn't be in for another two weeks. We went back to the control room and sat down. The stooge who had been locked in came out with us, much chastened. It got hotter.

Four days later we were a sorry-looking lot. No one had spoken for twelve hours. We'd thrown away all our clothing with metal fasteners, all rings, wrist chronometers and radios, because the metal was too hot to bear. The refrigerator in the storeroom had afforded some relief until it broke down. We were in a bad way. And one by one the crew started to crack. Hume began to giggle quietly to himself, on and on and on. Fuzzy lay still like some great hairy animal, panting silently. The captain sat unmoving with an insanely complacent smirk on his excuse for a face. No one dared move or speak because of the agonizing impact of the hot air on their bare flesh when they did so. There was no relief, no help for it. By now the sodium cargo was molten, the mag burning wherever it could find air—and it found air every time it got a bulkhead hot enough to work on it. The bulkheads weren't built for that sort of thing. They could take any kind of hammering when they were fairly cool, but that damn alloy couldn't take it when it got much over a thousand degrees. The hull resisted nicely enough, more's the pity. We'd have been happy to see the mag burn its way through into space.

No one noticed the faint rumbling sound any more, once we had doped it out as merely the opening up of new bulkheads, feeding more air and more mag to the voracious fire. But all of us started weakly at the tremendous shuddering crash that echoed suddenly through the ship. The captain began to laugh crazily. We looked at him numbly.

"She's still working," he whispered hoarsely. "And that finishes us. The ship was getting off balance. The automatic equalizing chutes just opened. All the mag on the port side's open to the fire now." He waved weakly at the temperature board. Every needle on it had begun to climb.

Hume said something that made my flesh creep. "I wish I had the guts to kill myself."

Another two days. The crew sprawled around, asleep or unconscious or dead. I came to for a little while, I remember, because I started coughing weakly. Hume, in a last effort to accomplish something, had opened a water valve he'd discovered in the storeroom, thinking it would cool us off. It puffed into steam where it touched metal, and the air was full of it. Somehow someone else—Fuzzy, I think—managed to turn it off.

Then there was a time when someone began shaking me and shaking me. I didn't see how I could be alive, but I must have been because I felt the heat again. It was Hume. He had lost about thirty pounds. He had a red beard. Red eyes.

"Whassamarrer?"

"The gauges! They're ... they're going down!"

I lay there for a long time, not able to react. He crouched over me, a thin line of moisture creeping out of the corner of his mouth.

"The holds are cooling down!" he said again and began shaking me.

I sat up, blinked at the board. It took quite a while for me to focus my eyes, but when I saw he was right I somehow found the energy to get my feet under me, climb upright.

It was unbelievable, it was past all hope, but it was true! Hume started giggling again, and this time it didn't annoy me because I giggled, too.

"The mag," he said. "You see? Why'n hell didn't we think of that before? Mag's a good conductor. When the ship equalized herself, the rest of the mag smashed down on what was burning, soaked up heat, distributed it so much that it lowered the temperature below kindling point!"

"Throw another log on the fire," I crooned, "an' the fire goes out!" And then the rest of it occurred to me.

"Th' sodium!" I said. "See what happened? It dumped onto the hot mag, vaporized. The vapor conducted the heat to the ship's hull. She's radiating it off! If it wasn't for that, the temperature would just get to a certain point and stay there, and we'd have gotten roasted anyway, fire or no fire!"

We hugged each other gleefully and then started working on the rest of the crew.

"Well, that's all there is to it. We rode in to Titan on the super-efficient wreck. We were all of us more dead than alive, but what the hell—as long as there was life enough left to bring back." The second officer of the new passenger liner stood up and stretched himself.

"So they restored the office of chem super?"

"Yep. But now those boys really know their stuff. Man—you ought to see the examinations they have to pass to get that kind of money for doing nothing! I'd sooner work for pay all along the line than work for nothing trying to learn that much about a job I might flunk out of anyway."

"Just a second," I said. "A couple of things I'd like to know. What happened to Hume and Fuzzy?"

"Both got the jobs they wanted. You'd be surprised how hard they studied their chemistry!"

"Not under those circumstances I wouldn't," I said. "Er ... one thing I don't understand. You said that the ship was thrown off balance when one half of the mag cargo was ignited. How come? Where'd the weight come from?"

The second officer fastened his collar. "Very shrewd of you, my lad. Can you keep something to yourself?"

"I can try."

He sat down again and put his head close. "The *Maggie Northern* didn't put her own fire out. I did."

"*You* did?"

"Yeah. Now wait a minute—don't go giving me credit for it. I turned plumb yellow. I got hysterical. I couldn't stand to see those boys gasping out their lives for days on end. Most of all, I guess, I couldn't stand the idea of dying that way myself. That 'log on the fire' business was my idea. If half the cargo would burn and kill us slowly, I assumed that if the whole cargo burned we'd die fast. I dumped the rest of the cargo on the fire. Maybe some of them saw me, but no one noticed. Well, it turned the trick, and it wasn't the kind of thing I'd bring out at the inquest if nobody else did."

"Completely automatic," I murmured. "I've sure changed my opinion about these useless jobs. You guys can get along swell without brains!"

Poker Face

WE ALL HAD to get up early that morning, and we still hadn't sense enough to get up from around the poker table. We'd called in that funny little guy from the accounting department they called Face to make it a foursome with the three of us. It had been nip and tuck from nine o'clock on—he played a nice game of stud. But tonight there was no one lucky man, and when Harry jokingly bet a nickel on a pair of fours and Delehanty took him up on it, the game degenerated into penny-ante. After a while we forgot whose deal it was and sat around just batting the breeze.

"Screwy game," said Delehanty. "What's the use of squattin' here all this time just to break even? Must be your influence, Face. Never happened before. We generally hand all our money over to Jack after four deals. Hey, Jack?"

I grinned. "The game still owes me plenty, bud," I said. "But I think you're right about Face. I don't know if you noticed, but damn if that winning didn't go right around behind the deal—me, you, Face, Harry, me again. If I won two, everyone else would win two."

Face raised an eyebrow ridge because he hadn't any eyebrows. There wasn't anything particularly remarkable about his features, except that they were absolutely without hair. The others carried an AM stubble, but his face gleamed nakedly, half luminous. He'd been a last choice, but a pretty good one. He said little, watched everyone closely and casually, and seemed like a pretty nice guy. "Noticed that, did you?" he asked. His voice was a very full tenor.

"That's right," said Harry. "How about it, Face? What is this power you have over poker?"

"Oh, just one of those things you pick up," he said.

Delehanty laughed outright. "Listen at that," he said. "He's like the ol' mountain climber who saw a volcano erupting in the range he'd scaled the day before. 'By damn,' he says, 'why can't I be careful where I spit?'"

Everybody laughed but Face. "You think it just happened? Would you like to see it happen again?"

They stopped the hilarity. We looked at him queerly. Harry said, "What's the dope?"

"Play with chips," said Face. "No money, no hard feelings. If you like, I won't touch the cards. Just to make it easy, I'll put it this way. Deal out four hands of stud. Jack'll win the first with three threes. Delehanty next with three fours. Me next with three fives. Harry next with three sixes. Each three-spread will come out hearts, diamonds, clubs, in that order. You, Delehanty, start the deal. Go on—shuffle them all you like."

Delehanty was a little popeyed. "You wouldn't want to make a little bet on that, would you?" he breathed.

"I would not. I don't want to take your money that way. It would be like picking pockets."

"You're bats, Face," I said. "There's so little chance of a shuffled deck coming out that way that you might as well call it impossible."

"Try it," said Face quietly.

Delehanty counted the cards carefully, shuffled at least fifteen times with his very efficient gambler's riffle, and dealt around quickly. The cards flapped down in front of me—a jack face down, a six, and then—three threes; hearts, diamonds, clubs, in that order. Nobody said anything for a long time.

Finally, "Jack's got it," Harry breathed.

"Let me see that deck," snapped Harry. He swept it up, spread it out in his hands. "Seems O.K.," he said slowly, and turned to Face.

"You deal," said Face woodenly.

Harry dealt quickly. I said, "Delehanty's s'posed to be next with three fours—right?" Yeah—right! Three fours lay in front of Delehanty. It was too much—cards shouldn't act that way. Wordlessly I reached for the cards, gathered them up, pitched them back over my shoulder. "Break out a new deck," I said. "Your deal, Face."

"Let Delehanty deal for me," said Face.

Delehanty dealt again, clumsily this time, for his hands trembled.

That didn't matter—there were still three fives smiling up at Face when he was through.

"Your deal," whispered Harry to me, and turned half away from the table.

I took up the cards. I spent three solid minutes shuffling them. I had Harry cut them and then cut them again myself and then passed them to Delehanty for another cut. I dealt four hands, and Harry's was the winning hand, with three sixes—hearts, diamonds, clubs.

Delehanty's eyes were almost as big now as his ears. He said, "Heaven. All. Might. Tea." and rested his chin in his hands. I thought he was going to cry or something.

"Well?" said Face.

"Were we playing poker with this guy?" Harry asked no one in particular.

When, by a great deal of hard searching, I found my voice again, I asked Face, "Hey, do you do that any time you feel like it, or does it come over you at odd moments?"

Face laughed. "Any time," he said. "Want to see a really pretty one? Shuffle and deal out thirteen cards to each of us, face down. Then look them over."

I gave him a long look and began to shuffle. Then I dealt. I think we were all a little afraid to pick up our cards. I know that when I looked at mine I felt as if someone had belted me in the teeth with a night stick. I had thirteen cards, and they were all spades. I looked around the table. Delehanty had diamonds. Face had hearts. Harry had clubs.

You could have heard a bedbug sneeze in the room until Harry began saying, "Ah, no. Ah, no. Ah, no," quietly, over and over, as if he were trying to tell himself something.

"Can they all do things like that where you come from?" I asked, and Face nodded brightly.

"Can everyone walk where you come from?" he returned. "Or see, or hear, or think? Sure."

"Just where do you come from?" asked Harry.

"I don't know," said Face. " I only know how I came and I couldn't explain it to you."

"Why not?"

"How could you explain an internal-combustion engine to an Australian bushman?"

"You might try," said Delehanty, piqued. "We's pretty smart bushmen, we is."

"Yeah," I chimed in. "I'm willing to allow you the brains to do those card tricks of yours; you ought to have enough savvy to put over an idea or two."

"Oh—the cards. That was easy enough. I felt the cards as you shuffled them."

"You felt with my fingers?"

"That's right. Want proof? Jack, your head is itching a little on the right side, near the top, and you're too lazy to scratch it just yet. Harry's got a nail pushing into the third toe of his right foot—not very bad, but it's there. Well, what do you say?"

He was right. I scratched. Harry shuffled his feet and said, "O.K., but what has that got to do with arranging the cards that way? Suppose you did feel them with our hands—then what?"

Face put his elbows on the table. "As for arranging the cards, that was done in the shuffle. You grasp half of the deck in each hand, bend them, let them flip out from under your thumbs. If you can control the pressure of each thumb carefully enough, you can make the right cards fall into the right places. You all shuffled at least four times; that made it that much easier for me."

Delehanty was popeyed again. "How did you know which cards were supposed to go in which places?"

"Memorized their order, of course," said Face. "I've seen that done in theaters even by men like you."

"So've I," said Harry. "But you still haven't told us how you arranged the deal. If you'd done the shuffling I could see it, but—"

"But I *did* do the shuffling," said Face. "I controlled the pressure of your thumbs."

"How about the cuts?" Delehanty put in, finding that at last we had him on the run. "When Jack dealt he handed the pack to Harry and me both to be cut."

"I not only controlled those cuts," said Face calmly, "but I made you do it."

"Go way," said Delehanty aggressively. "Don't give us that. How're you going to make a man do anything you like?"

"Skeptical animal, aren't you?" grinned Face; and Delehanty rose slowly, walked around the table, caught Harry by the shoulders and kissed him on both cheeks. Harry almost fell off his chair. Delehanty stood there rockily, his eyes positively bulging. Suddenly he expectorated with great violence. "What the dirty so and forth made me do that?" he wanted to know.

"Chummy, ain't you?" grinned Harry through his surprise.

Face said, "Satisfied, Delehanty?"

Delehanty whirled on him. "Why you little—" His fury switched off like a light going out. "Right again, Face." He went over and sat down. I never saw that Irishman back down like that before.

"You made him do that?" I asked.

Face regarded me gravely. "You doubt it?"

We locked glances for a moment, and then my feet gathered under me. I had a perverse desire to get on all fours and bark like a dog. It seemed the most natural thing in the world. I said quickly, "Not at all, Face, not at all!" My feet relaxed.

"You're the damnedest fellow I ever saw," said Harry. "What kind of a man are you, anyway?"

"Just a plain ordinary man with a job," said Face, and looked at Delehanty.

"So am I," said Harry, "but I can't make cards sit up and type-write, or big, dumb Irishers snuggle up to their fellow-men."

"Don't let that bother you," said Face. "I told you before—there's nothing more remarkable in that than there is in walking, or seeing, or hearing. I was born with it, that's all."

"You said everyone was, where you come from," Harry reminded him. "Now spill it. Just where did you come from?"

"Geographically," said Face, "not very far from here. Chronologically, a hell of a way."

Harry looked over my way blankly. "Now what does all that mean?"

"As near as I can figure out," said Face, "it means just what I said.

I come from right around here—fifty miles, maybe—but the place I came from is thirty-odd thousand years away."

"Years *away?*" I asked, by this time incapable of being surprised. "You mean 'ago,' don't you?"

"Away," repeated Face. "I came along duration, not through time itself."

"Sounds very nice," murmured Delehanty to a royal flush he had thumbed out for himself.

Face laughed. "Duration isn't time—it parallels it. Duration is a dimension. A dimension is essentially a measurement along a plane of existence. By that I mean that any given object has four dimensions, and they extend finitely, along four planes—length, width, height, duration. The last is no different from the others; nor is it any less tangible. You simply take it for granted.

"When you're ordering a piece of lumber, for instance, you name its measurements. You say you want a two by six, twelve feet long. You don't order its duration; you simply take it for granted it will extend long enough in that dimension to suit your needs. You would build better if you measured it as carefully as you do the others, but your life span is too short for you to care that much."

"I think I can savvy that," said Harry, who had been following carefully, "but what do you mean by saying that you came 'along' duration?"

"Again, just what I said. You can't move without moving along the plane of dimension. If you walk down the street, you move along its length. If you go up in an elevator, you move along its height. I came along duration."

"You mean you projected yourself into the fourth dimension?" asked Henry.

"No!" said Face violently, and snorted. "I told you—duration is a dimension, not another set of dimensions. Can you project yourself into length, or height, or into any one dimension? Of course not! The four are interdependent. That fourth-dimension stuff you read is poppycock. There's no mystery about the fourth dimension. It isn't an impalpable word. It's a basis of measurement."

I said, "What's this business of your traveling along it?"

Face spread out his hands. "As I said before, duration is finite. Suppose you wanted to walk from Third Street to Fifth Street. First you'd locate a sidewalk that would take you in the direction you were going. You'd follow that until it ended. Then you'd locate one that would take you to your destination. Where the one stopped and the other started is Fourth Street. Now if you want to go twenty blocks instead of two, you simply repeat that process until you get where you're going.

"Traveling along duration is exactly the same thing. Just as you enter a street at a certain point in its length, so you encounter an object on the street at a certain point in its duration. Maybe it's near the beginning, maybe near the end. You follow it along that dimension—you don't project yourself into it. All objects have two terminations in duration—inception and destruction. You travel along an object's duration until it ceases to exist because you have reached the end of it—or the beginning. Then you proceed to find another object so that you may continue in the same direction, exactly as you proceeded to find yourself another sidewalk in your little trek across town."

"I'll be damned," said Delehanty, "I can understand it!"

"Me, too," Harry said. "That much of it. But exactly how do you travel along duration? I can get the idea of walking beside a building's length, for instance, but I can't see myself walking along beside ... er ... how long it lasted, if you see what I mean. Or do I see what I mean?"

"Now you're getting to something that may be a little tough to explain," said Face. "You have few expressions in your language that could cover it. About the clearest way for me to put it is this: My ability to travel in that particular direction is the result of my ability to perceive it. If you could only perceive two dimensions, length and breadth, you would be completely in the dark about the source of an object which dropped on you from above. If you couldn't sense the distance from here to the door—if you didn't know the door existed, nor the distance to it, you wouldn't be able to make the trip. I can see along duration as readily as you can see up and down a road. I can move along it equally readily."

"Do you stay in one place while you travel duration?" I asked suddenly.

"I can. I don't have to, though. You can go forward and upward while you curve to the left, can't you? Mix 'em any way you like."

Harry piped up. "You say you came thirty thousand years. How is that possible? You don't look as if you're much older than I am."

"I'm not," said Face, "in point of years existed. That is, I didn't live those years. I—passed them."

"How long did it take you?"

Face smiled. "Your question is ridiculous, Harry. 'How long' is a durational term. It involves passage of time, which is a convenient falsehood. Time is static, objects mobile. I can't explain a true state of affairs from the basis of a false conception."

Harry shut up. I asked him something that had been bothering me. "Where did you come from, Face, and—why?"

He looked at me deeply, that eyebrow ridge rising a trifle. "I came—I was sent. I came because I was qualified for the job. I was sent because—well, someone had to be sent, to restore the balance of the city."

"What city?"

"I don't know. It had a name, I suppose, but it was forgotten. Do you name your toothbrush, or your bed sheets, or anything else that has been nearly part of you all your life? No one ever left the city, no one ever arrived at it. There were other cities, but no one cared about them, where they were, who their people were and what they were like, and so on. There was no need to know. The city was independent and utterly self-sufficient. It was the ultimate government. It was not a democracy, for each individual was subjugated entirely to the city. But it was not a dictatorship as you know the term, for it had no dictators. It had no governing body, as a matter of fact. It didn't need one. It had no laws but those of habit and custom. It ran smoothly because all of its internal frictions had been worn smooth by the action of centuries. It was an anarchistic society in the true sense of anarchism—society without need of government."

"That's an impossibility," said Harry, who had a reputation as a minor barroom sociologist.

"I came from that city," Face reminded him gently. "Why is it impossible? You must take certain things into account before you make such rash statements. Your human nature is against such an organization. Your people would be like lost sheep—possibly like lost wolverines—under such a set-up. But my people were not like that—not after centuries of breeding for the most desirable traits, living circumscribed ways of life, thinking stereotyped thoughts. Imagine it if you can.

"Now the city was divided into two halves, like the halves of a great brain. For every death there was a birth; for every loss there was a gain or an equal loss on the other side. The equation was kept balanced, the scales level. The city was permanent, inexorable, immortal and static."

"What did they do with their spare time?" asked Harry.

"They lay in their cubicles until they were needed."

"Were there no theaters, ball games—nothing like that?" asked Delehanty.

Face shook his head. "Amusement is for the relaxation of an imperfect mind," he said. "A mind that has been trained to do one thing and one thing only needs no stimulation or change of pace."

"Why was the city so big?" asked Harry. "Good gosh, a civilization like that doesn't *mean* anything. Why didn't it simply degenerate into the machines that ruled it? Why keep all those humans if they must live like machines?"

Face shrugged. "When the city was instituted, there was a population of that size to allow for. Then, it had a rigid human government, and there was crime and punishment and pain and happiness. They were disposed of in a few generations—they were not logical, you see, and the city was designed on the philosophy that what is not logical is also not necessary. By that time the city was too steeped in its own traditions, there was no one left to make such a radical change as to cut down on the population. The city could care for that many—likewise it could not exist as it was unless it did care for that many. Many human offices were disposed of as they became unnecessary and automatic. One of these was that of controller of population. The machines took care of that—they and the unbreakable customs."

"Hell!" said Delehanty explosively. "I wouldn't go for that. Why didn't the people push the whole thing over and get some fun out of life?"

"They didn't want it!" said Face, as if he were repeating a self-evident fact, and was surprised that he had to. "They had never had that sort of life; they never heard or read or saw anything of the sort. They had no more desire to do things like that than you have to play pattycake! They weren't constituted to enjoy it."

"You still haven't told us why you left the place," I reminded him.

"I was coming to that. In the city there was a necessity for the pursuance of certain knowledges, as a safety measure against the time when one or another of the machines might need rebuilding by a man who understood them.

"One of these men was an antiquarian named Hark Vegas, which is really not a name at all but a combination of sounds indicating a number. His field was history—the development of all about him, from its earliest recorded mythologies and beyond that to its most logical sources. In the interests of the city, he so applied himself to his work that he uncovered certain imponderables—historical trends which were neither logical nor in harmony with the records. They were of no importance, perhaps, but their existence interfered with the perfection of his understanding. The only way he could untangle these unimportant matters was to investigate them personally. And so—that is what he did.

"He waited until his successor was thoroughly trained, so that in any eventuality the city would not be left without an antiquarian for more than a very little while, and he studied carefully the records of the city's customs. These forbade any citizen's leaving the city, and carefully described the boundaries thereof. They were so very old, however, that they neglected to stipulate the boundaries along the duration dimension, since duration perception was a development of only the past four or five thousand years. As an antiquarian, Hark Vegas was familiar with the technique. He moved himself out along the duration of a metallic fragment and thus disappeared from the city.

"Now this unheard-of happening disturbed the timeless balance of the city, for Hark Vegas was no longer to be found. Within seconds of his disappearance, news of it had reached the other half of the city, and the group of specialists there.

"The matter involved me immediately for several reasons. In the first place, my field was—damn it, there's no word for it in your language yet. It's a mental science and has to do with time perceptions. At any rate, I was the only one whose field enabled him to reason where Hark Vegas had gone. Secondly, Hark Vegas was my contemporary in the other half of the city. We would both be replaced within a week, but during that week there would be one too many in my half of the city, one too few in his—an intolerable, absolutely unprecedented state of affairs. There was only one thing to do, since I was qualified, and that was to find him and bring him back. My leaving would restore the balance; if I were successful in finding him, our return would not disturb it. It was the only thing to do, for the status quo had to be maintained at all costs. I acquired a piece of the metal he had used—an easy thing to do, since everything in the city was catalogued—and came away."

Face paused to light a cigarette. The man smoked, I noticed, with more sheer enjoyment than anyone I had ever met.

"Well," said Harry impatiently, "did you find him?"

Face leaned back in a cloud of blue smoke and stared dreamily at the ceiling. "No," he said, "And I'll tell you why.

"I ran into a characteristic of dimensions that was so utterly simple that it had all but escaped me. Let me give you an example. How many sides has a cube?"

"Six," said Harry promptly.

Face nodded. "Exactly. Excluding the duration dimension, the cube is a three-dimensional body and has six sides. There are *two* sides as manifestations of each dimension. I think I overlooked that. You see, there are four dimensions, but eight—*directions!*"

He paused, while the three of us knotted our brows over the conception. "Right and left," he said. "Up and down. Forward and backward—and 'beginningwards' and 'endwards'—the two directions in the duration dimension!"

Delehanty raised his head slowly. "You mean you—didn't know which *way* to go?"

"Precisely. I entered the durational field and struck off blindly in the wrong direction! I went as far as I reasoned Hark Vegas had gone, and then stopped to look around. I found myself in such a bewildering, uproarious, chaotic world that I simply hadn't the mental equipment to cope with it. I had to retreat into a deserted place and develop it. I came into your world—here, about eight years ago. And when I had begun to get the ways of this world, I came out of hiding and began my search. It ended almost as soon as it had begun, for I stopped searching!

"Do you know what happened to me? Do you realize that never before had I seen color, or movement, or argument, or love, hate, noise, confusion, growth, death, laughter? Can you imagine my delighted first glimpses of a street fight, a traffic jam, a factory strike? I should have been horrified, perhaps—but never had I seen such beautiful marvels, such superb and profound and moving happenings. I threw myself into it. I became one of you. I became an accountant, throttling down what powers I alone of all this earth possess, striving for life as a man on an equal footing with the rest of men. You can't know my joy and my delight! I make a mistake in my entries, and the city—this city, does not care or suffer for it, but brawls on unheeding. My responsibilities are to myself alone, and I defy my cast-steel customs and laugh doing it. I'm living here, you see? Living! Go back? Hah!"

"Colors," I murmured. "Noise, and happy filth, and sorrows and screams. So they got you—*too!*"

Face's smile grew slowly and then flashed away. He stared at me like some alabaster-faced statue for nearly a full minute, and then the agile tendrils of his mind whipped out and encountered mine. We clutched each other thus, and the aura of our own forces around us struck two men dumb.

"Hark Vegas," he said woodenly.

I nodded.

He straightened, drew a deep breath, threw back his head and laughed. "This colossal joke," he said, wiping his eyes, "was thirty-eight thousand years in the making. Pleased to meet you—Jack."

We left then. Harry and Delehanty can't remember anything but a poker game.

Nightmare Island

THE GOVERNOR TOOK a sight between two leaves of carefully imported mint, lining the green notch up with the corner of the bamboo verandah and the bowed figure of the man on the beach. He was silent so long that his guest became restless, missing the easy drone of the governor's voice. That was the only thing to do, he thought, watching the old man pressing the cool glass against his cheek, peering through the leaves at the beachcomber; the only thing a man could do in this dreary, brilliant group of little islands—you could only talk. If you didn't keep a conversation going, you thought of the heat and surf-etched silences, and the weary rattle of palm fronds, and that brought you back to the heat again. God, he thought suddenly, the governor dresses for dinner in this heat, every last damn day.

"Poor crazy devil," muttered the governor.

His American visitor asked, "Who?"

The governor gestured with his glass toward the sea and the beachcomber, and then sipped.

The American swiveled and stared. The beachcomber stood dejectedly with the surf tumbling about his knees, and the sun was sinking so rapidly that his shadow crept and crawled along the beach like something with a life of its own. A trick of the light seemed to make the man's flesh transparent for a split second, and it appeared to the American that the man was a broad-shouldered skeleton standing there staring out to sea. A slight shift of shades showed him up again for what he was, the thin husk of a man, sharp-boned, stringy.

The American grunted and turned back toward his host. "What's the matter with him?"

The governor said, "Him? He just doesn't give a damn any more. He lost something and he can't—I can't let him—get it back."

"What did he lose?"

The governor regarded him gravely. "You're a businessman. You deal in dollars and cents and tons— You wouldn't believe me if I told you, and you might not let me finish."

The American opened his mouth to protest, but the governor held up his hand and said, "Listen to that."

The beachcomber's cracked wail drifted out over the cluttered beach and the whispering surf. "Ahniroo!" he cried. "Ahni- Ahniroo!" Then for a long while he was silent, and it grew darker. Just as the sleepy sun pulled the blanket of horizon over its head, they saw the beachcomber's shoulders slump. He turned and walked up the beach.

The American squinted at him. "I take it he isn't as crazy as he looks?"

The governor shook his head. "You can put it that way."

The American settled himself more comfortably. He didn't care about the 'comber particularly, or the governor either, for that matter. But he had to stay here another forty-eight hours, and there would be nothing to do until the mail steamer came except to sit and talk with the old boy. The man seemed to have at least one good yarn to tell, which was promising.

"Come on—give," he grinned. "I'll take your word for it. Don't forget, I'm not used to this kind of country, or the funny business that goes on in it. Who is he, anyhow? And why is he calling out over the water? Gives me the creeps. Who's Ahniroo—or what is it?"

The governor leaned back and looked up at a spider that would probably drop down someone's collar before the evening was over, and he said nothing for quite a while. Then he began:

Ahniroo was a . . . a friend of the fellow's. I doubt that any man has had a friend like that. As far as the man himself is concerned—yes, you may be right. Perhaps he isn't quite all there. But after what he went through, the surprising thing is that he can talk fairly sensibly. Of course, he's peculiar there, too—all he'll talk about is Ahniroo, but he does it quite rationally.

He was a seaman, much like any other seaman. He had relatives ashore and was going to marry one of these years, perhaps; and there was a visit to the place where he was born, some day, when he could walk into the town with a hundred-dollar bill in every pocket of a new suit. Like other seamen he saved his money and spent it and lost it and had it stolen from him, and like some other seamen he drank.

Being on the beach really started the whole thing for him. A sailor's unemployment is unlike any other kind, in that it is so little dependent on the man's whereabouts. A silk mill worker must starve around a silk mill before he can get his job, but a seaman can starve anywhere. If he is a real seaman, he is a painter and a general handyman, a stevedore and roustabout. Chances are that he can drive a truck or play a little music or can turn his hand at any of a thousand semiskilled trades. He may not know where he will eat next, but he can always find a bit of drink to warm him or cool him as the weather dictates. But Barry—our beachcomber over there—didn't care much for eating, and didn't do much of it for quite a while, except when it was forced on him. He concentrated on the drinking, and the more he drank the more reasons he found for drinking, until he couldn't walk or sleep or work or travel or stay still without a little snort or two as a persuader. Not so good. He lost a lot of jobs ashore and afloat. When he had a job he'd guzzle to celebrate, and when he lost one he'd guzzle to console himself. You can imagine what happened.

It hit him in a small town on the Florida coast. He had just been fired from a little four-thousand ton freighter that ran coastwise and found that stopping in such half-forgotten whistle stops paid expenses. It was on the North American continent, but aside from that it hardly differed from these islands. It was hot and humid and a long, long way from anywhere else.

And Barry found himself sitting on the edge of a wooden sidewalk with his feet and his soul in the gutter, with no money and no job and no food in his stomach. He felt pretty good, being just halfway between a binge and a hangover. He stared for twenty minutes at a painted stone in the dusty road, just because his eyes happened to be directed that way. And before long a scorpion crept out from behind the stone and stood looking at him.

It was like no other scorpion he had ever seen. It was no larger than any other, and the same dark color, but instead of the formidable pincers, it had *arms*. They were tiny and perfect and pink and soft, and had delicate hands and little diamond specks of fingernails. And—oh, yes, no joints, apparently. They were as sinuous as an elephant's trunk. It was such an unheard-of thing to see that Barry stared at it for a long moment before he let himself believe what he had seen. Then he shook himself, shrugged drunkenly, and said:

"I'll be damned!" And then, addressing the strange scorpion, "Hi!"

The scorpion waved one of its perfect, impossible arms, and said, "You will be!" and then, "Hi yourself."

Barry started so violently that he came to his feet. The liquor he had been sopping seemed to have collected in his knees; at any rate, those members were quite liquid and buckled under him, so that he fell on his face. He remembered the scorpion scuttling away, and then his forehead struck the painted stone and the lights went out for him.

Barry had been a strong man, but after two years of nursing from flat bottles, you wouldn't have known it. He was no beauty. He had a long leather face and purple nose. His eyes were nearly as red as their lids, and his broad shoulders were built of toothpicks and parchment. Skin that had been taut with the solid muscle under it was now loose and dry, and fitted him as badly as the clothes he wore. He was a big fellow—six foot three at least, and he weighed all of a hundred and twenty-seven pounds.

The scorpion was the start of it, and the crack on the skull brought it on full strength. That's right—the horrors. The good old creeping, crawling horrors. When he came to and hauled his ragged body back up to the sidewalk, he found himself in a new world, horribly peopled by things he couldn't understand. There were soft white wriggling things—a carpet of them under his feet. Standing at bay in the doorway of a general store down the street was a gryphon, complete with flaming breath, horns and tail, frighteningly real, lifted bodily from an old book that had frightened him when he was a child. He heard a monstrous rustle over his head, and there was a real life prototype of Alice-in-Wonderland's buck-toothed Jabberwock, and it was out to get him. He shrieked and tried to run, and fell choking and splattering into the Slough of Despond from "Pilgrim's Progress." There was someone else in there with him—a scantily clad girl on skis from the front cover of a Paris magazine. She laughed and turned into a six-legged winged snake which bit at him viciously and vanished. He scrambled to his feet and plunged sobbing down the dusty road, and people on the sidewalks turned and stared and said, "Crazy with th' heat," and went on about their business, for heat madness was common among beached sailors in that country in August.

Barry staggered on out of town, which wasn't very far, and out among the sand dunes and scrub and saw grass. He began to see things that he could not describe, devils and huge spiders and insects. In the angry blaze of the sun he slumped to his knees, sobbing, and then something clicked in his mind and he collapsed from sheer psychic exhaustion.

It was night, and very cool, when he woke again. There was half a moon and a billion stars, and the desertlike dunes were all black velvet and silver. The black and the gleam were crowded with strange life, but it was worse now than it had been in the daytime, because now he could feel what he couldn't see. He *knew* that twenty feet away from him stood a great foul buzzard that stared steadily at him, and yet he could not see it. It was more than a fearsome sensation that the thing was there; he could feel each feather, every wrinkle of the crested, wattled neck, each calloused serration on its dry yellow legs. As he stared tremblingly into the mounding distances, he felt the grate of a bison's hoof as it eyed him redly, ready to charge. The sound of a wolf's teeth impacted on his skin rather than his eardrums, and he felt its rough tongue on its black lips. He screamed and ran toward the town, guided by his omnipresent seaman's instinct, dodging and zigzagging among the silver dunes. Oh yes—he had 'em. He had the horrors really thoroughly.

He reached town about eleven at night. He was pretty much of a mess—covered with grime, cut and bruised and sick. Someone saw him leaning rockily against the sun-dried wall of a gin mill, trying to revive himself with the faint clinking of glasses and the fainter odor of liquor that drifted from inside. Someone else said, "Look at the hulk; let's feed him a drink." It was a lucky break for Barry; with his metabolism in the pickled state it was, he would most certainly have dropped dead if he had not had that snifter.

They led him in and gave him a couple more, and his garbled mutterings were amusing to them for a time, but after a while they went home and left him cluttering up a round table with his spent body.

Closing time—which meant the time when there was no one left around to buy a nickel beer—came, and the bartender, a misplaced Louisiana Cajun, came over to throw the sailor out. There was no one else in the place but a couple of rats and some flies. One of the rats had only two legs and wore a collar and tie even in that heat. The other rat had some self-respect and scuttled under the beer pulls to lap suds, being a true quadruped with inherited rat reflexes.

The two-legged rat's name was Zilio. He was a small oily creature with swarthy skin, a hooked nose supported by a small mustache, an ingratiating manner and a devious way of making a living. His attention was attracted toward Barry by the barkeep's purposeful approach. Zilio slid off his stool and said:

"Hold it, Pierre; I'm buying for the gentleman. Pour a punch."

The name did not refer to the ingredients of the drink but to its effect. The barkeep shrugged and went back to his bar, where he poured a double drink of cheap whiskey, adding two drops of clear liquid from a small bottle, this being the way to mix a Zilio punch.

Zilio took it from him and carried it over to Barry. He set it on the table in front of the seaman, drew up a chair and sat close to him, his arm on Barry's shoulder.

"Drink up, old man," he said in an affected accent. He shook Barry gently, and the sailor raised his head groggily. "Go on," urged Zilio.

Barry picked up the glass, shaking and slopping, and sipped because he had not energy for a gulp.

"You're a sailor, eh?" murmured Zilio.

Barry shook his head and reared back to try to focus his disobedient eyes on the oily man. "Yeah, an' a damn good one."

"Union member?"

"What's it to you?" asked Barry belligerently, and Zilio pushed the glass a little closer. Barry realized that the smooth, swarthy character was buying a drink, and promptly loosened up. "Yeah; I belong to the union." He picked up the glass.

"Good!" said Zilio. "Drink up!"

Barry did. The raw liquid slid down his throat, looped around and smashed him on the back of the neck. He sank tinglingly into unconsciousness. Zilio watched him for a moment, smiling.

Pierre said, "What are you going to do with that broken down piece o' tar?"

Zilio began to search Barry's pockets diligently. "If I can find what I'm looking for," he said, "this broken down piece of tar is going to be removed from the rolls of the unemployed." Another minute's searching uncovered Barry's seaman's papers. "Ah—able seaman—quartermaster—wiper and messman. He'll do." He stood back and wiped his hands on a large white handkerchief. "Pierre, get a couple of the boys and have this thing brought down to my dock."

Pierre grunted and went out, returning in a few minutes with a couple of fishermen. Without a word they picked up the unconscious Barry and carried him out to a disreputable old flivver, which groaned its way out of sight down the dusty road.

Zilio said, "'Night, Pierre." He handed the bartender two clean dollar bills for his part in the shanghai, and left.

When Barry swam up out of the effects of Pierre's Mickey Finn, he found himself in all too familiar surroundings. He didn't have to open his eyes; his nose and sense of touch told him where he was. He was lying in a narrow bed, and the sparse springs beneath him vibrated constantly. His right side felt heavier than his left, and he rolled a little that way, and then the weight shifted and he rolled back. He groaned. How did he ever get working again?

He opened his eyes at last, to see what kind of a box it was that he had shipped out on. He saw a dimly lit fo'c's'le with six bunks in it, only one of which was occupied. The place was filthy, littered with empty beer cans, dirty socks, a couple of pairs of dungarees, wrapping paper from laundry parcels, and cigarette butts—the usual mess of a merchant ship's crew's quarters when leaving port. He closed his eyes and shook his head violently to rid himself of this impossible vision—he didn't remember catching a ship, *knew* he was on the beach, and was good and sick of seeing things he could not believe. So—he closed his eyes and shook his head to clear it, and when he did that he groaned in agony at the pain that shot through it. Oooh—that must have been a party. Wow! He lay very still until the pain subsided, and then cautiously opened his eyes again. He was still in a ship's fo'c's'le.

"Hey!" he called weakly.

The figure on the lower bunk opposite started, and a man pushed his head into the light that trickled in from the alleyway.

"Hey, where am I? Eh—when is this?"

Apparently the man could make sense out of the vague question. "Tuesday," he said. That meant nothing to Barry. "Ye're aboard th' *Jesse Hanck*. Black oil. Far East."

Barry lay back. "Oh," he moaned.

The Hanck ships were famous—or was it notorious? They were old Fore River ships, well-deck tankers. They were dirty and unseaworthy, and they were hungry ships and paid ordinary seaman's wages to their petty officers, grading it on down from there. Twenty-eight lousy dollars a month. No overtime. Eighty-six-day runs.

Barry got up one elbow and said half to himself, "What did I do—*ask* for this job?"

The other man rolled out and sat on the edge of his bunk, putting on a tankerman's safety shoes. "Damfino. Did you ever meet a guy called Zilio?"

"Ah— Yeah."

The man nodded. "There you are then, shipmate. He gave you a drink. You passed out. You wake up aboard this oil can. That's Zilio's business."

"Why the dirty—I'm a union member! I'll tie this ship up! I'll have her struck! I'll report her to the Maritime Commission! I'll—"

The other man rose and came across the fo'c's'le to lean his elbows on Barry's bunk and breathe his gingivitis into Barry's face. "You'll do your work and shut up. When you sober up enough to look around, you'll find out you're sailing without seaman's papers. If you're a good boy and play along with the seahorse that calls himself a chief mate, you'll get them back. Step off the straight and narrow and you'll be beached somewhere without your livin'. An' listen—better dry up with that union talk. You got picked up by a fink-herder and shipped on a fink ship. They don't go for that around here, that fellow-worker stuff."

"Yeah?" Barry swung his feet over the side of the bunk and had to clutch his pounding head. "I'll jump ship in Panama! We got to go through the canal!"

"Ain't nobody jumpin' no ship in Panama nowadays, friend. They'll send out a fifth-colyum alarm fer you from the ship an' you'll spend somethin' like fifty years in a military bastille. Besides—time you get to Colon you won't want to be jumpin' ship. Better cool off now. G'wan back to sleep. I got the eight to twelve. You got the twelve to four."

So Barry went back to work again. He spent his days and nights in the utmost misery. The packing around the posthole beside his bunk had kicked out some years ago, and every time the weather got a little drafty, his bunk shipped water. The food was atrocious, and the crew was composed of bootblacks, kids on vacation, ex-tenant farmers, and one or two bonafide seamen like himself, either outright finks or shanghaied wrecks. But all of this didn't stack up to his horrors. They persisted and they grew.

It isn't often a man gets them that badly, but then it isn't often that a man lets himself get into the state that Barry was in. He walked in a narrowing circle of ravenous beasts. When he slept he dreamed horrible dreams, and when he lay awake he could feel tiny, cold, wet feet crawling over his body. He was afraid to stand a lookout watch by himself, and the mate had to batten down his ears for him before he would go out to the fo'c's'le head at night. He was dead sure that there was something horrible hiding in the anchor engine, ready to leap out at him and wrap him up in the anchor cables. He was just as afraid to be in a roomful of men, because, to his sodden eyes, their faces kept running together fluidly, assuming the most terrifying shapes. So he spent his hours off watch hovering in the outskirts of smaller groups of men, making them nervous, causing them to call him Haunt and Jonah.

He found out what the eight-to-twelve man had meant when he'd said that Barry wouldn't feel like jumping ship in Panama. A day before they made the canal, those who might make trouble were called to the second mate's room, each secretly, and fed rotgut liquor. They hadn't learned—not one of them. It was a Mickey again. When they came to, they were in the Pacific.

The *Jesse Hanck* steamed well out of the usual steamer lanes. The Hanck fleet were charter boats, and they saw to it that they were always behind schedule sufficiently to enable the captains to pad the fuel and store consumption accounts enough so that pockets were lined all around, except for those of the crews. A thoroughly rotten outfit. At any rate, Barry had his little accident eight days out of the canal.

The ship was shuffling along somewhere on the tenth meridian, and it was hot. It was one of those evenings when a man puts clothes on to soak up perspiration and rips them off thirty seconds later because he can't stand the heat of them; when sleeping on deck is just as bad.

The men bunked all over the place, throwing mattresses down on the after boatdeck, swinging hammocks from the midship rigging, crawling under the messroom tables, which were out on the poop now—sleeping anywhere and everywhere in impossible attempts to escape the cruel heat. Calling the watch was a hit-or-miss proposition; you might find your relief and then again you might wake the wrong man from a rare snatch of real sleep and get yourself roughed up for your mistake.

Barry came off watch at four that morning. He turned in somewhere back aft. He never got up for breakfast anyway, and when the eight-to-twelve ordinary seaman tried to call him for lunch at eleven-thirty, he couldn't be found. It was one-thirty before the bos'n missed him. Sometime between four in the morning and one in the afternoon, then, Barry had left the ship.

It gave all hands something to talk about for a couple of days. The captain wrote up a "lost at sea" item in the log and pocketed Barry's wages. An ordinary seaman was given Barry's duties with no increase in pay. Barry was forgotten. Who cared, anyway? Nobody liked him. He wasn't worth a damn. He couldn't steer. He couldn't paint. He was a lousy lookout.

Barry himself always gets that part of his story garbled. How a man trained at sea, capable in any emergency of looking out for his own skin, no matter what the weather or his state of sobriety, could possible *fall* off a ship at sea is beyond understanding. I don't believe he did. I think he jumped off. Not because of the way he was being treated aboard that slave ship; he hadn't self-respect enough left for that. It must have been his horrors; at any rate, that, according to him, is the last thing he remembers happening to him aboard the *Jesse Hanck*.

He had just drifted off to sleep, when he was aroused by some shipboard noise—the boilers popping off, perhaps, or a roar from the antiquated steering engine. At any rate, he was suddenly dead certain that something was pursuing him, and that if he didn't get away from it, he would be horribly killed. He tried, and then he was in the water.

As the rusty old hull slid past him in the warm sea, he looked up at it and blinked the brine out of his failing eyes and made not the slightest attempt to shout for help. He trod water for some moments, until the after light of the tanker was a low star swinging down on the horizon, and then he turned over on his back and kicked sluggishly to keep himself afloat.

Now delirium tremens is a peculiar affliction. Just as the human body can be destroyed by a dose of poison, but will throw off an overdose, so the human mind will reach a point of supersaturation and return to something like normality. In Barry's case it was pseudosanity; he did not cease to have his recurrent attacks of phantasmagoria, but he became suddenly immunized to them. It was as if he had forgotten how to be afraid—how, even, to wonder at the things he saw and felt. He simply did not care; he became as he is today, just not giving a damn. In effect, his mind was all but completely gone, so that for the first time in weeks he could lie at ease and feel that he was not mortally afraid. It was the first time he had been in real danger, and he was not afraid.

He says that he lay there and slept for weeks. He says that porpoises came and played with him, bunting him about and crying like small children. And he says that an angel came down from the sky and built him a boat out of seaweed and foam. But he only remembers one sun coming up, so it must have been that same morning that he found himself clutching a piece of driftwood, rocking and rolling in a gentle swell just to windward of a small island. It was just a little lump of sand and rock, heaped high in the middle, patched with vegetation and wearing a halo of shrieking sea birds. He stared at it with absolutely no interest at all for about four hours, drifting closer all the while. When his feet struck bottom he did not know what it meant or what he should do; he just let them drag until his knees struck also, and then he abandoned his piece of wood and crept ashore.

The sun was coming up again when Barry awoke. He was terribly weak, and his flesh was dry and scaly the way only sea-soaked skin can be. His tongue was interfering with his breathing. He lolled up to his hands and knees and painfully crawled up the sloping beach to a cluster of palms. He collapsed with his chin in a cool spring, and would have killed himself by over-drinking if he had not fallen asleep again.

The next time he pushed the groggy clouds from him, he felt much better. He was changed; he knew that. He was basically changed; he felt different about things. It took him quite a while to figure out just how, but then it occurred to him that though he was still surrounded with the monsters and visions and phantoms of his own drink-crazed creation, he did not fear them. But it was more than that. It was not the disinterest he had experienced out there when he was adrift. It was a sullen hatred of the things. It was an eagerness to have one of them come near enough for him to attack. He crouched by the spring and looked craftily about him, trying to find an object to kill and tear.

He found it. Near him was a coconut. He picked up a stone and hurled it, and cracked the coconut. He caught it up and drank greedily from the streaming cracks, and then broke it and ate the meat until it made him sick. He was enormously pleased with himself.

All around him the ground pimpled and dimpled, and from the little depressions what he thought were strange plants began to grow. They were sinuous stalks, and they seemed to be made of two rubbery sheaths that wound about each other spirally, forming a tentacle-like stem, and spreading out at the tip in two flashy extensions like snail's eyes. He reached out and touched one as it grew visibly, and it writhed away from him and began clubbing the ground blindly, searchingly. He'd never dreamed up anything like this before. But he was certain he had nothing to fear from them. He got up, kicking one out of the way disgustedly, and began to climb the central hill for bearings. Just as he left, one of the growths spurted up out of the ground, curved over his head and smashed wetly down on the spot he had just vacated. He didn't even look over his shoulder. Why should he, for a figment of his imagination? The mistake he made was that the things were real. Just as real, my friend, as you and I!

Barry, poor crazed wreck, couldn't realize it then, because the growing, writhing trunks all around him were mixed and mingled with things of his own creation, dancing and gibbering around him. There were things harmless and beautiful, and things too foul to mention, and it is little wonder that the stemlike things were of little importance.

Barry went on up the hill. He picked up a thorny stick, quite heavy, and strode on, casually swiping at the monsters, real and imaginary. He noticed subconsciously that when he struck at a unicorn or a winged frog, it would vanish immediately, but when he swung at a growing tentacle it would either duck quickly or, when struck, twist into a tight knot about its wound. He even looked back and noticed how the stalks kept pace with him, sinking back into the ground behind him and sprouting ahead. It still meant nothing to him.

A few hundred yards from the top he stopped and sniffed. There had been a growing, fetid odor about the place, and he didn't like it. He connected it somehow with the smell of the ichor that exuded from the wounded stalks after he had slashed them, but he was incurious; he didn't really care. He shrugged and finished his climb.

When he had reached the top he stood a moment wiping his forehead with his wrist, and then sighted all around the horizon. There were no other islands in sight. This one was small—nearly round, and perhaps a mile by a mile and a quarter. He spotted two more springs and a tight grove of coconut and breadfruit. That was encouraging. He stepped forward as a rubbery trunk poured out of the ground and lashed at his legs with its two prehensile tentacles. It missed.

A puff of wind bearing an unspeakable odor brought his attention back to the crest of the hill. It was nearly round, almost exactly following the contours of the island, and fell in the center to form a small crater. Down at the bottom of the crater was a perfectly round hole, and that was the source of the noisome smell.

Barry walked down toward it because he happened to be facing that way and it was the easiest way to go. He was halfway down the slope when two points of what looked like pulpy flesh began to rise out of the hole. They seemed to be moving slowly, but Barry suddenly realized that it was an illusion due to their enormous size. Before he could bring himself to stop, they had risen twenty feet in the air. They began leaning outward, one directly toward him, the other across the hole, away from him. They grew thicker as they poured upward and outward, and finally they lay flat on the slope and the near one began licking up toward him.

It was the most frightening phantasm that had yet presented itself to Barry's poor alcoholic brain, but now he would not be frightened. He stood there, legs apart, club at the ready, and waited. When the thing reached his feet he raised himself on his toes and brought the thorny club down with all his strength on its fleshy tip. It winced away and then poured back. He hit it twice more and it retreated. He ran after it and smashed it again and again. It suddenly rocketed up in the air, as did its mate from the other side of the crater. They struck together with a mighty wet *smack!* and stood there, a pale-green, shining column of living flesh, quivering in the sunlight. And then, with unbelievable speed, they plunged into the ground, back into their hole. Barry dropped his club, clasped his hands over his head and smirked. Then he turned and went back to his spring.

And all the way back, not another trunk showed itself.

He slept well that night under a crude shelter of palm leaves. Not a thing bothered him but dreams, and of course they didn't bother him much any more. His victory over the thing in the crater had planted a tiny seed of self-esteem in that rotten hulk of a man. That, added to the fact that he was too crazy to be afraid of anything, made him something new under the sun.

In the morning he sat up abruptly. At his feet was a pile of breadfruit and coconuts, and around him was a forest, a wall of the waving stalks. He leaped to his feet and cast about wildly for his club. It had disappeared. He drew his sheath knife, which by some miracle had stayed with him since he left the *Jesse Hanck,* and stood there, palisaded by the thickly planted, living stems. And he still was not afraid. He took a deep breath and stepped menacingly toward the near wall of stalks. They melted into the ground before he reached them. He whirled and rushed those behind him. They were gone before he could get within striking distance. He paused and nodded to himself. If that was the way they wanted it, it was O.K. He put away his knife and fell to on the fruit. The stems ranked themselves at a respectful distance, as if they were watching. And then he noticed something new. Deep within his brain was a constant, liquid murmur, as if thousands of people were talking quietly together in a strange tongue. He didn't mind it very much. He'd been through worse, and he wasn't curious.

After he was quite finished he noticed a rustling movement in the wall surrounding him. The creatures were passing something, one to the other—his club! It reached the stalk nearest him; it was taken and laid gently by his side. The stalk straightened and dropped into the earth quickly as if it were embarrassed.

Barry looked at the waving things and almost grinned. Then he picked up the club. Immediately the things on one side of him melted into the ground, and those on the other side doubled in number. A couple of them began sprouting under his feet; he jumped away, startled. More sank into the earth from his path, and more sprang up behind. He looked at them a little uneasily; it occurred to him that they were a little insistent, compared with his usual disappearing monsters. He walked away from them. They followed; that is, they massed behind him, sprouting in his footsteps. And the murmuring in his mind burst into a silent cacophony; gleeful, triumphant.

He wandered inland, followed by his rustling company of pale-green stalks. When he turned aside they would spring up around him, and it was no good trying to press through. They made no attempt to harm him at all. But—they were *forcing* him toward the hill! Perhaps he realized it—perhaps not. Barry, by this time, was totally unhinged. Any other man could not have lived through what he did. But his peculiar conditioning, the subtle distortion of his broken mind, gave him the accidental ability to preserve himself. Certainly he himself could take no credit for it. His fantastic world was no more strange to him than ours is to us. If you or I were suddenly transported to that island, we would be as frightened as—well, a gorilla in Times Square, or a New Yorker in an African jungle. It's all a matter of receptivity.

And so he found himself marching up the central slope being driven gently but firmly toward that monstrous thing in the crater by his entourage of pale-green stalks. They must have been a weird-looking company.

And the thing was waiting for him. He came up over the crest of the rise, and the tip of one of the two great green projections curled up over his head and lashed down at him. He threw himself sideways and belted it with his club as it touched the ground. It slid back toward the hole. He took a step or two after it. It was huge—fully sixty feet of it stretched from him to the hole in the center of the crater. And no telling how much more of it was in there. At the first movement from the thing, there had been a rustle behind him and every one of the stalks had dropped from sight.

As Barry ran forward to strike again, a shape shot up out of the ground at his side, whipped around his leg and flung him down. He rolled over and sat up, to see the other great green arm come swooping down on the stalk that had tripped him and—saved his life. The two huge tentacles slapped together, twisted the slender stalk between them, and began to pull. The stalk tried to go underground, and for a moment held, while its spiraled body stretched and thinned under tons of pull. Then the ground itself gave, and with a peculiar sucking sound, the stalk came up out of the earth. And for the first time Barry saw it for what it was.

The "root" was a dark-green ovoid, five or six feet long, about two and a half feet thick at the middle. It was rough and wrinkled, and gleamed with its coating of slime. The stalk itself was nearly eight feet long. The creature hung for a moment in the twin tentacles of its captor, and then it was enfolded, the bulge of it sliding visibly down the two arms which had closed together and twisted, forming a great proboscislike tube. And Barry heard it scream, deep down in his mind.

Barry rose and scrambled back over the crest of the hill. It had occurred to him that the monster in the crater had struck at a victim—himself—and that the stalk had sacrificed itself to save him. Having a victim, it would be satisfied for the time being. He was right. Peering back, he saw the great column rise in the air and slip swiftly back into its hole. And he realized something else, as the two tips disappeared underground. The divided proboscis—the ability to rise from and sink into the earth—why, the big fellow there was exactly the same as all the rest of these creatures, except for its huge size!

What was it? Why, Barry never knew exactly, and though I took a great deal of trouble to find out, I never bothered to tell him. There they were; more than that, Barry did not care. He still doesn't. However, as closely as I can discover, I think that the creatures were a species of marine worm—one of the *Echiuroidea,* to be exact—*bonellia viridis.* They grow large anywhere they grow, but I've never heard of one longer than four feet, proboscis and all. However, I think it quite possible for a colony to develop in a given locality, and mutate into greater size. As for the big one—well, Barry did find a thing or two out about that monster.

Barry went back down the hill and headed for cover. He wanted to sit somewhere in the shade where he would not be bothered by such things. He found himself a spot and relaxed there. And slowly, then faster and faster, the stalks began to spring up around him again. They kept their distance, almost respectfully; but there was a certain bland insistence in their presence that annoyed Barry.

"Go away!" he said sharply.

And they did. Barry was utterly astonished. It was the first really human reaction that had struck him in weeks. But the sight of these curious creatures, so dissimilar to anything that he had ever heard about, obeying him so implicitly, struck some long-buried streak of humor in the man. He roared with laughter.

"Hello."

His laughter cut off and he peered around. Nothing.

"Hello." The sound seemed to come from no specific direction— as a matter of fact, it seemed to come from no direction at all. It seemed to come from inside him, but he hadn't spoken.

"Who said that?" he snapped.

"I did," said the voice. He looked around again, and his eyes caught a movement down low, to his left. There, just peeping out of the ground, were the twin tendrils that tipped the ubiquitous stalks.

"*You?*" asked Barry, pointing.

The creature rose another two feet and swayed gently. "Yes."

"And what the hell might you be?"

"I don't understand you. What is hell?"

"It speaks English!" gasped Barry.

"I speak," agreed the monster. "What is English?"

Barry rose to his knees and stared at it. "What are you?" he repeated.

"Man."

"Yeah? What does that make me?"

"You are different. I have only your words for everything. Your name for yourself is Man. My name for myself is Man, too. I have no name for you."

"I'm a man," asserted Barry, half truthfully.

"And what would you say I am?"

Barry looked at it carefully. "A damned nightmare."

223

The thing said seriously, "Very well. Hereafter we shall be known as nightmares. I shall tell all the people."

The thought of actually having a conservation with this unpleasant-looking beast struck Barry again and almost overwhelmed him. "How the devil can you speak with me?"

"My mind speaks to your mind."

"Yeah! Gee!" was the only comment Barry could think of.

"What are you going to do?" asked the creature.

"Whatcha mean?"

"You have proved yourself against the Big One. We know you can destroy him. Will you do it soon, please?"

"The Big One? You mean that thing in the crater?"

"Yes."

"What can I do?"

"You will know, all-powerful one."

Barry looked around to find out who was being addressed in such prepossessing terms, and then concluded that it was he. He puffed his chest. "Well," he said, "I'll make a deal with you. Get me a drink and I'll fix you up."

It was an old mental reflex, one he had used all over the coast to get himself plastered when offered any kind of a job, aside from shipping out. His technique was to demand more liquor until he was so drunk he was of no value to any kind of an employer; and they would go away and leave him alone.

The stalk said, "It shall be done."

A whirring telepathic signal sounded in Barry's brain, and two or three dozen of the things leaped out of the earth.

"The master desires a drink. And pass the word; hereafter we are to be known as nightmares. It is his wish."

The stalks dropped out of sight, all but the one Barry was talking with.

"Well; that's something like service," breathed Barry.

"All things are yours for the service you will do us," said the nightmare.

"This is the damnedest thing," said Barry, scratching his head.

"Why didn't you talk to me before?"

"I did not know what your intentions were, nor whether or not you were an intelligent animal," said the nightmare.

"Y'know now, huh?"

"Yes, master."

"Hey— How come none of 'em talk to me but you?"

"I differ slightly from the rest. See those birds?"

Barry looked up at the wheeling, screaming cloud of gulls and curlews. "So?"

The nightmare gave a peculiar telepathic whistle. The birds wheeled and hurtled downward toward them. In an instant the glade was filled with them. Barry was cuffed and slapped by their wings as they crowded about him. He snatched at a large bird, caught it by the leg, and promptly twisted its neck.

At the nightmare's sudden signal, the rest of the birds turned and fluttered and soared up and away.

"Why did you do that?" asked the nightmare.

"I'm going to eat it."

"You eat birds?"

"Why not?"

"You shall have all you want. But as I was saying—I am different from these others. Of all of us, I alone can call the birds. Apparently, only I may speak with you."

"Seems like. I can—hear the others, but I dunno what they're driving at. What about this Big One? Where'd he come from?"

"The Big One was one of us. But he differed also. He was a mutant, like me, but he is unintelligent. He eats his own kind, which we cannot do. He is very old, and every time he eats one of us, he grows larger. He can't move from the crater because it is rockbound, and he can't burrow through it. But the larger he grows the farther he can reach. If you were not going to kill him, he would grow until he could reach the whole island, or so they say. It used to be, a thousand years ago, that he could travel our roads—"

"Roads? I didn't see no roads."

"Oh, they are underground. The whole island is honeycombed with our burrows. We never put more of ourselves above the surface than our proboscis. We catch our food that way, feeling about the ground and the water's edge for small plants and animals. We can dig, too, almost as fast as we can travel through our roads— Here's your drink."

Barry watched fascinated as a column of stalks approached, bearing gourds of coconut shells filled with water, coconut milk, and breadfruit juice. Never a drop was spilled, as the stalks progressed. Two or three would sprout swiftly, lean back, toward the gourd bearers. They would take the burden, bend swiftly forward and pass it on to some newly sprouted nightmares, and then sink into the ground and appear ahead.

"Why don't they carry it underground?" asked Barry.

"It might not suit you then, master. You live in the sun, and the foods you have eaten have grown in the sun. It shall be as you wish it."

Barry extended his hand and a coconut shell full of cool water was deposited in it. He sipped once and threw it down. "Call this a drink?" he roared. "Get me a *drink!*"

"What would you like?"

"Whiskey, damn you! Gin, rum—beer! Wine, if you can't find anything better." The more he thought of it, the thirstier he got. "Get me a drink, you—what's your name?"

"Ahniroo."

"Well, get it anyway." Barry slumped sullenly back.

"Master—we have none of these things you ask. Could we perhaps make one of them?"

"Make one? I don't—wait a minute." Barry did a little thinking. If he had to make a drink—brew it up, wait for it to ferment, strain it—well, he'd just as soon do without. But it seemed as if these goofy critters were aching to work for him. "O.K.—I'll tell you what to do."

And so Barry gave his orders. He knew very vaguely what to do, purely because he had some idea of what alcoholic drinks were made out of. And it passed the time pleasantly. He had plenty to eat and drink and never had to lift a finger to get it. For the first time in his life he had the kind of existence he'd dreamed about—even if it was mixed up with nightmares.

The base of his brew was coconut milk. He'd heard somewhere that an otherwise innocuous drink would ferment if you put in a raisin and closed the container tightly. No raisins, though. He tried several things and finally got fair results with chunks of breadfruit dried on the rocks in the sun. They were put into a plugged coconut shell, the opening carefully filled with a whittled wooden stopper and sealed with mucus from the hides of the nightmares. Barry wasn't finicky.

It was a pleasure to watch them work. They cooperated admirably, grouping about a task, each supplying one or both of the "fingers" at the tips of their proboscis. To see a coconut held, plugged, doctored with a breadfruit and sealed up again, was a real pleasure, so swiftly and deftly was it done. Barry had only to whittle one plug when the knife was taken from him and three of the stalks took over the task, one to handle the knife, two to hold the wood. And do you know how many coconuts Barry had them prepare? By actual count, according to Ahniroo—over nine thousand!

And when it was done, Barry announced that it would be, anyway, six months before the stuff was worth drinking. The nightmares, in effect, shrugged that off. They had lots of time. One of them was detailed to mark off the days; and in the meantime they waited on Barry hand and foot. No mention was made of the Big One. And Barry lay and dreamed the days away, thinking of the binge he was going to go on when he could get his hands on nine thousand bottles of home brew!

"Governor," said the American, as the old man stopped to light a cigar, "tell me something. Isn't it a little tough to believe this drunkard's yarn? That business of the worms having intelligence and talking with him. Isn't that a little strong?"

The governor considered. "Perhaps. But once you get over the initial surprise of an idea like that, try taking it apart. Why shouldn't they be intelligent? Just what is intelligence anyway?"

"Why"—the American fingered his Adam's apple uneasily—"I'd say intelligence was what we have that makes us the leading race on the planet."

"Are we, though? We're outnumbered by thousands of other species—worms, for instance, if numbers is your idea of racial supremacy. We are not as strong as the elephant or as quick as the antelope—strength and speed have nothing to do with supremacy. No, we use our intelligence to make tools. We owe our position on earth to our ability to make tools."

"Is that intelligence—tool-making?"

The governor shook his head. "It is one of the ways to use intelligence."

"What about these worms of Barry's, then—why didn't they have cities and literature and machines?"

"They didn't need them. They were not overcrowded on the island. There was plenty to eat for all. The only menace they had was the Big One, and even that wasn't a complete menace—he could have lived another twenty thousand years without endangering the life of any but those who wandered too close. His presence was a discomfort. As to their literature—how can we know about that? Barry was a seaman, and a very low-type seaman, an ignoramus. What did he care about the splendid brains that Ahniroo and his people might have had? Intelligence of that sort must have produced superb developments along some lines. Barry never bothered to find out.

"No, you can't judge the intelligence of a race by its clothes or its automobiles or its fancy foods. Intelligence is a cellular accident affecting the nervous cysts of certain races. It might strike anywhere. It seems as if it is a beautiful jest handed about by the gods, like a philanthropist giving away beautiful grand pianos to uneducated children. Some may learn to play them. Some may build intricate machines with the parts. Most would destroy them, one way or another. What do you think our race is doing with its great gift? Well?"

The American grinned. "Better get on with your story."

Well, for those six months Barry lived in the lap of luxury. Yes, raw sea birds and coconut and breadfruit and clams can be luxury, once you're used to them. It isn't what you have that makes luxury, anyway; it's how it's given to you. A raw albatross, carefully cleaned and cut up, is as great a luxury when it is brought to you in style as is a twelve-dollar French meal that you have to cook yourself. Barry had nothing to kick about. He had never felt better in his life; he hadn't sense enough to realize that it was largely due to his being on the wagon. He dreamed about coconut shells filled with rare old Scotch now, instead of winged dragons and snakes.

The months went by far faster than he realized; it was a real surprise to him when Ahniroo came to him one morning bearing a coconut.

"It is ready, master."

"What?"

"The drink you asked to have us make for you."

"Oh boy, oh boy! Give it here."

Ahniroo leaned toward him and he took the nut. A jab with his knife drove the plug in, and he took gulps. One went down and the other went immediately out.

"*Phhhtooey!* Ahni, take this some place and bury it. Holy sweet Sue! It takes like th' dregs of a city dump!"

Ahniroo took the nut gravely and swayed away. "Yes, master."

Barry sat there running his tongue around the inside of his mouth to get rid of the taste. The tongue moved more and more slowly; he stopped; he swallowed twice, then he leaped to his feet. "Hold it!" he bellowed. "I've drank worse'n that an' paid money for it. Bring that back. Bring fifty of 'em." He snatched the nut and drained it. It was alcoholic, after all. It tasted like nothing on earth, but it had a slight wallop.

Three hours later found Barry sprawled out amid a litter of broken coconut shells. There was a peaceful smile on his long horsy face, and in his mind was unalloyed bliss. Ahniroo bent over and touched the back of his neck with a slimy tentacle. Barry rolled his head and lay still again. Ahniroo was very persistent. Barry finally rolled over and sat up, promptly falling over the other way and lying prone again. Ahniroo and two of his fellows helped to roll him over on his back and sit him up again. Ahniroo shook him gently for some eight minutes until he began to grumble.

"Master—it is time! Come, please; we are waiting."

"Time? What time?"

"Your promise, all-powerful one. We have fulfilled your desire. You promised us you would kill the Big One when we had brought you a drink. You have had your drink, master."

Barry clapped his hand to his brow and winced. Promised? Was that what— Then this wasn't all for nothing? He had to pay off? The full import of it struck him. He was deputized to rid the island of that monstrosity that lived in the crater!

"Now let's be reas'n'ble," he coaxed. "You can't make me do that job, now; y'know y'can't, huh?" Getting no answer from Ahniroo, he said belligerently, "Listen, bean pole, you can't push me around. S'pose I don't even try to do that job?"

Ahniroo said quietly, "You will. You have promised. Come now."

A shrill signal, and Barry found himself lifted bodily and set on his feet. Spluttering and protesting, he was shoved by a solid wall of nightmares towards the hill. Twice he tried to simply quit—sit down, the way he had on the tank ships when he thought he was getting the runaround. The *Echiuroidea* did not understand modern labor methods. They picked him up and carried him when he would not walk. And once he tried to run away. They let him—provided he ran toward the hill. He finally settled to a hesitant plodding, and marched along, wishing the island was ten times as big and he was twenty times smaller.

When they reached the top of the hill, the nightmares disappeared into the ground, all but Ahniroo. Barry was in tears.

"Ahni—do I hafta?"

"Yes—master."

Barry looked toward the hole. It was sixty feet away and thirty feet in diameter. "Big, ain't he?"

"Very."

"How's about a little drink before I go down there?"

"Of course, master!"

Ahni gave his signal. In a few minutes a stream of coconuts began to pop out of the earth. They were the only thing of Barry's that Ahniroo would allow to be transported underground.

When fifty or sixty had arrived, Barry broke and drained three. "I tell you, Ahni," he said, "just you keep 'em coming. I'll need 'em."

He gave a hitch at his belt and started down the slope, a coconut in each fist. There was no sign at all of the Big One. He walked to the edge of the pit and looked down, trying to hold his breath against the smell of the thing. Yeah—there he was, the little rascal. He could just see the tips of his proboscis.

"C'mon up and fight!" Barry yelled drunkenly.

Still no movement. Barry grinned weakly and looked back toward the edge of the crater. Ahniroo was there, watching. Barry felt a little foolish.

"Come on," he coaxed. "Here; have a drink." He cracked open a coconut and let the fluid run into the pit. There was a stir of movement, and then silence.

Ahni's mental voice came to him. "The Big One is not hungry today."

"Maybe he's thirsty then. Roll me down a couple dozen nuts, pal."

The obedient nightmares shoved at the pile of doctored coconuts. They came rolling and bouncing down the slope. He broke them and pitched them in—about thirty of them. He had not countermanded his order—they were still coming up there.

The Big One thrust up a tentacle, waved it and let it slump back. The last few drinks were getting Barry down. He was long past the stage where he knew what he was doing.

"Hey! My pal wants more! Come on—fill 'em up! He's a big feller—he needs a man-size drink. Couple o' you guys give me a hand!"

Two stalks immediately appeared beside him. He gave no thought to the fact that he was possibly leading them to their deaths. The three began breaking coconut shells and pouring the contents into the pit.

Now just why this happened I could not say. Perhaps the Big One was allergic to alcohol. Perhaps it tripped up his coordination so that he couldn't control a movement once it started. But suddenly, with a wheezing roar, the Big One rose up out of his lair.

It is all but impossible to describe that sight. The proboscis alone was fully one hundred and twenty feet long, and it rose straight up in the air, twisting slowly, and then fell heavily to the ground. It lay on the floor of the crater, reaching from the center pit all the way up and over and well down the hill. If it had fallen on Barry it would have crushed him instantly beyond all semblance of a man. And it didn't miss him by much. The two tips of the proboscis were out of sight now, but the whole mass, eighteen feet thick, pulsed and twitched with the violent movement that must have been going on at the extremity.

Barry fell back aghast, in that instant cold sober. Ahniroo's message cut through his awed horror:

"The bristles, master! Cut the bristles!"

Barry drew his knife and ran to the edge of the pit. The actual body of the thing, that thick ovoid part, was just visible, and he could see the bristles—the powerful muscled projections by which the creatures, all of them, burrowed. But the flesh about the Big One's bristles was soft and flabby—it had been decades since he had been able to use them. Barry leaned over and hacked hysterically at the base of one of them. The steel slid through the layers of tissue, and in a moment the bristle hung loose, useless. Barry flung himself aside to avoid a foul gush of ichor, and drove for the other bristle. He couldn't do as much to this one; it sank into the side of the pit, trying to force the great body back into the hole. The earth yielded; the bristle whipped up through the ground and smacked into the Big One's side. That was its last anchorage, and its last refuge was gone.

Immediately the crater was alive with the wavering stems of Ahniroo's kind. Like ants around a slug, they fastened to the gigantic body, dragged and tore at it, tied it to earth. Barry danced around it, his mind drink-crazed again; he waved a full coconut shell aloft in one hand and with the other cut and slashed at the prone monster. He laughed and shrieked and sang, and finally collapsed weakly from sheer exhaustion, still murmuring happily and humming to himself.

Ahniroo and some others carried him back down and laid him on the beach. They washed him and put soft leaves under his body.

They fed him continuously out of the huge stock of coconut shells. They almost killed him with kindness. And for his sake, I suppose, they shouldn't have left him on the beach. Because he got—rescued.

A government launch put into the cove to survey, since these days you never can tell what salty little piece of rock might be of military value. They found him there, dead drunk on the beach. It was quite a puzzle to the shore party. There he was, with no footprints around him to show where he'd come from; and though they scoured the neighborhood of the beach, they found no shelter or anything that might have belonged to him. And when they got him aboard and sobered him up the island was miles astern. He went stark raving mad when he discovered where he was. He wanted to go back to his worms. And he's been here ever since. He's no use to anyone. He drinks when he can beg or steal it. He'll die from it before long, I suppose, but he's only happy when he's plastered. Poor devil. I could send him back to his island, I suppose, but— Well, it's quite a problem. Can I, as the representative of enlightened humanity in this part of the world, allow a fellow human being to go back to a culture of worms?

The American shuddered. "I—hardly think so. Ah—governor, is this a true yarn?"

The governor shrugged. "I'll tell you—I was aboard that launch. I was the one who found Barry on the beach. And just before we lost sight of the island, some peculiar prompting led me to look at the beach again through my glasses. Know what I saw there?

"It was *alive!* It was one solid mass of pale-green tentacles, all leaning toward the launch and Barry. There was an air about them— the way they were grouped, their graceful bending toward us—I don't know—that made me think of a prayer meeting. And I distinctly heard—not with my ears, either—'Master, come back! Master!' Over and over again.

"Barry's a god to those damned things. So are the rest of us, I imagine. That's why they were too frightened by us to show themselves when we went ashore there. Ah, poor Barry. I should send him back, I suppose. It's not fair to keep him here—but damn it, I'm a man! I can't cater to a society of— Ugh!"

They sat silently for a long while. Then the American rose abruptly. "Good night, governor. I don't—*like* that story." He smiled wryly and went inside, leaving the old man to sit and stare out to sea.

Late that night the American looked out of his bedroom window uncomfortably. The ground was smoothly covered with a rather ordinary lawn near the governor's house. Farther back, there was night-shadowed jungle.

The Purple Light

I WAS TAKING *No. 14* back to the base when it happened. The figures painted on her scarred molyb hull didn't mean we had fourteen
ships. It was one of the four cans—and I means cans—that com-
prised our charter service. In the six years we had been operating,
we had bought and rebuilt seventeen wrecks, and had seen the end
of thirteen of them. One more just at this time would finish us. We
couldn't stay in business with less than four spaceships, what with
the sudden influx of mining machinery into the asteroid belt and the
competition of two more freight lines in our territory. And here I
was about to wash the old *Kelli NX*.

The purple light had flashed on. There were half a dozen signals
of the sort on the little one-man cargo carrier—warnings for lowering air pressure, fuel shortage, synth-grav system troubles—I always
thought that was a funny one. You'd fly up off the deck plates, and
smack your sconce on the overhead, and when you came to, the silly
signal light was on to tell you something was wrong with the synth-
grav!—even humidity changes and fuel shortage. But the big purple
light on the forward bulkhead was something different again.

It was a very bright and a very pretty shade of purple and it said,
in effect, "Somewhere around here is an atomic power plant whose
U-235 is just at the ticklish point where the disintegration will be
too fast for its ordinary energy output. There is about to be an explosion that will make a light bright enough to read a postage stamp
by from here to the moons of Mars; and if there is anyone around
here just now he'd be foolish to loiter."

Out here in space, you know, it wouldn't make any noise. I wasn't
afraid of being startled. Nor was it the kind of an explosion that
would butter me over the bulkheads, the way they put it on toast in
cafeterias—with a brush. Because there wouldn't be any bulkheads.

Or any me. There would be a lot of light and heat and a squib in a trade journal about Rix Randolph, expressman, and how he had been a little careless with his '235.

Now it was perfectly evident what I had to do. Also that I had to do it fast. Cut off my power, stop the uranium action. Just possibly the disintegration would slow a trifle, enough to lower the output below the danger point. And if that didn't work—bail out. Slip into the ancient but reliable spacesuit strapped to the bulkhead there and get away in one sweet hell of a hurry. I don't know why I thought there was any choice in the matter. The suit was fueled and provisioned for twice the distance from here to either Terra or Port of Eros.

I hopped to the control panel, threw over the three levers that controlled the neutron-streams and their generator. The whisper of escaping steam faded out of the water jackets, and my stomach lurched as acceleration cut out. I looked up at the purple light again. It was still on.

Too late!

I ran to the bulkhead, opened the chest plates of the spacesuit, climbed in, got the arms controls working and flipped the switch that lowered the helmet, closed the plates, and cut down the artificial gravity of the floor plates. It seemed to take an eternity to operate, though it could only have been a couple of seconds; and in that couple of seconds I did a lot of thinking.

That purple light, for instance. There were some bright boys in the ship-designing business, and they had even these old cans nicely enough equipped. The warning device was a result of the labors of that Edison of the spaceways, old Dr. Fonck. He'd invented the attachment to a U-235 plant that emanated a static quench-field to act as a governor to the neutron-streams that activated the uranium. It made the neutron-streams that much more inefficient, but who cared about that with all that power to throw around? The important thing was that it blanketed the disintegration to some extent. If the thing was going to blow up with the fury that only an atomic explosion or a supernova can show, it would at least start to blow up slowly. That is, when the reaction started to accelerate beyond control, the quench-field got in the way of the countless millions of neutrons, tending to add a positron to them, and convert them into useless, harmless hydrogen nuclei. It meant a slowing down of the whole process, until the neutrons came too fast. Then—lights out.

But at the same time it gave the poor sucker in the ship, or wherever else the plant was, a few minutes grace in which to get away from there. It also gave that purple light a chance to tell him about it. Not much of a warning, of course. Once that kind of a reaction starts, it can't be stopped. The signal was rather like tying a guy to a chair and then telling him, "See that dark character over there? He has a gun aimed at your head and is about to pull the trigger." You were grateful for the warning; at least you'd know about it before you were shot. Maybe even some miracle would happen to untie you. But in the case of the atomic explosion, it would have to be a miracle in speed.

I thought of something else as I released the suit with me inside it from the bulkhead straps. It was the ship, the business—all it meant to me. I was partners in it with my brother, and it had been killing work. Years of it, borrowing for a measly new piece of equipment; twenty-hour stretches with welding arcs and pressure testers, trying to make our old tow-ins spaceworthy; cutting out competition by going profitless, working for nothing and half-starving besides, just to keep the little service extant. With my hand on the air-lock door I paused. I knew that. This was the finish of the business. I knew that. It wouldn't finish the way I would if I stayed here another two minutes. Not fast and clean like that. There would be desperate councils of war with my brother. Bankruptcy proceedings. Sheriff's sales. Months of litigation. No job in the meantime. Relief. I'd never taken something for nothing in my life.

I slumped against the door and flipped open my face plate.

The neutron-field wasn't confined to the power compartment. It was a spherical field about the ship, not directly attached to the power plant. Didn't have to be. As long as it was as close as possible to the plant, as long as it was most concentrated near the neutron-streams, it had its delaying effect on the inevitable explosion. I watched the forward bulkhead glumly, and the light over it. It would come roaring up from there. I wondered vaguely if I would be able to see it coming. Bail out, chowderhead, I told myself desperately. The business is gone; why do you have to go, too? But I didn't move. What's the use of saving a skin if the very guts are gone out of it? I couldn't go on any more. I knew I shouldn't run out on my brother this way, but—What would he do in my place? What would anyone do? Fonck himself couldn't stop it now. No atomic plant can generate a quench-field powerful enough to stop its own explosion. My face was clammy. I decided I didn't want to see it coming, and walked over to the forward bulkhead.

When I did so the purple light dimmed. I stared at it, shook my head. Maybe my eyes—no. It remained dim, but it wasn't getting any dimmer. The other lights looked all right. I walked back to the after companionway, looked along it. Those lights were O.K., too. Now what—Oh! Oh! Now the purple light was brilliant! Any second now. I stumped over to the forward bulkhead again. I'd meet it halfway—damn the miserable, stupid business and the balky relic of a ship anyway! They'd finish Rix Randolph but they'd find him on his feet! I knew what it felt like now to die with a grand gesture.

I stood with my legs apart, eyes closed, fists clenched, directly under the purple light. I wish that little French girl in Port of Eros could see me now, I thought. "All right," I said steadily. "I'm—ready."

Nothing happened for about ten seconds. About that time I discovered I'd been holding my breath. I let it out with a whistle. Still nothing happened. All of a sudden I felt like a melodramatic damn fool. Which I was. I opened my eyes. The purple light was dim, almost out.

"I got to get out of here!" I screamed, and headed for the air lock, slid the door open. As I whirled to close it, I saw the light gleam out brightly again. I stopped dead, fighting with myself, fighting fear with curiosity.

Every time I got near the forward bulkhead the light grew dim. Every time I drew away from it it got brighter. Now—why?

I went, like a fear-frozen sleepwalker, over to the light. It dimmed. "No!" I breathed. "Don't tell me—Bodily aura? Hell, that's ghost story stuff! But—" It certainly looked like it, though. Well—why

238

not? A man was a hunk of matter; matter was a mess of electric charges, positive, negative, neutral. Was I, by some crazy chance, made up of precisely the right combination of electric charges to increase the quench-field around the U-235 up there? Aw, it was crazy! But—The light did dim when I approached the power plant. The indicator was extraordinarily sensitive—had to be, to record the atomic acceleration in there fast enough to do any good. Maybe then if I got close to it—crawled in next to the plant, it would swing the scales!

With a sob I tore open the repair doors in front of the water jacket, squeezed myself in, hugging the plates. It was hotter than the furnace in Hell's cellar in there, even with an insulated spacesuit on. But what did I care about that? I was going to die anyway. I might as well die doing something about it.

But I'd already done it. The purple glow faded and died, and I knew I was safe. I kissed the hot plates, and I'll have scarred lips for the rest of my life because of it. I broke down and cried like a baby.

It must have been an hour later when I crawled out and pulled myself together. As I climbed out of the suit and strapped it up and turned on the grav again, I thought deliriously of being alive again. Yes, and not only that—rich! Any way you look at it—suppose I was, as I had guessed, possessed of a neutral electric charge? Why, the biggest passenger lines in the System would bid against each other for me! And more—if I handled it right, I could grab me the Space Prize for the most important contribution to space commerce when this five-year period was up—five hundred thousand bucks, no less, on the very strong chance that my adventure had some hint in it that the lab boys could develop into something salable. No more worries! No more debts!

And that's how I came in to Eros, laughing like a loon and calling up every newspaper and laboratory in the place. They sent their scientists to look over the old can, and they wined me and dined me and after they found what they found in the ship they very nearly laughed me out of the System. Why?

Well, it's this way. The purple light signal was all right. The quench-field was all right. And there *had* been an imminent atomic explosion in the ship. But not in the ship's power plant. I shouldn't have thought of bailing out. I shouldn't, being a mere space pilot, have tried to think I was an atomic physicist. And—I shouldn't have opened my face about it. Because that atomic explosion was building up in the power plant of my *spacesuit*. And I killed it by crawling into the heart of the ship's big and potent quench-field.

Artnan Process

SLIMMY COB AND his hair stood up short, tough and wiry. His eyes were slitted like his mouth, both emitting, from his dark face, thin lines of blue-white. "Blow!" he gritted, and his finger tightened on the trigger of the snub-nosed weapon he held.

The other man in the ship raised his face by making his pillar of neck disappear into great hunched shoulders. I was afraid of this, he thought, and his fingers froze over the control panel. "Better put that toy away," he said softly.

"I want a chance to unload it," said Slimmy, and he moved the muzzle coldly across the back of Bell Bellew's hairless skull. "And I'll sure get my chance unless you get out of that bucket seat and let me land the ship. Ain't kiddin', son."

Bell grinned tightly, jammed his knees into the recesses provided for them under the board, and with one dazzling movement threw two switches. The gravity plates under Slimmy's feet went dead and those in the overhead whipped the little man upward. He hung there, spitting and swearing like an angry kitten. Wrenching one pinned arm away, he aimed and fired. An opaque white liquid squirted downward, lathering the big man's skull, running down over his ears and eyes, down his neck. Bell swore chokingly, clawing at his face. He felt swiftly over the panel, his practiced fingers finding the right switches as if they were tipped with eyes. Slimmy fell heavily to the deck plates, and Bell pounced on him.

Great fingers wrapped themselves around Slimmy's throat, through which gasped the words, "Dammit! Why didn't I try to kill you outright instead of poisoning you?" His jaws champed, and his slot of a mouth closed as his slitted eyes opened wide and began to pop.

On the arid, shining planet below the silver ship, three naked, leather-skinned Martians crouched around a compact recording instrument, their implacable logical minds cubbyholing the above happenings. Their recorder, receiving by means of a tight beam vibration from the control room of the Earthlings' ship, showed in its screen every detail of the chamber, clearly sounded every word. A slight drift of the ship above moved it away from the spy beam, and the signals faded out. One of the Martians bent swiftly to the instrument while the others spoke in their high, monotonous voices.

"They are unaccountable as ever," said the first. His words were spoken syllable by syllable, with no emphasis on any of them, with no rise or fall of tone at the end of his sentence. The language of Mars is necessarily that way, since Martians are tone-deaf.

"It is beyond understanding," said the other, "that these two humans, who have come from the Solar System to this planet of Procyon, should have lived so amicably together until the day they arrive here on Artna, and then strive to kill one another."

"At least," said the first, "we have discovered their purpose in coming here."

"Yes. I trust that they will meet with no success."

"If they fail, they will have done no more than we have. The Artnans are far from hostile, but guard their secret closely. However, it seems reasonable to me to dispatch these Earthmen. Their presence here accomplishes nothing for us."

The third Martian turned from the still-dead recording machine at this. "I would advise against that," he piped. "He," by the way, is a term of convenience. Martians are parthenogenetic, or self-germinating females. Variation of racial strains is accomplished by a periodic mutual absorption. "Earthmen, involved and unnecessary as their thought-processes are, have achieved a certain degree of development. Hampered by such inefficient and wandering mentalities, they could only have developed so far by possessing some unexplained influence over the laws of chance. Should that quality be used here, they might discover the secret we are after—how the Artnans produce U-235 so cheaply that they can undersell Martian and Terrestrial atomic fuel."

"There is reason in that," said the first Martian, than which there is no higher compliment to a Martian. "If we cannot discover the secret ourselves, we may conceivably secure it from any who get it before us." He turned back to his machine, but to no avail. The little silver ship had disappeared over the horizon, and the Martian spy ray was strictly a sight-line proposition.

When the blue began to show through Slimmy's tanned skin, Bell Bellew let go the little man's throat, took one wizened ear between each great forefinger and thumb, and began to rap on the deck plates with Slimmy's skull. A little of this, and the gun toter called it quits. Bell sat on his prostrate shipmate and grinned broadly.

"Get off," wheezed Slimmy. "I feel all crummy, lying under this big pile of—"

Bell put a hand under his chin and slammed the wiry head on the deck again.

"O.K.—O.K. You got me. Now what?"

"What was it you loaded that gun with?" asked Bill.

"Zinc stearate, lug, in an emulsion of carbohydrates and hydrogen oxide. I couldn't think of anything you needed more or liked less."

"Soap and water," nodded Bell. "Couldn't believe it, that's all, coming from you." He climbed off. "Enough horseplay, little one. We got to get to work. We're over the horizon, anyway. That spy ray of theirs won't see any more of this dray-ma."

Slimmy got his feet under him uncertainly, and shook his spinning head. "Now that we're here, what do we do?"

"We land as near as we can get to the Artnan's transmutation plant and see if we can get a gander how to make U-235 out of U-238."

"You really believe they can do that?"

"They must. I used to think they mined it, but they don't. Artna has an atmosphere much like Earth's, except that there's more xenon and neon and less nitrogen in the air. Also considerable water; and you know as well as I do that '235 can't exist where there's water."

"I dunno," said Slimmy. "The fact that they produce so much, so cheaply, is a contradiction in terms. Uranium is a little more plentiful here than it is on Earth, but it has less than Mars. And the ratio of '238 to '235 is 140 to 1, same as anywhere else. Damn, boy," he burst out suddenly, "won't it be something if we crack this racket?"

"Sure will," breathed Bell.

The simple words bore a weight of profound meaning, for in spite of their skylarking tendencies, Cob and Bellew never belittled the importance of their mission. Its history went back nearly five hundred years, to the ill-fated days when Earth first flung her pioneer ships out into space, to bring back their tales of other, older civilizations. They found the dead remains of titans of Jupiter, and they brought back miles of visigraph records from the steaming swamps of Venus. But from Mars they brought undreamed-of power; a beam of broadcast energy from the old red planet that seemed inexhaustible. Earthmen were free to come and go; Earthmen saw the broadcasting towers that gave them their power, and the measureless stores of purest U-235 that fed it. The only thing they were not allowed to see was the plant which supplied the '235. Earth did not care much about that—why should they? They got power from Mars for a fraction of what it cost them to produce it themselves, so they took the Martian power and shut down their own plants.

Of course, there were one or two small rights which the Martians exacted in exchange—little matters concerning the rights to Earth's mineral resources, occasional requests to the effect that Earthmen must stop researches in certain directions, must prevent the publication of certain books, must limit their travel in certain directions ... The edicts came far apart, and were applied with gentle and efficient firmness. Occasionally a group of Earthly hotheads would find reason to resent the increasing Martian influence. They were disciplined, usually by the greater mass of their own race, the hypnotized sheep who blathered of "beneficent dictatorship"; quoted interminably the Mars-schooled leader of men who burned his speeches into the souls of all—Hyatte Grove, who said, "To Mars we owe our power, our transportation, our every industry. To Mars we owe our daily bread, our warless, uneventful, steadily progressive lives. The Martian power beam is the beating heart of our world."

Earthmen outnumbered Martians ten to one. Martians outlived Earthmen eight to one. The advantage was with Mars. The Martian conquest was applied without blood, without pain. There was no war of worlds, no great fleet of ray-equipped ships. There was just the warming, friendly power beam, and the great generosity of Earth's "Elder Sister." Generation after generation of men lived and died, and each of them was gradually led deeper into the slow-spun web of the red planet. Earth entered into a new era, one of passive peace, submission, slavery.

Some men knew it for what it was, and did not care. Some cared, but could think of nothing to do about it. Some did something about it, and were quietly killed. Most of humanity didn't bother about what happened. You were born and cared for. You grew up and were given a job. You were comfortable. Sometimes you were allowed to marry and have children, if it was all right with Mars. Married or single, there was room for everyone. When you were too old to be useful, you begged and were cared for by your fellows—that was easy, for everyone had so much. Then you died, and they dropped your carcass into the disintegrating furnaces. So what difference could it make whether man or Martian ran the show?

When man owned the Earth, you were told, he made a mess of it. No one killed now, or stole or broke any law. It was better. No one thought very deeply or clearly; no one had ambition, pride, freedom. That was better, too—for Mars. Mars grew fat on Earth's endeavor.

But some Earthmen didn't know when they were well off. They read the forbidden books, and studied the forbidden sciences, and most of them were killed off before they could add anything; but some did, and in a few centuries they had accomplished something. They knew these things:

Earth had a soul of her own, and they were determined to restore it to her.

Mars was the master—but Mars herself was a slave! And power had enslaved the red planet even as it had Earth. A thousand years and more before the first clumsy Earth ships had landed on Mars. Mars, too, had had great plants for the transmutation of '238 into '235. But one night an object was found on the Great Plain near the city of Lanamarn. It had appeared without a whisper; it was an irregular cylinder containing various simple objects—spheres, cubes, triangular and square plane surfaces of a tough alloy. Each was marked by a symbol. The Martians experimented with the things, drew some shrewd conclusions, and deposited other objects in the cylinder, replacing the cap. There was a shrill whine; on removing the cap again, the Martians found that their offerings had disappeared and were replaced by still other objects, each of which also bore a symbol.

After long and painstaking effort, a written language was established between Mars and the mystery from space which had sent the cylinder. The Martians learned that it had come from Artna, a planet of the Procyon system, and that the method of transmission was by way of the probability wave, a scientific refinement beyond the understanding even of Mars. It worked on the principle that matter cannot be destroyed; if it is annihilated in one portion of space, it must necessarily appear somewhere else. The transmission is instantaneous; as soon as it is negated at its source, it simply occurs at its destination.

And the Artnans had a proposition, to wit: Perhaps there was some little thing the Martians would like in return for the boron which showed up so strongly on the Artnan's teleospectrographs. The Martians sent out a sample of U-238 and asked if the Artnans could transmute it, in bulk, to U-235. The Artnans could, and did. They cheerfully sent plans for construction of a tremendous plant on the plain. U-238 was dumped into hoppers, stored by machinery in bins deep in the heart of the apparatus, and disappeared. Elsewhere in the plant pure '235 poured out in pulverized, greenish-black abundance.

So Martian transmutation plants shut down, and Mars used Artnan atomic fuel exclusively. While boron was cheap, the arrangement was greatly to Mars' advantage. But the Artnans easily realized their advantage when they had cornered the power market, and they jumped the price. They kept it at just the level that would make it impossible for the Martians to reopen their own plants, until they had nearly exhausted the Martians' supply of both uranium and boron. They would accept no substitute for the boron; Mars faced an extreme economic reversal when the fortunate fact of communications with Earth was established. Hence Mars' economic penetration of Earth's resources; and now, Mars could afford to sit back and enjoy her position. Earthmen slaved in the boron mines; cargo after cargo of Terrestrial uranium was freighted to Mars to feed the maw of the gigantic "transmutation" plant on the Great Plain.

All this was discovered by Earth's spies, the dozens who came back out of the hundreds of thousands that sought the information. In two centuries, nine attempts were made on Earth to design and build a ship which could travel to Procyon fast enough to spare its crew the misfortune of dying of old age before the ship reached there. Eight crews of workers were discovered and killed or dispersed, put to work in the mines by wandering, gently thorough Martian investigators. The ninth ship got away—a physical impossibility, as the Mars-hating element on Earth freely admitted. Mars gave them no permission to build and launch the little silver craft; but the Martian investigators stretched the probability and did not discover the hidden factory.

Perhaps it was purposeful. Perhaps Mars was curious to know whether Earthmen could find the secret of Artnan transmutation. Mars couldn't. Even now that they had Earth's vast resources at their disposal, the Martians would be happy to free themselves from the Artnan monopoly of transmutation. They remembered with bitterness the carefully outfitted body of operatives who had entered the transmission chamber and had gone to Artna via the wave, in place of a scheduled cargo of boron. The Artnans, with their next shipment of '235, included the six-legged, two-foot long body of an Artnan and a polite note thanking the Martians for the inclusion of the *corpses!* and expressing regret that no living thing could traverse space time via the wave; also a reminder that the latest boron shipment was slightly overdue.

All of which flashed through Bell Bellew's mind as he stood beside Slimmy Cob and stared down at Artna. It had been a long trip— three years or so, even with the slight space warp stolen by workers in Martian shipyards. But Slimmy was good company, even if he did prefer horsing around to anything else in the world. They had both been picked for that quality, among many others. The reason was that the Martian mind is completely without humor, and the less

Martians could understand the two men, the better it would be.

"Do you see what I see?" asked Slimmy after a long moment.

Bell followed the little man's pointing finger. Down in a hollow, nearly invisible from above, lay the squat shape of the Martian space cruiser.

"I do. I wouldn't worry about that, Slimmy. I expected that they'd be here."

"Why?"

"As I told you—I don't think it was just luck that got this ship off Earth, out of our system. I think the Martians let us."

"Yeah." There was disbelief in Slimmy's voice. "The Martians have always treated us that way—let us do as we pleased, when we pleased. Wipe the rest of that soap off, Bell; it's addled your brain."

Bellew gave Slimmy a playful pat that brought him up against the opposite bulkhead, and went back to the controls. "Let me know when you sight anything that looks like the Great Plain transmutation plant," he said. "We can start from there."

The planet was but slightly larger than Earth, with an astonishingly smooth topography. There were no mountain ranges, and yet there were no true plains. The whole planet was surfaced with small rolling hillocks. Most were sandy; there was little vegetation. The Artnans, whose metabolism was a mineral one, had no agriculture.

After an hour or two Slimmy grunted and came away from the forward observation port and switched on the visiplate, tuning in the buildings he had spotted. "There she be, cap'n," he said.

Bell studied the great pile of alloy. "You got to give credit to those Martians," he said. "They certainly built theirs the spit an' image of this one."

"Not quite," said Slimmy, swinging the range finders. "Look there—see that ... that— What is it anyway?"

"Sort of a shed," said Bell. "One flat building, not more than three feet high, and all of ten miles square!"

A warning signal pinged, and their eyes swiveled toward it. A yellow light blinked among the studs on the panel. "Vibrations," gritted Bell, and put a thousand feet of altitude under them so fast that he heard Slimmy's kneecaps crackle. They circled slowly over the shed, feeling carefully ahead of them with delicate instruments, and charted the hemisphere of tight-knit waves that roofed the flat structure.

"What is it?" asked Slimmy.

"Dunno. Let's sit down and see if we can find out."

The ship settled down gently, her antigrav plates moaning. Bell followed the curve of the vibration field at a safe distance, and came down in a depression a hundred yards from its invisible edge.

"Air O.K.?"

"Sure," said Slimmy. "Just like home. Temperature's just under blood heat. Come a-walkin'!"

They strapped on side arms and went out, using the air lock for safety's sake. They topped a rise and stood a moment looking at the shed. It was barely visible from the ground, and there wasn't a sign of life anywhere about.

"Wonder why the sand don't drift over the thing," said Slimmy.

"This might be why," Bell grunted. He was staring at a line in the sand across the path. On their side of it, the sand puffed and tumbled in the light breeze. Toward the shed, however, there was apparently no moving air. "See that line? Unless I'm 'way off my base, that's the edge of the vibration field." He scooped up a handful of sand, stepped cautiously close to the line and tossed it. The sand fanned out, drifted over the line and—disappeared.

Slimmy tried it for himself before he commented. "I would gather," he said dryly, "that the Artnans would rather not have anyone look into that shed."

"Something like that," said Bell. "Look!" The crest of a nearby dune detached itself and scrabbled on six scrawny legs toward the line. It shot between the startled Earthmen, over the line, almost to the low wall of the shed before it turned up its pointed tail and burrowed quickly under the sand.

"What was that?" asked Slimmy.

"An Artnan, from what I've heard."

"Nasty little critter," said Slimmy. "Hey—the field didn't seem to bother it any, Bell."

"So I noticed. Seems that the field has been set up for the benefit of you and me. And maybe even for our Martian friends over there."

As they turned back toward their ship, Slimmy said pensively, "What we just saw is justification for the Laidlaw Hypothesis, if it makes any difference to you."

"What do you mean?"

"Speaks for itself, doesn't it? Laidlaw said that the inhabitants of any Solar System have a mutual ancestor, parallel evolutions, and similar metabolisms. You know yourself that Martians, Earthmen, Venusians and the extinct Jovians are all bipeds composed mainly of hydrocarbons. That field was set up to keep such molecular structures out. The sand here is apparently something of the sort. The Artnan who ran through the field was something different. We'll catch us one sometime and find out just what makes him tick."

"Yeah. You got something there. What interests me, though, is what's in that shed. If we guessed right about who it was put up for, then the shed must cover something they want to keep Solar noses out of. Ah—it wouldn't by any chance be what we're looking for, would it?"

Slimmy's eyes glowed. "The transmutation plant? Could be, pal; could be. It's adjacent to the Prob.-wave transmitter. It's screened against Earth or Martian interference."

"Huh!" Bell ran a thick forefinger up behind his ear. "We got a problem here, little man. We toss ourselves through nine-odd light years of space and wind up flat-footed in front of a killer-wave thrown up around a cubist's idea of a beanfield. I sort of expected a city—machinery, people, maybe."

"It's not simple," said Slimmy. "Howsomever, let's see if you can make your brains go where you flat feet fear to tread. Let's go to work on the Martians. From the looks of things, they've been messing around here for quite some time."

"Want to go right to work, don't you?" grinned Bell. "Always wanted to get a Martian alone away from his playmates so you could tie a half hitch in his eyestalks! O.K., buddy—where do we find us one?"

"If I know Martians, there ought to be a couple sniffing around our ship by this time."

There were.

They were lined up in front of the air lock, their spare bodies quivering with the palpitation peculiar to their race, and with their eyestalks pointing rigidly toward the approaching Earthmen, points together, in the well-known Martian cross-eyed stare. They had, of course, sensed the body vibrations of the men quite some time ago; the very fact that they were there meant that they were ready for a showdown.

"Hi, fellers," said Slimmy laconically, flipping the butt of his atomic gun to make sure that it was loose in the holster.

"What are you doing here?" piped the Martian on the right.

"We're rick-bijitting for a dew-jaw," said Slimmy immediately. He had studied the masterworks of the ancients in his extreme youth.

"Yes," said Bell, taking the cue. "We willised the altibob, and no sooner did we jellik than—*boom!* here we are."

The Martians regarded them silently. "You do not tell the truth," one of them said.

"It ain't a lie," Bell dead-panned.

The evasion served its purpose, for to them, anything that was not a lie was the truth, and vice versa. Their hearing apparatus was partly sensitive to air-vibration and partly telepathic. Bell's last statement was the truth and they knew it was the truth; that convinced them. They'd die before they admitted they didn't know what the men were talking about.

"What are *you* doing here?" Slimmy countered, before their machinelike minds could work on the problem.

The Martians stiffened. "It is not for you to ask," said one of them.

"Aw, don't be like that, son," drawled Bell. "Haven't Martians always told Earthmen that Mars takes only its just due, and does nothing for Earth but good?"

"Yeah," said Slimmy. His inflection was drawn-out, lowering, and meant "That's a lot of so-and-so!"

But to the Martians "Yeah" meant "Yes," and that was that. "Why should things be different here? You don't have to hide the fact that you're looking for the same thing we are; maybe we can make a little deal."

"Sure—come in and set awhile!" Bell pushed past the Martians and unlatched the airlock. He knew that turning his back on the enemy was bad tactics, but it was good diplomacy. Besides, fast on their feet as Martians were, no one in the Universe could draw, aim and fire faster than little Slimmy Cob.

Slimmy walked around the Martians, not between them, and sidled into the ship. He apparently faced the Martians merely to talk to them. "Sure—come on in. Maybe we can give each other a hand. We can decide later what to do if we get the information we're after."

Three sets of eyestalks intertwined briefly, and then the three spindly Martians bent and entered the silver ship.

The Martians squatted in a row against the starboard bulkhead, sipping Earth's legendary cocola through glassite straws and coming as near to a feeling of well-being as was possible to these unemotional logicians. Slimmy's sharp eyes had noticed that one of them was taller than the others, the second taller than the third. Knowing that Martian names, being in the semi-telepathic Martian language, were unpronounceable to humans, he had dubbed them Heaven, Its Wonders, and Hell.

"Have another coke," said Bell heartily.

Its Wonders passed his empty flask. Bellew flashed a glance at Slimmy and Slimmy nodded. The Martians were getting nicely mellow; a carbonated drink plasters up the Martian metabolism with amazing efficiency. Intoxication, however, is not befuddlement to a Martian. It merely makes him move slower and think faster. If he drinks enough, he will stop altogether and turn into a genius for an hour or so. The idea of gassing the Martians up was to disarm them as to the human's motives; for they knew that no human would dare to try to pull the wool over a drunken Martian's eyes.

The Martians accepted the drink as a gesture of good faith, for they knew that they would soon be unable to navigate. It was the pipe of peace between them, with the Earthmen paying the piper, which was the way any deal with Mars seems to work out. So when the pale-blue flush began to blossom across their leathery hides,

Slimmy went to work on them.

"Look fellers," he said bluntly, "there's no sense in our cutting each other's throats for a while yet. If you've guessed what we're here after, you've probably guessed right. We know that Martian '238 isn't transmuted into '235 on Mars. We know it's done here, in that flat building under the killer field over there. All we want to know is how it's done, and whether or not the method can be used in our System."

"What has that to do with us?" asked Hell.

"I'll take the question as a feeler," Bellew cut in. "You want to find out how much else we know. All right. We know that more than half of Terrestrial and Martian industry is being diverted to the production of boron to pay for the Artnans' processing of '238. We know that Martian domina ... er ... control of the Solar System won't be complete unless and until the Artnan process of transmutation is made the property of Mars; for every indication shows that the cost of the Artnan process must be practically nothing. We know that the Martian Command did not have the process when we left the System three years ago, and we know that you don't have it yet because we wouldn't have found any Martians here if you had."

Heaven said, "What do you want to find the process for?"

"I might say that we of Earth would like to return to Mars some of the many kindnesses she has done us," said Slimmy around the tongue of his cheek. "And I might say that it's none of your damn business. I'll do neither, and simply say that I won't insult your intelligence by considering the question."

Three sets of eyestalks fumblingly sought each other out and, intertwining, connected their owners in a swift, silent conference. Coming out of the huddle, Heaven addressed the humans. "We have certain information bearing on the matter at hand. How can we be assured that it will be to our benefit to share it?"

Bell answered that. "I've no idea how long you've been here, but it seems as though you haven't got on the right track yet. I don't know whether we'll be able to find the process with your information and our brains. If we can, well and good. If we can't, what have you lost?"

"We will share it," decided Its Wonders instantly. "All we know is this: The Artnans are a race totally unlike anything in our System. They have a mineral metabolism, feeding on ores and excreting sulphides. Their culture is beyond our understanding; they seem beyond the reach of Solar reasoning. They have made no attempt to drive us away from the planet. They have also made no attempt to communicate with us, in spite of the fact that they must know we are Martians and that it is with Martians that they trade. The vibration field around the transmutation plant cannot be penetrated by anything but light; it even excludes a spy ray. There is no way of estimating the extent of their science or their civilization. They exist mainly underground; for all we know, this may be an artificial planet. There is a possibility that their science is no more advanced than ours, but that it has simply progressed along other lines. The trade with Mars may be a major or a very minor industry with them. It is completely impossible to tell. That is all we have been able to discover."

"That might help," said Bellew, "and it might not. We'll work on it. Now. There's one more little point we have to take care of. How can all concerned be sure that there is no dirty work? How do we know that we will not be killed if we get the secret; how do you know that we will not kill you for it if you beat us to the gun?"

"We can promise," said Its Wonders in his spark-coil voice.

"Won't do, chum," said Slimmy. "No reflection on you, but in spite of the fact that a Martian has never been known to break his word, we don't want you establishing precedents. Bad for the racial morale. Got any other ideas?"

Bellew sometimes wished that Martians could add inflection, voice control, to their speech. You couldn't tell whether they were sore, happy, insulted—anything. He shook his head quickly at Slimmy—the little man was pushing things a little.

However, Its Wonders didn't seem annoyed by the refusal of his word. "We could," he said, "destroy each other's weapons."

"Would you agree to such a proposition?"

"Yes," chorused the three Martians.

Once they were together again in their emasculated ship, Slimmy and Bell compared notes.

"What's their ship like?" Slimmy wanted to know.

"Smooth," said Bell. "An Ikarion 44, with all the fixin's. Got that old-style ether-cloud steering for hyper-space travel, though—you know—the one that builds etheric resistance on one bow or the other to turn the ship when she's traveling faster than light? We can outmaneuver them if it comes to a chase."

Slimmy grinned. "That bootleg ether rudder of ours is so perfect because it's so simple, but it's not the easiest thing in the world to adapt to an Ikarion. How's their spatial steering?"

"Same as ours," answered Bell. "So all we need is the process and a small start. Fat chance . . . By the way—remember what Its Wonders said about the killer field's stopping a spy ray? That was a slip on his part. I got looking for one when I was busting up their big guns. They have one, sure enough—a neat, little portable, sound and visiscreen; and I'll bet my back teeth it records. We got to watch our mouths."

"Yeah." Slimmy walked over and drew himself a flask of cocola, then came and sat on his bunk next to Bell.

Bell was surprised to find that on the way Slimmy had snatched up the cellotab and stylus. He took it, shielded it closely, and began to write as he talked about the Martian ship. In a few minutes he passed the tablet to Slimmy. It read:

"A laugh for you. Heaven and Its Wonders no sooner got out of here than they began to pump me about why you'd tried to kill me just before we landed. We were right; they saw you shooting me with the water pistol and it threw their mental gears into six speeds at once. Couldn't understand why you didn't kill me or why I didn't kill you for trying. Suggested that if I wanted to slip you the double-x, they'd see to it that you were killed. Gave me a phial of Martian paralysis virus. They told me that if we found the Artnan secret, if I killed you with the virus, I'd be protected when they brought me back to the System."

"Yep," said Slimmy aloud as he reached for the stylus, "them Martians are certainly nice fellers."

Bellew motioned to Slimmy to duck the cellotab, winked, stretched and said, "You think we ought to grab some sleep?"

Slimmy said, "Why, sure," with admirable promptness, considering that both of them had had the sleep-centers removed from their brains by outlaw Earth surgeons in preparation for the trip.

While Slimmy pulled off his shoes, Bell went to a locker and slid two pairs of thick spectacles under his tunic, along with two disks of the same material as the lenses. He switched off the lights, pulled his own bunk out from the bulkhead over Slimmy's, dropped a pair of spectacles and a disk on the little man's chest, and rolled into bed. Both men clipped the disks to their bunklights, switched them on, and donned the glasses. Martians, possessing vision far into the ultra-violet, are blind to the reds merging into the infrared which is so prevalent on their own planet. If the spy ray was functioning—and of course it was—all the screen showed was a lot of nothing on a background of the same, and all the amplifier picked up was the tiny whisper of a busy stylus.

"Been thinking about those Artnans," wrote Bell. "What do you suppose is the reason for their building that transmutation shed on the surface of the planet if their civilization is underground?"

"To be near the transmitter, I'd imagine. Far as I know, a probability wave can't operate below ground."

"Seems likely. What's your guess about the process?"

"That, bud, is our little stymie. The Martians have tested the ground right clear up to the edge of the killer field for vibrations from machinery. They heard the footsteps and the burrowing of the Artnans, and the noise from the Prob.-wave transmitter and receiver. But that's all. Artnan workers—not more than eight or ten at a time—tend whatever's in that shed. Now and then a blast of artificial wind rushes through the shed. Right afterward big suction intakes gather up a powdery material and collect it in the hoppers which feed '235 into the transmitter. Then the wind blasts back with a slightly heavier powder. There's also a little vegetative sound—spores popping and what-not—but our Martian friends don't know whether there is some plant life in the shed or whether the vibrations come from the flora outside. That's lot of info to get from ground vibrations, but you know Martian detection instruments."

"Wonder what the Artnans do with the boron they get from

Mars?" Slimmy wrote after a silent interval.

"Eat it, I guess. For all we know, the whole setup that has made Earth a slave and put Mars on the economic rocks may be just a sideline to the Artnans. Maybe it's candy to them, or a liquor industry. That's something we'll never know as long as the Artnans act so unsociable."

"They don't behave like an outfit that's trying to keep a monopoly," Slimmy scrawled. "Seems to me their very treatment of us and the Martians is their way of telling us, 'We found the process. If you want to dig it up for yourselves, go to it.' They don't seem to give much of a damn whether we do or not."

"Seems sound enough. I wish we could get some slant on their psychology. Their reasoning is so alien to anything we have in our System. Old Laidlaw was right."

Bell handed this to Slimmy and then snatched it back excitedly. *"The Laidlaw Hypothesis!"* he underlined. "That's the answer! Laidlaw said that each Solar System had civilizations and cultures with a common ancestor, which ancestor was peculiar to the System. For that reason there is no way of predicting in what direction a new system's fauna will evolve. The Artnans are mineral eaters, right? Then, according to Laidlaw, their plants have a corresponding metabolism, and so has every other living thing in the system! Do you see what I'm getting at?"

"No," said Slimmy aloud, forgetting himself. Bell snatched the pad and belted the little man's mouth with it before he wrote:

"It isn't an apparatus process, dope! The Artnans don't transmute '238 into '235 by electrochemistry or radiophysics or any other process we ever heard of! Those Artnans in the shed aren't scientists or even mechanics! They're *gardeners!*"

"Plants?" Slimmy's amazement dug the stylus deep into the cellotab. "How can plants transmute one isotope into another?"

"An Artnan might like to know how an Earth plant can change light and water and minerals into cellulose," wrote Bell. "Now; plant or mold or fungus—what sort of a place might it come from?"

"Not here," was Slimmy's prompt reply. "The atmosphere is slightly humid. Water and pure '235 don't mix. Any plant that gave off atomic fuel that way would blow itself from here to Scranton. It must have been brought here from an airless planet or satellite too hot or too cold for water to exist."

"Is there such a body in this system?"

In answer, Slimmy rolled out of his bunk and went to the chart desk, returning with a sketched astro map of the system.

"Two," he wrote on the edge of the chart. "This one"—an arrow indicated a large planet far away from the double sun—"and this peanut here. A ninety-six-day year, son, and it's hot. I mean, but torrid. Don't tell me anything from there could live here, if at all."

"Might, if it's a mold, or a bacterium. Temperature wouldn't make much difference to a really simple metallic mold. It's worth a try. How do we get out there without taking our three little playmates with us?"

They thought that over for a while, and then Slimmy giggled and wrote, "Buddy, I feel an awful attack of Martian paralysis coming on!"

Bell snapped his fingers, lay back in his bunk and roared with laughter.

Heaven, Its Wonders and Hell squatted excitedly before the portable spy-ray set in the center of their control room, watching the scene it pictured. Slimmy's head protruded from a small iron lung built into the bulkhead, and his head was stretched back so far that the skin on his neck seemed on the breaking point. His face was bluish; there was a thin line of foam on his lips, and his breath whispered whistling through the annunciator.

"Traitorous creature," piped Its Wonders. "He has taken our advice and inoculated his companion with the disease."

Heaven waved his eyestalks. "Where is that Earthman, anyway?"

A loud *thuck! thuck!* answered his question, as Bell Bellew banged on the insulated gate to the Martians' air lock. Heaven reached out a long, jointless arm and pressed a panel; the door opened.

"Hey," Bell roared before he was well into the room, "you guys better come a-runnin'. My partner's went and got himself some Martian paralysis and he can't last much longer." Bell permitted himself a leer.

"What has that to do with us?" Heaven wanted to know.

"Everything. He has the secret of the Artnan process. His voice is gone now; all he can do is gurgle. I ain't telepathic; you are. His gurgles ought to make some sense to you."

"You stupid primitive," squeaked Its Wonders. "What do you mean by inoculating him and endangering the secret? If he dies with it, we may never discover it!"

Bell looked sheepish. "Well, it was this way," he said. "Slimmy figured it all out. Said it was simple once you got the idea—one of those things that's so evident you can't see it. I asked him what it was. He wouldn't say. Said he'd tell me if his life was in danger, but not before. It was too dangerous for both of us to know. I got to thinking. If we got back to Earth with the secret, we'd have no chance of keeping it from Mars. Mars would take the process and kill us for our pains. Why should I get myself killed? If I tied in with you, I had your promise of protection. So I slipped him the virus, thinkin' he'd tell me the process when he knew what was the matter with him. But it hit him too fast. I can't understand a word. Come on— he may be dead before we get there!" So saying, the big Earthman turned and bolted out of the Martian ship.

The Martians held a shrill consultation and then took out after Bell, their thin claws eating up the distance. Bell was running with everything he had, but the Martians passed him before he had gone an eighth of the way. They were not even breathing hard.

Martian paralysis is sure death to the people of the red planet. When Bell got to the ship he found the three Martians pressing as close to Slimmy as they dared, which was about five feet. They were straining to hear what Slimmy was mumbling, and stared annoyedly when Bell burst in.

"Get away from him," Bell wheezed. "Dammit, now you'll never get the information. He'd die before he'd tell it to a Martian."

"Be quiet!" snapped Hell. "He is past that. The paralysis strikes first at the eyes, then at the hearing. He doesn't know who is here."

Slimmy's tortured voice broke from moans into words. "Bell ... process ... electrolization of ... dying, I guess ... lousy Martian ... process ... electrolization of—" Suddenly he made a tremendous

259

effort, lifted his head, and said in a perfectly normal, conversational tone, "We're rikbijitting for a dewjaw." Then his head snapped back and he lay still.

Bell blundered over to the after bulkhead, ripped open the cold locker, and tossed three flasks of cocola to the Martians. "Drink up," he snapped. "You're going to need all your brains from now on if you're going to savvy *that*." He waved a hand toward Slimmy, who was babbling busily away about fortissing a sanzzifranz.

The Martians sucked away eagerly at the frothy liquid; willing to do anything that would sharpen their senses.

So Slimmy muttered and the Martians guzzled, and in forty minutes Bell stopped passing out cocola and went to the iron lung and opened it, and Slimmy climbed out, rubbing his neck and cussing softly.

"That was a long haul, Bell," he complained.

"You did fine, kid," said Bell. "I must remember to slip you the real thing sometime."

"What are we going to do with these disgustingly intemperate creatures?" asked Slimmy, indicating the Martians.

They were propped up against the bulkhead, limp eyestalks registering their impotent rage. They were absolutely helpless, though their implacable brains were clicking away like high-speed calculating machines.

Bell thought, and snickered: "You stick around and watch 'em. I'm going to take a ride. I'll leave fifty gallons of coke with you. They're too plastered to keep you from opening their ugly faces and pouring more coke in. Don't let them sober up. Just keep telling them that they'll drink it or you'll drown them in it."

Together they lifted the limp bodies and dropped them in the sand outside. "We ought to knock them off," said Slimmy.

"I thought of that. But if you could see farther than your excuse for a nose, you might remember that we have nothing but a shrewd guess as to the accuracy of our idea about the process. If we're wrong, these guys might come in handy again."

"Anything you say," said Slimmy reluctantly. "I'll take good care of them until you get back. After that, I can't promise. Take care of yourself, incidentally."

"Worry not, little man. Ought to be back inside of fifty hours. So long." He slapped Slimmy's back and dove back into the ship.

The port closed with a clang, and the silver ship rose, circled twice, and dwindled to a point before it slipped under the horizon. Slimmy looked after it longingly and then turned to the helpless Martians.

"Time for your bottles, babies," he said, and went to work pouring the cocola into their gullets.

Bell followed the planet's surface until he was sure he was out of sight of the drunken Martians, and then curved up and away into space. As soon as he was out of the planet's effective space warp, he slipped into hyperspace and traveled toward Procyon and its dark companion at many times the speed of light. Watching his chronometers closely, he spun dials and flipped switches in each phase of acceleration and deceleration, and then went spatial again not two thousand miles from the inner planet. In spite of the almost perfect physical insulation of the craft, it was already growing warmer in the control room. Bellew set up a small warp around the ship to convert the heat into light that could be sent back toward the twin suns, and then began circling the planet. Delicate instruments felt into the depths of every crater, every boiling sea of rock on the hot little world. Bell let the ship fall into an orbit, and with one eye glued to a teleo-spectrograph and the other to his detector instruments, he searched every inch of area as it passed beneath him. The hunt didn't take long—there was uranium aplenty down there. There were great pits of U-236 and '37, something he didn't know existed in the Universe, so rare are they.

But—and his teeth flashed in a wide grin as he saw it—there were correspondingly great masses of both '238 and '235. He brought the ship close to the surface, cloaked in its light-building warp, near a fiery plain where both isotopes could be detected. Through a screened telescope he saw what he was after—a field of writhing growth, nearly hidden by a fine dust of spores. They weren't plants—they were molds; and at enormous magnification he observed their life cycle as they ate into the uranium, turning the rarer isotopes into their structures, throwing out all impurities, including U-235. Their rate of metabolism was astonishingly fast; and when a colony of them had exhausted all the uranium near it, the molds cast off their spores and died. The spores, heavily encysted, drifted about in the hot gases at the surface, until the nearness of their food drew them to the planet's semi-molten surface. Then they sprouted, fed, spored and died again.

Bellew let his ship settle even more, and dropped a tube of berylu-steel from the hull to a drift of spores. A few of them were drawn upward by the suction he set up; then, tube and all, he snapped the ship into space. Once out there, he experimented briefly and thoroughly with his prize. The mold certainly filled the bill. The cysts apparently could stay alive without nourishment indefinitely. They germinated readily at any temperature, as long as they were in the presence of uranium. Happily, Bellew slipped into hyperspace and dove back toward Artna.

The search of the inner planet and the capture of the spores had taken considerably longer than Bell had expected; he was twenty hours overdue when at last he sighted the great Artnan probability wave transmitter. He cast about anxiously for the spot where he had left Slimmy and the Martians. There was nothing there but tumbled sand.

Bell flung the ship down and, through a telescope, examined the ground. There had been a scuffle, apparently, and if Bell knew Slimmy, it must have been a pip, in spite of the fact that Martians are three times as strong as any human.

"A hell of a mess," he murmured, and swung the ship toward the hollow where lay the Martian cruiser.

Landing next to it, he hunted through Slimmy's locker until he found what he wanted, concealed in a cleverly devised secret compartment. Then he opened the air lock and strode over to the Martian ship.

The port swung open as he approached. Its Wonders stood there, apparently suffering little from what must have been quite a hangover. "What do you want?"

"Slimmy. What have you done with him?"

"Your companion is safe. He will be returned to you alive if you give us what you went away to get."

"You've killed him!"

Its Wonders stood aside. "Come in and see for yourself."

Bell pushed past him. Slimmy was there, looking very sheepish in the iron grip of the other two Martians.

"Hiya, boy," he said.

"Slimmy! What happened?"

"What happened to you in Cincinnati that night we spent at Bert's place?"

Bellew remembered the occasion. He wasn't proud of it. He'd tried to outdrink half a dozen boron miners and had failed rather miserably. He remembered with distaste the oily feeling at the pit of his stomach, and how liquor had suddenly turned from one of the greater pleasures of life into nothing more nor less than an emetic. "What's that got to do—"

"They fooled me, that's all. After you'd been gone about eight hours or so they stopped trying not to swallow the stuff and began to get greedy. I missed the gag—I fed it to them as fast as they would take it. They all got sick. Very sick. Then they started to sober up, and I had to feed 'em more while they were still weak. Gallon for gallon, they threw off what I fed them. I don't know how they did it—they sure can take it. Anyhow, I ran plumb out of cocola. We shoulda killed 'em."

"We will," said Bell grimly, his jaw bunching. "O.K., fellers—let him go now." He reached casually into his pocket and pulled out a blue-steel automatic blaster. The Martians stiffened indignantly.

"Where did you get that?" said Heaven. "We had your promise to allow us to destroy every weapon you had aboard. You destroyed all of ours. How is it that you kept that?"

Again Bell found himself wishing that a Martian could express emotion. He'd have given anything to know just how mad the tall Martian was.

"This," said Bellew, stepping aside to let the released Slimmy past him, "is what we call, on Earth, an ace in the hole."

The Martians started and stopped a concerted rush at Bell as he glanced over to see if Slimmy was safe in the silver ship, and then turned to them again.

"Nice to've known you," he said, and backed out.

As the Earth ship rose gently away from Artna, Slimmy looked happily up from the controls. "You know, Bell, in spite of the fact that it was a dirty trick to hold out that blaster after giving our word, I'm glad you did it."

Bell looked at the blaster and grinned, moving toward the refuse lock. "Swing her a little left," he said, sighting through a port. "You got the wrong idea, chum." He dropped the gun into the lock, closed the upper door, and put his hand on the dumping lever. "We promised to let them destroy all our deadly weapons. They did. Am I glad to do *this!*" and he threw the lever. The gun curved down and dropped right in front of the air lock of the Martian ship. Three lanky figures pounced on it, and a jet of soapy water shot futilely up at them.

Biddiver

I T I S E V E N T R U E R in fact than in fiction that more important business is transacted in palaces of pleasure than is ever handled in austere offices. Such a deal was taking place in such a hangout between two swarthy individuals who sat in a semiprivate room just off the dance floor of the Purple Pileus, the most expensive drinkery in the most exclusive section of the richest city on three planets.

"I thought you might like it," said one of the two men. "Inside and out, it's a standard model—two wheels, gyro-stabilized, antigrav plates to support it while the wheels drive it; conventional controls. Old George Carrington himself couldn't tell it from the latest Carrington '78."

"What's that to me?" said the other. "I'm satisfied with the cars I have."

"You won't be, Eric, when you've seen this one. It's just a little bit special."

"With a special price on it, hey?"

"Nothing you couldn't afford. You can have it for a present if you'll play ball with me. I mean"—he added at the other's quick glance—"if you'll allow me to play ball with you."

"What's your proposition?"

"Something like this—I am cut to the quick when my own brother is victimized by such a creature as The Fang. A terrible thing. The finest ship in your fleet, wasn't she? And pirated, burned to a cinder, crew and all, by that spectacular criminal with the melodramatic name. *Tsk, tsk!*"

"Get to the point," growled Eric. "Even if I had nothing to do with my time, you'd still be wasting it."

"I'll get there," said his brother happily. "That piracy—it was particularly tough on the insurance company, wasn't it? The cargo

265

was insured for ten times the value of the ship, which in itself was plenty."

"It cost me ten times the value of the ship," said Eric shortly.

"Of course it did. I read the record of the investigation. A government man stood by a sealed meter and watched the stuff being pumped into the tanks. Only thing is, one of my men was watching the flow in your secret chamber under the loading platform. Every drop that went into the ship wound up in the tank it came from. Two million barrels of lucasium, the finest atomic fuel yet synthesized. The insurance company paid you for it; then you sold it to Martian Spaceways, whose stock you control, at a phony high price 'justified' by the shortage created by The Fang's highjacking."

Eric's knuckles whitened against the background of the blue champagne in his glass; otherwise he gave no sign of having heard.

"Before I go on," continued his brother easily, "I want to point out that my death will result in the delivery of two cans of sound film to the government. They tell the whole story. I'll run off a print of them for you any time you'd like to see them. In other words, it'll pay you to see that nothing happens to me."

"The air in here," said Eric absently, "smells of blackmail."

"Perish the thought!" said the other primly. "Have I demanded anything?"

"Not yet," said Eric. "And to tell you the truth, that's what bothers me a little. I know the way you work—I should, by this time—and I don't doubt that you have the film you mentioned. You're the only man I ever heard of who was oily enough to get it. What else can you want but a payoff?"

"I want to help you. I want to fight this menace shoulder to shoulder with you. After all, blood is thicker than water. Never let it be said that Budd Arnik wouldn't risk half the danger that threatens his brother."

"I get it. For half the 'danger,' half the profits. Right? You got a busy liver, son, building up all that gall. The answer is *no!*"

Budd stretched out his legs, shoved his hands deep in his pockets and smiled at his brother. "When I said I could help you, I meant it. You've set yourself up a nice racket there, but you always did lack imagination. You haven't begun to tap the possibilities. Now, about that car I was trying to give you, because I like you so much. It's— well, look!" He pointed at the glass brick wall, through which could be seen the exquisitely landscaped driveway which led up to the Purple Pileus.

A beautifully clean vehicle swept in at the gate, just one long, lean sliver of chrome and iridescent blue. There was bulk there, and weight, but it took an engineer to spot it, so fine were its ultra-streamlined curves. Its two wheels, which thrust themselves far ahead and behind the car, were individually sprung, and supported the great teardrop about six feet off the ground. Both wheels ran inside a tread which moved on shaped tracks, so that they were rounded in front and sharply pointed in the rear. From the ground up, then, each fore-and-aft cross section of the machine was a perfect stream-line. The car came to a whispering stop at the entrance, and the wheels retracted, setting the hull swiftly and gently to the ground. A lovely sight.

"Carrington '78," said Eric. "What about it?"

"Just the thing for the man about town, isn't it? To look at, it is simply the right vehicle for a man of your position. The one I have parked outside is exactly the same in every respect—with a slight difference. It has every feature of a stock car with just one or two more."

"Such as—"

"A momentum neutralizer. An automatic refueling screen—repels large bodies, sweeps in small ones for transmutation into air, food, fuel. And—an armament. Why, I couldn't begin to tell you—"

"You don't have to," snapped Eric. "What the hell use is a car like that to me? Or—to my organization?" He sipped slowly, digesting the items Budd had just reeled off. "What's the idea of all that gadgetry on a surface car?"

"The idea is that it isn't a surface car, obviously. Why, that machine will operate practically forever without having to stop for fuel and supplies. It will fly. It will push the speed of light between here and anything you can see with a telescope. Don't you see, or is it that you won't admit it? It's the perfect getaway. The perfect front. Piracy?

Pal, you haven't touched the subject. For example, suppose you ship a cargo of automobiles to Mars, and there is another regrettable incident like The Fang's little coup. The ship just might explode gently enough to strew that portion of space with parts of the cargo. Thereafter, any other ship on the same run, sighting an automobile afloat in space, would pay little attention—until the automobile began spouting atomic shells and setting up a sleep-destroying field.

"Outlets for the stuff? Well, there's the colony on Neptune— remember? It was a prison once, and they revolted just for the privilege of staying where they were to colonize like free men. I don't have to tell you about Mars and Venus and the asteroid colonies. We'd do all right."

"On principle," said Eric. "I hate to confess it, but you really have something there." He beamed. "Yes, you most certainly—" The two swarthy heads moved close together over the table.

Neither of the Arnik brothers was in a position to see the man who stepped out of the blue Carrington and strode purposefully into the Purple Pileus. Protecting his jauntiness with a hundred-dollar bill, he evaded the grim headwaiter's intention of locking him out, and marched up to the bar.

He was a most extraordinary figure, from the top of his mauve streamlined hat, through his iridescent vest to his flexi-glastic shoes. He barely cleared five feet. His body was tubby but his arms apparently couldn't understand that, for they were long and scrawny. From his brow to an inch below his eyes, his nose turned up; from there on, down. His short upper lip slanted sharply toward his tonsils, which had the effect of making his chinlessness positively jut. He ordered *lyanka*, which is the Martian word for "equalizer," with the air of a man who couldn't possibly hold even one but who has just had three. The large bill on the bar overcame the barkeep's desire to protect a customer against himself, and the man was served. He slurped from the goblet and looked around him.

"So this is the top. This is the—wha' you call—ul-timate."

"This is the Poiple Pileus," said the bartender.

"Oh, yeah ... yeah ... I know. What I mean, this's what people work up to. People put down numbers in books, maybe, drive transports—stuff like that, five hours a day, five days a week, week in, week out." He ran out of breath and inhaled some *lyanka* with his air. "People ... *fft* ... 'scuse me ... all got the idea someday they'll be rich. When they get rich, they come to a place like this. *Fft.* What I want to know is, why? Get just as drunk at Casey's Hardwater Store."

"Casey's ain't exclusive," the barkeep pointed out.

"Take me, now," said the fantasy on the paying side of the board. "Biddiver's my name. Two days ago I'm on the assembly line up at General, and somebody name of Phoebe Biddiver dies. Yesterday I got two million bucks, free and clear. Today I buy everything I ever thought I wanted and go every place I ever wanted to see. An' now what?"

"What?"

"An' now I don't know what to do tomorrow." The bartender was fascinated by the way the teardrops proceeded down Biddiver's amazing nose. One drop would dash almost halfway, and then hesitate, daunted by the hump. Then it would be joined by another teardrop, and the two, merging, would surmount the obstacle and slip down to hang glittering over the disappearing lip until a sob came along to shake them off. "I ain't done nothin' to nobody," complained Biddiver brokenly. "I don't want to do nothin' to nobody. What did I do to deserve this?"

"Guys what don't want to do nothin' to nobody," said the bartender, in a philosophic flash, "most generally don't amount to nothin'."

"What do you mean?"

"Just what I say. This place, now, it crawls with big shots. Every one of them walked up to the top on other guys' faces. Take that Fang feller now, that's in all the papers. Bad egg, sure. But at the top all the same. Sneaks up on a tanker on the Earth-Venus run, swipes the cargo, burns the ship and the crew, and disappears. Then he tells three planets an' the whole Belt, speakin' through every ultraradio set that happens to be turned on, that he is The Fang, an' he is the one who done it, an' he'll do it again whenever he feels like it. Not a direction indicator in the System can locate where he's broadcasting from. See what I mean? He's smart an' he doesn't give a damn about who he roughs up. Now look. See those two guys in that semi-private over there? They're the Arnik brothers. One's a shipper an' the other's a kind of freelance gorilla. They operate the same way as The Fang. They must like it or they wouldn't keep it up." He nodded sagely. "If I had as much change as you do, I wouldn't get down in the mouth about it. The main idea in gettin' really rich is to be rich in the first place; then you make your money, take people out, lose 'em and come back with their bank accounts. I seen it done right here."

Biddiver shook his head weakly. "I don't think I could be that kind of a heel."

"You can be. Rich people can't afford to be nice about things. Only guys who work for a living can do that, an' even then they got to watch themselves or they'll get took over." He peered at Biddiver, judging expertly his state of insobriety, and then pointedly took away his goblet, rinsed it and put it away.

Biddiver took the hint because, by now, he wasn't feeling so good. He waved the change from his bill back to the bartender and weaved out. The barkeep pocketed the money, shaking his head sourly, quite unaware of the fact that his little speech had created an interplanetary menace.

Biddiver somehow reached the Carrington and nudged the door open. He sprawled into the driver's seat and touched the starting lever. The door locked as the machine rose up on its two wheels, gyroscopes whirring ever so faintly. On each side of Biddiver, an upholstered arm swung upward until it embraced him in foamy comfort. He pressed the panel which presented itself to his right forefinger; the brakes released themselves and the machine started forward. Pulling gently with his right and then his left hand, he turned the car and wheeled it out of the gate and into the street. Plastered as he was, he realized that in this machine he had one thing that it would take him a long, long while to tire of. He pressed the accelerator under his finger, and as he passed the 150-k.p.h. mark the speedometer's mechanical whisper cut in— "One sixty— One sixty-eight— One eighty—" He loved the sleepy surge of the car, its metrical obedience. "Damn if she won't up an' take off one of these days," he muttered as he leaned over to turn on the radio.

And when he flipped the switch she did take off.

"What I don't understand," said Eric Arnik, "is why you bother to come to me at all. You have the goods on me, to a certain extent; you have the car and you have some rather sweet ideas on how to use it."

"Oh, that." Budd inspected his stylishly scalloped fingernails. "I have to have a lot of research done, you see. I could have it taken care of easily enough, but news gets around, you know. You have all the facilities in your little undercover laboratories. If I work along with you, I can get it done right and fast. Particularly since you realize how much it will be to your own interest."

"What sort of research?"

"On the car, of course. You don't think I built it myself, do you? It was like this— I ran across a bright old fellow who had a few ambitious ideas along the lines of auto design. I asked him if he could build something like this baby of mine. He could and he did, but he was curious about why I wanted it and was fool enough to ask me some questions. Luckily for all concerned, he died of natural causes."

"You mean you just naturally slipped him a ticket out?"

"Something like that," said Budd carelessly. "Terrible, the filtrable viruses that can get accidentally into a man's air conditioning unit. Anyway, here I am with the car and no plans or blueprints of any kind. I'll have to get it to someone who can knock it down and duplicate it. That's up to your boys."

"I see. Is the car really on the up-and-up? I mean, have you tested it?"

"And how." A gleam of enthusiasm crept across Budd's deadpan face. "Come on—let's get out of here. I'll show you." Eric paid the bill and they left. When they were seated in the big blue Carrington Budd said, "Oh—by the way. I can't show you any altitude yet. The one thing the old boy hadn't quite perfected was the Heaviside screen."

"He didn't?" Eric's face flushed with anger. "Damn it, what good is the car to us without that? You expect my technicians to build a

Heaviside unit small enough to fit into this jalopy? Why, the smallest one ever built weighs more than three tons!"

"Take it easy, pal," soothed his brother. "There are a lot of new principles involved in this wagon. Your boys are pretty good—they ought to get a lead after looking over the rest of the equipment."

"I hope so. Damn that Heaviside business anyway."

"You ought to be glad that the layer's there, chum, and that science knows a way to synthesize one for spacecraft. Did you ever hear what happens to a man when he's exposed to unfiltered cosmic radiation?"

"I heard." Unaccountably, Eric Arnik shuddered. Budd started the car.

Biddiver was in that enviable state of inebriation in which he could not be surprised. When he threw the switch to get some music and nothing happened, he did what any trained driver will do—glance far ahead through the windshield to see if the road is clear enough to allow him to investigate his controls for a few seconds. Only there wasn't any road. He blinked carefully and looked again, and there still was no road. Just a blankness, with a silly little cloud in the middle of it. He suddenly realized that he was looking into the sky; but he was looking, not up, but *ahead* into it. He grunted surprisedly and hauled at the left chair arm. The cloud ahead disappeared and was replaced by a rapidly expanding relief map. It struck Biddiver as a little ominous; he pulled at the right chair arm until the windshield framed a horizon.

For no reason at all he was reminded of a satire, centuries old, which he had read, concerning a college boy who yielded to the temptation of his evil companions, drank a glass of beer and staggered out of the saloon with delirium tremens. "Been a good boy all m' life," he reflected bitterly, "because I couldn't afford to be any other way. And now—four drinks, an' this." He wagged his head, hauled back on both arms at once. When he saw the little cloud again, he let go and slumped down in his seat. He was quite convinced he was dreaming, but he didn't want to dream about a crack-up in a flying automobile, and he felt he would far rather bump the cloud. He went quite peacefully to sleep then, ignoring the new whispering voice that joined that of the speedometer:

"Four hundred twelve k.p.h.—"

"Altitude twenty-three thousand fifty—"

"Four eighty-three k.p.h.—"

"Altitude twenty-five thousand, thirty-three—"

But he woke, completely sober, when the car hurtled through the Heaviside layer.

Twenty minutes after the second Carrington '78 pulled away from the Purple Pileus, it swept back again and two men leaped out. One was flushed and one was pale, but both were furious. They pounced on the frightened doorman.

"Where's my car? What happened to the other Carrington?"

"Wh—Mr. Arnik, I—" His eyes bulged in terror. He had heard of the Arniks. "A gentleman drove off in it. He had only stayed a half hour or so. His car was exactly like—"

"That's what you think," spat Budd, hurling the man down the resilient plastic steps. The brothers went in and collared the bartender.

That worthy was a true philosopher; that is, his morbid view of life extended to himself as well as to his fellow man. He came along uncomplainingly when it was demanded of him, which was immediately after he had said that he had spoken with the man who drove the Carrington. They whisked him to Eric's shipping offices, into an inner room, and down an elevator whose entrance was under Eric's desk. Far underground he was seized by a staff of highly trained men who lived out their lives in secrecy underground because they dared not show their faces above.

The bartender was given four injections in rapid succession and for the next six hours was subjected to the most thorough of grillings. He was powerless to tell anything but the truth. Highly detailed information about the man in the other Carrington was fed, item by item, into a monster card-sorting machine. His name; height; weight; probable age; dress; accent; timbre of voice; physical peculiarities; each of these was gone into with incredible nicety.

The machine dealt in probabilities; if a man of a given height and weight reacts in such and such a way to such a statement, uttered so, then he may have spent a specified number of years in any one of eight professions. Each of these was taken in order, compared with other characteristics, canceled out or in. Each result was checked and rechecked, compared with every other result. At the end of the grilling, the Arniks had a complete dossier on Biddiver, as well as a slightly conventionalized full-length portrait. Looking at it, they doubted that their machine was working correctly, but it hadn't failed so far.

"Well," said Budd, scratching his head, "we know what we're after. Where is it?"

"It's probably well out of the way," said Eric. He turned away to give orders about the disposal of the mindless wreck that had been the head bartender of the Purple Pileus. He would be found dead days later, after wandering through the city, starving because he was incapable of realizing it, freezing because he couldn't understand that he needed shelter. "You see," he went on, staring at the picture, "from what you tell me, the space-travel mechanisms on the car had their master switch where any other Carrington has its radio. This guy was apparently one of those people who can't breathe unless a radio's pounding their ear. Drunk as he was, you can bet that the first thing he did after he started the car was to turn on the radio. As soon as he did that, he took off. He hasn't crashed; I'd have heard about it if he had. He hasn't been seen flying around, either. He must have gone—straight up."

"And the car isn't shielded against the cosmics. So—"

"So they probably got the rat. I hope."

Budd shook his head. "You can't count on it. What that radiation did to him depends on factors that no one's been able to chart. I hope it killed him. Maybe it didn't—but what's the difference? That car's as fast as anything in space. By this time it's reached terminal velocity and is 'way out of reach. I'm out an automobile, I guess. Oh, well. I should kick. At least I'm where I know my dear brother will look out for me." He smirked at Eric and the way he made an infinitesimal move toward his shoulder holster and then visibly thought better of it.

"I can just barely stand you," gritted Eric after a taut moment. "Don't make it any tougher for me by your lip."

Somewhere in space, a chrome and blue automobile raced the green light of Earth. Biddiver was quite dead now, if death is complete loss of personality, of human hopes and dreams and desires. There was another at the controls, certainly, one who moaned and gibbered and mewed at the stars spread about him, one who snatched and pawed at the sensitive, unprotesting controls before him. But it was not Biddiver, any more than the car itself was the ores and gases and fluids from which it was fabricated. The car was new, and even newer was the creature at the controls.

After those first mad moments, he quieted to stare with his new, scarlet eyes at the car, the dials and meters that now presented themselves in place of the conventional dashboard that had slid up out of sight when the car had reached the thousand-k.p.h. mark. He fingered the upholstery with an animal's preoccupied attention, touched metal and glass and fabric with listless hands. Then he looked down at himself, snarled, and began to strip the clothes from his body. He worked slowly, systematically, from his shoes upward, ignoring clasps and slides, depending on the invariable rule that each chain has a weakest link. His flesh had a greenish cast, and it puffed tautly everywhere except near the joints, which were all simply skin on bone. When he had tossed the last tatter over his shoulder, he put both hands to his head and wiped off his frowsy mane. The hair came quite easily off the puckered skull. He giggled then, and went to sleep for three Earth days.

"Who's The Fang?" asked Budd Arnik, a couple of weeks after he had bulldozed his way into the titular vice-presidency of Eric's shipping firm. "I've seen some sweet write-ups about him in the telefacsimiles. He's a crazy Martian. He's an exiled scientist from another solar system. He's a refugee from a sunspot. Everybody has a different idea about him, except you. Seems funny, somehow," he went on, affecting the lightly sarcastic tone which he knew infuriated his brother. "The gentleman steals a cargo which is not aboard a ship, destroys the vessel, and leaves you with your pockets full of money. I wouldn't be curious if I didn't happen to know that you've made no big payoffs to anyone recently. If you'd hired the guy, it would have cost you plenty. If you didn't, why should he scuttle a ship with a nonexistent, heavily insured cargo, and then announce to the Universe that he is The Fang and will be heard from again?"

"You found out about the payoff," growled Eric. "Why bother asking me any questions at all? Figure it out for yourself."

"I will," promised his brother smoothly. "Which reminds me— I have an idea that'll make us some money, if The Fang can be depended on to do a little more work for us. Can he?"

Eric hesitated and then said, "Pretty much."

"Ah," said Budd. "Well, you know that uranium mine on Pallas?"

"Mm."

"Well, there's a lot of money tied up on it. That uranium, you know, is about forty per cent 235. U-235 from Pallas supplies most of the System, since it's so easy to refine. There's still plenty of market for it, you know. Lucasium is more efficient, but it's a hell of a lot more expensive. Now—here's my idea. Just to see if The Fang has any kind of reputation as yet, we'll have him threaten the colony. We'll set a price—not too much; maybe they'll pay it—and tell 'em to set it adrift in space, static, right there in the Asteroid Belt. By the time it has moved more'n a couple hundred miles toward the Sun, it'll intersect the orbits of quite a few planetoids. One of our boys can be roosting there in a small ship to pick it up."

Eric sent him a glance. "Is that what you meant when you said you had imagination?"

"Yeah. Why?"

"I'm surprised, that's all. It's not bad. Let's get going."

In a very few days they had a ship outfitted. It was decided that Budd would take her out to the Belt. As they stood in the control room just before the take-off, Budd asked:

"You're going to get in touch with The Fang?"

"I'm doing that right now," said Eric. "You are The Fang."

"I'm *what?*"

For once in his life Eric Arnik actually laughed. "Certainly. The incendiary explosion of the tankship was done by time bombs."

"But—that voice?"

"No trouble. It was recorded and transmitted from little sets set adrift in space. Any signal transmitted simultaneously from three sources widely separated makes a direction indicator run around in circles." He chuckled. "One transmitter was dropped from the ship a day before she blew up. Another was in my office. The third was in an orbit around Eros. They were timed to transmit The Fang's message twenty days after the explosion, just about when it would be discovered. I told you you could have figured it out for yourself. All I had to do was to give my hypothetical criminal a name like 'The Fang' so that the feature writers would pick it up and plaster it around. That's what you're doing now, dope. Just follow the course that's in the co-ordinator over there. The automatic releases will take care of everything for you. You'll drop atomic bombs in the path of Pallas, so that the asteroid will strike them just when its rotation will put the mines on the point of impact. The message is already recorded. Your course takes you within the gravitic field of Jupiter; one of the transmitters will swing around behind the old boy. One will be here, and one will be attached to the bombs.

Budd was aghast. "So that's— Holy Kitt! And I was the guy who said you had no imagination!" He looked at his brother as if he had never seen him before, and then something of his cockiness returned to him. "May I ask the master some questions?"

Eric looked at the chronometer. "Fire away. You have twelve minutes."

"How did the signal blank out all others in every ultraradio set in the System?"

"I can't tell you exactly, because I'm not a radio man. One of my boys fixed it up. The general idea is that every wave frequency has a corresponding negating frequency—another wave that vibrates node to trough with the original, and cancels it out. My signals were transmitted in every frequency; they sounded above and below the ones that were canceled."

"How about the time lag between all those transmitters? They were an awful long way apart."

"A silly question, son. You know ultraradio. Those vibrations think the speed of light is a minus quantity!"

Budd rubbed his neck. "So I'm The Fang. I can't get over it. By the way, chum, I wouldn't try killing two birds with one stone on this trip. You're liable to be the other bird. I'm talking to a buddy of mine every twelve hours, until I come back. If I miss a single call, those cans of film will get to the Feds."

"Damn it," said Eric mildly. He walked to the bulkhead, pressed a panel. A section slid open; he lifted out a compact little piece of destruction in the form of an atomic bomb. "I was hoping you wouldn't think of anything like that," he said. "This was for you. Oh, well."

Budd grinned. "Better luck next time. So long, pal. See you anon!"

When the air-lock gates had hissed to a close, he threw a master switch set into the chronometer housing, lit a cigarette and sat down to read and look at visirecordings until he had something to do. The chronometer clicked softly, and the ship hurtled away. It was only then that a certain detail occurred to Budd—namely, that whether or not the miners of Pallas and their paymasters agreed to The Fang's terms, they were doomed, for the eggs would be laid. Their planetoid would strike the hovering nest of bombs when, in all probability, they would be looking for some sort of an attacking ship. Now, what was the good of that?

He reflected a moment, and then laughed aloud. This was all that the System needed to learn that The Fang was a force to be reckoned with! Budd had the bright ideas, but it took a brain like Eric's to really stretch them out. After this, The Fang could dictate to the Universe!

"My own brother," Budd chortled. "But, oh Lord, what a man!"

He had changed; he knew that. The tearing radiations that had thrust his new being into the System had left him memories of puffed green flesh, bony joints, and a bald, rough skull. The transition was complete now. Blue-white hair covered the obese body. It was a good three feet long and beautifully silky. It fell down on each side of his scarlet eyes, down from his cheeks, his chin. It mantled his whole frame, ending in a great puff at his knees. The erstwhile chitinous structure of his fingernails was now flexible, sentient flesh, so that, from the tip of each finger and thumb a dexterous tentacle about four inches long extended.

It was a new and glorious world that this creature regarded. To him, radiant heat was a color, and electricity was a color, and every vibration between them on the electromagnetic spectrum was a shade. Thought itself was a visible, physical thing to him. Thought strikes the average telepath like a hand on the arm of a paralyzed deaf-mute, but to the creature in the Carrington it was as easy to sense as the handshake of a friend.

His interest in the interior of the car was soon exhausted, and he spent many days drinking in the immensities of space. He looked with understanding and the truest kind of appreciation on mighty Jupiter and the speckled Belt. His eyes sensed rather than saw Neptune and frozen Pluto. Then, having had his fill of infinity, he turned again to his small world and himself.

He regarded the car and its workings not with the eye of science, but with that of the most superb logic. The ape regards three turns of rope around a beam as a Gordian knot. A lay human being regards an atomic power plant as a hopelessly involved technical jumble. Not the silver-silk being in the Carrington, however. He crawled into the power compartment, and with the joy of a man who has just found a book he loved in his childhood, he followed leads, inspected coils and bars and casings. In a locker he found tools of every kind, spare parts of every description, and with them he went to work.

The powerful and delicate tentacles at his fingertips worked with a speed and precision impossible to a human hand. Here he found a busbar a few millimeters too thick for the light load it carried; there he saw a mechanical task which could be performed electrically with less drain on the power source. He looked carefully at the wheel-driving mechanism, and after an hour's work on it, went forward to the control chair and re-calibrated the throttle indicator; for now the machine could not be operated safely on the ground unless it drew less fuel, due to its new efficiency. He regarded the antigrav apparatus with some amusement, for it seemed primitive to him. Hooking his leg around the wheel driveshaft, he drew a set of tools equipped with spring clips toward him, shut off the unit, and rebuilt it.

The car kept him busy for some days, and then there was little else he could do to it; and so he turned his brilliant eyes inward on himself. He was a creature without precedent. Of the human basic urges, he had none. He could not know hunger, for the car supplied him with food tablets as they were needed. Fear did not exist. Wealth, power, shelter—these things were impossible conceptions, for he had been born with them all.

He remembered little or nothing about Biddiver. He sent his metrical mind back along the past few days, searching for clues as to his origin and that of the automobile. Almost all of it had been blanked out. There was, however, a recent experience—a voice had spoken to him, and he had thought it authoritative. He knew himself to be talented and superior, for had he not improved on the work of a people who manifested a high degree of scientific knowledge? Then the words he had heard from that source must be the thought-image of a Power past even his understanding. If he could only remember when—and where—

That voice had said, "Guys that don't want to do nothin' to nobody most generally don't amount to nothin'. Big shots—every one of them walked up to the top on other guys' faces. The Fang— at the top now." There were details about The Fang; the creature suddenly found it difficult to remember whether he had heard of or been The Fang. "Arnik ... Arnik brothers—" That was a recurring thought-pattern that brought with it a wondering distaste. There was more, but it was these things that were most significant. Why?

He opened his eyes and stared through the windshield. All of it had something to do with the third planet, the green one. There was a message for him in that voice from the past. He set about the problem as if it were put together with nuts and bolts.

Arnik—big shots—these, and the things about them, were somehow unpleasant thoughts. There was pleasure, however, in improvement. Unpleasant things were made pleasant by improvement. The Arniks, then—

He paused. Everything about him—the car, the stars and planets, the food he ate and the air he breathed, each of them had a purpose. But he himself—why was he there? The speedometer was there because it had something to do—a function. Had he a function? He must have, he reasoned, or he would not be there. He regarded the green planet thoughtfully, running his pointed yellow tongue over his lips. Where it parted the long hair, two great white tusks showed. He laid his hands on the arms of his chair, and the tentacled tips curled over the ends, lightly touching the controls. He knew what he had to do.

And that is how the philosophy of a bitter bartender became a space dweller's driving creed.

Budd Arnik found time a little heavy on his hands until his ship approached the Belt, and then he spent most of his time at the forward port. He dared not touch the controls, for his course was timed and plotted and automatically steered, and a fraction of a degree one way or the other would defeat the whole plan.

Power off, the little ship swung into the Belt and into the orbit of Pallas. Then a few gentle nudges this way and that, to brake her and steady her in that untenable position, stasis in space. The most advanced of calculating machinery had been employed to check this one tiny dot on the astro chart. She hung there for twenty-two hours, awaiting just the right split second to drop her deadly load. Budd only felt the infinitesimal lurch because he had waited so long for it—that tiny swaying as automatic grapples let the bombs go, repelled them a few feet so they would be clear of the mass of the ship. Then the artificial gravity and momentum neutralizer cut in, a relay clicked, and the ship looped over and fled back toward Earth.

Budd slipped into the pilot's chair with a sigh. This leg of the trip would be a little more exciting. Although the automatic pilot would take him unerringly back to his starting point, the explosion on Pallas would occur long before he got there, and space would be crawling with Tri-planet Patrol ships. He knew he could outmaneuver and outrun any of the ships, but he knew he wouldn't have a chance against an ultraradio torpedo or a sleep-destroying field. Particularly the latter, for the range of the field was tremendous, and the penalty of being snared in one was agonizing death from lack of sleep. He had to rely on his detector beams to warn him of any approaching ship.

He slept frequently for lack of anything else to do, woke for a few minutes, checked over his gauges, and dozed off again. And in one of these periods he dreamed.

He dreamed that a hollow, insistent voice, just like that of The Fang on Eric's recordings, was calling him insistently. "Arnik! Arnik! Arnik!" He was conscious of his own effort to rouse himself, and found he could not. "Arnik!" said the voice. "Answer! What are you doing? What was the meaning of those bombs dropped in the path of Pallas?"

And he dreamed that he was bound down by gentle but irresistible forces, so that he could only cry out against them; but the only cry he could make was the truth. "We are bombing the mines."

"Why?" The voice was a glittering steel probe, picking away at his brain.

"To create fear of The Fang. To make The Fang's commands law."

Question by remorseless question he was forced to tell the whole story. And then, suddenly, he found himself free to awaken. He sat bolt upright, streaming sweat, sputtering profanity, and carrying the most terrific headache in the memory of man.

"I'm gettin' the crawlin' willies," he muttered, and then realized that the detector alarm signal was shrilling. He glanced at the dial. It had been ringing for two hours and twenty-seven minutes. He shook his head, nearly shrieked at the pain, and snapped the switch. The signal cut itself off. From another dial he read the bearing and distance. He swiveled about, unlimbered a short-range visiscope, and turned it on. Sharp and clear, the image of the offending vessel showed up on the screen.

Only it wasn't a vessel. It was an automobile—an iridescent blue Carrington '78.

Budd Arnik grunted, looked again and grinned. "Well, well," he chuckled. "Imagine meeting you here!" It was a one-in-a-quadrillion chance, he thought. That ugly-looking lug who had accidentally swiped his car had probably gone nuts and died when he broke through the Layer. By some fluke the car had quit with a corpse at the controls and must now be caught in somebody's orbit—probably old Jupiter. And of all people in the Universe, he, Budd Arnik, had to be the one to find it!

He cut off the automatic pilot and took over, swerving toward the car. It was traveling in the same direction but in a slightly different plane. He focused the visiscope and read off the range from the gauge. The car was nineteen kilometers ahead. He put on a burst of speed, overtook and circled the automobile. As far as he could see, it was totally unharmed. He grinned happily, edged closer, and reached for the magnetic grapple control. But before he could touch it, the car suddenly faded away from the screen. Budd swore and fiddled with the controls, bringing it quickly back into focus. It had jumped four kilometers when he came close. He crept in again, watching carefully. When the range closed to one kilometer, the car jumped again. Budd frowned. Was that dope still alive in there?

He lifted his ship above the car and began to settle down toward it. And again the car jumped away. "What the hell," growled Budd. "If he don't like me, why don't he turn tail and run?"

He tried it again, and only then did he think of a repellor field. He hadn't known that the car possessed one, but then there were probably half a hundred gadgets on that wagon that he knew nothing about. Most big spacecraft carried such fields in case of emergency repairs in space, to guard the hull against small meteorites when the ship was not able to navigate clear of them.

Budd shrugged. "There's more ways of killing a cat than stuffing it in a knee boot," he growled. He took some sights, punched cards with the results, and fed them into the co-ordinator. When he had his position, he lined his ship up with the car on his course, and moved forward. The car leaped away, and Budd followed grimly, the car preceding him exactly a kilometer ahead. The two crafts soon attained their terminal velocity, and Budd turned the controls over to the mike.

He walked over to the ultraradio, noticing that he was an hour or so late for his usual communiqué to Eric. That gentleman's face flashed furiously on the screen. Budd smiled back at it.

"Well?" roared Eric. "What the hell have you got to be so happy about? Why you double-crossing rat!"

"Easy, pal," soothed Budd. "I been busy. I've got a present for you."

"Take your present and ram it up—"

"*Tsk, tsk,*" tsked Budd. "All this excitement over a little tardiness! Listen, goon. Remember that car we had swiped from us at the Purple Pileus?"

"Yes, I remember and I don't give a damn about it."

"No? Well, give a look!" Budd walked away from the radio, switched on the visiscope. "Can you see what I've got in tow?"

"No, I can't. Now stop your hogwash and tell me what sort of monkey business you're up to!"

Budd sobered. "What are you talking about?"

"Don't play innocent," snarled Eric. "What was the idea of blanketing *my* signal?"

"When? What signal?"

"The F—" Eric stopped apoplectically, remembering that he was on the air and that the System was full of ears. "The signals we arranged," he said, as if talking to a four-year-old. "Remember?"

"Yeah—"

"They were blanked! The one in my office, I— Hey! You don't really mean to tell me that you actually *don't* know what happened?" He peered out of the screen at Budd's amazed face, rubbed his ear, and went on with a desperate sort of patience. "O.K. then. My transmitter was blanked, and so were the others, apparently. Instead of that, I got *this!*" His face disappeared, and a recording screen was shoved up against the transmitter. "Now watch!" said his voice, and the recorder glowed. It showed a typical radio show, a dancing chorus, a vapid female singing dourly. Suddenly the scene disappeared and a truly terrible voice rasped forth.

"I am The Fang," it said melodramatically. "I have come again to warn the world. But not, as was expected, to warn you of myself, but of my masters."

There was a long, significant pause. Budd's throat felt very dry.

"I was ordered to destroy the mines on Pallas. I have disobeyed, for my masters want power they cannot control. I also warn my

284

masters that I will not rest until they are as I am!" With the last two words, the screen came alive with a picture.

"God!" said Budd, his eyes bulging.

The screen went dead and was moved away. Eric's face reappeared. "There's something for you to look forward to," he said snidely. "Hurry home, babe." He signed off.

"The son," growled Budd. "He looks almost happy about it. Great sweet sidesway what a face!" He slumped into a fearful heap in the pilot's chair.

As Budd expected, the car's repellors cut out when it had been shoved well within Earth's gravitic field. He grappled it to his ship's side and landed neatly on the stage in front of the Arnik Shipping Co. His first act on alighting was to release the car and try the door. It opened readily. He recoiled a little at the heap of rags that littered the stained control seat, and then he shrugged and climbed in, kicking them out the rags, and the odd bones they covered. Budd Arnik wasn't picky. As the ground crew disposed of the spaceship, Budd tested the controls. They seemed to be all right. He waved to the foreman and the car slid smoothly down the ramp.

He could have taken a solenoid car out to Eric's place and saved twenty minutes, but he was too tickled at having got his car back. He swept out of the city, lulled by the whispering speedometer; and when he had the highway to himself, he leaned over to the conventional radio switch and then pulled back on the arms. The car soared up effortlessly. He put it down again and raced to his brother's place.

Eric was waiting fretfully at the door. "Dammit, why didn't you take the solenoid?"

"Brother," said Budd easily, "when you've spent as many weeks as I have being toted around by a machine that did your thinking for you, you'll be glad of the chance to be the boss for a change."

Eric stared over his shoulder at the house, shrugged nervously and climbed into the car. "Place gives me the jitters," he complained. "Go ahead then—drive. I want to talk to you."

Budd wheeled the Carrington around in its own length and rolled onto the highway. Drifting along at a hundred and eighty, he turned to Eric. "What's this about jitters? Something new for you, isn't it?"

Eric looked sheepish. "Yes. No." He swore fluently. "Budd, you're a phony. You're in this up to your neck." He sent a glance Budd-ward from the corners of his eyes. "And I don't know that that isn't the silver lining they told me about in school, come to think of it. If I get it, you'll get it, too. Anyway, you're a phony. You're up against something you can't laugh off, this trip."

"You're talking a lot of nonsense," said Budd. "You're all shot, man. I've never heard you go on like this. What's under your skin?"

Eric began in a low voice that got increasingly higher and hoarser, until he wound up in a piping whisper. "We create, for our own ends, one master criminal. Said master criminal consists in ultraradio transmitters set adrift in space and in time bombs. We do one little job with our hypothetical criminal's aid. We start another one. Our make-believe monster promptly goes on strike because he doesn't like our greed. And you ask what's under my *skin!*" He gasped for breath, then went on, in a crazed monotone, "And I've been having dreams. Dreaming with my ears and my eyes while I'm wide awake. I hear that ... that *thing* laughing. I keep seeing that face. That's what's going to happen to us, you damn fool; don't you see?"

Budd went right on grinning; then Eric suddenly realized that the grin was frozen there. Budd said hoarsely, "Yeah. I know. I heard things, too. Merciful heavens!" he burst out. "We can't let it get us! Shut up about it!"

Eric's gaze dropped between his feet. He clamped them nervously, held it there. "If it was anything we could understand, we'd know what to do ... but you can't tell about those things. It might hit you one way, me another, and yet we're brothers. You just can't tell. Anything might happen—" Eric, due to his morbid attention to his feet, and to the artificial gravity in the car, did not notice Budd's turning on the radio, or the swift leap of the machine off the road. "Who can tell what it did to that ugly Biddiver fellow? How can we know what he is now? You can't predict anything, you can't even guess—"

"What are you talking about?" snapped Budd.

"Biddiver—the guy that swiped your fancy car by mistake. Biddiver—The Fang."

Budd's face turned a sick gray. "Biddiver is—The Fang?"

"Certainly. That was easy enough to find out. He's altered—God, yes; but it's him all right. Didn't I tell you? I guess I forgot. I'm shot to hell." He shook his head, and sweat flung from his forehead. "The card-selector—you know, the one we used on that barkeep. It gave us a portrait and a description. With The Fang I reversed the process. He's slightly changed, but underneath all that . . . that fur—he has the same bone structure. It clicks . . . it couldn't be anyone else. Somewhere he's cruising around in that damned automobile. Sooner or later, he'll get us."

"Not 'that' damned automobile," said Budd, and laughed hysterically. "'*This*' damned automobile. I tried to tell you about it when I was out there in space. I thought I picked it up and brought it back. I see now—it brought me."

Eric raised his head, stared out of the side window, and screamed. The Carrington was a thousand kilometers up and going higher. Budd forced the control arms downward violently; the nose of the car tipped up instead. He sat like a statue, blood pouring from where he had bitten through his lip. Eric dove for his gun, snatched it out, put it to his temple.

A white-furred arm reached almost casually from behind them, lifted the gun out of Eric's hand. "Don't do that," said The Fang gently. "Not at this stage. I want you changed. I want you made like me. That," he added, "is what I am for."

They turned slowly and faced the creature. "Do not be frightened," droned The Fang. He was regal, magnificent as he stood there, in front of the door to the power compartment where he had been hiding. His luminous eyes were separately articulated, and one fixed on each of the men, held them. His long face hair was swept away on each side from his chrome-yellow mouth, baring the great tusks.

He held them there while the machine swept up and outward, the whine of air outside growing fainter as the air thinned. Stratosphere—ionosphere—and the Heaviside. The Fang watched with puzzlement growing in his eyes as Eric shrieked and died, as Budd groveled in pain and then hung limply on the back of his seat. The Fang picked him up carefully and laid him on the deck. Something was happening to the man. He tried to scream, and his legs kicked out. He tried to strike out with an arm, and his head whipped back against the floor. His eyes widened, the flesh between them thinning, the eyeballs beginning to fuse. He died, then, for no human being can live when his medial division starts to go to pieces. Humans are built to operate with two sets of limbs, two eyes, two ears, two nostrils—the radiations found that the path of least resistance in Budd Arnik was to do away with that medial line, and it couldn't work.

So The Fang was left, keening over the twisted bodies, mourning that he had not done it the right way, horrified because he had been mistaken—for he only wanted to help. Perhaps one day he will find his function.

The Golden Egg

WHEN TIME ITSELF was half its present age, and at an unthinkable distance, and in an unknowable dimension, he was born.

He left his world so long before he came to earth that even he did not know how long he had been in space. He had lived so long on that world that even he could not remember what he had been before his science changed his race.

Though we can never know where his world lay in space, we know that it was in a system of two mighty suns, one blue and one yellow. His planet had an atmosphere and a great civilization and science beyond humanity's most profound visions. He spoke little of his planet because he hated it.

Too perfect. Their sciences fed them, and controlled the etheric currents that gave them comfort, and carried them from place to place, and taught them, and cared for them in every way. For many aeons there were members set apart to care for the machines, but in time they died out, for they were no longer needed. There was no struggle and no discomfort and no disease. There were therefore no frontiers, no goals, no incentives, and eventually no possible achievements, save one—the race itself, and the changes possible to it.

Step by step the thing was done. Limbs were not needed and wasted away from long-lived, lazy bodies, and were replaced, redesigned, or forgotten. And as the death of an inhabitant became more rare, rarer still became the advent of new life. It was a mighty race, a powerful race, a most highly civilized race, and—a sterile race.

The refinement went on endlessly, as occasional flashes of initiative appeared down through the ages. What was unnecessary was discarded, and what could be conceivably desirable was attained, until all that was left was a few thousand glittering golden ovoids, supermental casings, functionally streamlined, beautiful and bored. The beings could move as and if they wished, through air or time or space. Everything was done for them automatically; each was self-sufficient and uncooperative. Brains they were, armored in a substance indestructible by anything less powerful than the heat of the mightiest of suns or by the supercosmic forces each could unleash at will.

But there was no will. There was nothing for them. They hung in small groups conversing of things unimaginable to us, or they lay on the plains of their world and lived within themselves until a few short aeons buried them, all uncaring, in rubble and rock. Some asked to be killed and were killed. Some were murdered by others because of quibblings in remote philosophic discussions. Some hurled themselves into the blue sun, starved for any new sensation, knowing they would find there an instant's agony. Most simply vegetated. One came away.

He stopped, in a way known to him—stopped in space so that his world and solar system and corner of the cosmos fell away from him and left him free. And then he traveled.

He traveled to many places and in many ways, as his whims dictated. He extended himself at times around the curve of curved space, until the ends of him were diametrically opposite; and then he would contract in a straight line, reforming countless millions of light years from the point of his extension; and his speed then was, of course, the speed of light cubed. And sometimes he dropped from his level in time to the level below, and would then lie poised and thoughtful during one cycle, until he was returned to the higher level again; and it was thus he discovered the nature of time, which is a helical band, ever revolving, never moving in its superspace. And sometimes he would move slowly, drifting from one gravitic pull to another, searching disinterestedly for the unusual. It was in such a period that he came to earth.

A goose found him. He lay in some bushes by a country road, distantly observing the earth and analyzing its elements, and the goose was a conventional one and blindly proud of its traditional silliness.

He ignored it when it approached him and when it rapped his shell curiously; but when it turned him over with its beak he felt that it was being discourteous. He seized it with a paralyzing noose of radiations, quickly read its minuscule mind for a way to annoy it, and then began pulling its tail feathers out to see how it would react. It reacted loudly.

Now, it so happened that Christopher Innes was on that country road, bringing the young'un home from Sunday school. Chris was an embittered and cynical mortal, being a normal twelve-year-old who had just learned that increasing age and masculinity made for superiority, and was about to be a teenager and find out differently. The young'un was his five-year-old sister, of whom he was jealous and protective. She had silly ideas. She was saying:

"But they *tol'* me in school last week, Chris, so it mus' be so, so there. The prince came into the palace an' everyone was asleep, an' he came to the room where *she* was, an' she was asleep, too, but he kissed her an' she woke up, and then everyone—"

"Aw, shut your fontanel," said Chris, who had heard that babies shut their fontanels when they started to grow, though he didn't know what one was. "You believe everything you hear. Ol' Mr. Becker tol' me once I could catch a bird by putting salt on its tail, an' then whaled me for loadin' up a twelve-gauge shotgun with rock salt and knockin' off three of his Rhode Island Reds. They tell you that stuff so they'll have a chance to hit you afterward."

"I don't care, so there," pouted the young'un. "My teacher wouldn't hit me for b'lieving her."

"Somebody will," Chris said darkly. "What's all that racket, I wonder? Sounds like a duck caught in a fox trap. Let's go see."

Chris stopped to pick up a piece of stick in case he had a trap to pry open, and the young'un ran ahead. When he reached her he found her jumping up and down and clapping her hands and gurgling, "I told you so! I told you so!" which is the most annoying thing any woman can say to any man.

"You tol' me whut?" he asked, and she pointed. He saw a large white goose digging its feet into the ground, straining to get away from its invisible bonds, while behind it lay a glittering ovoid. As they watched, a tail feather detached itself from its anchorage and fell beside two of its prototypes on the ground.

"Chee!" Chris breathed.

"They tol' me that story, too!" chortled the young'un. "About the goose that laid the golden egg. Oh, Chris, if we take that goose home an' keep um, we'll be rich an' I can have a pony an' a hundred dolls an'—"

"Chee," Chris said again and gingerly picked up the golden egg. As he did so the goose was released suddenly, and its rooted claws shot it forward face first into the earth, where it lay stunned and quonking dismally. As only a farm child can, the young'un caught its legs together and picked it up in her arms.

"We're rich!" breathed Chris and laughed. Then he remembered his assertions and frowned. "Aw, it didn't lay no egg. Someone lost it an' this ol' goose jus' found it here."

"It's the golden-egg goose! It is too!" shrilled the young'un.

Chris spat on the egg and rubbed it with his cuff. "It's sure pretty," he said half to himself, and tossed it into the air. He must have stood there open-mouthed for two full minutes with his hands out, because it never came down. It vanished.

They found out later that the goose was a gander. Neither of them ever quite got over it.

"It might be interesting," thought the armored brain to himself as he lay in the stratosphere, "to be a biped like that for a while. I believe I will try it. I wonder which of the two is the more intelligent—the feathered or unfeathered ones?" He pondered a moment over this nice distinction and then remembered that the boy had armed himself with a stick, while the goose had not. "They are a little ungainly," he thought, then shrugged mentally. "I shall be one of those."

He plummeted down to earth, braked off, and shot along just over the surface until he came to a small town. A movement in a tiny alley caught his attention; a man there was leveling a gun at another across the street. Unseen, the being from space flashed between them, and his path intersected that of the bullet. It struck his smooth side and neither left a mark nor changed his course by a thousandth of a degree as it spun into the street four feet below him. The intended victim went his way unharmed, and the man in the alley swore and went to his room to take his gun apart wonderingly. He had never missed a shot like that before!

Just outside the town the brain found what he had been looking for—a field under which was a huge mass of solid rock. He came to rest in the field and dropped from sight, sinking through sod and earth and granite as if it had been water; and in a matter of minutes he had cut himself a great underground chamber in the rock, with high arched walls and a vaulted ceiling and a level, polished floor. Hovering for a moment in midair, he tested the surrounding countryside for its exact chemical content, sending out delicate high-frequency beams, adjusting them fractionally for differences in molecular vibrations. The presence of a certain fine harmonic at any given frequency indicated to him the exact location of the elements he needed. There were not many. These bipeds were hardly complex.

"A type—a type," he thought. "I must have something to work from. I gather that these creatures are differentiated from each other in certain ways."

He slipped up through the roof of his chamber and went back to the town, where he found a busy corner and hid up under an eave, where he could watch the people passing.

"Those smaller ones must be the males," he ruminated, "the ones that strut and slink and apparently do little work and wear all those blatant colors and so ridiculously accentuate the color of the oral orifice. And the large, muscular ones, I suppose, are females. How drab."

He projected a beam that would carry thought impulses to him. It touched the mind of a young man who was mooning after a trim blonde just ahead of him. He was a hesitant and shy young man, and a passionate one, and the battle he fought within himself, between his inclinations and his diffidence, almost dislodged the creature in the eaves.

"Whew!" thought the golden ovoid. "An emotional monstrosity! And it appears that I was a little mistaken about males and females. How very quaint!

"I shall be one of the males," he decided at length.

Wisely, he searched about until he found a girl who was suffering from every "osis" in the advertisements, as well as an inferiority complex, acne, bunions, and tone-deafness, knowing that her idea of an ideal man would be really something. Inserting gentle thought tendrils into her mind, he coaxed her to dream a lovely dream of her ideal man as she walked along, and carefully filed away all the essentials, disregarding only the passion the dream man showered on the poor starved creature. Enveloped by the dream he had induced, she walked into the path of an automobile and was rather badly hurt, which was all right, because she later married the driver.

The brain sped back to the laboratory, nursing his mental picture of a muscular, suave, urbane, sophisticated, and considerate demigod, and began to assemble his machinery.

Now the brain had no powers, as such. What he had was *control*. The engineer of a twenty-car train would be stupid even to dream about hurling such a train at a hundred and twenty miles an hour along a track if had to do so himself with his own physical powers. But with his controls the thing is easy. In the case of the brain, his controls were as weak compared with the final results of it as is a man's arm compared with the two thousand horsepower delivered by a locomotive. But the brain knew the true nature of space: that it is not empty, but a mass of balanced forces.

Press two pencils together, end to end. As long as the pressure is even and balanced the effect is the same as if the pencils were just resting their ends together. Now get some tiny force to press on the point where the pencils come together. They snap out of line; they deliver a powerful resultant, out of all proportion to the push which upset the equilibrium, and you probably break a knuckle. The resultant is at right angles to the original equalized forces; it goes just so far and then the forces come together in equilibrium again, knuckles notwithstanding.

We live in a resilient universe; the momentary upset is negligible, since the slack is taken up to infinity. Such a control had the brain from space. Any and every form of energy—and matter is energy—was his to control, to any degree. The resultant from one tiny upset balance could be used to upset another; and a chain like this could be extended *ad infinitum*. Fortunately, the brain knew how not to make mistakes!

He made his apparatus quickly and efficiently. A long table; tanks and small bins of pure elements; a highly complex machine with projectors and reflectors capable of handling any radiation that can be indicated on a circular spectrum, for compounding and conditioning the basic materials. The machine had no switches, no indicators, no dials. It was built to do a certain job, and as soon as it was completed it began working. When the job was done it quit. It was the kind of machine whose perfection ruined the brain's civilization, and has undoubtedly ruined others, and will most certainly ruin more.

On the surface of the table appeared a shadow. Cell by cell appeared as the carbon-magnesium-calcium mixtures were coordinated and projected by the machine. A human skeleton was almost suddenly complete—that is, an almost human skeleton. The brain was impatient with unnecessary detail, and if there were fewer vertebrae and more but finer ribs, and later, a lack of appendix, tonsils, sinal cavities, and *abductors minimi digiti,* then it was only in the interest of logic. The flesh formed over the skeleton, fiber by perfect fiber. Blood vessels were flat, their insides sealed to each other until the body was complete enough to start distributing blood. The thing was "born" with a full stomach; it began its functions long before it was complete enough for the brain's entry.

While it was forming, the brain lay in a corner of the room reasoning it out. He knew its construction and had carried it out. Now he asked the reasons for its being this way, and calculated its functions. Hearing, sight with light, communication by vibrating tissues, degree of telepathy, organs of balance, possible and probable mental and physical reflexes, all such elementary things were carefully reasoned out and recorded on that fathomless brain. It was not necessary to examine the body itself or to look at it. He had planned it, and it would be as he had planned. If he wished to study any part of it before it formed, he had his memory.

The body lay complete eventually. It was a young and strong and noble creature. It lay there breathing deeply and slowly, and under its broad, intellectual forehead its eyes glowed with the pale light of idiocy. The heart beat firmly, and a tiny switch in the left thigh developed and disappeared as the cells adjusted themselves to each other. The hair was glossy and black and was in a pronounced widow's peak. The hairline was the line separating the two parts of the head, for the top part was a hinged lid which now gaped open. The white matter of the brain was formed completely and relaid to make room for the metal-encased creator.

He drifted up to the head of the table and settled into the open skull. A moment, and then it snapped shut. The young man—for such he was now—lay quiet for a long while, as the brain checked the various senses—temperature, pressure, balance, and sight. Slowly the right arm raised and lowered, and then the left, and then the legs rose together and swung over the edge of the table and the young man sat up. He shook his head and gazed about with his rapidly clearing eyes, turned his head stiffly, and got to his feet. His knees buckled slightly; he grasped the table spasmodically, not bending his fingers because he hadn't thought of it yet. His mouth opened and closed, and he ran his tongue over the inside of his mouth and lips and teeth.

"What an awkward way to get around," he thought, trying his weight on one leg and then the other. He flexed his arms and hands and hopped up and down cautiously.

"Agh!" he said waveringly. "A-a-a-gh-ha-agh!" He listened to himself, enchanted by this new way of expressing himself. "Ka. Pa. Ta. Sa. Ha. Ga. La. Ra," he said, testing the possibilities of linguals, gutturals, sibilants, palatals, labials, singly and in combination. "Ho-o-o-o-owe-e-e-e!" he howled, trying sustained tones from low to high pitch.

He tottered to the wall, and with one hand on it began padding up and down the room. Soon the support was no longer necessary, and he walked alone; and then he went faster and faster and ran round and round, hooting strangely. He was a little disgusted to find that violent activity made his heart beat fast and his breathing harder. Flimsy things, these bipeds. He sat panting on the table and began testing his senses of taste and touch, his muscular and oral and aural and visual memories.

Chauncey Thomas was an aristocrat. No one had ever seen him in patchy pants or broken shoes. They would, though, he reflected bitterly, if he didn't get a chance to steal some soon. "What de hell," he muttered. "All I ast is t'ree meals a day and good clo'es, an' a house an' stuff, an' no work to do. Heh! An' dey tell me I can get t'ings by workin'. It ain't worth it. It just ain't worth it!"

He had every right to be bitter, he thought. Not only do they throw him down three flights of stairs in the town's most exclusive apartment house just because he was sleeping on the landing, but they stick him in jail for it. Did he get a chance to rest in jail? He did not. They made him work. They made him whitewash cells. That was hardly right. Then they gave him the bum's rush out of town. It was unfair. What if it was the ninth time they had booked him? "I got to find me another town," he decided. He was thinking of the sheriff's remark that next time he was run in the sheriff would pin a murder on him if he had to kill one of his deputies to do it.

Chauncey turned his slow, unwilling feet onto the Springfield Turnpike and headed away from town. The night was two hours old and very warm. Chauncey slouched along with his hands in his pockets, feeling misunderstood. A slight movement in the shadows beside the road escaped his attention, and he never realized that anyone was there until he found himself picked up by the slack of his trousers and dangling uncomfortably from a mighty fist.

"I ain't done nothin'!" he squalled immediately, resorting to a conversational reflex of his. "Le's talk this over, now bud. Aw, come on, now; you got nothin' on me. You—*awk!*"

Chauncey's mouthings became wordless when he had managed, by twisting around in his oversize clothes, to see his captor. The vision of a muscular giant, at least six feet five, regarding him out of fathomless, shadowy eyes as he held him at arm's length was too much for Chauncey Thomas. He broke down and wailed.

The naked Apollo spun the bum about in midair and caught him by the belt. He plucked curiously at the worn jacket, reached down and tore a piece of leather out of the side of an outsize sport shoe as if it had been made of blotting paper, studied it carefully, tossed it aside.

"Lemme go!" shrieked Chauncey. "Gee, boss, I wasn't doin'

nothin', honest I wasn't. I'm goin' to Springfield, I'll get a job or somethin', boss!" The words burned his mouth as he said them, but this was an emergency and he had to say something.

"Gha!" grunted the giant, and dropped him on his ear in the middle of the road.

Chauncey scrambled to his feet and scuttled off down the road. The giant stood watching him as he slowed, made a U-turn, and came running back under the influence of a powerful hypnotic suggestion emanating from that great clean body. He stood awed and trembling before the newborn one, wishing he were dead, wishing he were away from there—even in jail.

"Who-who are you?" he faltered.

The other caught Chauncey's shifty eyes in his own deep gaze. The hobo's shaken mind was soothed; he blinked twice and sat down on his knees beside the road, staring upward into the inscrutable face of this frightening, fascinating man. Something seemed to be crawling into Chauncey's mind, creeping about there. He felt himself being drawn out; his memories examined; his knowledge of human society and human customs and traditions and history. Things he thought he had forgotten and wanted to forget popped up, and he felt them being mulled over. Within a few minutes the giant had as complete a knowledge of human conduct and speech as Chauncey Thomas had ever had.

He stepped back, and Chauncey slumped gasping to the ground. He felt depleted.

"Get up, bum," said the big man in Chauncey's own idiom.

Chauncey got up; there was no mistaking the command in that resonant voice. He cringed before him and whined: "Whatcha gonna do wit' me, boss? I ain't—"

"Shut up!" said the other. "I ain't gonna hurt you."

Chauncey looked at the immobile face. "Well ... I ... I guess I'll be on my way."

"Aw, stick around. Whatcha scared of?"

"Well ... nothin' ... but, who are you, anyway?"

"I'm Elron," said the giant, using the first euphonious syllables that came to mind.

"Oh. Where's yer clo'es? You been rolled?"

"Naw. Well, yeah. Wait here for me; I think I can—"

Elron bounded over the hedge, not wanting to astound the little tramp too much. From Chauncey's mind he had stolen a mental photograph of what Chauncey considered a beautiful outfit. It was a plaid suit with a diamond-checked vest and yellow shoes; a wing collar and a ten-gallon hat. Slipping into his underground laboratory, Elron threw back the casing of the complex projector that had built him his body, and made a few swift adjustments. A moment later he joined Chauncey, fully clad in Chauncey's own spectacular idea of tailoring to taste.

"Hully gee!" breathed Chauncey.

They walked along the road together, Chauncey quite speechless, Elron pensive. A few cars passed them; Chauncey automatically and without hope flung a practiced thumb toward each. They were both surprised when a lavish roadster ground to a stop ahead of them. The door was flung open; Chauncey slid in front of Elron and would have climbed in but for Elron's grasping him by the scruff of the neck and hauling him back.

"In the rumble, lug," he ground out.

"Nuttin' good ever happens t' me," muttered Chauncey as he followed orders. He had seen the driver. She was lovely.

"Where are you bound?" she asked as Elron closed the door.

"Springfield," he said, remembering from something Chauncey had said that the town was on this road. He looked at this newest acquaintance. She was as tiny and perfect as he was big and perfect, and she handled the car with real artistry. Her eyes were deep auburn to match her hair. Judging by human standards, Elron thought her very pleasing to look upon.

"I'll take you there," she said.

"T'anks, lady."

She looked at him quickly.

"What's up, babe?" he asked.

"Oh—nothing. Don't call me 'babe.'"

"Okay, okay."

Again she flashed him a look. "Are you—kidding me?" she asked.

299

"What about?"

"You look—oh, I don't know."

"Spill it, sister."

"Oh, sort of—well, not like the kind who calls girls 'babe.'"

"Oh," he said. "You mean—you'd say it different, like." He was having trouble with Chauncey's limited vocabulary.

"Something like that. What are you going to do in Springfield?"

"Just look around a little, I guess. I want to see a city."

"Don't tell me you never saw a city!"

"Listen," he snapped, covering up his error by falling back on one of Chauncey's devices, "it ain't worryin' you any, is it? What do you care?"

"Oh, I'm sorry," she said acidly. He sensed something strained about the silence that followed.

"Mad, huh?"

She looked at him scornfully and sniffed.

The trivial impasse intrigued him. "Stop here," he ordered her.

"*What?*" she asked furiously.

He leaned forward and caught her eye. "*Stop here!*"

She cut the ignition and the big car slid to a stop. Elron took her shoulder and turned her to him. She almost struggled but hadn't time.

Tendrils of thought stole into her brain, explored her memories, her tastes, her opinions and philosophies and vocabulary. He learned why it was *déclassé* to address a woman as "babe," and that among civilized people ten-gallon hats were not worn with wing collars. He liked the language she used a little better than Chauncey's harsh inadequacies. He learned what music was, and a great deal about money, which, strangely enough, was something that almost never crossed Chauncey's mind. He had learned something of the girl herself; her name was Ariadne Drew, she had a great deal of wealth she had not earned, and she was so used to being treated according to her station in life that she was careless about such things as picking up hitchhikers on the road.

He let her go, snatching the memory of the incident from its place in her mind, so that she started the car and drove off.

"Now what on earth did I stop for?"

"So I could check up on that rear tire," he ad-libbed. He thought back about things he had discovered that might interest her. Clothes were a big item.

"I must apologize," he said to her, word for word in her own vernacular, "for this hat. It's just too, too revolting. I saw a cute little number the other day in a shoppe on the avenue, and I mean to get it. My dear, I *mean!*"

She glanced aghast at his noble profile and bulging shoulders. He chatted on.

"I saw Suzy Greenfield the other day. You know Suzy. Oh, she didn't see *me!* I took care of that! And do you know who she was *with?* That horrible Jenkins person!"

"Who *are* you?" she asked him.

"I hear that Suzy is—What? Who am I? Oh, yes; about Suzy. You've probably heard this awful gossip before"—she had!—"so stop me if you have. But she told her husband—"

"This is as far as I go," snapped the girl, wheeling the car over to the curb.

"Well, I—" Elron sensed that the right thing to do would be to get out of the car. He opened the door and turned to her.

"Thank you for the lift, darling. Let me know if I can do the same for you sometime." He stepped up onto the walk, and she slammed the door and rolled the window open.

"You've forgotten to polish your fingernails," she said nastily, and slammed the car into gear.

"Now what the hell did you do?" asked a voice at the side. Chauncey was looking longingly after the roadster.

"Don't swear," said Elron. "It's vulgar. You are very crude, Chauncey. I don't want to have you around. Good-by, darling." Could Elron help it if Ariadne Drew called everybody "darling"?

The little bum stood open-mouthed, staring after the Greek god in his noisy plaid suit, and then followed slowly. "Dat mug'll bear watchin'!" he muttered. "Hully gee!"

Elron, with his new-found knowledge of human affairs, had little trouble securing a few dollars from a man he passed on the street—all he had to do was to demand it—and getting a hotel room for his body. From Ariadne's mind he had found out what handwriting was, and he signed the register and paid for a room without a hitch. Once his body was parked conventionally in bed, he popped the head open and slipped out. He felt that the body would relax a little better without him.

He drifted out of the window and hung for a while high above the town, searching for a familiar vibration—the impulses of Ariadne's mind. Freed from the cumbersome human body, Elron was far more sensitive to such things. He wanted to observe Ariadne now because he wanted to check up on his performance.

He caught it soon. It was to him as a gentle perfume is to us. He whisked over to the outskirts of the city and settled down toward a massive red brick pile surrounded by lovely landscaping. He circled it twice, finding her exact place in the house, and then dropped down the chimney. He hovered just above the artificial logs in the fireplace and began his eavesdropping.

Ariadne was sitting in her extravagant living room, chatting with—of all people—the redoubtable Suzy Greenfield. Suzy was a small-souled, graceless girl with the ability to draw a remark out of any given acquaintance, and by ardent agreement she could cull enough back-biting comment to keep her busy for weeks. She looked like a buck-toothed sparrow, dressed like a sweepstakes winner from Dubuque, and had a personality as soothing as the seven-year itch.

"Well, what have you *heard* today?" she asked expectantly.

Ariadne was gazing into far distances, and she only smiled. "Oh, Ari," said Suzy, "come on! I know something must have happened today from the way you're acting. Please; you never tell me *anything!*"

Ariadne, being a woman, ignored this untruth and would have changed the subject had not Elron, in the chimney, gently stroked certain of her brain convolutions with his intangible tentacles. She stared up suddenly, turned to Suzy. Elron could have had her reaction directly, but he was interested in the way she would express it to another and in the way the other would receive it.

"If you must know," said Ariadne, "I met someone today. A man." She sighed. Suzy leaned forward happily. When she was not all mouth she was all ears.

"Where?"

"Picked him up on the road. Sue, you never saw such a pair as those two. They looked like a couple of comedians. One was a tramp—at first I thought they both were. The little one got into the rumble and the nice handsome one rode in front."

"Handsome?"

"Darling, you don't *know!* I've never seen—"

"But you said they were comic!"

"*Looked* comic, dear." In the fireplace the golden-armored brain gave the equivalent of a nod and sent a thought current out to Ariadne. As if answering a question, she said, "He would have looked *so* nice in a soft gray suit and a Homburg. And—I don't know what he is, but I think he should be an adventurer. A sort of poet-writer-adventurer."

"But what *was* he?"

Ariadne suddenly felt it possible to speak of other things. She got Suzy started on the peccadilloes of her long-suffering spouse and soon had completely eclipsed all thought of her volatile mystery man. Elron was gone.

Back at the hotel, the ovoid hovered over his sleeping body and thought bitter thoughts. He was ashamed of himself for underestimating the subtle nuances of human behavior. He had succeeded in making something ridiculous out of this biped he had created, and the fact annoyed him. There was a challenge in it; Elron could control powers that would easily disintegrate this whole tiny galaxy and spread its dust through seven dimensions, if he so wished it; and yet he was most certainly being made a fool of by a woman. It occurred to him that in all the universes there was nothing quite as devious and demanding as a woman's mind. It likewise occurred to him that a woman is easy to control as long as she always has her way. He was determined to see how closely a man could resemble a woman's ideal and still exist; and he was going to do it with this man he had made himself responsible for.

It was a long and eventful three months before Ari Drew saw Elron again. He went away in his ten-gallon hat and his blatant plaids and his yellow shoes; and he took away with him his conversational variants and Chauncey the bum. He went to the greatest city of them all and sought out people who knew about the things that he must be to achieve the phenomenal status of a man good enough for Ariadne.

He found it a fascinating game. In the corridors of universities, in prizefight training camps, in girls' schools and kindergartens and gin mills and honkytonks and factories he cornered people, spoke with them, strained and drained and absorbed what their minds held. Sorting and blending, he built himself an intellect, the kind of mentality that awed lightweights like Suzy Greenfield, who spell Intellect with a capital I. Instead of trying to suit each man's speech by using each man's speech, he developed a slightly accented idiom of his own, something personal and highly original. He gave himself an earthly past, from a neatly photostated birth certificate to gilt-edged rent receipts. He sounded out the minds of editors and publishers, and through the welter of odd tastes and chaotic ideology therein he extracted sound and workable ideas on what work was needed. He actually sold poetry.

While his body slept in luxury, his mind hurtled over the earth, carried by its illimitably powerful golden shell. Elron could lecture a New York audience on the interesting people he had met in Melbourne, Australia, and the next day produce a cablegram from one or two of those people whom he had visited during the night. Scattered all over the earth were individuals who believed they had known this phenomenal young man for years.

It was at one of those pale-pink and puffy poetry teas that Ariadne saw Elron again. Suzy gave the tea as a current-celebrity show. Ari came gracefully late, looking lovely in something powder-blue, chastely sophisticated. Elron was scheduled to speak—something about "Metempsychosis and Modern Life." Ari was scheduled to sing. But she—

He was watching for her. He was dressed in soft gray, and the Homburg awaited him by the door. Her entrance was as ever in the grand manner, and all realized it; but for her it was that breath-catching experience of realizing that she was putting on the show for just one person in all that crowded room. She'd heard of him, of course. He was the "rage," which is a term used in polite society to describe current successes. Would-bes and has-beens are known as outrages.

But she had never seen him that she remembered. He rose and stood over her and smiled, and he wordlessly took her arm, bowed at the hostess, and led her out. Just like that. Poor Suzy. Her protruding teeth barely hid the tiny line of foam that formed on her lips.

"Well!" Ariadne said as they reached the street. "That was a terrible thing to do!"

"*Tsk, tsk!*" he said, and helped her into his new sixteen-cylinder puddle-jumper. "I imagine Suzy will get over it. Think of all the people she'll be able to tell!"

Ari laughed a little, looking at him strangely. "Mr. Elron, you're not . . . not the same man that—"

"That you picked up on the pike three months ago, dressed like a comedian?"

She blushed.

"Yes, I'm the man."

"I was . . . rude when I left you."

"You had a right to be, Ariadne."

"What happened to that hideous little tramp you were traveling with?"

"Chauncey!" Elron bellowed, and the trimly uniformed chauffeur swiveled around and nodded and smiled.

"Good heavens!" said Ariadne.

"He doesn't offend any more with his atrocious diction," said Elron precisely. "I found it possible to change his attitude toward work, but to change his diction was beyond even me. He no longer speaks."

She looked at him for quite a while as the huge car rolled out into the country. "You're everything I thought you might possibly be," she breathed.

He knew that.

That was their first evening together. There were many others, and Elron conducted himself perfectly, as befitted a brilliant and urbane biped. Catering to every wish and whim of Ari's amused him, for she was as moody as a beautiful woman can be, and he delighted in predicting and anticipating her moods. He adjusted himself to her hour by hour, day by day. He was ideal. He was perfect.

So—she got bored. He adjusted himself to that, too, and she was furious. If she didn't care, neither did he. Bad tactics, and something that supercosmic forces could do nothing about.

Oh, he tried; yes, indeed. He questioned her and he psychoanalyzed her and he even killed off all the streptococci in her bloodstream to see if that was the trouble. But all he got was a passive resentment from her. Half as old as time itself, he knew something of patience; but his patience began to give way under the pressure applied by this very human woman.

And, of course, there was a showdown. It was one afternoon at her home, and it was highly spectacular. He could read her mind with ease, but he could know only what thoughts she had formed. She knew he annoyed her. She also knew she liked him immensely; and for that reason she made no attempt to analyze her hostility toward him, and therefore he was helpless, tangled in her tenuous resentment.

It started with a very little thing—he came into the room and she stood at the window with her back to him and would not turn around. She did not speak or act coldly toward him, but simply would not face him. A very petty thing. After ten minutes of that he strode across the room and spun her around. She caught her heel in the rug, lost her footing, fell against the mantel, and stretched becomingly unconscious on the floor in a welter of broken gew-gaws. Elron stood a moment feeling foolish, and then lifted her in his arms. Before he could set her down she had twined her arms around his neck and was kissing him passionately. Poor, magnficent thing, he didn't know what to do.

"Oh, Elron," she blubbered. "You brute! You struck me. Oh, darling! I love you so! I never thought you would do it!"

A great light of understanding burst for Elron. *That* was the basic secret of this thing called woman! She could not love him when he acted in a perfectly rational way. She could not love him when he was what she thought was ideal. But when he did something "brutish"—a word synonymous with "unintelligent"—she loved him. He looked down at her beautiful lips and her beautiful black eye, and he laughed and kissed her and then set her down gently.

"Be back in a couple of days, darling," he said, and strode out, ignoring her cries.

He knew what to do now. He was grateful to her for amusing him for a while and for teaching him something new. But he could not afford to upset himself by associating with her any longer. To keep her happy he would have to act unintelligent periodically; and that was one thing he could not stand. He went away. He got into his huge automobile and drove away down the turnpike.

"It's a pity that I'm not a man," he reflected as he drove. "I'd really like to be, but—Oh, I can't be bothered keeping track of anything as complicated as Ariadne!"

He pulled up at the outskirts of a small town and found his laboratory. Once inside, he lay down on the table, popped open his skull and emerged. Going to the machine in the corner, he added and took away and changed and tinkered, and the glow began to form again around the still body. Something was happening inside the skull. Something took shape inside, and as it happened the skull slowly closed. In three hours Elron the man climbed off the table and stood looking about him. The golden egg flew up to his shoulder and nestled there.

"Thank you for this ... this consciousness," said Elron.

"Oh, that's all right," replied the ovoid telepathically. "You've had it for some months, anyway. Only I've just given you what you needed to appreciate it with."

"What am I to do?" asked the man.

"Go back to Ariadne. Carry on from where I left off. You can—you're a man, perfect in every cell and gland and tissue."

"Thank you for that. I have wanted her but was never directed—"

"Never mind that. Marry her and make her happy. Never tell her about me—you have history enough to carry you through your lifetime, and brains enough, now, to do the work you have been doing. Ari's been good to me; I owe her this much."

"Anything else?"

"Yes. Just one thing; but burn this in your brain in letters of fire: A woman can't possibly love a man unless he's part dope. Be a little stupid all the time and very stupid once in a while. But *don't* be perfect!"

"Okay. So long."

"Be happy ... er ... son—"

Elron the man left the laboratory and went out into the sunlight. The golden egg settled to the floor and lay there an hour or so. He laughed once within himself and said, "Too perfect!"

Then he felt terribly, terribly lonely.

Two Percent Inspiration

DR. BJORNSEN WAS a thorough man. He thought that way and acted that way and expected others to exceed him in thoroughness. Since this was an impossibility, he expressed an almost vicious disappointment in incompetents, and took delight in pointing out the erring one's shortcomings. He was in an ideal position for this sort of thing, being principal of the Nudnick Institute.

Endowed by Professor Thaddeus MacIlhainy Nudnick, the institute was conducted for the purpose of supplying brilliant young assistants to Professor Nudnick. It enrolled two thousand students every year, and the top three of the graduating class were given subsistence and a considerable salary for the privilege of entering Nudnick's eight-year secondary course, where they underwent some real study before they began as assistants in the Nudnick laboratories.

Bjornsen never congratulated an honor student, for they had behaved as expected. He found many an opportunity of delivering a kick or two in the slats to those who had fallen by the wayside; and of these opportunities, the ones that pleased him the most were the ones involving expulsion. He considered himself an expert disciplinarian, and he was more than proud of his forte for invective.

It was with pleasurable anticipation that he summoned one Hughie McCauley to his office one afternoon. Hughie was a second-year student, and made ideal bait for Bjornsen's particular line of attack. The kid was intelligent to a degree, and fairly well read, so that he could understand Bjornsen's more subtle insults. He was highly sensitive, so that he could be hurt by what Bjornsen said, and he showed it. He lacked sense, so that he continually retorted to Bjornsen's comments, giving the principal blurted statements to pick meticulously apart while the victim writhed. Hughie was such perfect material for persecution that Bjornsen rather hated to expel him; but he comforted himself by recalling the fact that there were hundreds of others who could be made to squirm. He'd take his time with Hughie, however; stretch it out, savor the boy's suffering before he kicked him out of the school.

"Send him in," Bjornsen told the built-in communicator on his luxurious desk. He leaned back in his chair, put the tips of his fingers together, lowered his head so that only the whites of his eyes were visible as he stared through his shaggy brows at the door, and waited.

Hughie came in, his hair plastered unwillingly down, his fear and resentment sticking out all over him. The kid's knees knocked together so that he stumbled against the doorpost. There was a gloss of cold sweat on his forehead. From previous experience, he had no difficulty in taking up the front-and-center position before the principal's desk.

"Y-yes, sir!"

Bjornsen made a kissing noise with his wrinkled lips before he spoke, threw back his head and glared. "You might," he said quietly, "have washed your ears before you came in here." He knew that there is no more painfully undignified attack for an adolescent, particularly if it is not true. Hughie flushed and stuck out his lower lip.

Bjornsen said, "You are an insult to this institution. You were in a position, certainly, to know yourself before you applied for admission; therefore, the very act of applying was dishonest and insincere. You must have known that you were unfit even to enter these buildings, to say nothing of daring to perpetuate the mistake of the board of examiners in staying here. I am thoroughly disgusted with you." Bjornsen smiled his disgust, and it was a smile that perfectly matched his words. He bent to flip the switch on the communicator, cutting off its mellow buzz. "Yes?"

"Dr. Bjornsen! Professor Nudnick is—"

The annunciator's hollow voice was drowned out in the crashing of a hard, old foot against the door. Nudnick kicked it open because he knew it could not be slammed, and he liked startling Bjornsen. "What sort of nonsense is this?" he demanded, in a voice that sounded like flatulence through ten feet of lead pipe. "Since when has that vinegar-visaged female out there been instructed to announce me? Damn it, you'll see me whether you're busy or not!"

Bjornsen had bounced out of his chair to indulge in every sort of sycophantism short of curtsying. "Professor Nudnick! I am delighted to see you!" This was perfect. The only thing that could possibly increase Hughie McCauley's agony was to have an audience to his dismissal; and what better audience could he have than the great endower of the school himself? Bjornsen rubbed his hands, which yielded an unpleasant dry sound, and began.

"Professor Nudnick," he said, catching Hughie's trembling shoulder and using it to thrust the attached boy between him and Nudnick, "you could not have picked a better time to arrive. This shivering example of negation is typical of the trash that has been getting by the examiners recently. Now I may prove to you that my recent letter on the subject was justified."

Nudnick looked calmly at Hughie. "I don't read your letters," he said. "They bore me. What's he done?"

Bjornsen, a little taken aback, put this new resentment into his words. "Done? What he hasn't done is more important. He has neglected to tidy up his thinking habits. He indulges in reading imaginative fiction during his hours of relaxation instead of reading books pertaining in some way to his studies. He whistles in corridors. He asks impertinent questions of his instructors. He was actually discovered writing a letter to a ... a *girl!*"

"*Tsk, tsk,*" chuckled the professor. "This during classes?"

"Certainly not! Even he would not go that far, though I expect it hourly."

"Hm-m-m. Is he intelligent?"

"Not very."

"What kind of questions does he ask?"

"Oh—stupid ones. About the nature of a space-warp, whatever that may be, and about whether or not time travel is possible. A dreamer—that's what he is, and a scientific institution is no place for dreamers."

"What are you going to do with him?"

"Expel him, of course."

Nudnick reached over and pulled the boy out of Bjornsens's claw. "Then why not post him as expelled and spare him this agony? It so happens, Bjornsen, that this is just the kind of boy I came here to get. I'm going to take him with me on a trip to the Asteroid Belt. Salary at two thousand a month, if he's willing. Are you, what's-your-name?"

Hughie nodded swimmingly.

"Eh." Beckoning the boy, Nudnick started for the door. "My advice to you, Bjornsen," grated the scientist, "is as follows. Keep your nose out of the students' lives on their off hours. If you must continue in these little habits of yours, take it out in pulling the wings off flies. And get married. Take this advice or hand in your resignation effective this date next month."

Hughie paused at the door, looking back. Nudnick gave him a quick look, shoved him toward Bjornsen. "Go ahead, kid. I'd like it, too."

Hughie grinned, walked up to Bjornsen, and with a quick one-two knocked the principal colder than a cake of ice.

They were eight days out now, and these were the eight:

The day when the unpredictable Professor Nudnick had whisked Hughie up to his mountain laboratory, and had put him to work loading the last of an astonishingly inclusive list of stores into the good ship *Stoutfella*. Hughie began to regard the professor as a little less than the god he had imagined, and a little more as a human being. The old man was perpetually cheerful, pointing out Hughie's stupidities and his little triumphs without differentiating between them. He treated Hughie with a happy tolerance, and seemed to be more delighted with the lad's ignorance than by his comparatively meager knowledge. When Hughie had haltingly asked if he might take a suitcase full of fiction with him, Nudnick had chuckled dryly and sent him off to the nearest town with a pocketful of money. Hughie arrived back at the laboratory laden and blissful. They took off.

And the day when they heard the last broadcast news report before they whisked through the Heaviside layer. Among other items was one to the effect that Dr. Emil Bjornsen, principal of the Nudnick

Institute, had resigned to accept a government job. Hughie had laughed gleefully at this, but Nudnick shook his shaggy old head. "Not funny, Hughie," he said. "Bjornsen's a shrewd man. I've an idea why he did that, and it has nothing to do with my ... our ... ultimatum."

Struck by the scientist's sober tone, Hughie calmed down to ask, "What did he do it for?"

Nudnick clapped a perforated course card into the automatic pilot, reeled its lower edge into the integrator, and checked his controls before switching them over to the "Iron Mike."

"It has to do with this trip," he said, waving the kid into the opposite seat, "and it's about time you knew what this is all about. What we're after is a mineral deposit of incalculable value. How it is, I don't know, but somewhere in that mess of nonsense out there"— he indicated the Asteroid Belt—"is a freak. It's a lump like the rest of the asteroids, but it differs from the rest of them. It must've been a wanderer, drifting heaven alone knows how far in space until it got caught in the Belt. It's almost pure, through and through—an oxide of prosydium. That mean anything to you?"

Hughie pushed a couple of freckles together over his nose. "Yeah. Rare Earth element. Used for ... lessee ... something to do with Nudnick Metal, isn't it?"

"That's right. Do you know what Nudnick Metal is?"

"No. Far as I know it's a trade secret, known only to the workers in the Isopolis Laboratories." The Isopolis Laboratories were half heaven and half prison. By government grant, the great Nudnick plant there turned out the expensive metal. It was manned by workers who would never again set foot outside the walls—men who did not have to, for everything they could possibly want was supplied to them. There was no secret about the way they lived, nor about anything in the fifty-square-mile enclosure except the process itself. "Nudnick Metal is a synthetic element, thousands of times denser than anything else known. That's about all I remember," Hughie finished lamely.

Nudnick chuckled. "I'll let you in on it. The metal is the ideal substance for coating spaceships, because it's as near being impenetrable as anything in the Universe. This ship, for instance, is coated with a layer of the stuff less than one one-hundred-fifty-thousandths of an inch thick, and yet is protected against practically anything. We could run full tilt into an object the size of Earth, and though the impact would drill a molten hole thirty miles deep and most likely kill us a little bit, the hull wouldn't even be scratched. Heh. Want to know what Nudnick Metal is? I'll tell you. Copper. Just plain, ordinary, everyday Cu!"

Hughie said, "Copper? But what makes it— How is it—"

"Easy enough. You know, Hughie, it's the simple things that are really effective. Try to remember that. Nudnick Metal is *collapsed* copper; collapsed in the way that the elements of the companions of Sirius and Procyon are collapsed. You know the analogy—pile wine-glasses into a barrel, and there'll be a definite, small number of glasses that can be packed in. But crush them to fine powder, and then start packing. The barrel will hold thousands upon thousands more. The molecules of Nudnick Metal are crushed that way. You could build four hundred ships this size, from stem to stern of solid copper, and you'd use less copper than that which was used to coat this hull.

"The process is only guessed at because copper is synthesized from the uranium we ship into Isopolis ostensibly for power. As you just said, it is known that we import prosydium. That's the only clue anyone but I and the Isopolites have as to the nature of the process. But prosydium isn't an ingredient. It's more like a catalyst. Of all the elements, only prosydium can, by its atomic disintegration, absorb the unbelievable heat liberated by the collapse of the copper molecules. I won't go into the details of it, but the energy thus absorbed and transmuted can be turned back to hasten the collapsing process. The tough thing about prosydium is that it's as rare as a hairy egg, and so far no one's been able to synthesize it in usable quanities. All of which makes Nudnick Metal a trifle on the expensive side. This lump of prosydium in the Belt will cut the manufacturing cost way down, and the man or concern or planet that gets hold of it can write his—its—own ticket. See?"

"I will," said Hughie slowly, "if you'll say all that over again a

few thousand times a day for the next couple of years." The boy was
enormously flattered by the scientist's confiding in him. Though he
himself was not qualified to use it, he knew that the information he
had just received was worth countless millions in the right quarters.
It frightened him a little. He wanted to keep the old man talking,
and so reached for a question. "Why do we have to sneak out in a
little ship like this? Why not take a flotilla of destroyers from Earth
and take possession?"

"Can't do things that way, son. The Joint Patrol puts the kibosh
on that. You can blame the jolly old idealism of the Interplanetary
Peace Congress for that, and the Equal Armament Amendment. You
see, Mars and Earth are forced by mutual agreement to maintain
absolutely equal armament, to share all new developments and to
police space with a Joint Patrol. A flotilla of Earth ships taking off
without the knowledge or consent of the Patrol constitutes an act of
war. War is a nasty business for a lot of people who weren't in on
starting it. We can't do it that way. But if I turn over the location of
my find to the Patrol, it becomes the property of the Joint Patrol,
neatly tied up in red tape, and it doesn't do anybody any good—
particularly the Nudnick Laboratories. However—here's where we
come in.

"If an independent expedition lands on, or takes in tow, any body
in space that is not the satellite of a planet, said body becomes the
sole property of that expedition. Therefore, I've got to keep this
expedition as secret from Earth as from Mars, so that Earth—and
Nudnick—can get the ultimate benefit. In two months my little treasure will be in opposition with Earth. If I have taken it in tow by
then, I can announce my discovery by ultraradio. The signal reaches
Earth before it reaches Mars; by the time the little red men can send
out a pirate to erase me, I am surrounded by a Patrol Fleet, and quite
safe. But if Mars gets wind of what I am up to, son, we are going to
be intercepted, followed, and rubbed out for the glory and profit of
the red planet. Get it?"

"I get it. But what's all this got to do with Bjornsen?"

The old scientist scratched his nose. "I don't know. Bjornsen's a
most peculiar egg, Hughie. He worked most of his life to get to be

principal of the Institute, and it seems to me he didn't do it just for the salary and prestige attached. More than once that egocentric martinet tried to pump me for information about what I was doing, about the Nudnick Metal process, about a hundred things of the sort. I'm sure he hasn't got any real information, but he might possibly have a hunch. A good hunch is plenty to put a Martian ship on our tail and a lot of money in Bjornsen's pocket. We'll see."

And then there was the day when Hughie had made bold enough to ask Nudnick why he had picked him for the trip, when he had his choice of thousands upon thousands of other assistants. Nudnick unwrapped his white teeth in one of his indescribable grins.

"Lots of reasons, son, among which are the fact that I delight in displeasing the contents of Bjornsen's stuffed shirt, and the fact that I dislike being bored, and since I must needs make this trip myself, I might as well be amused while I am cooped up. Also, I have found that baby geniuses are inclined to be a little cocky about what they know, and the fact that they knew it at such a tender age. A trained assistant, on the other hand, is almost certain to be a specialist of sorts, and specialists have inflexible and dogmatic minds. Bjornsen said that one of your cardinal crimes was that you relaxed in fantasy. I, with all of my scientific savvy, can find it in me to admire a mind which can conceive of the possibility of a space-warp, or time travel. Don't look at me that way—I'm not kidding you. I can't possibly imagine such a thing—my mind is far too cluttered up with facts. I don't know whether or not a Martian ship will pick up our trail on this trip. If one does, it will take fantastic thinking to duck him. I'm incapable of thinking that way, so it's up to you."

Hughie, hearing the old man's voice, watching his eyes as he spoke, recognized the sincerity there, and began to realize that he carried an unimaginable responsibility on his shoulders.

On the fourth and fifth days out, there was little to do and Hughie amused both of them by reading aloud, at Nudnick's insistence, from some of his store of books and magazines. At first Hughie was diffident; he could not believe that Nudnick, who had so outdone any fictional scientist, could be genuinely interested; but Nudnick put it as an order, and Hughie began to read, with many a glance at the old man to see if he could find the first glimmerings of derision. He found difficulty in controlling his voice and his saliva until Nudnick slowed him down. Soon he was lost in the yarn. It was a good one.

It concerned one Satan Strong, Scientist, Scourge of the Spaceways and Supporter of the Serialized Short-story. Satan was a bad egg whose criminality was surpassed only by his forte for Science on the Spot. Pursued particularly by the Earth sections of the Space Patrol, Satan Strong was always succeeding in the most dastardly deeds, which always turned out to be the preliminaries to greater evils which were always thwarted by the quick thinking of Captain Jaundess of the Patrol, following which, by "turning to the micro-ultra-philtmeter he rapidly tore out a dozen connections, spot-welded twenty-seven busbars, and converted the machine into an improved von Krockmeier hyperspace lever, which bent space like the blade of a rapier and hurtled him in a flash from hilt to point" and effected his escape until the next issue. Nudnick was entranced.

"It's pseudoscience," he chuckled. "I might even say that it's pseudological pseudoscience. But, it's lovely!" He regarded his withered frame quizzically. "Pity I don't have muscles and a widow's peak," he said. "I've got the science but I rather fear I lack glamour. Have you the next issue?"

Hughie had.

Then, on the sixth day, Hughie's reading was interrupted by a shrill whine from the forward instrument panel. A light flashed under a screen; Nudnick walked over to it and flipped a switch. The screen glowed, showing the blackness of space and its crystal points of light. He turned a knob; the points of light swung slowly across the screen until the tiny black ring of the juncture of the crosshairs encircled a slightly luminous spot.

"What is it?" Hughie asked, regretfully laying down his book.

"Company," said Nudnick tersely. "No telling who it is at this distance, unless they want to tell us about themselves by ultraradio. They're on our course, and overtaking."

Hughie stared into the screen. "You had this stern detector running all the time, didn't you? Gee— You don't think it's a pirate, do you?" There was something hopeful in Hughie's tone. Nudnick laughed.

"You want to see science in action, don't you? Heh. I'm afraid I'm going to be a disappointment to you, youngster. We can't travel any faster than we are going now, and that ship quite obviously can."

Hughie flushed. "Well, professor, if you think it's all right—"

Nudnick shook his head. "I don't think it's all right," he said. "Now that we have established that fact, let's get back to your story. To think that Captain Jaundess would be careless enough to let his betrothed get into the clutches of that evil fellow! What will he do to her?"

"But, Professor Nudnick—"

Nudnick took Hughie's arm and steered him across the control room to his chair. "My dear, overanxious young crew, the ship that is pursuing us presents no problem until it overtakes us. That will be in forty-eight hours. In the meantime, Captain Jaundess' girl friend is in far greater danger than we are. Pray proceed."

Most unwillingly, Hughie read on.

Forty-eight hours later, the brisk crackle of an ultraradio ordered them to stand by to be boarded in the name of the Joint Patrol. The destroyer pulled alongside, and a lifeboat carried a slim, strong cable around the *Stoutfella* and, through the mooring eyes, back to the Patrol ship. The cable was used because magnetic grapples are useless on a Nudnick Metal hull. A winch drew the craft together, and a "wind tunnel" boarding stage groped against the outside of the *Stoutfella*'s air lock.

"What are you going to do?" asked Hughie desperately.

"We are going to say as little as possible," said Nudnick meaningly, "and we are going to let them in, of course." He actuated the airlock controls; the boarding stage was hermetically sealed to their hull as the outer and inner doors slid back.

A purple-uniformed Martian yeoman stepped down into the room, followed by his equally ranking shipmate from Earth. The Martian swore and shut his nostril flaps on the sides of his stringy neck with an unpleasant click. "This air is saturated," he squeaked.

"You might have had the courtesy to dehydrate it."

"What?" grinned the Earth Patrolman. "And deprive me of the only breath of decent air I've had in nineteen days?" He drew a grateful breath, letting the moisture sink into his half-parched lungs.

The air in Patrol ships was always, since there was no happy medium, too dry for Earthlings and too humid for Martians; for the Martians, living for countless generations on a water-starved planet, had developed a water-hoarding metabolism which had never evolved a use for a water surplus.

"Who is in command?" piped the Martian. Nudnick gestured; the Martian immediately turned his back on Hughie. "We have orders from headquarters that this ship is to be searched and disarmed according to Section 398 of the Earth-Mars Code."

"Suspicion of piracy," supplemented the Earthman.

"Piracy?" shouted Hughie, his resentment at last breaking through. "Piracy? Who do you think you are? What do you mean by—"

Three tiny eyes in the back of the Martian's head flipped open. "Has this unpleasantly noisy infant a function?" he demanded, fingering the blaster at his hip.

"He's my crew. Be quiet, Hughie."

"Yeah—take it easy, kiddo," said the Earthman, not unkindly. "Orders are orders in this outfit. You got no fight with us. We just work here."

"Let them alone, Hughie," chimed in Nudnick. "We've little enough armament and they're welcome to it. They have every right." While the Martian stalked out, the scientist turned to the other Patrolman. "This is a Patrol Council order?"

"Of course."

"Who signed it?"

"Councilman Emil Bjornsen."

"Bjornsen? The new member? How has he the right?"

"Council regulations. 'If any matter should be put to a vote, the resulting decision shall be executed in the name of the president of the council, except in such cases where the decision is carried by one vote, when the order shall be executed in the name of the councilman whose vote carrried the measure.' Bjornsen, as the most recently appointed councilman, has the last vote. In this case the action was deadlocked and his vote carried it."

"I see. Thank you. I suppose you can't tell me who proposed this order?"

"Sorry."

The Patrolman moved swiftly about the room, covering every inch of space. In spite of his resentment, Hughie had to admire the man's efficiency. The kid stood sullenly against the bulkhead; when the man came to him, he ran his hands quickly over the boy, and with the skill of a practiced "dip," extracted a low-powered pellet-gun from Hughie's side pocket. "You won't want this," he said. "It won't kill anything but cockroaches and they're too easily fumigated." Glancing around swiftly to see if the Martian had returned from the storerooms yet, he clapped his hand over Hughie's mouth and whispered something. When the Martian came back, the Patrolman was finishing up on the other side of the room, and Hughie was staring at him with an affectionately resentful wonderment.

"Hardly a thing," complained the Martian shrilly, displaying a sparse armload of side arms and one neuro ray bow chaser. "Never heard of a Martian councilman sending a destroyer after a couple of nitwits on a pleasure cruise."

They saluted and left. In two minutes the ships drifted apart; in five, the destroyer was nothing but a memory and a dwindling spot on the stern visiscreen. Nudnick smiled at Hughie.

"*Tsk!* You certainly flew off the handle, Hughie. When that fellow took away your peashooter, I thought you were going to bite him."

"Nah," said Hughie, embarrassed. "He was O.K. I guess I didn't want the gun much anyhow."

There was a silence, while Nudnick inspected the inner airlock gate and then the air-pressure indicator. Finally Nudnick asked:

"Well, aren't you going to tell me?"

"What?"

"What it was that the Patrolman whispered in your ear. Or are you going to save it for a climax in the best science-fiction tradition?"

Hughie was saving it for just that. "You don't miss much, do you?" he said. "It wasn't nothing much. He said, 'There's a lousy little Martian private ship on your tail. Probably will stay on our spot on your visiscreen for a few days and be on top of you before you know it. Better watch him.'"

"Hm-m-m." Nudnick stared at the screen. "Anything else?" He spoke as if he knew damn well there was something else. Hughie blushed, robbed of the choicest part of his secret.

"Only just that Bjornsen's aboard."

"That still isn't all." Nudnick approached the boy, absolutely dead pan.

"Honest," stammered Hughie, wide-eyed.

Nudnick shook his head, put his hand in his pocket, gave something to Hughie. "There's just this," he said. "He slipped it into my pocket on the way out, just as easily as he slipped it out of yours."

Hughie stared at the gun in his hand with a delight approaching tears.

"A very efficient young man," said Nudnick. "You will notice that he unloaded it."

Three weeks later Professor Nudnick took it upon himself to disconnect the stern visiscreen because Hughie could not pry himself loose from it. The Patrolman had been right; the destroyer had dwindled there until it reached a .008 intensity and then had stayed right there for several days, after which it had grown again until the boy could make out the ship itself. It was no longer the destroyer, it was a plump-lined wicked little Martian sportster. He knew without asking that the little ship was fast and maneuverable beyond all comparison with the *Stoutfella*. It annoyed him almost as much as Nudnick's calm acceptance of the fact that they were being followed, and that there was every possibility of their never returning to Earth, to say nothing of locating and claiming the prosydium asteroid. He took the trouble to say as much. Nudnick merely raised his eyebrows to uncover his logic and said:

"Don't go off half-cocked, younker. Granted, the Martian is following us. I was apparently right about Bjornsen's hunch; he knows that I have been looking all over the system for prosydium and that it is rather unusual for me to go sailing off personally into space. Ergo, I must have found some. But he doesn't want me, or you. All he wants is the prosydium. He can get it only by following this ship. Until we tie on to something, we're as safe as a babe in a bassinet. So why worry?"

"Why worry?" The kid's brains almost crackled audibly in their attempt to transmit his worry to the scientist. "Here's something! Has it occurred to you that all the Martian has to do is to determine our course, continue it ahead on a chart, and then know our destination?"

"It has occurred to me," said Nudnick gently. "Our course will intercept Mercury in twenty days."

"Mercury!" Hughie cried. "You told me the prosydium was on an asteroid!"

"It is on an asteroid." Nudnick was being assiduously patient. "You know it, and I know it. But our course is for Mercury. That's all *they* know. If we lose them, we will change course for the Belt. If we don't lose them, we will go to Mercury. If they're persistent, we'll go back to Earth and try again some time, though I will admit there's only a billion to one chance of our slipping away without being followed again."

"I'm sorry," said Hughie after a while. "I have no business in trying to tell you off, Professor Nudnick. Only I hate like hell to see that Bjornsen guy keep you away from what you want to get. That heel. That lousy wart on the nose of progress!"

"End quotes," said Nudnick dryly. "Captain Jaundess."

"O.K., O.K.," said Hughie, grinning in spite of himself. "But I can't seem to get over that guy Bjornsen. He got in my hair for nearly two years at school, and now that he's kicked me out he seems to want to get under my scalp as well. I dunno—I never saw a guy like that before. I can't figger him—the way he thinks. That rotten business of ganging up on kids. He's inhuman!"

"You may be right," said Nudnick slowly. "You may just possibly be right." After a long pause, he said, "I picked the right assistant, Hughie. You're doing fine."

Hughie was so tickled by that remark that he didn't think to ask what provoked it.

Two days before they were due on Mercury, the professor heaved a sigh, glanced at Hughie, and connected up the stern visiscreen. "There you are," he said quietly. Hughie looked up from his magazine, dropped it with a gasp of horror. The Martian ship was not two hundred yards behind them, looming up, filling the screen. He sprang to his feet.

"Professor Nudnick! *Do* something!"

Nudnick shook his head, spread his hands. "Any ideas?"

"There must be something. Can't you blast them, professor?"

"With what? The Patrol took even our little neuro ray."

Hughie waved the defeatist philosophy aside impatiently. "There ought to be something you could do. Heck—you're supposed to be ten times the scientist that Harry Petrou is—"

"I beg your pardon?"

"Harry Petrou ... Petrou!" Hughie swept up the magazine, thrust the too-bright cover in the scientist's face. "The writer! The author of—"

"Satan Strong!" The dried-up old man let out an astonishingly hearty peal of laughter.

"Well," said Hughie defensively, "anyway—" Furiously he began to shout half-hysterical phrases. He was scared, and he had a bad case of hero worship, and he was also very young. He said, "You go ahead and laugh. But Harry Petrou has some pretty damn good ideas. Maybe they're not scientific. Not what you'd call scientific. Why doesn't anybody ever do anything scientific without studying for fifty years in a dusty old laboratory? Why does one of the greatest scientists in history," he half sobbed, "sit back and b-be bullied by a l-louse like Bjornsen?"

"Hughie—take it easy, there." Nudnick put out his hand, then turned away from those young, accusing eyes. "Things aren't done that way, Hughie. Science isn't like that—made to order for melodramatic adventures. I know—you'd like me to burrow into the air conditioner, throw a few connections around, and come out with a space-warp."

Hughie turned on the lower forward screen. It showed, blindlingly, the flaming crescent of the inner planet. They were descending swiftly toward the night-edge of the twilight strip, the automatic pilot taking care of every detail of deceleration and gravity control.

"You're quitting," said Hughie, his lip quivering. "You're running away!" And he turned his back to Nudnick, to stare at the evil menacing bulk of the Martian ship.

Nudnick sighed, went and sat at the controls, and took over the ship from the pilot.

After two silent hours, Hughie observed that Nudnick was preparing to land. He said in a dead voice:

"If you land, they'll catch us."

"That's right." Nudnick's voice was brisk.

"And if they catch us, they'll torture us."

"Yep." Nudnick glanced over his shoulder. "Will you obey my orders implicitly?"

"Sure," said Hughie hopelessly. His eyes were fixed in fearful fascination on the Martian ship.

"Start now, then. Get rid of all the metal on your clothes. Belt buckle, buttons—everything. You have fiber soled boots?"

"Mm-m-m."

"Put them on. Snap into it!"

An hour later the *Stoutfella* grated on a sandy clearing not far from a red and rocky bluff. The choking atmosphere of Mercury swirled about the portholes. Nudnick climbed out of the pilot seat and tore a pair of fiber boots out of a locker. He had already ripped his buttons off, tossed his wrist radio and identification ring on the chart table. "Come on!" he snapped.

"You ... we're not going out there?"

"You're damn right we are!"

Hughie looked at him. If this old man was willing— He shrugged, picked up a magazine. It seemed as if he—stroked it. Then he tossed it aside and strode with Nudnick into the airlock.

As the inner gate shut them out of the little world that the ship afforded, Nudnick clapped him on the back. "Chin up, kiddo," he said warmly. "Now listen—do exactly as I tell you. When we get outside, move as fast as you can toward that bluff. The Martians won't shoot as long as they think we have any information. Na—no questions—there isn't time! Listen. It's hot out there. As hot as the oven my dear old mother used to bake ten-egg cakes in. The air is not so good, but we can breathe it—for a while. Long enough, I guess. Ready?"

The outer gate slid back and they plunged out.

It was hot. In seconds acrid dust was packing on Hughie's skin, washing away in veritable gushes of sweat, packing the pores again. He saw the reason for taking off all metal clothing. He had left his identification ring on; it began to sear his hand. He tore it off, and blistered flesh with it.

The air lacerated his throat, stung his eyes. Somehow he knew the location of three things—the red bluff, the hovering Martian ship, and the professor. He pounded on. Once he tripped, went down on one knee. His breeches burst into flame. Nudnick saw and helped him slap it out. Inside the charred edges of cloth he caught a glimpse of his own kneecap, a tiny spot of bone amid a circle of cooked flesh, where his knee had ground into the burning sand.

Nudnick tugged at his elbow. "How far do you think we are?" he wheezed.

Hughie suddenly realized that Nudnick's old eyes couldn't see very far in this kind of heat; he had to be eyes for two people now. "Ship—hundred and fifty—yards—"

"Not—far enough! Go—on!"

They struggled on, helping each other, hindering each other. The ground rose sharply; Nudnick stopped. "Beginning of ... bluff ... far ... enough—" He began coughing.

Hughie held him up until he had finished. He began to understand. He had heard vague stories about Martian torture. Nudnick would rather die this way, then. They could have starved slowly in the ship. Maybe this was better—

Nudnick's shrill, dust-choked whisper reached him. "Martians?"

Hughie put one hand over his eyes and peered through the fingers. The Martian ship had settled down beside the *Stoutfella*. The port swung open, three figures, two tall and lanky, one short and shriveled. "Three ... coming ... two Martians ... Bjornsen." Talking was torture. Breathing was pulling living fire into the lungs. He heard a noise and looked down. Nudnick was clutching him and making the noise. Slowly he realized that the old man was laughing.

They lurched toward the three figures, clinging to each other. The two Martians grasped them, and just in time, or they would have fallen and died.

"Of all the crazy damn things to do!" shrilled Bjornsen. In spite of the blasting breeze, the insufferable heat, the old gestures returned to him, and he rubbed his hands together in that familiar, despised gesture.

Nudnick forced his eyes open and stared at the councilman worriedly, and then turned to each of the Martians. They were wilting a little bit in the heat, but their grip was still strong. Bjornsen spoke a few squeaky words in the Martian tongue, and the five of them began to struggle toward the ships.

Suddenly the Martian who had Hughie's arm began to cry out in a piercing, ululating whine. It was quite the most ghastly sound the boy had ever heard; he shuddered in spite of the heat and thrust at the creature. To his utter amazement the Martian slumped to the ground, arched his back as it began to scorch, screamed deafeningly and then lay still. Nudnick laughed cacklingly again and shoved at his Martian, tripping him at the same time. The second Martian stumbled, regained his balance, and then began screaming. In a matter of seconds he fell. He took longer, but died also—

Bjornsen stood in front of them, watching the Martians, and then, shouting agonized curses, began a stumbling run toward his ship.

"Damn it, he's going to make it!" cried Nudnick; and stooping, he caught up a hot stone and hurled it.

Straight as an explosive pellet it flew, and caught Bjornsen between his narrow shoulders. Bjornsen threw up his hands, trying wildly to keep his feet. Gibbering crazily, Nudnick threw another stone. It missed by twenty feet. Hughie caught the old man as he fell exhausted. When next he looked at Bjornsen, the councilman was, down on his knees, his hand clutching at the sill of the Martians' airlock. He sagged, writhed, and died there.

Hughie stood for five seconds, tottering; then he shook his head, bent and let the scientist's limp body fall across his shoulder. It took him an eternity to straighten up, and then eternities to locate his nearby ship and begin that long, long fifty-foot journey. Hughie knew later that if it had been five—three—feet more, he could not possibly have made it. But somehow he did—somehow he tumbled the old man into the lock, pitched forward on top of him. He scrabbled weakly around, found the lock control, pressed it.

Hughie screamed when he came out of it. Then he opened his eyes and saw that he wasn't in that fiery desert. He closed them again and realized that his knee hurt terribly. Then Nudnick was beside him, bathing his face, talking.

"Good stuff, kid. Fix you up in no time. Heh! Long chance just for a few tons of prosydium, eh? Well, we'll get it now. No one else around. No one else around."

"Bjornsen?"

"Dead. Remember? Like the Martians."

"Martians." The words brought horror into the heat-reddened young face. He raised his head and Nudnick slipped another pillow under it. "What happened to those Martians?"

Nudnick grinned. "They died of ignorance, son, and let that be a lesson to you." Hughie just stared. "You see, for generations now, Martians have lived on Earth and Earthmen on Mars. It made 'em forget something—that one little fact I was talking about before we landed. Water-hoarders, Hughie. *Martians can't sweat!* You see? A human can live beside a steak that's cooking, because he sweats. The evaporation cools him down. A Martian can't stand that kind of heat—he cooks like a steak!"

"But ... Bjornsen wasn't—"

"Ah. You're wrong there. Bjornsen *was!* A freak, Hughie. Look at Martians. Unemotional—logical—well, isn't that Bjornsen? Y'know, when I walked in on him when he was ganging up on you at the Institute, I heard him rub his hands together. I knew I'd heard it somewhere before, but I don't know just where. But the other day when you said he was inhuman, it clicked. Bjornsen didn't have no mamma and no poppa, kiddo. He came out of a Martian biochemical laboratory, or I miss my guess. Clever fellers, those Martians. Trained him from birth for that job. A key man in the middle of my little old institute. There may be more like him. I'll see to that. Heh! I won't be the first boss that's told his employees, 'Work up a sweat or get canned!'"

Hughie at last managed to grin a little. Nudnick kept on talking happily. "That knee'll be all right in a couple weeks. By that time we'll hook on to the prosydium. You're fixed for life, fella. Ah—hey, I've got a confession to make to you."

Hughie turned weak, amused eyes on him. The old man wagged his head. "Yep. About that prosydium. Didn't you wonder how I knew about it? I'll tell you. I was coming from Mars last year on a Martian liner. Very elegant. Humidifiers in every room. Radio. Recorded music. Lots of apparatus built into the staterooms. Would've delighted the heart of Satan Strong. Anyway, I got messing around. I . . . er—" He paused guiltily, then went on. "I sort of tore out some connections and spot-welded some busbars. Built me a dandy detectograph. Located that prosydium as we passed the edge of the Belt. Sheer luck. Spotted it, by golly, right from a stateroom in a Martian ship!"

Hughie laughed admiringly. "You old son of a gun," he said disrespectfully. "And you sneered at Satan Strong!"

"Me?" The old man shook his head and stood up. "Why should I sneer at Satan Strong? I *like* Satan Strong. I ought to. I *write* those stories!"

The Jumper

MY PILOT WAS ANNOYED with me, which was understandable, since he was an earnest young man and regretted the substitution of a Canadian medical officer for three fifty-pound bombs. Bombs would do his work over Germany, he reasoned; and they would do it without observing him and his gunner, without making constant notations in a military blank book. But the war office wanted these observations of R.A.F. lads under stress, and to us, the war office was at the top of the heap.

I wasn't subjected to his annoyance long, more's the pity. The youngster guided us skillfully through the black over Europe to within forty miles of our objective and then swallowed a German tracer that puffed in through the cowling. He screamed and threw up his hands, and we went into a dive with benefit of engines. A Me-110 whipped past with a sound for all the world like a mighty belch, and the right auxiliary petrol tank spewed flames all over the fuselage. It all happened bloody fast, and there was nothing to be done, so I went over the wall. Pulling my ripcord a few seconds later, I saw the pale gleam of the gunner's 'chute moving about me in a great circle. That's the way it was, because I couldn't see that I was spinning—and I couldn't see anything but his 'chute, and the meteor that had been a slim blue-gray bomber. It crashed tremendously a couple of minutes later, and the *whump* of the concussion jerked at my shroud lines. The intensity of the dead lad's purpose must have carried him through, for the flaming carcass carried its basket of eggs right into the middle of a crowded railroad yard, as I saw by the flash and the flame.

Then Archy opened up on us, and I thought that was just about the outside edge. Five hundred guineas' worth of H.E. and shrapnel for two men dangling from parachutes. Myself, I might try my aim with an automatic rifle at a Hun in a 'chute. I used to be a pretty fair duck hunter. But shrapnel? Deuced unsporting. I had the nasty feeling that the gunner and I had been reduced to a bet on a bottle of beer between two bored Jerries.

Archy shared half a dozen rounds with us. I was too busy spilling wind out of the silk to see how the other chap made out. He was taking his chances on riding it straight down. I miscalculated my altitude, what with Jerry banging away and all that spilling , and I came down pretty fast. Landed with a bit of a bump and broke both of my legs. The umbrella dragged me cross country because I couldn't roll over, and the jarring compounded one of the fractures. I lay down then, when the silk fouled on a sapling, and wished that the fall had knocked me out. Just by crazy chance, the gunner came down within twenty feet of me. His 'chute seemed to set him down like a thistle seed. The breeze quit and let him fold up gently, but not before I saw that shrapnel had taken his shoulders out from under his head. Then the great white 'chute billowed down over both of us.

They treated us pretty well at the camp. I call it a camp because it's known as a camp to the press, but it was really a castle. Polish. We had the run of two-thirds of the place, including a wide garden. Keep your eyes away from the walls and you'd think you were in England, though no Englishman would let his garden run riot the way this one was. This one had been so well planted that it was all the better for its neglect. I used to clump about it after my legs had knit well enough to bear my weight. Jerry had done more than was humanly possible for that right leg. A less skilled medico would have amputated and thereby given me more of a limp but a lot less pain. I suppose it's better to have your own limbs in any condition, but there were times when I didn't think so.

The whole set-up had all the elements of being bearable. They fed us adequately, and anybody can get used to *ersatz* coffee made from tulip bulbs and turnips. They allowed us half a dozen Tommies to keep the rooms and mess hall clean, and they were decent about letting packages from home get through. Well, the German military is that way, anyhow. There's a new government in Berlin, a new Germany in men's minds and on the maps; but it hasn't killed the traditionalism of the armed forces. To the Prussian mind, an officer is an officer, be he German, English or Guatemalan, and as such he is entitled to respect and subordination. He may be a prisoner, but if he is, no man without rank may give him orders. The party would like to do something about that, but the party is a little too shrewd to interfere with the military during wartime. Wait till it's over; then the factions will blossom out. Then the army will have its chance to even up a few scores—and it will, it will.

Richter was a party man. Richter had reached the ripe old age of twenty-two and had six devoted and bloody years of party work behind him. At sixteen he had reported his uncle and aunt to the Nazis because they had made some derogatory remarks about the leader. Richter was in an ideal spot to spy on them since they were supporting him. He made it his business to investigate the family of his childhood sweetheart, found that the girl was one-eighth Jewish, held the fact over her head until he was tired of her, and then had her sent to a camp equipped with sundry abrasions and a condition associated with so much bitterness that not even mother love would override it. He was a charter member of the *Jugend;* he had worn his brown shirt with pride and plain clothes with poisonous efficiency. He had clung to the *Landwehr* as long as he could, on the theory that his loyal talents were of more use to the party in spying on his associates than in pulling a more honest trigger. He was in the army now, but he had been sent to the prison to check up on its administration; a fact that he made no bones about. He was tall and broad, with rotten teeth and eyes set too close together, and I do believe he bleached his hair.

But he was a private. He used his low rank on German and British officers alike, begging to be disciplined for his insubordinate conduct so that he could send in a lying report to Berlin. He was sly—he clung impeccably to the letter of his Soldier's Manual. But the spirit of it—that was his toy. The Jerries loathed him as only soldiers can loathe political theorists. The English—well, at least they had the freedom of being his admitted enemy.

I ran afoul of him the very day I first got out of bed. I was sitting in the garden, smoking my pipe, a pair of crutches on one side of me and an R.A.F. flight commander on the other. We were talking quite casually about something he had read when we realized that Richter had pussyfooted up behind us. McCarthy, the flier, went right on talking. "—and that's something I've noticed in all his books," he said. "I have to agree with him. There is nothing on earth quite as revolting as a criminal doing as he pleases under the holy name of patriotism. A man who would do that would report his relatives to the authorities. More—he would eavesdrop on his superiors. Richter," he said without turning, "Captain LaFarge's pipe has gone out. Light it for him like a good chap."

Richter came around where we could see him. He was speechless with rage. Indirection and irony were completely foreign to his malignant mind; they baffled and hurt him.

"I haf not a match," he said stiffly.

"Very well," said McCarthy. "Carry on, then," and he waved the German away. McCarthy gazed after him. He was English— Northumberland—and a brilliant man. He had been a corporation lawyer before the war, and was the kind of soldier that Goebbels tries to teach Germany to disbelieve in. "That creature," said McCarthy softly, "is going to figure prominently in a murder very soon. He'd better see to it that he's the party of the first part."

I laughed loud enough to annoy Richter, for he must know that we were talking about him. "Is he always like that?"

"That, or worse," said McCarthy. He spat. "I don't know if there'll be an exchange so I can get out of here, but if I do, I have a pretty little problem posed for myself. I'm certain that I could find this place from the air. There's an air field not three hundred yards from here— military objective. Knowing that, would I bomb the whole layout on the off-chance of killing all the English here, if I knew I'd get Richter in the process?"

"Hardly," I said. "You *can't* dislike a man so thoroughly that you'd slaughter a hundred of your own to get to him."

"Can't I, though?" He rose. He was a steady sort, and it surprised me to see that his hands were trembling. "You'll find out for yourself soon enough." He glared at the gate through which the Nazi had disappeared, wiped his palms on his trousers. "Well, I'm going to wash up. Dinner in ten minutes, you know."

"I'll be along," I said. He went into the building, and I sat there watching a flight of Me's coming in from the west, watched them circle to get the wind and drop down until the high garden wall concealed them from me. I remember thinking that perhaps McCarthy was letting the prison get the better of him.

Richter came back, with his usual arrogant marching stride. He halted in front of me—I could almost hear a master sergeant yelling, "*Halt!* One—*two!*" as he did it—and extended a box of matches.

"Oh. Thank you, Richter."

He waited until I had begun to light my pipe, right-faced, and marched back to the castle. On the way he put out his hand, caught up my crutches, dragged them thirty yards away, and dropped them. I called him, furiously, but he apparently did not hear me.

I finished lighting my pipe because there was nothing else I could do. I knew he would be somewhere where he could watch me, ready to enjoy it if I called out for help, for I couldn't move without the crutches. I knew he was praying that I would, rather than call out, crawl in the dirt until I could reach them. So I did neither.

It was a long wait. Because I was just out of the hospital, there was no place set for me at table, and I was not missed until after nightfall. Obermeier found me. He was the prison adjutant.

"Captain LaFarge!"

He floundered through the weeds. "Captain! Why have you not to your room reported?"

"I've been delayed," I said. "If you'll be good enough to fetch me my crutches, I'll go in with you."

He peered at me through the gloom, his fat cheeks shining with sweat. It goes hard with these men if there's a prison break. "Krodges?" He looked up and down the bench.

"Over there," I said. He brought them to me.

"How is this that they are over there the krodges?"

"I must've dropped them. Silly of me, wasn't it?"

He looked carefully all around the dark garden and suddenly sat beside me. "Herr Captain," he whispered, "that Richter—did he—"

"It was what we call a practical joke," I said. "Very funny. If one of the British did it, you can't expect me to tell you his name, can you?" He blinked at me owlishly. "And if it was Richter, I gather that what he wants is a complaint against him for an action to which there were no witnesses. That being what he wants, we'll do otherwise." I climbed to my feet; Obermeier was gentleman enough not to try to help me. "Forget it," I said.

He walked slowly beside me. Finally he said, "If the British like you all are, Germany and England friends is."

"All the British *are* like me," I said.

"This I am not allowed to believe," he grinned, and went inside.

I missed osteomyelitis by a hair, and in a couple of months could navigate by myself. I had a lump on one leg and a limp in the other, and one of my ankles was rigid, while the other refused to be. The result was a syncopated shamble in which Richter took the greatest delight. When I was alone in the garden he used to patrol the wall with an automatic rifle, mimicking me. He had mimicry down to a fine art. Not only physical things like my gimpy walk, but Morris' lisp and poor old Ruffing's *tic doloro* and Beauchamp's voice. Richter spoke a regurgitative sort of English, and I had, at times, to admit that his imitations were as clever as they were crass. He was careful; to the prison authorities he was never guilty of anything tangible. To the prisoners he was a torturer and a tyrant.

McCarthy asked me about that one day. "You used to be a psychologist," he said. "What would you call that warp of Richter's?"

"'Warp' is scarcely the right term," I said. "Richter isn't a normal man gone haywire. He's a nicely integrated personality. He's rational, controlled, quite sane. There's no excuse for his ingrained criminality. Nothing causes it—it just growed. It's a little something of his very own."

"I've heard wonderful things about psychoanalysis," said McCarthy thoughtfully. "Couldn't we perhaps—"

"No," I said. "Psychoanalysis isn't the high-speed panacea the novelists would have us believe. A thorough analysis of a fairly normal man takes three years and costs upward of six hundred pounds. It demands a hell of a lot of work, and incidentally, the complete and utterly sincere cooperation of the subject. I can just see Richter giving us that!"

McCarthy pulled at his lip. He was acting rather strangely, I thought, as if he were on the point of laughing uproariously—or screaming. His features were drawn, and he moved stiffly, which was rather odd for a man who had been doing the most bewildering gymnastics only three minutes ago. He was remarkably fit, and a very able tumbler, and he had a routine he used to go through that he called a round-off-back-handspring-layout-back-somersault with a full twist, which I assure you was as amazing as it sounds. He moved metrically and gracefully, and the spot he appropriated each evening for these gyrations had become marked with his gymnastic spoor—a depression where his leading hand struck on the round-off, two bare patches in the grass where his feet struck, two lighter ones where his hands touched on the handspring, two sets of footprints marking the somersault. McCarthy was very much a creature of habit.

"Three years!" he said disappointedly. "Isn't there something faster than that?"

"A well-placed blow on the side of the jaw," I said.

McCarthy tossed his head in irritation. "You know he never does his filthy work in close quarters," he said.

"What's he done now?"

In answer he extended the hand he had been holding behind his back. It dripped dark blood. A slender steel spike had entered his palm and was sticking up out of the back of his hand. I took his wrist gently. "Good Lord! What is it?"

"An icepick," he said. "I never saw the damned thing. That's what I get for working out on the same spot of ground every evening. Anyone could tell to a fraction of an inch where my hand would come down. The pick was buried point up right where I was due to hit. It went through my hand and broke off. I was already into the handspring when I felt it, and I imagine I tore it up a little when my hands came down the second time."

I set up a yell for Obermeier and swiftly yanked the pick out of his hand. "Let it bleed free," I said, "The dirty—"

The adjutant took him inside and had him bandaged up. I sat there foaming and wondering why a man with a pick through his hand would come to me and start up a casual conversation about psychoanalysis. Perhaps he was just cold-blooded. More likely he had to say something to somebody before he dropped dead with rage. McCarthy was a peculiar bird.

Down at the end of the garden I could see Richter patrolling the top of the wall. He turned toward me, grinned, pulled out a white handkerchief, elaborately bandaged his hand with it, grinned again, and resumed his patrol.

I began to think seriously about whether or not there *was* something faster than psychoanalysis, that you could use on a man who kept out of range of a well-placed blow on the side of the jaw.

You wouldn't think that a creature like Richter could be in any way sensitive, but he was, to an extraordinary degree. Not to any of the humanities, not to music, but to—well, let me tell you how I first noticed it.

He was standing in the corner of the garden wall, leaning casually on his rifle, but so poised that he could club it and kill any prisoner who made a move toward him. He was enjoying himself thoroughly, singing a rasping paraphrase on a popular wartime song—something about "The little old church where England stood." There was no escaping his voice, no ignoring his ingeniously improvised lyrics. We tried loud talking, but it petered out. There was no going inside, out of earshot, for the polite but inflexible prison routine demanded our presence in the garden.

But for once in his life Richter was caught napping. Obermeier came out of the castle and was halfway across the garden before the private saw him.

"Richter!" barked the adjutant. Richter stopped singing, paled visibly, and dropped his rifle. They stood staring fixedly at each other, arms hanging loosely, legs apart. In German, Obermeier said, "Richter! You are on guard duty, no?"

Richter didn't move.

"When has the army allowed a guard on duty to indulge in light opera?" Obermeier was furious, but his native caution was in high gear. He meticulously avoided any reference to the song, or to Richter's obvious reasons for singing it, knowing that if he did, the party would be informed that he was turning pro-British. He had caught Richter in a petty departure from regulations, and for that alone he was reprimanding him. What astonished me was that Richter did not snap into attention. He mouthed silently when Obermeier spoke, glared unmoving when he ceased.

"Attention!" blasted Obermeier. "What ails you, man?"

Richter's face worked, but he didn't move. Obermeier flushed angrily, opened his mouth to speak, closed it and scratched his neck instead. Then he turned on his heel and started back up the path. And then that astonishing thing happened. Richter started up after him. He was ten yards behind, but he walked step for step with the adjutant. I heard one of the imperials say, "Look at th' blighter! He's aping his own officer now!"

The gravel path took a right-angle turn up near the building. As he reached it, Obermeier called, "Teubner! Rausch!" I assumed he was calling a couple of guards to take care of Richter. And then he turned the corner.

And ten yards behind him, Richter called, "Teubner! Rausch!" in exactly the same tone of voice, exactly as loud, and *exactly at the same time* as Obermeier. So perfectly synchronized were the two voices that the effect was like having two radios playing the same program in the same room. Most of us heard it, for we were between the two of them; but I am certain that Obermeier did not, for his own voice drowned out that of Richter. It was something considerably more than mimicry. It was uncanny. But even more so was that when Obermeier took the turn in the path, Richter also made a right turn. It took him off the walk, through a bed of tulips, and briskly into a heavy marble bench. His kneecap struck it with a sickening crack, and over it he went. He did not put out his arms as he fell, and he brought up with his head against the concrete edge of a lily pool. And there he lay, cold as a cake of ice, blood slowly trickling over the yellow cement. The crash of his fall made Obermeier turn his head; he took one look, trotted to the castle and disappeared inside. A few minutes later Rausch and Teubner came out on the run, gathered him up and carried him inside.

McCarthy ranged up beside me as I stood smiling, staring at the patch of Richter's blood. "What the devil do you make of that?"

"Richter overplayed it," I said noncommittally.

He looked at me shrewdly. McCarthy was very fast on the uptake. "You have an idea, haven't you, LaFarge? You know what happened just now?"

"Well," I said slowly, "it does remind me of something. I've seen French-Canadian loggers in Quebec act that way. Jumpers, they call them. I've heard of it happening to members of certain Siberian tribes. In Malaya they call it *latah*. But damn if I ever heard of an Aryan being like that. I don't know why he shouldn't, though, come to think of it. No one knows much about it."

"But what on earth is it?" asked McCarthy impatiently.

"Oh, it's a peculiar kind of hypnotism. For some reason, certain persons are subject to attacks of what you might call 'abject imitativeness.' Their minds slip into rapport with that of another individual, and they have to imitate him. Sometimes they don't realize what they're doing, more often they do and can't help it."

"That's the most extraord'ry thing I ever heard," said McCarthy. "What starts it?"

"Depends on the individual. Generally a jumper'll start imitating someone when his attention is suddenly and forcibly attracted to another person. Richter's was, you know. He was shocked and surprised when Obermeier bellowed at him. Did you notice that he was entranced all the while that Obermeier faced him, and as soon as Obermeier turned he began to move in perfect synchronization with him? Some jumpers get the condition so badly that they slip into a state of *latah* for no reason at all."

"How long does it last?"

"Seconds or weeks. I remember reading about a Malayan who followed his high priest around that way for two solid months. The priest decided that the man was possessed, and that he himself was haunted. But he couldn't get anyone to kill the fellow, because the tribal laws prohibited laying hands on a priest, and the tribe regarded the two of them as one and the same person. So the priest walked up a river bank, made a sharp turn and started across a cane bridge. The man in *latah* made the right turn at the same time, but there wasn't any bridge. He cured his *latah* all right. The poor beggar drowned."

McCarthy grunted and got out his pipe. "Drowned, did he?" he said around the stem. "Hm-m-m. I find that most interesting."

Thinking it over, I did, too.

What account Richter gave to the adjutant for his peculiar actions, I'll never know. He was on sick leave for three days, and in the guard-house for four, and he was much sobered when he resumed his duties. The prisoners and the guard left each other tensely alone, but we knew that it was only a matter of time before he would start his peculiar brand of torture again. He did, and he started on me.

My legs were still shaky, and I was making my way over to my favorite bench one afternoon when I became conscious of a faint creaking. For a nasty moment I thought it was me, for with every step I took I heard a creak; a long one for my right leg, a short one for my left. I stopped; so did the noise. I took two more steps. *C-r-r-r—ik!* Puzzled, I looked around me, and saw Richter standing just inside the old summerhouse, airily looking at all the world but me. He had one hand on the doorknob, and it was that door that needed the oiling, not my leg. I ground my teeth and said nothing; and all the way over to the bench he kept up the crude stunt. I made myself so busy packing my pipe that I jumped when I realized McCarthy had seated himself beside me.

"I saw that," said Mac casually, nodding toward the summerhouse.

"Yep," I said. "Here we go again."

Mac shook his head. "Things are going to be a bit different," he said. "Let's us make that jumper jump."

"Have you been thinking about that, too?" I grinned.

"Right-o. Let's see what we can do with him before he gets too rambunctious." He swiftly outlined his plan. It was a honey.

I got up and limped over to the summerhouse. "Richter!"

He stood sullenly at attention, his little pig eyes roving up and down me, finally settling insultingly on my crooked leg.

339

"How do you feel?" I said conversationally.

He looked out at the castle, saw that the coast was clear, and leaned up against the doorpost. "*Gut,*" he grunted, and spat out the door just past my head.

The finest of the filthy spray settled on my cheek. I gasped with rage, got a four-handed grip on myself. "You know, you remind me of my cousin Julius in Winnipeg," I chatted.

He regarded me with a sort of disgusted wonder on his face as I gabbled on in disconnected sentences. He was completely at a loss. Just as he was about to burst into my prattle, I heard a faint tap on the wall of the summerhouse. I don't think I have ever moved faster in my life.

I reached out, took him by the shoulders and hauled him out of the door, spinning him around at the same time. McCarthy, who had been stealthily circling the building while I held the Nazi in conversation, leaped out of hiding with a rush, four feet in front of us. Richter froze, scared out of his wits.

For an interminable moment I was in doubt. Mac and the German held each other's eyes while I held Richter's shoulders, and all three of us were afraid to breathe. Then Mac knotted his jaw, turned around and walked off. Richter shuddered, moaned a very tiny moan, and—followed him.

"Got him!" I cried happily.

"Good stuff," said two voices, speaking as one. It was an astonishing effect. Mac stopped and turned around. "What are we going to do with the blighter?" they asked me.

"Can't do much with the two of you as close together as that," I said. "Steer him into the wall."

"Right-o," they said in unison. Mac gauged his distances, walked up to the corner of the summerhouse, left-faced and disappeared around the corner. Richter marched up to the wall, hit it with a bump, and kept on marching futilely. I moved over to where I could see both of them.

"How's this?" asked Richter. It was Mac speaking, but he was too far away for me to hear the low-voiced question. Talk about your wireless transmission!

"That's dandy," I said. They both stopped and turned; Mac came back to me while Richter plowed through flower beds. When the Englishman reached me, Richter was well out in the open spot where Mac used to do his tumbling.

"Now what?" asked Mac.

"Now Herr Richter is going to put on a bit of a show," I said gleefully. "See if you can make the silly fool get his gun out."

He began fumbling about the region of his side pocket. He had to make eight or ten passes, but finally got it right.

"Up in the air," I said. "Just once."

The Mauser roared. Richter, carefully guided by Mac and me, holstered it and stared raptly into the sky. A thudding of boots, and Rausch skidded to a stop in front of him. In rather low German, he wanted to know what the hell. Fortunately, Mac's German was flawless.

"Didn't you see it?" said Richter. "A Hawker Hurricane!"

Rausch was big and dumb. He stared up into the sky, and then said he didn't see any airplane.

"Of course you don't," said Richter. "I shot him down." He beckoned Rausch closer and whispered, "It was Rudolph Hess flying back." Rausch went a little popeyed. "He had to get out," said Richter. "The British Isles have been torpedoed and sunk." They gazed solemnly at each other, and then Richter burst into rich Northumberland laughter. He slapped Rausch on the back, and Rausch, suddenly conscious that he was being kidded, uttered a complementary guffaw, took a deep breath, forced out another laugh, and then beat a hasty retreat.

"Halt!" snapped Richter. "Come back here, my friend. I want to tell you a fine English joke I learned from one of these dirty prisoners. You don't speak any English, do you?"

Rausch shook his head.

"All the better," said Richter jovially. "Now listen to me. The next time you see Herr Obermeier, you say these words in English." He repeated a phrase a few times, and the gullible Rausch said it over and over until he had it right.

I have always regretted that I wasn't around when Rausch walked into Obermeier's quarters and said, "Thumbs up, you old prince!" (I think it was "prince" he was told to say.) "There'll always be an England!"

Richter stood out there humming an air called "The Tinker He Went Walking" that Mac hadn't learned in Sunday school until Obermeier erupted violently out into the garden. "Richter!"

"Ja! Heil Hitler!"

"Heil Hitler!" sputtered the adjutant. "Are you responsible for sending that blockhead in to me with those seditious utterances?"

Richter put a finger to his lips. "There's going to be a revolution," he said gravely.

"A revolution? Traitor! Marxist! Jew!"

"It is the truth, Herr Obermeier. Look." And Richter rose off the ground in a perfect back somersault. Obermeier stepped back in alarm. Richter spread his hands and smiled. "You see? There was a revolution. I revolved, no?"

Obermeier's face went into travail and delivered a laugh. Once he had laughed out loud he found that it was an easy and pleasant thing to do, and he roared until the tears ran down his cheeks. "Richter," he gasped after a time. "I have thought hardly of you. I have never credited you with a sense of humor." His features suddenly went wooden. "But this is war. This for such foolishness is no time."

Richter said easily, "Hate is all the stronger if you give it a rest. I respectfully suggest to the adjutant that the prisoners should be served beer this evening."

"A profound thought," said the adjutant, after thinking it over. "That will do, Richter." He eased his conscience by speaking very severely. "And hereafter curb your nonsense!" He went briskly into the castle. As he went through the door his voice drifted back— "Revolution. Hah! *Das is gut!*"

"What are we going to do with the fool now?" asked Mac. I looked out at the fine young specimen of Aryan manhood and grunted. "Pity we can't send him to Berchtesgaden," I said. "I'd like to pull that

'There'll always be an England' gag on der Fuehrer."

"That would be jolly—fine." Mac swayed suddenly, mumbled something.

"What?" I asked.

"Jolly—*Ach! Ich neine*—" He shook his head drunkenly.

"Mac!" I rapped. "Mac! What's the matter?"

Sirens suddenly screamed outside the walls. As they died down I heard the growl of many motors. Torn between Mac and the noises outside, I dragged him to the door and looked up. There was a clutter of aircraft in the sky, attack bombers and pursuits. A formation of Messerschmitts climbed into the sky, and three lovely P-37s howled down to meet them.

Mac said, "Feel deuced queer, old boy. I—" Suddenly he whipped away from me, snarling. "*Schmutzig Englisch schweinhund, du!*" he spat, and he clawed at his hip, pulled a nonexistent Mauser out of his nonexistent holster, filled me full of imaginary holes. Every time his forefinger twitched there was a report outside. Richter had his gun out, was banging away at the garden wall. The sound of his shots was lost in the unholy racket from above.

"Mac!" I screamed, shaking him, slapping him. "Mac! What's—"

He closed his eyes, opened them slowly. "This bloody thing works both ways," he gritted. "The damned—goosestepper's—fighting—" He rallied and said briskly, "What's going on—air raid?"`

"Yes. Mac, are you all right?"

"I can hold him off, I th—Ah-h-h! *Heil, mein Fuehrer! Der fleigand*—" He drifted off into a hopeless jumble of words. Then, "LaFarge," he said, "remember I said I'd like a chance at that air field if I ever get out of here? Well, I probably won't, but maybe I can give someone else a break. I'll wager those lads up there don't know they have anything like that right under them. Are the Huns sending up any planes from here?"

I looked out. "No. Dammit, you're right! They've got it camouflaged. They don't want it bombed, and it's likely because they have a man-sized gasoline dump around here!"

"We've got to—get word—" He groaned, came back strongly. He seemed to be putting up a tremendous battle. "Richter's getting the knack of it," he said grimly. "For a minute there I thought I was out in the garden. I ran my tongue around my mouth and felt a lot of rotten teeth. Ugh!" He shuddered. "Got—shaving mirror?" I had one of those unbreakable trench mirrors in my tunic. Mac waved me outside. "Give it to the Hun," he said. "Right hand. Hurry, now, I don't know if I—" And he went into one of those bilingual paroxysms. I ran out to Richter.

As I thrust the mirror into his hand he eyed me viciously, reached for his gun, paused, grinned. "Good stuff, chum," he said. "Thumbs—*für der Reich*—be an England!"

It occurred to me what Mac had wanted him to have the mirror for. Heliograph. But what was the use of that puny flash of sunlight? How could it attract the attention of a pilot in a dogfight? Off chance. Why didn't he want me to get out there and signal? I glanced around, saw guards on the walls, Obermeier running around like a brood hen. Richter *might* not be noticed, standing there in the garden with the mirror in his palm. I hobbled back to the summerhouse and ducked inside.

"Give me your watch," said Mac. For the moment he was completely himself. I handed it to him, and he moved into the doorway where the late, bright afternoon sun streamed in. He let it play on the back of the watch, threw a spot on the ceiling, and began twitching his wrist steadily. Out in the garden Richter stood firm, eyes upward, right hand extended. Mac began to send.

Dot-dash-dot. Dot-dash. Dot-dot-dash-dot. R.A.F.

I don't know how long that went on. Mac and Richter were engaged in a monumental struggle, weaving now and then on their feet, features working, sweat—and all the while, almost without a break, Mac sent those three letters. Twice he screamed in pain, and both times it was in Richter's guttural tones. McCarthy. Renfrew McCarthy, of Northumberlandshire. Never was there such a man!

Once Richter threw the mirror from him, and I had to limp out and put it in his hand again. And Mac kept sending.

There was a growing, screaming roar. I looked up and saw a Messerschmitt 110 on the tail of a P-37. They seemed to be heading right for us, coming down, coming incredibly fast. At about two hundred feet, the Curtiss began to pull out of it. The Me began to try. The Curtiss made it. The Me didn't. God bless the Nazis for building ships that are sloppy on the turns! The Me whipped low over my head, crashed into the garden wall. The P-37 groaned upward, lost speed, stalled into a wingover, and began to circle at about eight hundred feet.

"Mac!" I screamed. "He's seen us! He's seen us!"

Mac, his face green-white and beaded, chuckled hoarsely and kept sending. Fascinated, I watched that bouncing spot of light on the ceiling. Now it said. "*Cam.—air field—300 yds—SSE.*" He repeated it, repeated it again. Now he was sending, "*Castle—munition dump.*" And then the two of them were mixed: "*Camstle—300 munition—SSE.*"

"Mac—are there munitions in the castle?"

"No, dammit, Richter's sending that! I think I'm driving him under, LaFarge! But—he's going to see to it that if bombs are dropped, we get them, too!"

The circling P-37 waggled its wings and started to climb. I could almost feel the crisp bur of its radio, calling for bombs. A flight of Blenheims swelled up out of the west, wheeled toward us.

"Right-o, Mac," I said quietly. "We better get as near underground as we can." I put an arm around him. He leaned so heavily against me that my legs hurt me. He was dead beat. "Chin up," I gritted, and began dragging him across the garden.

Outside the walls there was a flash of flame, and the ground shook. It shook again, and again. Ahead of us, Richter floundered crazily. When we reached the castle door I propped Mac against the jamb and looked back while I got my wind.

The whole skyline was aflame. There was gasoline there, but plenty. A huge Kurier waddled into the air, and a Hurricane cut it down, and I wondered why in hell they tried to get that monster into the air at a time like this. A bomb landed just outside the wall and blew it inward, and the debris swept Richter off his feet. I mean that word for word. I looked at his body and saw that he was all broken up about it. When the rubble hit Richter, Mac shrieked and passed out.

I'd no sooner got him inside when the next load of eggs were laid on the roof right over our heads. Richter's message had been right. There was an ammunition dump in the castle. The whole bloody business came crashing and crushing down on us. So they got us and most of the other imperials. But we got an air field and an ammunition dump. And Richter. We got game, set and match.

Story Notes

by Paul Williams

Theodore Sturgeon sold his first short story in May 1938, to the McClure Newspaper Syndicate. He was 20 years old, a seaman in the merchant marine. In January of 1939 he moved to New York City and began to write full-time. The only markets he successfully sold to were the newspaper syndicate, which primarily bought short-short stories from him, and, beginning in May 1939, two magazines edited by John W. Campbell, Jr.: *Astounding Science-Fiction* and *Unknown* (the latter specialized in fantasy and horror).

Sturgeon shipped out again between July and October of 1939, doing some writing while at sea, and then returned to New York. In March of 1940 he married his high school sweetheart Dorothe Fillingame, and moved from Manhattan to Staten Island (his birthplace). Their daughter Patricia was born in December 1940, and in June 1941 the three of them left New York and moved to the British West Indies, to manage a resort hotel in Jamaica owned by Sturgeon's mother's family.

Sturgeon's last McClure story was published in March 1940. He did some writing for hire in 1940 and 1941, primarily scripts for comic books, but most of his income until he left New York was from selling stories to *Astounding* and *Unknown*. Sturgeon's bibliography shows him appearing regularly in the two magazines over a five-year period, but this is misleading. In fact, the move to the tropics, which was intended to make it easier for him to write, resulted in his doing no writing at all between July 1941 and April 1944. All of the Sturgeon stories that appeared in *Astounding* and *Unknown* in 1941, 1942, and 1943 were written and sold by June of 1941.

The first volume of *The Complete Stories of Theodore Sturgeon* covered the period from December 1937, when the story he sold in May 1938 was penned, until spring of 1940. The stories in this second volume were all written between April of 1940 and June 1941. All were published in *Astounding* or *Unknown* except for "The Anonymous," presumably submitted to Campbell and rejected, and "Two Sidecars," an unpublished story that contains no fantasy or science fiction element and therefore could not have been aimed at Campbell. There is evidence that Sturgeon wrote other non-fantasy stories during this period, but no manuscripts survive. It is also probable that he submitted a few stories to other fantasy magazines, but without success.

The period covered in Volume 1 was well documented in Sturgeon's correspondence; he was writing regularly to his mother, who was living in Scotland, and to his fiancée in Philadelphia. By contrast, there is almost no documentation of the chronology, or circumstances of writing, of the stories in this volume; Ted had stopped writing to his fiancée now that she was his wife and living in the same house, and he wrote much less frequently to his mother. No other correspondence (or record-keeping) survives. As a result, the sequence of stories in this volume is somewhat arbitrary. "Cargo" belongs near the beginning; "The Jumper" near the end; and some of the other stories can be dated at least within a few months. But the precise order of composition is unknown. (Campbell did not necessarily publish them in the order received.)

"**Cargo**": first published in *Unknown,* November 1940. Probably written in June, 1940. Sturgeon's introduction to the story in his 1948 collection *Without Sorcery* reports:

The story of the origin of "Cargo" will gladden the heart of the string-saver. The reader may remember that in "The Ultimate Egoist" the protagonist at one point debated the advisability of going to sea. In the first draft of that tale, he actually did, and for some three thousand words found himself on a tankship on which weird things happened. I realized suddenly that I was getting far away from my story, and cut back. But instead of throwing away these extraneous pages, I saved them and expanded them: "Cargo" is the result.

Some surviving manuscript pages among Sturgeon's papers confirm this, although in fact the primary contribution of the "Egoist" pages seems to be paragraphs 2–6 of "Cargo" and the general idea of a story about strange events on a renegade oil tanker engaged in war profiteering. Sturgeon's papers also yield the first few pages of a 1939 story (probably never finished) again about a renegade tanker and a skipper referred to as the Old Man.

The rich detail in the story is attributable to the author's extensive experience as a merchant seaman between 1937 and 1939, serving primarily on "coastwise" oil tankers—New York to Texas and sometimes further south. No Atlantic crossings. (Although in 1937 Sturgeon fantasized about a trip to Spain on an oil tanker. He told his mother, in a letter written at sea on September 6, *I hope to be in Europe within the next month or so, but I doubt whether I'll be able to see you. I'll only be in port 18 hours and it will be a Spanish port at that. The whole idea is strictly mercenary on my part, because the oil companies are paying huge bonuses to crews entering the* [Spanish Civil] *war zone. As for the theoretical side of it, you can be sure I'll ship on a cargo of Loyal oil. Texas Co., like all the others, sells to both sides.*)

"Cargo" was also included in the last collection of Sturgeon stories published in his lifetime, *Alien Cargo* (1984). Introducing the story in that book, TS wrote:

—either alien, or very definitely not alien, just different. Depends on how you use the word. Also written in '39 or early '40; England was at war, and I wrote out of my experience in the Merchant Marine. Also, it was a fun story. Later on, I stopped writing fun stories for a very long time. I got pretty grim, I did ... (I can't think of any period when Sturgeon was actively writing for which this comment seems accurate.)

In an undated letter probably written in late August, 1940, Sturgeon told his mother: *You notice this missive is written in two types. I just got this, my precious, back.* (He's referring to his typewriter with a script typeface, on which he wrote most of these early stories.) *It wrote my baby masterpiece, "Cargo," and then quit—absolutely refused to write another word until it was rebuilt. I didn't mind—it was a great big check for a lovely yarn about a crummy old outlaw tankship that was taken over by war refugees—all the Little People who didn't like bombs and shells and thought that this country would be a nice haven. Ye ed. was nuts about it, bought it on sight, and begged me for a sequel.* (Sturgeon's concern for his mother—he urges in the same letter that she return to the U.S. in order to escape the war in Europe—may have helped inspire the story-idea).

Unknown typically ran story blurbs (teasers written by the editor) in as many as three places: on the cover, on the contents page, and on the title page of the story. The title page blurb for "Cargo" read: THE OLD TRAMP STEAMER WAS UTTERLY DISREPUTABLE AND MANNED BY A CREW OF WANTED MEN. AND SOMEWHERE OFF THE COAST OF EUROPE SHE PICKED UP THE WEIRDEST CARGO ON RECORD!

"Shottle Bop": first published in *Unknown*, February 1941. This one is the descendant of a story called "Abraxas," written January 1940. The first seven pages of the earlier story survive among Sturgeon's papers, and they tell basically the same story as the opening pages of "Shottle Bop." On January 26, 1940, TS wrote to Dorothe:

> *Hope I never have to live thru another such week ... Sunday settled down to work on "Abraxas." Finished it Tuesday morning; no sleep Sun or Mon ... stopping only to eat, eating only oatmeal and cocoa because that's all there was ... took it down to JC, came home and passed out ... up at 9:30 that nite, over to Woodie's; bed again at 2, slept till 2 Wed. afternoon ... so to work again on "Salty Peanut." It came back. "Abraxas" came back. I'm working for nothing and the more I work the lousier it is and the less I eat ... you would ask me to write a letter instead of a card ... Wed. nite worked all nite. Thursday nite worked till twelve, went over to Martin's where I met my two protegés ... they wanted some back-number McClure releases so brought them home with me ... bull-session lasted until ten this morning ... so that's two more nites without sleep ... didn't known then about "Abraxas"; was hoping for a check. Hung around until 2nd mail, still nothing, called up JC who said come down and talk it over ... dead on my feet I went down, first to McClure's to pick up a life-saving finn for the rent ... they've owed it to me for two weeks but I was saving it for just this eventuality ... JC commented as I expected and feared he would; story had too many ramifications, spread out so much it couldn't support its weight ... tremendous amount of material in it; comedy, horror, Gnosticism, Basilidian Philosopy, possession, and so on ... hero wound up to be not only the Messiah but the f—ing Holy Ghost ... too big ... JC calmly suggests that I knock it down and make at least five shorts out of it ... so as soon as I get to bed, which is right after I finish this, will get to work on it ... and that means another two day stretch with oatmeal and cocoa ... good diet. Vitamins ABB₁CD and roughage ... pound of sugar every three days, can of milk every day. Thrive on it.*

The opening paragraph of "Abraxas" is: *Seems to me either you have an inferiority complex or you just don't admit you have one. Phooey. There, in its entirety, was my attitude on the day I bought bottles.*

At the time he began writing this story (the evidence from his correspondence is that he didn't write the published version till spring or summer), Sturgeon was living at 146 Tenth Avenue, Manhattan, not far from the Shottle Bop's fictional location.

TS's introduction to "Shottle Bop" in *Without Sorcery:*

This one almost disqualified the book-title. I maintain stoutly, however, that the plot strikes sorcery only a glancing blow. The verse was included as an experiment to see if I could get the two-bits a line the magazine was paying for poetry, with verse put into the body of a story. I didn't get it, a fact which has denied posterity, to its great benefit, several bushels of my doggerel. I think it pertinent to cite this story as an example of the "blind grope" technique of story telling. Start with a situation, give it a vaguely directional push, and let happen what may. If the author does not know what is to happen next, the reader cannot possibly know.

The blurb on the original magazine cover read: A VERY QUAINT LITTLE STORE, WITH A SIGN THAT SAID ONLY 'SHOTTLE BOP—WE SELL BOTTLES WITH THINGS IN THEM.' BUT THE THINGS IN THE BOTTLES WERE—THINGS!

"Yesterday Was Monday": first published in *Unknown,* June 1941. Because John Campbell had already selected it for his 1948 anthology *From Unknown Worlds,* this gem was not included in Sturgeon's first collection *Without Sorcery* (also 1948). It continued to be overlooked until *The Golden Helix,* 1979. Sturgeon's introduction to the story from the 1979 collection:

"Where do you get your crazy ideas?"

Every writer gets this question in various inflections, some of them downright insulting. Where this one came from is a mystery; why I set about writing it is another. Everything I had said about "The Ultimate Egoist" [earlier in the same collection] *applies to this one too: I was a beginner, I was unpracticed, I was eager—ready to write everything that came into my head. Often I would write myself into situations in which I had no idea where I was going or what might happen before the end. I do not recommend this as a technique; but if it does happen and you find a way out, you have written a story which doesn't 'telegraph' to the reader what the ending will be. If the author doesn't know, the reader can't.*

This is one of those. And also: it was fun to do.

"Yesterday Was Monday" is an example, like "Microcosmic God," of Sturgeon presenting an idea that is not new to fantasy or science fiction (or literature in general), but executing it so well that it is the Sturgeon version that leaves a permanent impression on anyone who encounters it. It seems likely that Robert A. Heinlein's short novel "The Unpleasant Profession of Jonathan Hoag" and the "heaven" sequences in *Stranger in a Strange Land* were influenced by this story; one also hears its echoes in the many "constructed realities" of Philip K. Dick, especially *The Cosmic Puppets* and *Time Out of Joint*.

"Yesterday Was Monday" was adapted as an episode of the television program "The New Twilight Zone."

Original magazine blurb (from the contents page): THE ACTOR SLIPPED BEHIND THE SCENES—TO FIND THE SCENE-SHIFTERS AT WORK BUILDING YESTERDAY AND TOMORROW!

"Brat": first published in *Unknown Worlds* (same magazine as *Unknown;* the title changed with the 10/41 issue), December 1941. It would be interesting to know whether this was written before or after the birth of the Sturgeons' first child (Patricia, born Dec. 21, 1940), but I have seen no hard evidence either way. I'm guessing it was written in anticipation rather than from first-hand experience—placing it as, perhaps, a summer 1940 story. In any case it's intriguing that in Theodore and Dorothe's divorce decree, the name of their second child is not Cynthia, as she has always been known, but Michaele.

Story introduction from *Without Sorcery:*

When this was written, I had the bad habit of running out all my copy in one draft, without a carbon. As a result, there were actually a half-dozen stories which I forgot entirely. Some appeared during the war when I was out of the country and could not get copies. When I returned I spent many a narcissistic night in reading my own stuff. It was with great joy that I ran across this one; I had absolutely no recollection whatever of having written it. I wandered around for days murmuring, "Did I write 'Brat'? Did I really?"

The above is a proper tribute to an underrrated story that in some ways is a breakthrough work: a true story of transformation (and thus one of the first truly characteristic Sturgeon stories), a transformation arising not through the author's preconceived plot but from something that happens to him and his characters as the tale tells itself.

There are times, however, when a literary caretaker wants to kick the author (who in turn, we can be sure, often feels the same way about the caretaker). In 1984, for *Alien Cargo,* Sturgeon wrote:

Not fun. A horrid little fantasy, derived from true-life observations by a man who loved children, but not children like this one. Those ones.

If you are reading these notes after reading the story in question—and if not, shoo, scram, go away, you're doing it wrong—you will immediately realize that this latter introduction was written by an author who had not recently read the story he was commenting on; who had, as it were, absolutely no recollection of what it was about emotionally. (Emotional content is primary in most Sturgeon stories—for example, the real power of "It," and that story's influence on later horror writers, lies not in the concept of the creature but in the emotional impact of the characterization and the setting.) Sturgeon couldn't have written this 1984 comment after actually rereading "Brat" and re-meeting its four characters.

Sturgeon's descriptions of his interactions with his paternal aunt Alice Waldo, in letters to his mother in 1938, suggest she may have been a model for the prissy Aunt Jonquil as she is portrayed at the start of "Brat."

Magazine blurb, from the contents page: 'BUTCH' LOOKED LIKE A NINE-MONTH-OLD BABY. BUT HE LIKED HIS STEAKS RARE, AND HIS COFFEE BLACK—AND TROUBLE IN MASSIVE DOSES!

"The Anonymous": unpublished. From the trunk left behind by Sturgeon on Staten Island in 1941 and returned to him in 1972. The typeface of the manuscript and the inscription on it saying "please note change of address" both identify it as having been written or completed circa August 1940.

The date is significant because the story (in my opinion) is so flat and energyless, yet seems to have been written during a period of time when the author was also producing excellent and exciting work. While many authors appear to grow in self-confidence (for better or worse) as their careers progress, Sturgeon from the beginning of his writing career found himself moving almost cyclically between real extremes of self-assurance and self-doubt. Highs and lows. Some of these cycles, in terms of his writing, were in periods of years (of writing a lot and writing nothing at all). But there is also considerable evidence in Sturgeon's correspondence of brief, intense fluctuations between energy and paralysis tormenting him even during relatively productive or prolific periods.

I've applied for a job with the British Purchasing Commission, he wrote his mother in December 1940, shortly before his daughter was born. *The idea is to establish some sort of regularity to my income, which, although ample, isn't steady enough to live comfortably on. My checks are large and fairly frequent, but just one reject can throw me out completely for weeks. The more work I do the worse I feel, the worse I feel the less money I make. Bounce two stories in a row—and science fiction is very hard to write—and I start having bad dreams when I'm wide awake. And I mean bad dreams—horror is my specialty. Can't sell sto-*

*ries while that goes on. But when I sell a couple a week or two apart, I
go on a spurt, and months go by in the life of Riley ...*

Sturgeon did submit his 1940-era rejects to other markets—the magazine *Weird Tales* for one, and no doubt other science fiction or fantasy
magazines—but not very persistently and certainly not successfully (he
sold no sf or fantasy to any magazine editor other than John Campbell
until 1946).

A comment in a letter from TS to his mother and stepfather March
20, 1938, after thanking them for sending his birth certificate and adop-
tion papers as requested, shows Sturgeon already chewing on the notion
of identity alteration: *For quite a while now I have had an idea buzzing
around in my sconce to the effect that someday, sometime, I would like
to change my identity—notice, I said identity, not just name, and disappear most melodramatically from the sight and mind of man. Sort of a
Jekyll-and-Hyde affair, you know; I've always thought that it would be
amusing to start a verbal war on some subject with myself through the
public press. Well, it's all conjecture and daydreaming; but like a good
scout I must be semper paratus. And don't worry about it; I'll most certainly keep you informed.*

"Two Sidecars": unpublished. Also from the trunk left on Staten Island.
The only specific mention in the surviving correspondence from 1940
and 1941 of Sturgeon attempting to write for markets other than *Astounding* and *Unknown* (and the Street & Smith comic books he wrote scripts
for) is in a letter to his mother dated April 22, 1941: *Another thing we
are hopeful about is the* Writer's Digest *contest, in which I entered two
stories. First prize of two hundred prizes is $250; all winning entries go
to* Liberty *magazine, and those that are printed there knock down an
additional hundred. It would make me very happy to win, I think!* This
story could have been for that contest, or could have been written much
earlier (anytime between August 1940 and spring 1941) for submission
to a non-fantasy market.

A sidecar, according to my dictionary, contains "brandy, an orange-
flavored liqueur, and lemon juice." This story and "Nightmare Island"
might raise the question of Sturgeon's own relationship with alcohol. He
did drink, of course, in his years as a merchant seaman, and afterward
(February 1940: *New Year's wasn't bad. I went to Philly, did the rounds
with Wally, got pleasantly tight four times in three days*), but there is no
suggestion in his correspondence that it was ever a problem for him. Nor

is there much specific evidence that he used alcohol to help him write, though he no doubt tried it. But his drugs-of-choice for writing seem to have always been coffee and sleep-deprivation (but in a 1952 letter included in the chapbook *Argyll* he also speaks of writing under the influence of dexedrine and "soggy with beer").

However, although alcohol wasn't the problem, the utter paralysis of the husband in this story in the face of his imminent loss of his wife is an eerie foreshadowing of the circumstances of Ted and Dorothe's divorce in 1945 (as described by Sturgeon himself in correspondence and later fiction).

"Microcosmic God": first published in *Astounding Science-Fiction*, April 1941. I date it as having been written after August 1940, based on a comment in a letter apparently written that month: *I'm only selling to one market*—Unknown, *I have five stories coming up in that, and one in* Astounding—*a sequel to "Ether Breather."* This suggests that "Microcosmic God," "Completely Automatic," and "Poker Face," all published in *Astounding* near the start of 1941, were written in the fall of 1940. "Microcosmic God" is further dated by the existence of five pages of an early draft, typed on the script (or italic) typewriter and with the return address that was used starting in mid-August 1940.

Sturgeon's 1948 comments on the story, from *Without Sorcery*:

This was written just at the beginning of the shooting phase of World War II, and is the result of mulling over a possible end product—in miniature—of dictatorship and isolationism. I have been asked repeatedly to do a sequel to this. I know better!

And his 1984 comments, from *Alien Cargo*:

I have always disliked this story—not for its basic idea, which has been called unique, but for its writing. Just out of my 'teens, I had not yet learned that nobody is ever and altogether good, and nobody is all bad. Ignorant of that, one can produce 100% purified vintage dyed-in-the-wool cardboard characters. The story's basic idea, however, is indeed unique, and many years later, at the Artificial Intelligence offices in M.I.T., a truly great scientist introduced himself to me, to tell me (as many scientists have) that he had gotten into science in the first place because of reading science fiction as a youngster, and further, that he had gotten into microbiology because of this one story. And this is a guy who might win a Nobel Prize! So ... what price literary judgments?

Science fiction historian Sam Moskowitz offers a different perspective in his book *Seekers of Tomorrow* (1967):

" 'Microcosmic God' ... had all the reaction of a bomb with a fast fuse. It was not that the idea was new; the concept of intelligent creatures in a microscopic world producing inventions at an accelerated rate relative to their own time span had been used in 'Out of the Sub Universe' by R. F. Starzl (*Amazing Stories Quarterly,* summer 1928), had been defined in complete detail by Edmond Hamilton in 'Fessenden's World' (*Weird Tales,* April 1937), and had been recognized as a poignant classic in Calvin Peregoy's 'Short-Wave Castle' (*Astounding Stories,* February 1934)—but Sturgeon did it best." [James Gunn in *Alternate Worlds* (1975) credits Fitz-James O'Brien's 1858 story "The Diamond Lens" as the first in the general category of "world in a microcosm" stories.]

Moskowitz goes on, drawing partly on his 1961 interview with Sturgeon: "The modest fame as master of fantasy which Sturgeon had attained with 'It' was far transcended by the acclaim brought to him by 'Microcosmic God.' Far from being pleased, Sturgeon was first annoyed and then infuriated. The kindest thing he could say for 'Microcosmic God' was that it was 'fast paced.' He deplored the fact that it did not have the 'literary cadence' of many of his other less complimented works and he deeply resented the fact that readers didn't even seem to get the point: that a superman need not be a powerful, commanding person.

"He failed to understand that he had struck the universal chord. Stories like 'Shottle Bop,' where you got what you wanted by 'wishing,' were good fun but nobody in this modern technological age believed them. On the contrary, a story like 'Microcosmic God,' where a man could get anything he wanted by logical scientific means, made possible the complete suspension of disbelief and utter absorption of the reader by the story. That was the story's appeal."

In any case, the extent and durability of the story's appeal were demonstrated in 1969, when members of the Science Fiction Writers of America were asked to vote on "the greatest science fiction stories of all time" (for inclusion in a book entitled *Science Fiction Hall of Fame*). "Microcosmic God" tied for #4 in total votes—one of the five best or most popular sf stories ever written (through 1965), according to a poll of "virtually everyone now living who has ever had science fiction published in the United States" (quote and voting results from Robert Silverberg's introduction to *SF Hall of Fame*).

"Microcosmic God" was included in the first paperback science fiction anthology published in the United States, *The Pocket Book of Science Fiction* (edited by Donald A. Wollheim) in 1943. As a result many readers associate it with their discovery of science fiction. ("The first [sf] story I read was 'Microcosmic God' by Theodore Sturgeon. It has sometimes occurred to me that it has all been downhill from there."—Gene Wolfe, in his introduction to *The Complete Stories of Theodore Sturgeon, Vol. I*)

John W. Campbell, Jr., summarized the story well in the March 1941 *Astounding* (in a section where the editor talks about next month's issue): "Theodore Sturgeon has a novellette coming up, too. The tale of a man who played god to a homemade microcosm and forgot that he still had to live and get along in his greater world himself." His blurb for the story when it appeared (title page) was: KIDDER HAD A SYSTEM FOR INVENTING THINGS IN A HURRY—AND HE THOUGHT HE HAD A SYSTEM FOR HANDLING THE RESULTS. HIS METHOD WAS INHUMAN—BUT HIS AGENT WAS HUMAN—AND DANGEROUS!

The unfinished early draft of "Microcosmic God," the text of which is included at the end of these story notes, reveals that the Neoterics evolved in the author's mind from ants ... and thereby makes a small link between this story and Sturgeon's 1953 classic "Mr. Costello, Hero"— which in turn suggests that in Sturgeon's universe Senator Joe McCarthy and Adolf Hitler may be perceived as examples of the archetype called Mad Scientist.

The early draft also reveals that "Microcosmic God" evolved out of a hoary "Sunday supplement reporter comes to interview eccentric inventor/scientist" plot frame that Sturgeon had been trying to use for several years (on the evidence of other unfinished story-beginnings found among the Sturgeon papers from the Staten Island trunk).

The second sentence of the early draft casually summarizes the main gimmick of "The Anonymous," suggesting, I guess, that when Sturgeon had something on his mind he didn't mind repeating himself. (In fact, as in the case of his reflex put-downs of "Microcosmic God," he was quite capable of repeating himself almost verbatim over a period of 40 years. The patience of his wives etc. is legendary.)

"The Haunt": first published in *Unknown*, April 1941. Sturgeon's interest since childhood in building crystal radios shows up in a number of his stories, notably "The Bones" and "The Martian and the Moron." Ghost stories ("Niobe," "Shottle Bop," "Ghost of a Chance") are another recurring theme. The following quote (from a letter TS wrote his mother in October 1937) could well have been included in the notes on "Cargo" or "Turkish Delight" (*Vol. I*), but I think it fits here as well:

This ship is supposed to be haunted, a propos of your remarks about the worker's influence on his product. It seems that two people have jumped overboard from the foc'sle head where I stand my lookout watches. And for apparently no reason. I had only one unusual experience up there, but it really was something to remember. One night about three AM *I was standing up there, absolutely groggy for want of sleep. I forget just why; I think that tank-mucking* [work in the gas tanks, under the influence of the fumes] *was responsible for it. Finally I could stand it no longer. I crawled down between the riding-chocks on the anchor-engine and went to sleep. Suddenly I found myself wide awake, in a cold sweat, and staring up into a threatening sky; I saw nothing that could have awakened me with such a start, and so lay back and dozed off. Immediately I awoke with such a jolt that it threw me right up on my feet, and then I heard, gradually fading away, and already almost imperceptible, the most extraneous possible sound for my environment. Of all impossible things, the skirling of bagpipes! I stood absolutely frozen, staring out over the bow, and there, dead ahead, at two hundred yards, the ugly stub snout of a Swedish freighter poked out of a fogbank, throwing two fountains of spray as she headed unerringly for our port bow. I whipped around to the bell behind me and rang three times ("Dead Ahead!") and yelled "Hard left!" as loud as I could bellow. Yes, we missed her, but only just. It was one of those awful moments that you dream about, but never see the end of. We practically scraped; to be more accurate, I should say that we missed her by about 40 feet. Later, when the excitement had died down, and I had taken the wheel, the mate told me that he had seen absolutely nothing until almost a minute after I rang the bell. What would have happened if those phantom pipes had not been so insistent?*

Note: I never sleep on watch any more!!

Magazine blurb (title page): IT SEEMED A GOOD IDEA TO CRACK THE CAST-IRON POISE OF THE GIRL BY A LITTLE SYNTHETIC HAUNT. SOUND EFFECTS, RADIO VARIETY, WERE INTENDED, BUT—

"Completely Automatic": first published in *Astounding Science-Fiction*, February 1941. Written fall 1940.

Two pages of an early draft of this story survive in Sturgeon's papers. As with the "Microcosmic God" draft, they show an author who has his basic story idea and is experimenting with how to tell it. It's possible that these two pages were all Sturgeon wrote before rethinking the story and writing it in its present form. The early draft does not have the "one space-sailor tells another a story" narrative structure. Instead the story starts with a new, green crewman meeting his bunkmate (and being razzed by him), a very skeletal version of the Babson-meets-Fuzzy scene in the finished story. This is followed by a long, incomplete clump of exposition, concerning the funkiness of the *Maggie Northern* and the recent elimination of the "Apprentice Chemical Controller" job aboard this automated ore-ship. One imagines Sturgeon stopping at the bottom of the second page and saying, okay, I think I'm ready to start writing now.

When Sturgeon wrote "Completely Automatic" and "Microcosmic God," he had already sold at least eight fantasy stories to *Unknown,* but his only science fiction sales were the two "Ether Breather" stories. He was still trying to find his voice as a science fiction writer.

Magazine blurb (from the title page): A YARN ABOUT A PERFECTLY AUTOMATIC SHIP, AND HER PERFECTLY INCOMPETENT CREW, HER HOPELESS, PRACTICALLY MINDLESS CREW TRAPPED BY HER PERFECT MECHANISMS WHEN THINGS WENT WRONG.

"**Poker Face**": first published in *Astounding Science-Fiction,* March 1941. Written fall 1940. Moskowitz in *Seekers of Tomorrow* says "Poker Face" is "historically important as one of the earliest science fiction stories based on the notion that otherworldly aliens [*sic*; actually in this case it's men from the future] are living and working among us." It could also be considered a forerunner of Arthur C. Clarke's vision of the perfect city at the end of time, lost in a self-sustained stasis.

Sturgeon (from *Without Sorcery*): *No one can change my conviction that there are people among us like "Face." Not necessarily people from his strange point of origin, but from many. The reasons these folk have for concealing themselves are more obvious than any they might have for self-advertisement. You do not attempt to alter what you see on your visits to a museum—or to a zoo ...*

And later, from *Alien Cargo:*

I'm so very glad to see this one back in print. Written sometime in early 1940, this and the next four were written in an extraordinarily prolific (for me) period in early 1940, during which my editor, the late John Campbell, hoarded them and pieced them out; I saw none of them in print until I returned to the States after managing a hotel in Jamaica, then, when the U.S. got into the war, working as a heavy equipment operator in Jamaica (for the Army) and in Puerto Rico (for the Navy). From

1940 until late '46 I wrote only one story (a novelette called "Kill-dozer!")—six solid years of "writer's block"—the worst I have ever known.

But about "Poker Face," 1940: I wonder what was in George Orwell's mind just then, eight years before he wrote his terrifyingly prescient 1984?

Sturgeon's account (written in 1984) requires a few factual corrections: his "writer's block" began in June 1941, when he moved to Jamaica; and he began writing again on a regular basis near the end of 1945.

When Sturgeon put together his first collection of stories in 1948, he evidently did some light editing on several of the stories (one, "Maturity," was substantially rewritten). The text included here is the book version. In the case of "Poker Face," two sentences have been trimmed from the middle of the first paragraph of the magazine version, four sentences cut from Face's description of how he arranged the cards, and, more significantly, there are several large cuts from Face's description of his future city, cuts that may help explain why Sturgeon remembered his story as being related to the dystopic vision of *1984*. The biggest cut starts at the end of the paragraph that starts, *"I came from that city."* In the magazine it ends, *Imagine it if you can—let me describe the life of an individual to you.* And goes on:

"He was born when he was needed. He was an individual from a mold. He was a certain weight, not the thousandth of a gram more or less than that of any of his contemporaries. He was fed the same food as they, slept exactly the same hours, learned precisely the same things at the same time. His pulse, mental powers, rate of metabolism, physical strength, range of vision—all were exactly the same as those of the same age. He needed no individual attention. He fought no disease, because there was no disease in the city. He was fed and clothed and housed by machines, and he was taught by them and quickly learned the way of them. When he was adult he was bred. When he was eighteen he had been schooled for two hours a day for eight years. He then spent one year working two hours a day tending one of the millions of machines that took their power from interstellar space and transmuted it into usable energies for the people and the structures. When he had finished that year he spent an hour each day for eight months in teaching the young the things he had observed about the work he had done. He gave instruction for twenty days less each year for twelve years and then died because he ceased to get fed, as there was nothing left for him to do. His body was transformed into raw materials of various kinds, with no waste. There was never any waste in the city.

"*Now the city was divided into two halves, like the halves of a great brain. One half was dedicated to the supply of power, and one to materials. There were forty-five million people in each half, equally divided in age and sex. The flawless smoothness of the city's operation depended on the maintenance of that exact balance between supply and demand, manufacture and the means to manufacture. For every death there was a birth* ... "

The paragraph that begins, "Face shook his head," originally ended with these added sentences: *Remember—it wasn't only that these people were educated that way and brought up in those surroundings. They were bred for those traits.*"

And slightly later, the paragraph that begins "I was coming to that," had these added sentences at the end: *Now the machines which supplied the people with everything from baby pap to muscle rubs, transportation to air conditioning, naturally covered such a vast number of highly specialized fields that it was necessary to maintain quite a number of men educated along these lines. There was only one of these men detailed to each field—astronomy, astrophysics, biology, and so on. He learned what his predecessor knew and spent the years of his life learning what else he might and teaching it to the next in line.*

No text was added or rewritten for the later version, although there are additions and light rewritings on the text of another *Without Sorcery* story, "The Ultimate Egoist."

Magazine blurb (title page): "FACE" WAS A REMARKABLE POKER PLAYER. EVEN MORE REMARKABLE THAN HIS FELLOW PLAYERS THOUGHT. IT WASN'T JUST THE WAY HE STACKED DECKS—

"Nightmare Island": first published in *Unknown*, June 1941, under the pseudonym E. Waldo Hunter. This was the exciting month that Sturgeon had four stories published at the same time, two in *Unknown* and two in *Astounding*. One story in each magazine was under his name; "The Purple Light," in *Astounding*, was published under the pseudonym Sturgeon had used earlier in *Unknown* (for "The Ultimate Egoist"), "E. Hunter Waldo." But "Nightmare Island" was credited to "E. Waldo Hunter." Campbell, in the next issue of *Unknown*, explained: "Waldo sort of forgot whether he'd put the 'Hunter' before or after 'Waldo' and we forgot to check. Hence the discrepancy of the name on 'The Ultimate Egoist' and 'Nightmare Island.'" Sturgeon, in a letter in that same issue, says, *It will no doubt surprise a great many people to learn that I was* *christened Edward Waldo, and that Hunter is my grandmother's maiden name. Of course, I was only a kid at the time.* The letter is signed, "E. Hunter Waldo Hunter."

Sam Moskowitz reports (based on his 1961 conversation with Sturgeon) that the idea for "Nightmare Island" was "derived from a reference in a 1910 edition of the *Encyclopaedia Britannica,* concerning the 'tube worm'."

The tropical setting of the story seems to conjure up Sturgeon's years in Jamaica, Puerto Rico, and the Virgin Islands, but in fact it was written (and published) before he left New York. He had, however, had some transient experiences in the tropics already, traveling through the Gulf and the Florida Keys as a merchant seaman. (To his mother, 12/3/37: *Now please don't try to tempt me away from the coastwise runs again; in the first place, they are ideal for winter weather, as we are so often south of Florida.* He had recently made what may have been his only Latin American run as a merchant seaman, stopping in Panama and Guatemala; but every trip between New York and Port Arthur, Texas took him through the Bahamian waters where this story probably takes place.)

Magazine blurb (contents page): ONLY A MAN WHO'D BEEN IN HIS CONDITION FOR A LONG TIME COULD HAVE UNDERSTOOD, ACCEPTED, AND ACTED REASONABLY ON NIGHTMARE ISLAND.

"The Purple Light": first published in *Astounding Science-Fiction,* June 1941, under the pseudonym E. Hunter Waldo. A science-fictional rewrite of Sturgeon's 1939 vignette "Watch My Smoke."

Magazine blurb (contents page): ONCE IN A WHILE, IT'S A SMART IDEA TO CRAWL RIGHT INTO THE MIDDLE OF TROUBLE!

"Artnan Process": first published in *Astounding Science-Fiction,* June 1941. Written early December 1940. TS to his mother, 12/6/40: *This morning I finished a science-fiction opus dealing with isotope-transmutation as she is done on the third planet of the Procyon system. It will with certitude bounce: I didn't like the idea before I started the yarn.* Same letter, now 12/12/40: *Ye ed. seemed to think highly enough of my vegetative-metabolistic transmutation process to pay me a hundred and a quarter for it. That pays the hospital bill and feeds us for a week, though it leaves damn little for Christmas.*

A manuscript fragment from the Sturgeon papers indicates that there was an earlier (probably incomplete) draft of this story, also starring

Slimmy and Bellew, in which Mars is not a factor; the cheap power deal is directly between Artna and Earth.

Introduction from *Without Sorcery* (1948):

This opus, sheer "spaced-opera," [sic; changed in the paperback version to "space-opera," a familiar sf term for clichéd or old-fashioned science fiction melodramas] is included here primarily because with it I can modestly take my place among the prognosticators. Based on the problem of isotope separation, it was written three years before the organization of the Manhattan Project. Major Groves' brain trust tried five methods to accomplish the trick of separating U-235 from U-238, in a mass of metal which was all chemically pure uranium. Here's one they never thought of ...

This year, incidentally, the layman is beginning to hear of the Probability Wave in connection with nuclear physics ...

Sometime in the mid-1950s (after reading a statement by Philip Van Doren Stern that said, "Never set pen to paper until you can state your theme in one single, simple declarative sentence"), Sturgeon began making a list entitled: *IN ONE SENTENCE—What Sturgeon stories said.* He only typed five entries, including one for this story, which says, *"Artnan Process": Any dictatorship is bad, even if beneficent.*

TS to Paul Williams, interview, December 6, 1975: *The only really important story I wrote in that so-called entertainment period was "Microcosmic God." It's a story I have never liked ... But that was a blockbuster. The other stories I wrote, they were fun, "The God in the Garden" and "Helix the Cat," all these funny kind of humorous things, "Biddiver" and all that, were lightweight amusing stories and they hadn't anything too heavy to say. What's that one about the Martian, and these two guys are so—they fed the Martians Coca-Cola until they got drunk?*

Magazine blurb (contents page): THE ARTNANS HAD A MONOPOLY ON THE U-235 BECAUSE OF A REFINING PROCESS. BUT THEY WERE PERFECTLY WILLING TO LET ANYONE FIGURE IT OUT—IF HE COULD!

"Biddiver": first published in *Astounding Science-Fiction*, August 1941. Sturgeon's "in one sentence—what Sturgeon stories said" for this one (circa 1954) was: *In the weakest of us lives a friendly giant.*

The insurance fraud at the start of the story harkens back to TS's first published story, "Heavy Insurance."

Sturgeon did own an automobile at the time he wrote "Biddiver"—*a deep maroon Buick coupé with chromium wheels and my initials on the doors* (letter to his mother, circa August 1940).

Another element of what Sturgeon later called his "optimum man" theme (he told David Hartwell in 1972 that his stories since 1945 *have all had this preoccupation with the optimum man*) begins to emerge here: the superman looking for a purpose ("Maturity," *More Than Human*).

Magazine blurb (title page): BIDDIVER WAS A LITTLE MAN WHO GOT RICH, GOT DRUNK, GOT INTO THE WRONG "AUTOMOBILE" AND—BECAUSE IT WASN'T AN AUTOMOBILE BUT SOMETHING ELSE— GOT CHANGED!

"The Golden Egg": first published in *Unknown,* August 1941. It would be interesting to know why John Campbell chose to run this story in his fantasy magazine rather than in his science fiction magazine.

The "phenomenal young man" aspect of this story makes it an early appearance of a recurring Sturgeon character, the superman/aesthete (Robin English in "Maturity," Horty Bluett in *The Dreaming Jewels*). The attractive adult male who knows nothing of the world (because he's a created human, or an alien, or an amnesiac) and has to be educated is another recurring character: for example, Nemo in "The Clinic," Anson in "The Other Man," the reborn Guy Gibbon in "When You Care, When You Love."

Sturgeon's unfinished manuscript "Cory Drew," dating perhaps from January 1940, also concerns a "very handsome" adult male newly created (in a laboratory by a couple of mad scientists), his childlike nature, and what happens when he meets a woman who falls in love with him. Ariadne Drew in "The Golden Egg" has the same last name as the hero of that unfinished effort. Sturgeon had evidently forgotten that he'd already used the name in "It" (which, although a very different sort of story, shares with "Egg" the driven, detached curiosity of its nonhuman entity).

One common thread in these "education" stories, illustrated by the comic sequence in "The Golden Egg" when Elron talks first like a hobo and then like a debutante, is Sturgeon's interest in how ordinary human behavior would appear to the proverbial "man from Mars," the outsider who knows nothing of our built-in cultural contexts and assumptions.

Why Sturgeon chose the name "Elron" is not known. He was certainly aware of and a reader of fellow sf writer L. Ron Hubbard.

Magazine blurb (title page): THE GOLDEN EGG WAS ANCIENT BEYOND MAN'S UNDERSTANDING—AND WANTED A MEASURE OF AMUSEMENT IN MAN'S SMALL WORLD—

"Two Percent Inspiration": first published in *Astounding Science-Fiction,* October 1941. In a 1953 essay, "Why So Much Syzygy?" (reprinted in *Turning Points,* Damon Knight, ed., Harper & Row 1977), Sturgeon describes his fiction as a series of investigations of "this matter of love," and lists the "love motivations" driving some of his stories: *In "Two Percent Inspiration" it was hero worship, a kid and a great scientist.*

1948 introduction (*Without Sorcery*): *The title, of course, is from the old saw about genius—"ninety-eight percent perspiration." I have since revised my conception of genius and now define it as an infinite capacity for taking beer. This story is the only one I ever wrote which has three (count 'em) plot twists at the end. I am proud of one thing in it: Satan Strong, Scourge of the Spaceways, Supporter of the Serialized Short Story, and Specialist in Science on the Spot.*

1984 introduction *(Alien Cargo): More early don't-give-a-damn fun; actually a lampoon on some of the more dreadful contemporary (1940) examples of science fiction. So come on and meet, Satan Strong* [etc.].

Although this seems to me a quite minor Sturgeon story, and granted the existence of many common sources (E. E. Smith's *The Skylark of Space,* for one), it is intriguing how much it anticipates, in tone as well as content, the excellent series of young adult science fiction novels Robert Heinlein wrote between 1947 and 1958. Heinlein's *The Rolling Stones* even features a space-going engineer who makes a living writing trashy sci-fi, possibly an acknowledgement of the influence of "Two Percent Inspiration."

The pre-story fragment surviving in Sturgeon's papers, in this one instance a kind of plot summary of "Two Percent" rather than a false start/early draft, seems worthy of inclusion here in its entirety. Read in conjunction with the story, it provides us a good glimpse of how Sturgeon transformed plot (note that the plot outline in this case also establishes the mood of the story) into narrative, circa 1941:

Professor Thaddeus MacIlhainy Nudnick, followed by ninety-three sections of the alphabet, was a genius. He found himself aboard the good ship Stoutfella, *named after a mythological character from the literature of the ancients who was always popping up in In-lish writings. Also aboard is a man-child by the name of Hughie, who was addicted to trashy literature in general and science-fiction in particular. Hughie was always pining away for an emergency, and dramatizing the possibility, particularly this trip; for he knew Professor Nudnick and some of his feats. He knew in his heart that come the emergency, the prof would take down the ultraradio, swiftly twist two wires, weld a connection, wind a coil, and—zooie! Everyone would be safe in the Betelgeuse system via space-warp. Or something.*

Comes the Emergency. The Earth-Mars Navigation Board, which is composed of an equal number of both races and decides by majority vote, is under the thumb of one Arthur Horn, who, oiled by Mars, has frightened the rest of the Earthmen on the Board to vote the way he wants. It seems that the Stoutfella *has discovered a huge deposit of prosydium, a rare-earth metal invaluable as an "atomic catalyst" in the molecular-collapse process for hardening copper. Nudnick is aboard to guide them to it; he spotted it by improvising a detector when he was travelling on a Martian pasenger liner. He has kept his mouth shut because if the existence of this unclaimed treasure were ever made known, it would precipitate a deadly war between the planets. Independently, Nudnick is trying to claim it for Earth; he can't acquaint the Earth Government of it for fear of their sending an armed fleet to seize it, which in space law is an act of war. He considers the headstrong government stupid fools for such characteristics. The prosydium asteroid is much nearer Earth than Mars anyway; once he has claimed it Earth can protect it. Anyhoo, this feller Horn has got some suspicions that Nudnick is up to something, and so has the* Stoutfella *stopped and completely disarmed on suspicion of piracy, knowing that when he later sends a private ship to squeeze the secret out of Nudnick, the old boy won't blast them, as he has every right to do. Nudnick annoyedly gives up his weapons, even to sidearms.*

The Stoutfella *proceeds; since Nudnick is wise to the fact that Horn is up to some monkey business, he leads Horn's little Martian-crewed ship a gay chase. He can't, however, keep this up forever; he is an old man and his ship will have to be fueled one of these days. The kid, meanwhile, is completely disgusted with the scientist. Keeps on quoting science-fiction to him, saying, "Why don't you blast 'em? Why don't you go into hyperspace? Why don't you make a light-deflector so the ship will be invisible? Why don't you do something really scientific?" The old guy just laughed at him and slapped him on the back. The kid tried a couple of things himself word for word out of the science-fiction rags, with little or no effect. Finally, with fuel almost gone, the* Stoutfella *is forced down on Mercury, on the twilight strip a bit toward the day side. It is hot and damn windy; the two of them sit the ship down and jump out, hightailing it for the mountings [sic]. The Martians come right away after them, land beside their ship and come ashore. A futile chase, and the Earthmen are caught. Halfway back to the Martian ship for torturing, the Martians drop dead. The only gadget Nudnick has whipped together is a beamed spy-ray, and he has forced the dying Martians to confess "all" about Horn, out there in the heat. Once back in the ship, explanation and delight.*

The opening scene of the completed story seems to draw partly on Sturgeon's childhood punishments at the hands of his professor stepfather, as described in his 1965 essay "Argyll," and perhaps also on the "bloody unfair" brutalization he and other cadets suffered at the hands of upperclassmen and officers at the Penn State Nautical School in 1936. However, the idealized brilliant professor Nudnick also probably derives to some degree from Sturgeon's childhood admiration of his Scottish stepfather Argyll.

Magazine blurb (contents page): A MARTIAN MIGHT BE AS GOOD AS ANY EARTHMAN IN MOST THINGS—BUT WHEN IT CAME TO A SHORT HIKE ON MERCURY—

"The Jumper": first published in *Unknown Worlds*, August 1942. Written before July 1941.

This is an early example of Sturgeon examining the psychopathic personality, who seems compelled to manipulate and irritate the people around him just because he can (see "When You're Smiling," "The Other Man"). The "jumper" is another fascinating, though unrelated, psychological or parapsychological conceit (Sturgeon may have learned of this when visiting his uncle in Canada). But unlike later Sturgeon stories, the psychological ideas are merely presented, not explored in a rigorous or imaginative fashion.

Magazine blurb (title page): THE NAZI PRISON GUARD WAS PLAIN NASTY—AND SOMETHING MORE. THE CANADIAN RECOGNIZED THE SYMPTOMS—AND MADE THE VICIOUS GUARD SIGNAL THE R.A.F. FOR HIM!

Corrections and addenda:

I have not had the opportunity to compare the texts of all the stories that were collected in *Without Sorcery* with their original magazine texts (manuscripts are unavailable for most of these stories). The reader is advised that there may be textual variants in such stories as "Microcosmic God," and "It" and "Ether Breather" from the first volume. We have used the *Without Sorcery* text as the source in this series for all stories included in that book.

A comparison has been made of the texts of the story "The Ultimate

Egoist" since the first volume was published. Sturgeon evidently went over the story carefully, removing (or adding) a word or a phrase from a sentence to improve the flow of the writing, and rewriting awkward sentences. The most significant changes are the dropping of a passage of reminiscence from the start of the paragraph that begins "Looking at Drip, putting sugar in his coffee" (*Vol. 1*, p. 295), and the conversion of the last two paragraphs of the story from past tense to present tense, which considerably heightens the dramatic effect.

The passage dropped from the magazine version reads: *I poured him a cup of coffee, thinking about the ships, thinking of the live surge of a steel deck, and the whip of a wind, and of a double rainbow by moonlight in the Caribbean. The pulsing rustle of valves and pistons. Aces backed up in a marathon stud game in the messroom. Heat in the fireroom, making your lungs too big for your chest. Breakdown in a hurricane off a rocky coast, and you smell death in the wind—death and kerosene. A load of high-test aviation gas, so your ship is a five-hundred-foot stick of dynamite. A Louisiana Cajun using his knife and a Boston Irishman using his feet. Breath of life, the very warmth in a man's blood, these things, once he's been to sea.*

With rare exceptions, Sturgeon did not revise his texts for book publication for his collections after the first one (he did revise his novels that were based on magazine material, *The Dreaming Jewels* and *More Than Human*). It is possible that he may have revised a story before it was anthologized by another editor, in the early years of his writing career, and that we may have missed such changes by working from the magazine text rather than the anthology text.

I have now examined the May 1947 issue of *Argosy* in which "Bianca's Hands" first apppeared and can confirm that the text is the same as in Sturgeon's collection *E Pluribus Unicorn*. The introduction to the story in the magazine reads, "It is with pride that *Argosy* presents the prize-winning story in our £250 competition. Its strange imaginative quality and the brilliance of its technique convince us of the author's sure mastery of the art of short story writing. The sinister and beautiful hands of Bianca will linger long in the memory of all who read this story. We congratulate the winner, Theodore Sturgeon, on a powerful and moving piece of work."

The editor would appreciate hearing from readers who have information about alternate texts or stories omitted from Sturgeon bibliographies, or who notice errors or omissions in these notes.

Microcosmic God
Unfinished Early Draft

HE OPENED THE door wide to me. He looked like the kind of man you forget easily because you see so many like him.

"Yes?" But his voice wasn't one to be forgotten.

"Mr. Samuel Kidder?"

"Yes?" A different intonation, a different attitude. He was a gentleman, and the force of his mind was an aura about him. I said, "I'm a freelance writer, Mr. Kidder. I've heard of you and your work and would like to do an article. May I—"

He stood aside. "Certainly. Come in." I did. I couldn't keep my eyes off him except to glance around the room and back again, and that was looking at him too, for this was his room, so much of the man himself. A weird place. Stacks of magazine fiction. A pulmotor. Velvet drapes. A platinum cigarette case on the same small table with a hookah, or water pipe. Window-frames like picture frames; windows scattered about the walls like pictures. There were plenty of things in the room, but there was no clutter. The place was different from all other places, but you wouldn't say it was a crazy place. The place was like the man that way too.

Kidder's papers had been read before the Geographic Society; the Psychical Society; the Institute for Psychological Research. He was an authority on atomic power; naval architecture; thermodynamics; Romansh literature. And yet he had, as far as anyone could find out, never graduated from any college or university. He had, or claimed, no titles. He was Samuel Kidder. *Mr.* Samuel Kidder. Period.

"What do you want to know, Mr.—"

"Egan," I said. "Just—who you are, why you do the things you do—you know. I'll write it. You say it. Just tell me what you'd like to read about yourself in a Sunday supplement."

"If I did," said Kidder, smiling, "I'd take up your time in talking about someone else." He motioned. "However—come on. I'll show you around."

I followed him. He flung aside one of the great drapes, stepped into a low doorway behind it. We found ourselves in a huge room with balconies on two sides. Kidder flipped a switch; scarlet light blazed from forty or fifty four-foot squares of plate glass set evenly around the walls. Brilliant as the light was, I could barely make out the features of the man beside me. It looked like hell, and I'm not trying to be funny.

"What is it?" I whispered the question, because I had to. You have to in a church too.

"Just red light with a lot of infrared thrown in," he said. "They can't see it. Don't know when they're being watched."

"Who can't?"

"The ants. Come over here." We went to the red-lit glass nearest the door. I had to stare for nearly a minute before I realized what I was looking at. An anthill, cross-sectioned, up against the glass. I looked around. The room was lined with them. It was like an aquarium, with ants instead. I made a surprised noise.

"Savages," said Kidder softly. He lifted a pointed stick from a rack over his head, began using it. "See there? That big black one?"

His pointer indicated a monster black ant which crept slowly along one of the bisected corridors in the anthill.

"Big," I said, for lack of anything else to say. "What is it—a queen?"

Kidder looked at me and back at the ant. "King," he said, and I saw his teeth flash redly in the light.

"I never heard of—" He silenced me with a wave of his hand, pointed with the stick. A smaller ant was coming the other way along the corridor.

"He better get out of the way," breathed Kidder.

He didn't. The big ant's antennae whipped out, struck the other's from side to side. Then he lunged forward, over the small one's back. His powerful mandibles caught just behind the other's thorax, sliced through. The king idled on, disappeared up a side corridor.

"And that's why he's king," said Kidder, as he pulled me over to the next window.

"Wait a minute," I said. "Hold on. What's the idea of all this? What did you mean by 'king' ant? I never heard of a king ant!"

"One thing at a time. 'The idea of all this' is a study of the mass psychology of my ants. As for the king ant—Yes, I know you never heard of one. These ants are—different. You never heard of one ant attacking another in his own hill, either, did you?"

"No; but then I don't know very much about ants."

"Forget everything you know about ants, then. These aren't really ants, you know. They're under treatment." Before I could ask anything more, he was pointing out a clodlike lump of grayish sand in the second ant village.

"The first temple," he said. "That's all there is here to differentiate this village from the last. It's all due to the presence of one ant, too. I call him John. He rates as something of a prophet among the rest. Know why? He is just barely sensitive to red light rays. Heh! He's—psychic!"

"I think," I said grimly, "I'll shut up and learn. Mr. Kidder, all this is Greek to me."

He laughed. He had a good laugh, which is a rare thing. Keep your ears peeled if you don't believe it. "You'd find it a little hard to take all in one dose, Mr. Egan. What I meant by saying that these aren't really ants is about what you'd say about the guinea pigs they tried insulin shock on. They weren't normal guinea pigs, with normal appetites and normal actions. They were temporarily something different. So with my ants, although my particular treatment is a far, far cry from insulin. About John here, my psychic ant. Watch him."

There was a great deal of activity around the clod Kidder had designated as a temple. By accident or design, one whole wall of it was formed by the glass, so it was easy enough to see everything that went on. A five-legged ant was holding off swarms of others who crowded in. As we watched the throng quieted down, seemed to be watching intently. The five-legged one turned around, facing us, and spread out his legs so that his quarter-inch black body lay on the floor of the temple.

"Watch the others," murmured Kidder. I did. One by one they imitated John's pose, sank their tiny fractions of inches to the pounded floor.

"I'm damned!"

Kidder looked at me for a long moment. "You are," he said.

"I've never seen ants like these!"

"No one has," he said. "There never have been any."

"They—they *think* like primitive men!"

"They think. Men are also creatures that think. At the risk of seeming to belabor a point, Mr. Egan, let me put it this way; men and these ants are creatures which think. Grant a living thing intelligence and it will conduct itself as a thinking being. Ant or human or anything else, there can be no basic difference. Varying details— yes. You don't plan the same period furniture for a sestoped that you do for a biped. You have no heating to plan for ant architecture, for ants are without body heat. For humans there is a whole art and science dedicated to clothing. For ants, there is an art and industry to oviparous eugenics. But by and large, the results are the same when the bases are the same."

"But—" I licked my lips, swallowed. "That may be true. But— ants! They can't think. They're creatures of instinct!"

"Quite right, Egan. Quite right. But not these ants."

"Why not?"

"Because they have intelligence. Come—I'll show you more." He took my elbow and led me to the next window.

MICROCOSMIC GOD

Theodore Sturgeon's body of work has had enduring impact on how science fiction is written and read. This second volume of *The Complete Stories of Theodore Sturgeon* offers multiple rewards.

The first is the pleasure of the stories themselves, all written in 1940 and 1941, a few never published in book form. The title story, "Microcosmic God," placed among the top five vote-getters when all living science fiction writers in 1969 (28 years later!) were asked to select "the greatest science fiction stories of all time." To the extent that fantasy is a separate form from science fiction, a story such as "Cargo" shows that Sturgeon is as much a fantasy writer as a master of science fiction.

This second volume of the collected stories of Sturgeon captures that moment in the author's career when he first began to think of himself as a "science fiction writer" and full-time professional writer. He was finding his voice and self-confidence, but he would soon lose both. Between June 1941 and May 1944 he found himself unable to write a word. The stories in this book, all written between Sturgeon's marriage in spring 1940 and his departure for Jamaica in late spring 1941, show an author hard at work trying to produce stories that would be acceptable to the one editor (John Campbell of *Astounding* and *Unknown*) who made it possible for Sturgeon to support his young family. They represent Sturgeon's first flowering, a time when he made a considerable and lasting reputation; but they also represent the final work he was able to do before distraction, doubt, and financial pressure interrupted his progress.

Theodore Sturgeon was born on February 26, 1918, in Staten Island, New York, and died in Eugene, Oregon, May 8, 1985. Primarily a resident of New York City and upstate New York, he also lived in Los Angeles for many years. He is the author of more than thirty novels and short story collections, and the winner of the International Fantasy Award for his novel *More Than Human,* the Hugo and Nebula Awards for the short story "Slow Sculpture," and the World Fantasy Life Achievement Award.

Paul Williams, series editor of *The Complete Stories of Theodore Sturgeon,* is founder of the rock music magazine *Crawdaddy!* and the author of *Bob Dylan: Performing Artist, Das Energi,* and *Outlaw Blues.* Literary executor for author Philip K. Dick, he supervised the publication of *The Collected Stories of Philip K. Dick.*

Books by Theodore Sturgeon

Without Sorcery (1948)
The Dreaming Jewels (1950)
More Than Human (1953)
E Pluribus Unicorn (1953)
Caviar (1955)
A Way Home (1955)
The King and Four Queens (1956)
I, Libertine (1956)
A Touch of Strange (1958)
The Cosmic Rape (1958)
Aliens 4 (1959)
Venus Plus X (1960)
Beyond (1960)
Some of Your Blood (1961)
Voyage to the Bottom of the Sea (1961)
The Player on the Other Side (1963)
Sturgeon in Orbit (1964)
Starshine (1966)
The Rare Breed (1966)
Sturgeon Is Alive and Well... (1971)
The Worlds of Theodore Sturgeon (1972)
Sturgeon's West (with Don Ward) (1973)
Case and the Dreamer (1974)
Visions and Venturers (1978)
Maturity (1979)
The Stars Are the Styx (1979)
The Golden Helix (1979)
Alien Cargo (1984)
Godbody (1986)
A Touch of Sturgeon (1987)
The [Widget], the [Wadget], and Boff (1989)
Argyll (1993)
The Ultimate Egoist (1994)
Microcosmic God (1995)